GREY EAGLE'S EMBRACE

"I wish now that I had done that morning what I wanted to do, but I was afraid it would send you racing after Joseph and Orion, begging them to take you to the fort," Grey Eagle said.

"What was that?" Diana came to a halt and watched him closely, feeling that his answer was terribly important.

He stopped also, then faced her, one hand running lightly down her arm. "I was so happy that you stayed, Diana. I wanted to take you in my arms, right there, in front of any who watched, and tell you so."

Her heart started thudding, a slow, happy thudding. Diana ran her tongue over her suddenly dry lower lip and did not ponder the wisdom of her next words. "Do it now."

The fingers that caressed her arm gripped her, and he brought his other hand up to her other arm. He stepped closer, so that their bodies almost touched, but just caressed her arms as he studied her face. Then, with a deep sigh, his powerful arms closed around her and he pulled her close.

"I am so glad you stayed," he whispered, his breath warm on her ear.

"So am I," she breathed. She raised her face to his, and their mouths met, tenderly at first, then with increasing urgency and passion . . .

Books by Jessica Wulf

THE IRISH ROSE

THE MOUNTAIN ROSE

THE WILD ROSE

HUNTER'S BRIDE

JOSEPH'S BRIDE

GREY EAGLE'S BRIDE

Published by Zebra Books

GREY EAGLE'S BRIDE

Jessica Wulf

Zebra Books
Kensington Publishing Corp.

http://www.zebrabooks.com

ZEBRA BOOKS are published by

Kensington Publishing Corp.
850 Third Avenue
New York, NY 10022

First Printing: October, 1998
10 9 8 7 6 5 4 3 2 1

Printed in the United States of America

ACKNOWLEDGMENTS

Thanks to Janet Grill for your excellent editorial help. Thanks also for your unshakeable faith in this story, and in my ability to tell it.

Thanks to Alex C. for inspiring me, so long ago. The dream never died.

Thanks to Eddie, just for being there. Your sweet spirit and constant loving affection helped my grieving heart to heal.

And my special thanks to Diane Headley for your help in brainstorming plot problems, for your insightful comments and suggestions, and for your enthusiastic reception of this story. This one is for you, my sister-of-the-heart. You wanted Grey Eagle—you got him.

—J.W.

Prologue

Near Fort Laramie, February 1851

"Fly, Franklin!" Diana Murdoch cried eagerly, encouragingly. As her father, Gideon, stood beside her, she threw her right arm up into the air, praying that the young golden eagle who so tightly clutched her leather-protected forearm obeyed her.

The eagle flapped his wings, his impossibly long wings, and she was keenly aware of how much bigger he was now than when she had first found him on the frozen prairie two months earlier, struggling to fly with a wounded wing. As children of all ages did, she took the injured bird to her father, with absolute faith that he could make everything better. After all, Gideon was a physician and surgeon.

And, with the eyes and heart of an adult, Diana knew that Gideon had surprised himself with the success of his efforts with the young eagle they had jokingly named after Benjamin Franklin, who had, eighty years earlier, espoused the wild turkey as the animal symbol of the infant United States rather than the eagle. Gideon agreed with Diana that the eagle had been a better choice.

Now, as they watched, Franklin fought to rise in the cold February air, his strong talons still gripping the leather guard Diana wore on her forearm. She closed her eyes, feeling the power of those talons, of his wings, feeling the power of his heart, of his life, of his very spirit. When he lifted off from her arm, her eyes remained closed, for she feared that the pain of watching the eagle she had come to love fly away forever would be too great. The cold wind blew wisps of hair around her face, and she felt as if that wind was lifting her away from the earth as surely as it bore Franklin aloft.

Now there was no fear.

On the wind, the woman's spirit followed the eagle into the blue heavens. Higher and higher they went, as if Diana were riding on his wings. Such feelings she had never known—joy at her patient's successful recovery, wonder at what he showed her from the unimaginable heights, calm acceptance of the impossible reality that she was truly flying with him.

Slowly, she opened her eyes, and, just for a second, had the strange sensation of falling. Then came the pain—the sharp, tearing pain—at the knowledge that nothing would or could ever be the same between Franklin and her again. Diana watched the eagle soar on the wind. She felt his soul-deep joy, and, at that, her own joy won over the pain of his leaving.

"Fare you well, Franklin," she whispered, her vision blurred by tears. She turned, blindly, to her father's comforting arms, and he held her close.

After a few minutes, Gideon led her in the direction of the fort. They had not gone far when Franklin's distressed cry rent the frozen air. Gideon stepped back as Diana whirled about and held out her arm in welcome. The young eagle slowed the motion of his now mighty wings and came to a gentle landing on the worn leather guard. He stared at her with his small eagle's eyes, blinking, as a strange cooing sound came from his strong beak.

The weight on her arm was an unwieldy burden, yet she managed to hold him up as she caressed the soft, tiny feathers between his eyes in the way she knew he liked. If Franklin had been a kitten, he surely would have purred. The thought brought a smile to her lips.

"I will love you forever, Franklin," she whispered, and brought her arm close to her body so that she could place a gentle kiss on the top of the docile raptor's head. "Now, go be an eagle."

Again, she threw her arm up and cried, "Fly!"

Again, Franklin flew.

This time, he flew far away, and although she sincerely wished him Godspeed, Diana's heart ached as her beloved eagle disappeared from view.

Several miles to the northwest, Grey Eagle Beaudine sat his horse and watched the eagle circle in the sky. The bird rode the wind currents as surely and as confidently as the sailing ships his father had described to him rode the waves of the seas he had never seen. Grey Eagle's spirit soared with the bird, as it always did, as it had all his life. He knew and accepted the Eagle as his spirit animal, had even been given the name of the Eagle by his father. Jedediah Beaudine had been dead for over five years now, cut down in a fierce battle with the Pawnee when he stayed behind to protect the fleeing women and children of a small Cheyenne encampment. Grey Eagle had never stopped missing his father, and took comfort from the mental image of Jedediah riding on the eagle's wings, free to go wherever he chose.

Grey Eagle watched the eagle fly higher yet, then turn to the north, where darkening storm clouds towered over the prairie. He drew in a deep breath, sniffing the cold air. More snow was coming, and before nightfall, if his nose was correct. The need to return to the Cheyenne encampment grew strong.

But he could not yet leave. The eagle was gone from sight, and still he stared at the clouds, hoping that the Woman would come to him again.

She had come to him the first time in the clouds, long ago, when he'd been but a boy on his first solitary vision fast, and now, even as a man, he always looked for her in the clouds.

Not often did he find her, but he never gave up hope. Sometimes she came to him in the flames of the campfire, sometimes in the drifting morning mist, sometimes in the sage-scented steam of the sweat lodge.

Always, she brought him peace.

In his visions, he never saw more of her than vague features, which included dark hair, dark eyes, and a smile that seemed somehow sad. He would know her, though, of that he was certain, just as he was certain he had not yet found her.

If it was possible to find her in the flesh.

Not even the wisest men in the village could tell him for certain whether she was a Spirit Woman, sent to watch over him, or a human woman whose spirit occasionally sought and touched his spirit. So he looked for her, everywhere he went.

Today, he looked in the clouds, and was rewarded. She came softly, forming in the coming storm. Her smile seemed lighter this time, not quite so sad. Grey Eagle reached for her, with one hand, and with his spirit.

The eagle called.

The bird had come back, and now flew toward him. Grey Eagle had the strange sense that the Woman in the clouds was watching the eagle. Somehow, her happier smile was meant for the eagle. He knew it, felt it, and wished the smile was meant for him.

The eagle flew high over his head and continued onto the south. The Woman in the clouds followed, her features dissipating as the clouds were borne on the furious gust of wind that now struck him. For a moment longer he watched. The wind blew his long hair around his shoulders and made him grateful that he had worn his thick coat made of a buffalo robe. The Woman was gone now, and, with a final cry that echoed on the wind, the eagle disappeared as well, leaving the man with a strange and haunting loneliness.

The snow was coming. Deep in thought, Grey Eagle turned his horse's head in the direction of the Cheyenne village.

Somehow, they were all bound together—the Eagle, the Woman, and he.

Someday, he would know how.

Chapter One

Diana Murdoch stood on the covered porch of the modest log house she shared with her father, absentmindedly smoothing the unfamiliar fur of a buffalo hide draped over the railing. The wind that blew against her face and rippled her wool skirts was from the north, and cold; she was grateful for the thick shawl around her shoulders. As she gazed out over the bustling parade ground of Fort Laramie, she tried to ignore the terrible sound of a hacking cough that came from inside the house, for she knew that she could not help the sufferer. No one could. She would never wish anyone harm, and yet, to the depths of her soul she wished that cough belonged to one of Gideon Murdoch's patients rather than to her beloved father himself.

"Diana."

At the sound of her father's quiet voice, she turned. Gideon stood in the doorway, leaning heavily against the frame. Even at forty-seven, with his hair touched by grey and his once robust body thinned by the hopeless struggle of his damaged heart and laboring lungs, Gideon Murdoch was a handsome man. The same cold wind that pushed against her skirts also ruffled

Gideon's hair—thick, wavy brown hair that he had passed on to her, his eldest daughter—and a powerful rush of love for her father filled Diana's heart, just as tears threatened to fill her eyes. She had to stop herself from reaching for him, for it would distress her father if she gave in to the tears.

Gideon pressed a handkerchief to his mouth then shoved the piece of cloth in the pocket of his trousers, but not before Diana saw the flecks of blood staining it. Now her heart grabbed with fierce sorrow and not a little fear. She was not a physician, but she knew her father didn't have much time left. Gideon would never fulfill his dream of reaching California.

She forced a smile to her face. "Yes, Papa?"

He nodded at the buffalo hide. "We were paid in hides again?"

"Yes. Two of them, in good condition. They were all the poor man had to offer as payment." Diana's mind touched on the aged Sioux who had come to Gideon in a desperate attempt to find a cure for the liver ailment that would eventually take the life of his equally aged and obviously beloved wife. Beyond giving the man a bottle of laudanum and instructions on its use, there was nothing Gideon could do for the woman. Diana sighed, saddened by the knowledge that such was often the case—aside from trying to keep them comfortable until death eased their suffering, many times little could be done for her father's patients. How did Gideon—or any physician—keep going in the face of so many painful losses?

"I'll take the hides to Angus later today," Gideon said.

At the mention of her uncle's name, Diana grimaced. "I'd rather we took them to Miles Breen, Papa," she said, referring to the fort's sutler. "Or to the Beaudine brothers, when they return from St. Louis. Any of them will give us a better deal in terms of trade."

"I know, daughter, but Angus is family, and struggling to get his trading post business going. We must support him."

"If he'd be fair with his trade and not water down his whiskey so much, he'd do better," Diana said sharply, her annoyance with her uncle and not her father. "How can he expect to compete with the Beaudines when he isn't an honest trades-man?''

"He will learn, Diana. Your aunt Phoebe has a gentling influence on him.''

Diana didn't agree, but she kept quiet. Phoebe—her father's sister—was a meek, soft-spoken woman who more likely feared her brutish husband than exerted a gentling influence on him. A rough voice interrupted her thoughts.

"Doc! Hey, Doc!''

Diana turned to see two heavily bearded men approaching on horseback. Both wore filthy coats—one made of a buffalo robe, the other of a red wool trader's blanket—and disreputable, wide-brimmed hats pulled low against the midday sun. She fought to keep her features straight as a whiff of their unpleasant body scents reached her nose. Conway Horton and Painted Davy Sikes always reeked; she wondered if either of them could remember the last time they had bathed. Thankfully, she wasn't often forced to share their company, as the two men spent most of their time in the wilderness, hunting buffalo and trading with the Indian tribes.

"We have need of your services, Doc,'' Painted Davy said as he pulled his mount to a halt at the porch railing. His mouth split in a wide, gap-toothed grin and he nodded at Diana. "Howdy, Miss Murdoch. Ain't you a pretty sight.'' Belatedly, he yanked off his hat, revealing a head of hair as dirty and matted as the growth of beard covering many of the intricate tattoos that decorated his pockmarked face and had given him his name.

"Mr. Sikes,'' Diana said, silently cursing the direction of the cold wind and trying not to breathe in through her nose. She looked past Painted Davy to Conway Horton and forced herself to be civil. "Mr. Horton.''

Horton only grunted, a sound that Diana thought suited the heavy-bodied, small-brained man perfectly. She did not like Conway Horton. The leering interest in his close-set, beady eyes when he looked at her made her feel unclean.

"Who is injured or ill?'' Gideon asked with a trace of impatience in his voice.

Painted Davy jerked a thumb over his shoulder. "Our little slave," he said cheerfully.

Diana frowned. *Who?*

Horton nudged his horse forward, and, for the first time, Diana noticed that he did not ride alone. A pair of thin, buckskin-covered arms circled his thick middle. Horton unsuccessfully fumbled with the rope that bound two small hands together in front of his belly and finally, with a muttered curse, jerked a wicked-bladed knife from his belt and sliced the bonds, drawing a little blood as he did. The small hands did not flinch, but fell weakly down.

Concerned, Diana stepped off the porch and shaded her eyes as she peered around Horton's smelly bulk.

"Get down," Horton ordered over his shoulder. He grabbed one of those thin arms and pulled, causing the person—the *slave?*—to fall to the ground. A young Indian landed hard, but not a sound came from his mouth. He struggled to a sitting position, then became immobile, staring straight ahead with dull, lifeless eyes, his dirty face expressionless except for his tightly clenched jaw.

"What's wrong with him?" Gideon asked as he stepped off the porch.

"Ain't a 'he,' " rumbled Horton. He spat a stream of tobacco juice, just missing the Indian. *"Her* right leg's broke bad, and she has a skin rash that ain't gone away."

Diana glared at him, then crouched down beside the shivering girl, who refused to look at her. In addition to worn knee-high moccasins, the poor thing wore only a ragged buckskin dress, and was as filthy as the two men were. Diana placed her shawl around the girl's shoulders. The girl's eyes widened, as if she was surprised, but she still would not look fully at Diana.

"We bought her from the Crow," Painted Davy explained as he climbed down from the saddle. He sounded very pleased with himself. "They think she's cursed 'cause of that damned rash and 'cause her leg won't heal. So does ol' Con, here." He snorted a derisive laugh. "He wants you to fix her leg, Doc, and get rid of that rash, so the curse'll be lifted. He don't want to poke his stick into a cursed hole."

"Watch your tongue in front of my daughter, Mr. Sikes," Gideon snapped.

"Sorry," Painted Davy grumbled.

The thought of Conway Horton's hands on the painfully thin girl—surely no older than eleven or twelve—who sat so stoically in front of her made Diana feel ill. With gentle hands, she eased off the filth-stiffened moccasin that covered the girl's right foot and calf. The girl tensed, but still made no sound.

Horrified, Diana saw that the leg had indeed been broken, but some time ago. The bone had been set wrong—if it had been set at all—and bent in an unnatural way just above the ankle. The girl had to be in constant pain. In addition, a light rash covered every inch of her exposed skin.

"She is your slave, you say?" Diana bit out harshly.

"Yeah," Painted Davy answered. Con Horton merely grunted.

"How much did you pay for her?"

"That was the sweet part of the deal," said Painted Davy, gloating. "One cast-iron skillet to the squaw of the brave who stole her from her people—that was all. We got her cheap."

So the girl wasn't Crow. God knew what horrors she'd suffered even before she fell into the cruel hands of Sikes and Horton. Diana wondered which tribe she had been stolen from. Jubal Sage, an old mountain man who, along with his young Cheyenne wife, Sweet Water, had befriended the Murdochs, once told them of the endless battles and wars between the various Indian tribes. Had this poor girl watched her family die before she was kidnapped and forced into slavery by the Crow? Diana's jaw tightened.

Whatever had happened, she was determined that the girl's suffering would end now. Conway Horton would not again touch the child with his large, dirty hands, nor would she ever endure the man's 'stick.' With a silent prayer for her father's support, Diana straightened and faced Painted Davy. When she spoke, it was a struggle to keep her anger and disgust from her voice.

"I'll give you those two buffalo robes for the girl." She pointed to the robes draped over the porch railing, then glanced at her father. Gideon's eyes widened, but he said nothing.

Painted Davy gaped at her. "You wanna buy her?"

"No!" barked Con Horton. "She ain't for trade."

Diana settled her cold, furious gaze on him, her hands clenched into fists, one of which she desperately wanted to plant in Horton's ugly face. "Her leg is badly injured, Mr. Horton. It should have been set properly long ago, when it was first broken. There's no guarantee my father can fix it. Then there's the rash. If he can't heal her, the curse will never be lifted."

"My daughter is right," Gideon put in. "I have no idea what is causing the rash—or if I can cure it—and I can tell by looking at that leg from here that it will never be right. The damage is too severe."

Painted Davy sauntered over to the railing and fingered the top buffalo robe.

"I ain't gonna trade her, Painted Davy." Horton's meaty hand tightened on the knife he still held. "I been waitin' to have her for over two months now."

Diana's lips pressed into a tight line. *Two months.* The child had been with those animals for two months.

"These are good robes, Con," argued Painted Davy. "We can trade 'em for whiskey—some of the good stuff, not that shit Angus MacDonald sells—and hole up with a couple of whores for a few days."

"Sikes!" Gideon warned.

"Sorry, Doc," Painted Davy snapped. "I'm tryin' to help your girl here." Then he turned narrowed, suspicious eyes on Diana. "Why do you want her?"

Diana shrugged. "I need assistance with my duties, both in the house and in the surgery. For those services, it doesn't matter if she's cursed." She couldn't keep a note of anger out of her voice.

"You just want a slave, too, Miss High-and-Mighty," Horton jeered.

"Not for the same reasons you do," Diana rejoined harshly. "I'll work her hard, but at least in my house she'll eat regularly and won't have to endure rape."

"It ain't our fault she wouldn't eat," Painted Davy protested.

"She's a slave, so I can do what I want with her," Horton interjected, his face flushed with anger. "You can't rape a slave, any more'n you can rape a whore."

The blood pounded in Diana's veins, urging her to violence. She ached to respond to that insistent call, and, if her father had not placed a calming hand on her shoulder just then, she might have.

Gideon spoke in a firm voice that brooked no argument. "She is a *child,* Mr. Horton, and a cursed one at that." He turned to Painted Davy. "Take the robes in trade for the girl and I'll add a keg of brandy to the deal. In turn, you can use the robes to trade for other . . . pleasures."

Diana stared at her father, grateful from the bottom of her heart for his support, in awe of his ability to turn a single word like 'pleasures' into an insult.

"The brandy you're offerin' ain't that watered-down sh— uh, stuff your brother-in-law sells, is it?" demanded Painted Davy.

"You have my word that it is not."

Painted Davy slapped his thigh in delight. "Then it's a trade, Doc!"

With a cruel jerk of his horse's head and a muttered curse, Conway Horton rode off across the parade ground, while Gideon and Painted Davy disappeared into the house to finalize their agreement. Diana stared down at the dirty, motionless Indian girl for whose life she had just become responsible and felt a sharp stab of anxiety. She whispered a prayer that she had done the right thing, and, before the words were finished, knew in her heart that no matter what happened now, she had.

Near a Cheyenne village,
seventy miles northwest of Fort Laramie

The eagle called, its eerie cry echoing off the cliff face. At the bottom of the cliff, Grey Eagle stood motionless as he stared into the mist created by the waters that tumbled over and down the cliff to land in the pool at his feet.

He had agreed—reluctantly—to act as protective escort for a group of women on an herb-gathering expedition, but now he was very glad he had done so.

The Woman and the Eagle had come to him.

She was there, in the mist, and it was fitting that the eagle be there as well. Grey Eagle raised his gaze to the sky and watched the eagle lazily ride the updrafts that caressed the face of the cliff. He felt a strange and wonderfully comfortable companionship with the eagle and the Woman, as if the three of them belonged together. Again, he searched for her vague, beloved face in the thundering waters, and was relieved to see that she had not left him.

"Who are you?" he whispered.

She only smiled, and the eagle called again. Grey Eagle fought the sudden urge to wade into the freezing waters of the pool, to join the Woman in the misty falls. The temptation was so powerful that, for one confused moment, he wondered if she was related to the legendary Sirens of the Sea. His frontiersman father, Jedediah Beaudine, had long ago told him stories of the great seas that divided continents, of sailing ships that flew over the waters like birds, of the Sirens—beautiful spirit women who lured unwary sailors to their watery deaths.

Then Grey Eagle shook his head, as if to shake away the thought. There was nothing of evil about his spirit woman. She would never harm him, of that he was certain.

The aching need to find her in the flesh tore at him. "Where are you?" he whispered pleadingly. "Tell me how to find you."

Another echoing cry of the eagle sounded, along with his name. "Grey Eagle."

Grey Eagle blinked. Had she answered him at last? He stared at her image, but found, to his dismay, that she was fading.

"Grey Eagle."

That soft voice did not belong to his beloved spirit woman. Disappointment flashed through him with painful intensity as the image in the mist vanished. He raised his eyes and saw that the eagle, too, was gone. Fighting to control his annoyance, Grey Eagle turned to face the human woman who was the cause of his earlier reluctance to accompany the group on its expedition.

Black Moon stood perhaps ten paces away, her hands held demurely in front of her, her large, dark eyes on him, a smile touching her lips. The deep green backdrop of a plump fir tree highlighted the soft golden color of her bead-decorated doeskin dress, which in turn highlighted the glistening black of her long braided hair.

She was breathtakingly beautiful.

Although Grey Eagle was aware of and could appreciate her beauty, his was a detached appreciation, like that he would feel for a beautiful flower. Because he considered something to be beautiful did not mean he wished to possess it—or her. Yet, he suspected that Black Moon wanted him to do just that— possess her. Over the last few months, in gentle and increasingly obvious ways, she had made clear her interest in him.

He did not return that interest, and for the life of him, could not explain why. Most of the men in the village found the lovely young widow very appealing; any of them would have been pleased and proud if she chose them. Grey Eagle fervently wished she would find another, one who could return her feelings.

"Who were you speaking with?" Black Moon asked, her sweet tone a shade away from being a demand. Her dark gaze darted about the area, a faint, grim frown touching her lips for just a moment.

"There is no one else here," Grey Eagle said tiredly. That was true; the Woman and the Eagle were gone.

"You were speaking to someone," Black Moon insisted. "Perhaps to the water spirits?" A teasing smile now lifted the corners of her mouth.

"Perhaps." Grey Eagle shifted the rifle he cradled in his arms, grateful that Black Moon seemed satisfied with his answer. "Are you and the rest of the women ready to go?"

"Yes."

Grey Eagle crossed the small clearing. When he reached her, Black Moon turned and matched her stride to his.

"It was kind of you to accompany us today," she said as

they walked. ''Most of the warriors would rather not guard a group of women.''

''To protect the old ones, the women, and the children is part of a warrior's duty.'' Even to Grey Eagle's ear, it sounded as if he were reciting a white man's school lesson.

''We are grateful,'' Black Moon said softly, with great feeling in her voice. She laid a small hand on his forearm, a daring action for a modest, widowed Cheyenne woman. *''I* am grateful.''

Grey Eagle glanced down at her, and was sorry he did. She looked up at him coyly, through the fringe of long lashes surrounding her eyes. She touched her bottom lip with the tip of her tongue before she spoke.

''I will think of a way to show you how grateful I am.'' The pressure of her fingers on his arm increased just a little.

''There is no need.'' Grey Eagle pulled away from her touch, thankful that they now approached the other women.

Black Moon said no more as she helped the women gather the bags and bundles of winter-dried herbs and sage. Just before they set out, she looked at him, and in that instant, all traces of gentleness were gone. The intense and calculating expression in her dark eyes surprised and troubled him, for it reminded him of a mountain lion he had once seen. The graceful cat had worn a similar expression just before it disembowelled an unlucky mule deer.

Then Black Moon affected a shy smile and turned to lead the way back to the encampment.

Uneasy now, Grey Eagle followed the group of women, all of his senses alert. Danger came in many forms—predators both animal and human, inhospitable terrain, a sudden and unfriendly change in the weather—and he was prepared for all of those. But he could not shake the troubling sense that one day, some kind of danger would come from the lovely and desirable Black Moon. How was he to prepare for that?

Even as he mentally put his feelings into words, he knew how preposterous was the idea that Black Moon would—or could—harm him.

Just the same, Grey Eagle whispered a prayer to the Spirit of the Eagle, and to his Spirit Woman, asking that they help him stay alert.

Chapter Two

"Di-an-a." Diana spoke the word slowly and pointed to her chest. She sat on the edge of her bed and smiled down at the sleepy Indian girl.

Much had been accomplished in the hours since Painted Davy left, taking with him his prized keg of brandy and his stench. The pretty girl who lay under Diana's blankets bore little resemblance to the scruffy urchin who'd been thrown down from Con Horton's horse.

The first order of business had been to give the child a bath, an experience she seemed to reluctantly enjoy. She had even allowed Diana to wash her straight, midnight-black hair, and accepted one of Diana's clean chemises, which was far too big for her scraped, bruised, and rash-covered body. Then, after giving her a dose of laudanum strong enough to render her unconscious, Gideon—with Diana's help—had done his best to repair the girl's damaged leg.

Because she was so thin, it had been easy for Gideon to locate the exact spot to strike with a surgical hammer. The poorly mended bone had snapped and was now correctly repositioned and secured with a splint made of box slats and clean bandages. Gideon could find no evidence of an illness or disease that would cause the rash, but he suspected an allergic reaction to something the girl had been exposed to for some time, since it had not healed in the two months she had been with Sikes and Horton.

The child had come out of her drug-induced sleep long enough to sip on some warm buffalo broth, and now looked up at Diana with dark, beautiful, weary eyes.

"Di-an-a," she repeated in a weak whisper.

Diana smiled and nodded. "Yes." Although certain that her English words would not be understood, she hoped her gesture would be as she pointed at the girl and asked, "What is your name?"

"Spah-roe." The girl's eyelids drifted closed. Her incredibly long black lashes only added to the dark circles under her eyes.

"What did she say?" Gideon asked from his position at the foot of the bed.

"It sounded like 'Sparrow,' " Diana answered in a soft voice as she pulled the blankets up to the girl's neck. "I'm probably saying it wrong. No doubt it's a native name, and translates to something completely different than Sparrow, but perhaps she'll understand that we mean to say her name." She looked down at the girl, who had again fallen into a deep sleep, and felt a pang of fondness. How had the child enaged her affections so quickly?

Through her courage? Through her stoic endurance of physical pain? Through her beauty, revealed when the filth had been washed from her thin body and long, thick hair?

For whatever reason, Diana was drawn to the girl called Sparrow.

She turned to her father as she moved away from the bed with the lighted candle in hand. "Thank you for backing me up today, Papa. I should have discussed it with you first, but I couldn't bear the thought of Horton having her, not even for a moment longer."

"Nor could I," Gideon responded. He led the way to the small parlor where a cheery fire crackled on the hearth. "That was quick thinking on your part, Diana, especially the pretension that the curse is valid. I'm proud of you." He sank into a wooden rocking chair positioned to take advantage of the fire's heat.

Gideon's words of praise warmed Diana's heart. Still, knowing they needed every penny they could earn, she asked, "Then you don't mind that I traded two valuable buffalo robes for a 'slave' we'll one day set free?"

"Of course not."

The warmth in her heart grew. "Thank you, Papa." She put the candlestick on a small table and settled onto the uncomfortable horsehair settee that had been provided by the Army. From a nearby basket on the floor, she took up her needle and the nightdress she intended to size down for Sparrow. The shabby buckskin dress the girl had been wearing now graced the refuse pile behind the house.

"She'll be in some pain for a few days," Gideon commented. "We'll give her small amounts of laudanum as needed. I'll see what I can do about fashioning a set of crutches for her, too; I don't want her putting weight on that leg for several weeks. And it will be interesting to see if that rash clears up now that she's clean and in a healthier environment." He leaned his head against the high back of the rocker and closed his eyes. Illness and exhaustion carved deep lines in his pale face.

The only sounds in the room were the crackling of the fire and the ever-present wails of the wind that blew against the outside walls and crept in around the windows and doors. Diana watched her father, her needle motionless, her heart now heavy with concern and sorrow. Gideon was dying; that she knew. The fatal seeds of damage had been planted in his heart years earlier by repeated bouts of rheumatic fever. She knew the course those seeds would take as they grew, for Gideon had explained it himself. His damaged heart would weaken until it could no longer function properly, which would cause fluids to gather in his lungs. Eventually, he would drown, most likely while lying in his own bed. The horrible cough—always so much worse at night—that plagued him was clear evidence of how far the damage had progressed.

Gideon did not have much time left.

Diana could not help but wonder if his broken emotional

heart was contributing to his decline, and if that—for her father—made the thought of his impending death easier to bear.

Her teeth clenched as she remembered the callous, uncaring words written by her mother in a letter that had been delivered by a courier only an hour ago.

As I've told you before, Gideon, Elinora and I will not join you until you have a suitable home established for us. A small log house on a barren Army post in the wilds of Indian Territory does not constitute a suitable home for two ladies.

After reading the letter he at first had been so happy to receive, Gideon had set the paper on the table without a word and gone to tend Sparrow. Diana read the short letter—not missing the insult to her in her mother's comment about *two* ladies—and had immediately penned a terse response, which now waited in the commanding officer's headquarters building, ready to go out with the dispatch leaving the next day for Fort Kearny and points farther east.

Papa is dying. Even if you have no wish to say good-bye to your husband, perhaps Elinora would like the opportunity to say good-bye to her father.

But now, as she watched her father rest, Diana doubted that her mother and younger sister could arrive in time for farewells, even if they left the very day her letter was received.

How Gideon Murdoch, kindhearted and compassionate Physician and Surgeon, had come to marry Felicia Webster, spoiled daughter of a wealthy merchant, Diana could not understand, nor had she ever. Felicia had never cared for or supported Gideon's calling; instead, she harangued him to join her father in his business. When Gideon made the decision to go West in the final and futile hope that a different climate would slow the deterioration of his heart, his wife remained in St. Louis with Elinora, surrounded by the luxuries provided by her doting parents, raising her younger daughter to follow in her dainty, polished footsteps.

From the time she was a child, Diana had filled the role as Gideon's helpmate, and she had done so gladly, not only because she adored her father but also because she understood and shared his calling as a healer. She had been the one to

assist with her father's patients, to keep his office and surgery—
and now his modest home—orderly and spotless, to study at
his side, knowing that society would never allow her to follow
completely in his footsteps as a documented and certified physician. She had been the one to offer comfort when he lost a
patient, as he too often did, as all physicians too often did.

She realized now that her mother had never intended to join
them in the West.

Her father knew it, too. Perhaps he had always known.

Diana didn't care if she never saw her mother again, but she
missed her sister. Despite their many differences, including the
seven years between them, Diana truly loved Nora. There was
a sense of duty there, too, she had to admit. She wanted to get
Nora away from their mother's influence, before her sister was
ruined beyond salvation. Diana didn't want to one day hate her
sister, as she had come to hate her mother.

A knock on the front door pulled her from her morbid
thoughts and caused Gideon to start. He looked about with
dull, dazed eyes.

"I'll see who it is," Diana said as she set aside her sewing
and stood. In passing her father's chair, she laid a hand on his
bony shoulder and fervently hoped that no one needed Gideon's
services tonight, for he would give them without complaint.
She opened the door; no potential patient stood there, but the
man who did offered her no relief.

Lieutenant Ransom Thatcher held his hat in his gloved hand.
An arrogant smile curved his mouth as the wind blew his
unkempt brown hair about his face, causing strands to catch
on the stubble covering his chin and cheeks. "Good evening,
Miss Murdoch," he said jovially.

Diana fought down a surge of irritation. Since her arrival in
Fort Laramie several months earlier, all of the unmarried officers had called upon her. She knew she was a true rarity—an
unmarried white woman on the frontier. Most of her would-be
suitors had taken her at her word when she gently explained
that she hadn't the time nor the desire for courting, not when
her father needed her so badly. Of course, none had actually
touched her heart, not even the kind and handsome Captain

Adam Rutledge. The captain was, thankfully, content to be her friend. Unfortunately, Lieutenant Thatcher was not.

"Am I needed?" Gideon called.

"No, Papa. This concerns me." Diana stepped out onto the porch and pulled the door closed behind her. The faint light that filtered through the curtained window gleamed off the brass buttons on Lieutenant Thatcher's Army-issue coat and showed his displeasure that she hadn't invited him in.

"A seriously injured patient is staying with us, and my father is not well. It's best that you leave," she said, her tone sharp as she pulled her shawl more closely around her shoulders. The wind was bitterly cold, and she wondered if they would awaken in the morning to find snow on the ground.

"I'll stay only a short while," Thatcher promised, then his voice fell to a low, seductive tone. "I couldn't wait any longer to call on you again, Miss Murdoch." He reached out to caress her upper arm.

Her irritation flared into anger, and Diana shrugged away from his touch. "There is no point in calling on me, Lieutenant. I've made it very clear that I do not, nor will I ever, welcome your suit. I would very much appreciate it if you would do me the courtesy of taking me at my word."

Thatcher's mouth tightened into a thin line, and an answering anger flared in his eyes. "Your father is dying, Diana," he said cruelly, for the first time taking liberties with her Christian name. "You're going to need a man—soon—and I need a wife. A wife will help my career, especially one like you: pretty, educated"—his gaze dropped to her chest—"curved in all the right places." He brought his gaze back up. "I intend to have you, so get used to the idea."

Diana stared at him, the warmth of her fury chasing the chill from her limbs. "You arrogant brute! You'll have nothing of me, except the palm of my hand across your face if you ever again dare to speak to me in such a manner." She pointed past him, her finger stabbing the night. "Get off my porch!"

Instead of obeying her, Thatcher grabbed her hand. "Your uncle Angus warned me you'd need breaking," he growled. "I look forward to it."

She jerked her hand from his bruising grip. "My uncle has no say regarding me, Lieutenant Thatcher, but we'll see what Colonel MacKay has to say about your behavior tonight. Now, *get off my porch!*"

Thatcher backed down the steps as he put on his hat. Again, his lips curved in a smile, this time a leering one. "I'll have you, Diana Murdoch. And, with the exception of Angus giving his blessing, no one will have anything to say about it." He laughed humorlessly and spun on his heel, then strode off into the night.

Diana watched him go, shaking with anger and not a little unnerved. Ransom Thatcher had crossed a line tonight, one to which he had never before come close. Tomorrow, she—and Gideon—would indeed talk to Fort Laramie's commanding officer. Was Thatcher's threatening treatment of her enough to get him transferred to another post, preferably one far, far away? She hoped so. With deep certainty, she knew he would not give up any other way. Grateful that both she and Thatcher had kept their voices relatively low, considering the force of their respective emotions, she turned and pushed the door open.

"Was that Lieutenant Thatcher?" Gideon asked. He stood near the short hallway that led to the bedrooms and on to the kitchen at the back of the house, holding the candlestick high.

"Yes." Diana bolted the door.

"Is everything all right?"

"For now." She managed a smile for her concerned father. "Let's get to bed; we both need some sleep."

For a moment, Gideon watched her, his steady gaze assessing, then he wearily nodded. "Thank you for sharing your bed with our little Sparrow, daughter. Wake me if she needs anything in the night."

"I will. Go on, now, Papa; I'll bank the coals."

Gideon nodded again before he went down the hall. The retreating candlelight sent strange shadows over the walls and ceiling. Diana watched until the closing of Gideon's bedroom door cut off the shifting light, then she moved to the hearth and crouched down. She stared into the flames, appreciative of the soothing heat that warmed her frozen hands and made its way through her thick wool skirts. Soon, though, the troubling scene with Lieutenant Thatcher replayed in the glowing coals, and Diana's stomach tightened.

Her father was dying.

Her mother—and possibly her sister—didn't care.

The life and welfare of an innocent, injured, vulnerable girl was in her hands.

Now she had to worry about the brutish, arrogant Lieutenant Thatcher as well.

"We'll see who has what to say, you bastard," Diana muttered as she grabbed the poker and stabbed at the traitorous coals. Then she realized what she had said, and a blush heated her cheeks, even though she was alone.

Because everyone had problems, Gideon had taught her, the problems one encountered in life were not cause for foul language or name calling. For all his problems, Diana had never heard her father swear. Yet, she could not help but wonder if Gideon ever felt as overwhelmed by the weight of his troubles as she felt tonight.

With both hands clasped around the wooden handle, Diana steadied the point of the poker on the stone hearth and rested her forehead against her hands.

Damn!

"And so, Colonel, I would appreciate it if you would make it clear to Lieutenant Thatcher that I wish him to keep his distance from me." Diana clasped her gloved hands more tightly in her lap, her gaze not leaving the stern visage of Colonel Henry MacKay. The sudden silence in the small office seemed oppressive, and weighed on her. She fought the urge to glance at Thatcher, who sat a few feet away from her, and was grateful for her father's comforting presence on the chair at her side.

"Well, Lieutenant, what have you to say for yourself?" MacKay demanded.

Thatcher jumped to his feet and stood at attention. "There is nothing I can say in my defense, sir," he said calmly. "I do not dispute Miss Murdoch's word."

Now Diana did look at him, not in trepidation but in astonishment.

Even the colonel seemed surprised. "Then why did you persist in pursuing her?"

"I mistook Miss Murdoch's reluctance to accept my suit for a woman's coquettishness, sir. I will not make such a mistake again."

"No, Lieutenant, you will not." Colonel MacKay stood. "I hereby order you to apologize to Miss Murdoch for your behavior, and to desist from all contact with her from this day forward."

"Yes, sir." Thatcher snapped around to face Diana, his boot heels clicking together, his hat held in one gloved hand. He did not look at her, but rather somewhere over her head. "I offer my apologies, Miss Murdoch," he said, his tone as formal as his stance. "I shall not trouble you again with my attentions."

The man sounded sincere, but his refusal to look at her gave Diana pause. Did she dare believe his uncharacteristic humility and remorse? "Thank you," she murmured.

Thatcher nodded, then turned to the colonel and waited.

"You are dismissed, Lieutenant," MacKay said.

"Yes, sir." Thatcher saluted, spun around, marched to the door, and let himself out.

"Thank you for your assistance in this unfortunate matter, Henry," Gideon said as he got to his feet. He clapped a handkerchief to his mouth in an attempt to stifle a cough.

With a quick, concerned glance at her father, Diana also rose.

"No need for thanks, Gideon," MacKay said, his brow furrowed with worry. "Let me get you some water."

Gideon waved the colonel's offer away. "No, but thank you. We must get back and check on our young patient."

"Ah, yes, the Indian girl." MacKay shook his greying head. "The poor child. Enslaved by the Crow, then by Sikes and Horton." He levelled his direct gaze on Diana. "It was kind of you to rescue her from their clutches."

Diana smoothed her gloves, embarrassed by the praise. "It wasn't a matter of kindness, Colonel. In addition to their cruelty toward her, they had immoral intentions. We simply could not leave her with them.''

"Well, many could have, and would have.'' The colonel took Diana's elbow and guided her toward the door. "You'll have no more trouble with Lieutenant Thatcher, Miss Murdoch. I'll see to it, with the help of Captain Rutledge.''

"Thank you, Colonel. And please relay my thanks to Captain Rutledge, as well.'' Diana stepped out onto the windblown porch. Her breath made a cloud in front of her mouth, and she pulled her cloak more tightly about her as she waited for her father to say his farewells.

The snow she had feared last night had indeed fallen, though not in great quantities. Whether the leaden skies would release more remained to be seen. Sections of the whitened parade ground were trampled from the earlier formations of reveille, and the never-ending wind blew little drifts over each clump and bump. Diana shivered. She would be grateful when spring truly came.

Suddenly, a strange sensation crept over her, one she felt was almost a warning. Another shiver raced down her body, but not from the cold. Slowly, she turned her head, and found Lieutenant Thatcher standing beyond the railing at the end of the covered porch. His malevolent gaze burned her with its hatred, and she knew then that his polite compliance in front of the colonel had been an act.

I'll have you.

Whether Thatcher spoke aloud into the wind or not, Diana did not know, but she clearly read the words as his lips moved. He may as well have shouted them. Then his mouth stretched into a grim smile. With a mocking salute, he turned and disappeared behind the building.

"Are you ready, Diana?'' Gideon asked.

Shaken, Diana faced her father, and, from his composed expression, knew that he had not seen Thatcher. She glanced back over her shoulder, wondering if she had imagined the lieutenant's presence, tempted to make certain that the snow on the ground at the end of the porch was indeed marked by boot prints. Instead, she took her father's arm and allowed him to lead her away.

As they approached their cabin, Diana saw movement beyond the window, and her heart sank at the possibility of yet another patient seeking her father's care. Gideon needed to rest, which his muffled coughs confirmed.

She opened the door and stepped into the parlor, with Gideon and a blast of the freezing wind following her. Gideon pushed the door closed as Diana nodded to the two women who sat on the horsehair sofa. She was relieved that neither Clara Steed, the chaplain's plump and sweet-natured wife, nor Belinda Mullen, who was married to the fort's top enlisted man, Master Sergeant Edward Mullen, appeared to be ill or injured. Still, because of her father's condition, she was not pleased to see them, especially the prim, pretty, and annoyingly self-righteous Belinda.

"Good morning, Diana," said that woman. "Dr. Murdoch." Her tone carried a trace of impatience, and her lips curved in the disapproving frown she often wore. Belinda Mullen was an attractive young woman, with pleasant facial features, big blue eyes, a generously curved figure, and golden hair. Upon first meeting her, most considered her husband very lucky, until Belinda opened her mouth. The difference between her pleasing appearance and her abrasive personality was startling and disconcerting. However, unlike most of the other inhabitants of Fort Laramie—male and female alike—Diana was not intimidated by her. In fact, she now had the irreverent thought that not a strand of Belinda's carefully arranged hair would dare step out of line, even in a high wind, and she struggled to keep from smiling at the thought.

"We hope you don't mind that we let ourselves in, Doctor," Clara Steed said anxiously.

"Of course not, Mrs. Steed," Gideon assured her. "That is why I don't lock the door. I wouldn't want anyone who might have need of me to be outside in this wind any longer than necessary." He shrugged out of his coat.

Diana hung her cloak on a hook, then faced the two women.

"Good morning, Clara. Good morning, Belinda. What brings you out on such a frigid morning? I hope no one is ill."

Belinda raised her chin. "We have come to see the heathen girl," she announced. "We must see to the salvation of her sinner's soul."

Diana's mouth tightened in irritation. Belinda Mullen took her Christian faith very seriously, as she did her self-imposed duty to ensure that everyone else believed as fervently as she did. "Our patient is but a child, Belinda," said Diana, "so she can hardly be called a sinner. She is also seriously injured, and, right now, sedated. It is not possible for her to receive visitors."

"For the sake of her immortal soul, it is indeed possible," Belinda snapped. "We must pray over her, and at once, especially if her life is in danger. Otherwise, she will have no hope of reaching the Glories of Heaven promised by our Father, should she die." Her blue eyes burned with the fervor of her conviction.

As she struggled to hold her tongue, Diana could not help but wonder if Belinda would truly welcome Sparrow into her Heaven. For all her preaching, there was little evidence of true Christian love in Belinda's actions and manner.

"She can have no visitors," Gideon said firmly.

"Surely for only a few moments, Doctor," said Clara Steed, her gentle tone a marked contrast to Belinda's aggressive one. "What harm can there be in praying over her?"

"I'm certain God can hear your prayers just as clearly from here, or from the chapel, as He can from our patient's bedside," answered Gideon. He sank into his rocking chair.

"Well, I suppose that is true." Clara sighed in disappointment, while Belinda emitted a disapproving and unladylike snort.

Again, Diana fought a smile. She had no doubt that both women were sincere in their desire to pray for Sparrow, but she also suspected that they were positively itching with curiosity to see the little 'heathen' for themselves. Just as she was about to ask—out of a reluctant sense of obligation—if the ladies would like tea, Gideon spoke again.

"The child's leg is injured, and she is also battered, bruised, and suffering from dehydration and malnutrition.'' His calm gaze rested on Clara. ''But it is not only for her sake that I refuse you admittance to her room.'' Now his gaze travelled to Belinda. ''For several months, she was a captive of the Crow tribe, then later, of Painted Davy Sikes and Conway Horton. In addition to the hurts I have mentioned, she is plagued with a rash, the cause of which I have not yet discovered.''

Belinda shuddered with revulsion.

Gideon continued. ''You ladies are merely trying to honor your . . . Christian duty . . . as you see it to be, but now is not a good time for a visit with our patient. I would never forgive myself if you were exposed to a contagious illness, or perhaps to an infestation.''

At that, Belinda shot to her feet, pulling the folds of her voluminous cape more securely around her. ''Thank you for your concern, Doctor. We will go now.'' She marched to the door.

''But I was just about to offer tea,'' Diana protested, unable to resist the naughty urge.

''We shall call again, my dear,'' Clara assured her, following in Belinda's footsteps. ''When your father feels more confident of the girl's condition.'' She paused at the open door, seemingly oblivious to the freezing wind that she allowed into the room. ''You are both so brave, to put yourselves at risk. I shall pray for you as well as for your poor little patient.''

The sincerity in Clara Steed's warm brown eyes instantly calmed the annoyed little imp inside Diana. ''Thank you, Clara,'' she said, meaning it. ''Divine assistance is always welcome.'' She glanced back at her father, who struggled with another bout of coughing, then turned to find Clara's gaze still upon her, now understanding and sympathetic.

''I know, child.'' Clara patted Diana's hand, and her voice dropped to a whisper. ''I will pray especially for your father.'' She pulled her hood over her head and hurried after Belinda.

Diana closed the door and rested her forehead against the wood for a moment, trying to give her father time to get his cough under control before she turned around. Although she herself had little faith that Divine assistance would be forthcoming, she knew that Clara Steed believed, and Diana took comfort from that. If anyone could reach the ear of God, the kindhearted and deeply faithful Clara could.

At last, Gideon drew a steady breath, and Diana turned around. "I think some fresh hot tea will be just the thing," she said, forcing a note of cheer into her tone.

Gideon nodded. "That sounds good."

"Your comments about contagion were brilliant, Papa." Diana dropped a kiss on Gideon's forehead, dismayed at how hot his dry skin felt. "I'm certain Mrs. Steed is sincere in her beliefs, but I have my doubts about Mrs. Mullen, for she tries too hard to prove to everyone that she is a believer. She would not have easily been persuaded to leave."

"No," Gideon said in agreement. "And our little Sparrow needs rest. It would do her no good to be subjected to the passionate exhortations of a fanatic."

Diana paused at the entrance to the hall that led back to the kitchen. "There is also no need to expose her to such, unless Sparrow indicates one. She may well be content with the spiritual and religious teachings of her own people."

"I agree with you, daughter." Gideon leaned his head against the back of the rocker. His thin face was white with fatigue, although it was not yet nine o'clock in the morning. "Just don't let Belinda Mullen hear you say that. She would not rest until she converted both you and Sparrow."

"I shall be the soul of discretion." Diana smiled and blew Gideon a kiss before entering the hall. She peeked into her bedroom and was satisfied to see that Sparrow appeared to be sleeping comfortably, then continued on to the small kitchen.

There, she allowed her shoulders to sag, and she clutched at the edge of the table as if the solid wood could give her breaking heart the strength it needed. A cry of anguish and sorrow welled up from deep within her, so strongly that she had to bite her lip to keep from screaming it out. Instead, she whispered, "Oh, Papa. How I shall miss you." Her eyes filled with tears, and Diana let them silently fall.

Chapter Three

Wearing only his breechclout, Grey Eagle ducked through the hide-covered door of the tipi and stepped out into the early-morning chill. Although the sky was light, the sun had not yet risen over the prairies to the east, and his breath made a cloud in front of his mouth. It was near the middle of April, and the spring season had proven to be as coy as a flirtatious woman— warm one minute, cold the next. Grey Eagle would be grateful when the spring ceased her teasing games and stayed warm.

The analogy brought another coy woman to mind. Several weeks had passed since the day he accompanied the group of women on their gathering expedition, and, much to his relief, Black Moon had not again approached him. He knew that another warrior had taken a gift of three fine horses to her brother, Two Bears—who was the male now responsible for her—in an offer for her hand, and that the horses had been refused. But he still clung to the hope that her infatuation with him had run its course. Black Moon had many ardent suitors. Surely she had forgotten about him.

He turned as another man came from the tipi. Like he, Jubal Sage wore only a breechclout. Grey Eagle surveyed the tall, lanky man who he considered a second father.

"You know, Jubal, you're mighty lucky you have that beard," he said in English, indicating the bushy grey growth that hung far enough from Jubal's chin to touch his chest. "It keeps you warm on mornings like this."

Jubal glared at him as he shoved a long lock of equally grey hair back from his forehead. "You drag me from the warmth of my bed and the arms of my wife to mouth off at me, Grey Eagle Beaudine? We'll just see 'bout that." He drew himself up, his good-natured indignation wrapped around him like a cloak. "I'll bet them beaver-hide gaiters Sweet Water made me against that new Bowie knife you're all puffed up about that I get to the river, wash up, and get back inside with my woman before you do."

Grey Eagle was partial to his knife, but it was easily replaceable, while the gaiters Sweet Water had fashioned for her husband were truly a work of art. "You've got a bet," he said, and sprinted for the freezing waters of the nearby river, with Jubal hot on his heels.

The great deal of whooping and hollering that accompanied the two racing men told Grey Eagle that he and Jubal would not be alone in their ablutions. The custom of the Cheyenne was that the men and boys of the village bathed first thing each morning in whatever water was near to hand, no matter the season or the weather, while the women and girls prepared the morning meal. Sometimes, like today, the bathing could be uncomfortably cold, but Grey Eagle also found the early-morning ritual invigorating and fun, for there was a certain boisterous camaraderie among the participants.

In deference to the inbred modesty of the Cheyenne people, the designated bathing spot was around a bend of the river and out of sight of the encampment. After flinging aside breech-clouts, the herd of men and boys splashed into the cold waters, which were fed by the melting snows of the nearby mountain peaks.

Grey Eagle dove deep and came up, then dove again. He worked his fingers through his waist-length hair and hurriedly scrubbed his body with sand grabbed from the riverbed. Jubal was moving as quickly as he was, and they both splashed out of the water at the same time. It took only a second for each to secure his breechclout, and they were off. Jubal pulled slightly ahead of him as they dashed through a stand of fir trees.

"Grey Eagle."

His name seemed to float on the very air, and Grey Eagle wasn't certain he had actually heard it. Distracted, he glanced about.

Jubal lengthened his lead.

"Please, I must speak to you."

Black Moon. For a moment, Grey Eagle considered running on, as if he had not heard her. But something had to be wrong for a woman to so boldly approach a man not her husband. Ignoring the pine needles that poked at his bare feet, he stopped and peered into the dense thicket of trees. Jubal's triumphant victory cry echoed in the cold air.

Mindful of her reputation, he called to her quietly, "What is it?" After a moment of silence, which was broken only by the wind whispering through the boughs and the distant shouts and laughter of the bathers, he tried again. "Where are you?"

"Come." Her voice led him deeper into the trees. Finally, Black Moon materialized from behind a boulder.

Breathless from the cold bath and the run, Grey Eagle waited as she approached. She was perfectly groomed and as lovely as ever, but he did not like the look in her eyes. It was ... predatory. The image of the hungry mountain lion flashed in his mind, and he fought the urge to step back.

"What is wrong?" he asked.

She said nothing as she closed the distance between them. Grey Eagle shivered, and not just because chilling trails of water ran from his wet hair down his body.

"What is it, Black Moon?" he asked more sharply.

She halted in front of him, very close. Only inches separated the rounded curves of her generous breasts from his chest. After allowing her gaze to roam boldly over his body, she looked up at him, and Grey Eagle found no trace of modesty or gentleness in her large dark eyes. Her lust was a tangible thing that reached between them and singed him. Perhaps most men would welcome her now, but he did not. Rather, he silently cursed himself for letting down his guard. It was fitting that he give up his knife to Jubal, if for no other reason than punishment for his own stupidity.

"There is nothing wrong, is there?" he asked bitterly. "You called me for no reason."

"There is a reason." Black Moon placed her hands on his chest and swayed toward him, her lips parted.

Grey Eagle grabbed her hands, and Black Moon pressed herself fully against him, grinding her hips against his, trapping his hands against her breasts. Under the softness he could feel the thundering of her heart. Her mouth moved toward his, and he turned his face away. Her lips brushed his cheek as he stepped back and set her from him.

"You shame yourself," he said, his voice firm and low. To his surprise, she showed no sign of shame, or even of embarrassment, at his words. She merely stared at him and ran her tongue over her bottom lip. In disgust, he turned away from her and broke into a trot. Her light, mocking laughter echoed through the trees, and Grey Eagle ran.

Later that same day—when night had fallen—and many miles away, Diana Murdoch drew the brush through her hair as she stared at her reflection in the old mirror hanging above the scarred table that served as her dressing table. At times like this, she mused, in a room lit only by candles, she looked very much her father's daughter.

Gideon had passed on to her his high cheekbones and squared jaw—which Diana privately wished wasn't so square on her— as well as his hazel eyes and thick brown hair. She wondered if her father's hair would ripple with the natural waves hers did if he grew it to his waist, as she had done. It was not evident now, but, in sunlight or at the right angle in lamplight, red highlights glistened in the dark depths of her hair, as they did in her father's. Her mother had always scorned Diana's hair as nondescript in comparison to the deep, rich auburn color with which both Felicia and Elinora had been blessed, but

Diana had come to like her own hair, perhaps because it was one more thing she shared with her beloved father.

Across the hall, Gideon began to cough, the terrible noise echoing from his room. Diana's grip tightened on the brush as she closed her eyes. Each hacking sound, each gasp for air, tore at her as if she were afflicted as well, and she fought the urge to pull her robe on over the chemise and petticoat she wore and rush to her father's bedside. But experience had taught her that Gideon did not want her to witness his battles to breathe, that he had grown self-conscious about disturbing her with the racket of those battles. She heaved a sigh of relief when the coughing ended.

Now a new sound came from the hall—a series of quiet thumps as Sparrow made her way toward the bedroom after a visit to the outside privy. Diana rose from the stool and moved to the door, opening it before Sparrow could knock. She smiled at the girl and beckoned her into the room, then closed the door and returned to her seat. With an eyebrow raised in question, she held the brush out to Sparrow.

Smiling shyly, Sparrow nodded and took the brush. She maneuvered to a position behind Diana and leaned her single crutch against the dressing table, then began to brush Diana's hair.

The brushing of each other's hair had become a bedtime ritual for the woman and the child, one Diana found soothing. Sparrow had gentle hands, and her silent ministration offered Diana respite from the relentless worry she felt for her father. Her eyes again closed, and she let her thoughts wander over the weeks that had passed since Sparrow had come to live with them.

Much had happened, and, in some cases, much had not happened.

In those four weeks, Sparrow had made great strides, and not only in relation to her healing leg. She had put on some badly needed weight, the mysterious rash had disappeared, and now, with her clean, shining hair, clear eyes, and rosy cheeks, the girl appeared to be a picture of health. Although Sparrow had agreeably worn the three simple 'white man' dresses—

two of calico and one of wool—that Diana had fashioned for her, she insisted upon wearing her hair in two neat braids, which was the style of her people. She called Diana by her first name, respectfully referred to Gideon as 'Doctor,' and, other than that, made no attempt to speak, except for the rare occasions Diana caught Sparrow murmuring to herself in her own language.

Try as she did, Diana could not get Sparrow to repeat any other English words, nor did the girl offer any words in her native tongue. They communicated well enough with hand gestures and facial expressions, yet Diana often had the sense that Sparrow understood far more than she let on. She had developed a strong affection for the girl, and hoped that, with time, Sparrow would become more willing to speak.

There had been no further trouble with Lieutenant Thatcher, but Diana had not forgotten the hate-filled look in his eyes as he stood in the wind at the end of the porch, nor his harshly uttered words repeating his vow that he would have her. She hoped that the passage of time would cool the lieutenant's ardor—for her or for revenge, whichever he now felt more strongly. To all outward appearances, that matter had been resolved.

Belinda Mullen had not visited again, although Clara Steed had come by a few times with offerings of fresh bread or a crock of nourishing soup and assurances of continuing prayer.

And, in the last four weeks, Gideon had come four weeks closer to his death.

In her heart, Diana knew her father did not have much time left—only weeks, perhaps only days—and there had been no word from her mother or sister. The familiar pain took her in its tight grip once again, and she pressed a fist to her mouth to keep from crying out.

"Di-an-ah."

Sparrow's young, soft voice soothed her, as did the girl's gentle hand on Diana's shoulder. Even in the dim candlelight, Diana could see reflected in the mirror the loving compassion in Sparrow's dark eyes. She managed a small smile, then sighed as Sparrow resumed her brushing.

The girl pulled Diana's hair back and began to braid it into a single thick plait, then suddenly, she gasped and her hands stilled.

"Netse!"

Diana looked again into the mirror, saw Sparrow's face reflected there, saw the shocked expression.

"What is it?" she asked fearfully. Her gaze darted about the small room; her ears strained for an unusual sound. She saw nothing, heard nothing, out of the ordinary.

Sparrow reached out with a shaking hand and touched the top of Diana's right shoulder, where the strap of her chemise did not cover it. *"Netse,"* she repeated in an awed whisper.

Diana almost sagged with relief. "Sparrow, it's only a birthmark." She realized that she had always before been wearing her nightdress when Sparrow brushed her hair. The girl had never seen her naked shoulder. Diana touched the small brown mark. "It is nothing—just a birthmark."

Sparrow's expression did not relax. Diana turned on the stool and faced her.

"I wish you could understand me, honey." She reached for Sparrow's hand. "The mark doesn't hurt me."

"Netse. Eagle. Mark . . . of . . . the eagle." Sparrow spoke slowly and distinctly, as if she were searching for the proper English words. Her voice carried a strange accent.

Diana stared at the girl, one part of her spooked, another—louder—part annoyed. "You speak English." Her fingers tightened on Sparrow's hand. "You speak English," she repeated, trying to keep a note of accusation out of her tone. "Why haven't you spoken before now?"

"Difficult . . . language . . . to speak." Sparrow's gaze fell. "Safer . . . not to."

Stung, Diana asked, "Safer? Even with me?"

Now Sparrow's head lowered, too. "I . . . sorry, Di-an-ah."

Instantly, all irritation fled. "Oh, honey." Diana drew Sparrow closer. "It's all right. I wish you had felt more comfortable about telling me sooner, but I'm sure you had your reasons not to." She frowned up at the girl. Where on earth had Sparrow learned English? "Surely you did not learn the language from Sikes and Horton."

"*Na-xáne, nahaa'e* . . . uncle . . . aunt . . . they teach me."

"Your uncle and aunt?"

A strange expression of pride moved over Sparrow's face. "All uncles and aunts. The Beaudines."

Diana gaped at her. "You are related to the Beaudines?"

"*Heehe'e.* Yes."

Of the hundreds of questions Diana longed to ask Sparrow, the first that came out was, "Which is your tribe?"

"*Tse-tsehése-stahase.*" As she spoke, Sparrow held out her left hand, palm down, and twice ran the fingertips of her right hand from wrist to fingertips, then extended the left forefinger and made a sawing motion across it with her right forefinger. "In your language, I am . . . Cheyenne." She leaned forward. "Where is . . . this place we are?"

"We are at Fort Laramie, at the confluence, uh, the joining of the North Platte and Laramie rivers."

"My uncles . . . here?" The eager hope on Sparrow's face tore at Diana's heart.

"No, but they will return."

Disappointed, Sparrow straightened. "Where . . . they go?"

"Joseph Beaudine and the Hunter went to St. Louis, with their mother, wives, sisters, and little Henry Jedediah, perhaps six weeks ago. They needed to tend to the family business there, and get supplies for their trading post here. Knute Jensen and his grandson, Thomas, are manning the post for the brothers. The Beaudines will be back before long, Sparrow. They have to be back before the trains of emigrant wagons bound for California and Oregon get here, and that will be soon. I, too, shall be glad for their return. I have missed them, especially the women and little Henry."

"Who is . . . little Henry?"

"The Hunter's son, born last fall."

Sparrow nodded in approval, smiling broadly. Then her expression sobered. "What of . . . Grey Eagle?"

Diana shook her head at the mention of the third—and, she now remembered, half Cheyenne—Beaudine brother, the only

Beaudine she had never met. "I don't know. He did not travel with them, at least not from here."

Sparrow muttered to herself in Cheyenne.

"What did you say?" Diana asked.

"Perhaps he is . . . with my people," Sparrow responded. Again, hope lit her young face. "Jubal Sage, he is here?"

Diana was not surprised that a niece of the Beaudine family knew her friend, Jubal Sage, and, no doubt, also knew his Cheyenne wife. Again, she shook her head. "He and Sweet Water are with her people. She is to have a child soon."

Great joy blazed in Sparrow's dark eyes. *"Ka'eshkone,"* she whispered. "A child." She grabbed Diana's hands. "I must go . . . *na-venovo* . . . my home, Di-an-ah."

A terrible sadness gripped Diana at Sparrow's eager, innocent words. Along with her father, she would also lose the young friend she had come to love. It was inevitable, she knew, but too soon, much too soon. She blinked, unable to speak for a moment. Then she said, "Of course you must go home, sweet child. As soon as your leg is healed. We will find your people."

"How long . . . for leg to heal?"

"Two, maybe three weeks, Sparrow. Not long." For the girl's sake, Diana forced a smile to her face. "Then we will see that you get home."

Sparrow threw her arms around Diana's shoulders. *"E-peva'e!* It is good!"

Carefully, Diana held her, relishing the closeness Sparrow had never before allowed. "I shall miss you very much," she whispered.

Sparrow patted her shoulder, then straightened, her gaze once more on Diana's birthmark. "You come . . . *na-venovo* . . . my home, with me."

"You want me to come to your village?" Diana asked incredulously.

With a nod, Sparrow lightly, almost reverently, touched the dark mark on Diana's shoulder. Her tone and expression became very somber. "Your father . . . soon will join the Great Spirit. You will not . . . be happy here."

Stunned at the girl's insight, Diana could only stare at her.

"You wear the mark . . . of the eagle," Sparrow said. "You belong with us."

Doubtfully, her heart hammering, Diana peered down at her shoulder. "I don't think the mark looks like an eagle. And I do not belong with the Cheyenne." She did not add that she had no idea where she would belong when Gideon died. Not in St. Louis, that was for certain, although she knew her father assumed that, because she had encouraged no suitors and therefore had no plans to wed, she would return to her mother's home when the time came. And just the thought of moving into the dark, repressive quarters of Uncle Angus and Aunt Phoebe made her blood run cold, for there her spirit might die, as Phoebe's had.

The sense of impending loss was suddenly overwhelming, and terrifying in its intensity. Diana whirled around on the stool and again faced the mirror, hoping that Sparrow would hear her unspoken message and finish with her hair, praying that Sparrow would say no more about the birthmark. How ironic that only moments ago she had wanted the girl to talk more.

Determined to change the subject, she asked, "Is Sparrow your name in Cheyenne?"

Sparrow apparently heard the unspoken message, for she again took up the long length of Diana's hair and, her manner nonchalant, continued with the task of braiding. "In the language of my people, my name is said *Xamáa-ve'keso*. It means 'sparrow,' or 'ordinary bird'."

"*Ox-a-mah-kay-so*."

Sparrow giggled. "*Xamáa-ve'keso*."

After a moment's hesitation, Diana asked, "May I continue to call you Sparrow?"

"*Heehe'e*."

"Does that mean yes?"

Sparrow nodded.

"*Heehe'e*," Diana repeated.

Again, Sparrow nodded, a small, pleased smile on her pretty face.

To Diana's relief, they spoke no more as they finished their preparations for bed. She could not help but notice that Sparrow had a new maturity about her, one that had developed only in the last few minutes. Diana felt a vague sense of discomfort, almost as if Sparrow knew something important and would not tell her what it was. She tried to ignore the odd sensation as she blew out the candle and settled under the blankets.

"Good night, Sparrow," she whispered.

"Good night, Di-an-ah. *Netse hé'e.*" Sparrow hesitated, then said, "That says . . . Eagle Woman." She turned on her side and faced away from Diana.

Eagle Woman.

The name sounded alien to Diana, and made her heart pound uncomfortably. *How could Sparrow know about Franklin?* The eagle had been returned to the wild—set free—weeks before Sparrow had come into Diana's life. How could the Cheyenne girl know about him? Again, Diana had the feeling that Sparrow was holding something back. Why did she also feel that she might not want to know what that something was?

Her life was going to change—unhappily, irrevocably, and all too soon—when her father died, and Diana needed no further worries or distractions from any quarter, including from her beloved little Sparrow.

In the dark of her room, under the warm comfort of her blankets, Diana touched the birthmark now covered by her nightdress, and shivered.

Sparrow could not know of the eagle.

It was not possible.

It was not possible.

Chapter Four

Grey Eagle poured water from a buffalo bone ladle over the heated rocks piled in the small pit, breathing deeply of the sage-scented steam that announced its creation with a hissing sound. His eyes closed as he drew the calming moisture into his lungs, as he relished the soothing warmth on his naked body. His long hair stuck wetly to his back. He pulled the thick, damp mass forward over one shoulder and continued his deep breathing.

A visit to the sweat lodge always soothed him, helped work the kinks out of his muscles, helped calm his mind. He took comfort from the ancient symbolism of using the elements of air, water, fire, rock, and earth to cleanse his body and mind. Today, he needed to cleanse both, even though he had done so just yesterday, after the scene with Black Moon.

He opened his eyes and scowled at the heated rocks, annoyed with himself as much as with her. Things would be so much easier if he could force himself to have some special feelings for her.

Black Moon was the most beautiful, most desirable woman in the village. She kept her lodge neat and clean, was a good cook and an industrious worker. From all accounts, she had made Stone Fox a good wife, until an unfortunate run-in with an angry buffalo bull had ended the man's life several months earlier. When her mourning period ended, many of the men in the village vied for the young widow's hand, but Black Moon instructed her brother, Two Bears, to send them all away. Yesterday morning, she had made it very, very clear why she gave those instructions.

She wanted Grey Eagle.

He had the sense that her infatuation for him had grown to the point of obsession. The scene of yesterday morning flashed in his mind, and he groaned to remember how easily he had fallen into her trap, how foolishly he had answered her soft calls.

Grey Eagle grabbed a fresh handful of sage and rubbed his chest vigorously, as if the herb could remove the memory of the feel of Black Moon's small hands on him. He knew that, as a widow, she was no maiden, but still, her aggressive attempts to seduce him had startled and disturbed him, for he had little doubt that she would not have stopped him had he attempted to take her right there among the fir trees. Cheyenne women were famous across the Plains for their chastity and modesty. Apparently Black Moon had none left, at least where he was concerned. The thought did not please him.

Even the tribal elders were beginning to add their own subtle pressures to Black Moon's more obvious ones. Grey Eagle had lived thirty summers, they said, and it was time he took a wife. The loveliest woman in the village was a worthy mate for one of the tribe's greatest warriors, they said.

Most of Grey Eagle's friends thought him crazy for not asking her to share his lodge and his life, but the simple truth was, the seemingly perfect Black Moon did not appeal to him.

He had long suspected that much of Black Moon's attraction to him was based on the fact that his father had been a white man. He was the son of the legendary frontiersman and trader, Jedediah Beaudine. That made him different from the rest of the men in the tribe, and perhaps, to Black Moon, more appealing. It was true that he had proven himself in battle, had counted many coups, was a good hunter and tracker, but he had accomplished nothing that several other eligible men in the tribe had not also accomplished.

Grey Eagle scrubbed his hands over his face to keep the sweat from his eyes, and breathed deeply of the moist air. It was his white blood and family name that drew Black Moon to him, he decided, that and the fact that he did not respond to her overtures with the enthusiasm she had come to expect from a man.

Perhaps that was what troubled him about her, what made him uneasy in her presence. Black Moon was wily, in a truly feminine way. She knew how to use her beauty to her own advantage, and did not hesitate to do so. He often felt that she was playing some secret game with him and the other men who wanted to court her—a game that reminded him of Matilda Greenlea.

Matilda, the daughter of the mayor of St. Louis, young, lovely, spoiled. Grey Eagle had met her during one of the winters he spent in St. Louis with his white family. He had been but seventeen, on the brink of manhood, and she, at fifteen, was far more worldly than he. In that case, it was his Cheyenne blood that had drawn Matilda. To her, he was exotic, and, because her parents disapproved, dangerous. She had toyed with him, had clearly enjoyed playing with his innocent heart. With the help of his surprisingly wise younger sisters, Grey Eagle had managed to escape the unfaithful clutches of Matilda Greenlea with most of his heart intact.

The same warning bells in his head that he had finally listened to with regards to Matilda rang with regularity when Black Moon was around, and Grey Eagle now always listened to those bells.

Besides, there was the woman in his vision, the woman who had haunted his dreams for years, whose face appeared to him in clouds, in flames, in holy steam. She had come to him more and more often in the past few months. But, aside from dark hair and sad eyes, he could not distinguish her features. He only knew that she was real, that she was *not* Black Moon, and that he had not yet found her. He would know when he met her, of that he was certain.

Grey Eagle grabbed the ladle and poured more water on the hot rocks, suddenly desperate to see his vision again, because she always brought him peace. His eyes closed as he poured yet another ladle, willing his Spirit Woman to come to him in the new steam. Over the hissing of the water he heard the faint cry of an eagle, and wondered if the Great Spirit was sending a message to him through his spirit animal. He sat perfectly still, feeling the heat and moisture on his body, breathing the warm, heavy, scented air, listening for another cry of the eagle, waiting for his Spirit Woman to come.

"Grey Eagle!"

His eyes snapped open.

The call came again. "Grey Eagle!"

Annoyance flooded through him as he recognized the voice of Two Bears, Black Moon's brother. No doubt she had sent him, even though both she and Two Bears knew that it was considered terribly rude to disturb a man in the sweat lodge for anything less than a true emergency. Grey Eagle took a few more fortifying breaths, then threw back the hide that covered the small door. He sat for a moment longer as the refreshingly cold air washed over him and dispelled some of the light-headedness he felt after staying so long in the heat and steam. Sure enough, Two Bears waited for him, a short and almost respectful distance away.

Grey Eagle clambered through the small opening and stood. The cold breeze felt wonderful against his naked body and chased the lingering dizziness from his head. He glared at Two Bears. "Why do you disturb me here?"

Two Bears flushed and straightened his shoulders. "My apologies, Grey Eagle."

The man was clearly embarrassed. Black Moon must have badgered him unmercifully, or he would not have come. Grey Eagle shook his head. Two Bears was going to have to bring his willful sister into line.

Grey Eagle turned to the nearby river, took two long strides, and threw his body out over the water in a nearly horizonal dive. As with the cold air, the shock of the even colder water braced him. He pushed his head above the surface, his face tilted toward the sky, and blinked the water from his eyes. Two Bears now stood on the grass-covered riverbank.

"What is so important that you had to disturb me?" Grey Eagle asked.

"I am here on behalf of Black Moon, my sister," Two Bears said formally. "She wishes you to know that were you to bring horses to my lodge, she would not send them away, as she has all the others."

The act of bringing horses to a woman's lodge was a proposal of marriage. The horses were a gift to the woman's father, or the male relative who was responsible for her. If the father or guardian kept the horses, the proposal was accepted. If the horses were sent away, the answer was no. Grey Eagle had no intention of taking horses to the lodge of Two Bears, but he had to choose his words with care. He wanted to give no insult. "Your sister flatters me."

Two Bears frowned. "That is not an answer."

"You did not ask a question." Grey Eagle stood up straight. The water reached just below his waist, and the current tugged at his legs. He stared at Two Bears, his challenge clear.

Two Bears shifted from one foot to the other. Finally he blurted out, "Do you intend to court my sister?"

In the Cheyenne culture, to ask such a direct question, leaving no way for Grey Eagle to save face if his answer was negative, was just as rude as disturbing him in the sweat lodge. He sighed. Neither Black Moon nor Two Bears was going to make this easy on him.

"Black Moon is an exemplary woman, Two Bears," Grey Eagle said, his tone as kind as his irritation would allow. "But she is not the woman for me."

Two Bears stiffened. His mouth tightened into an angry line, and he appeared to be about to say something. Instead, he spun on his heel and stalked off.

With a sigh of relief, Grey Eagle again ducked under the cold, cleansing water. Perhaps now, the matter would end. He rose from the river and made his way over the slick rocks to where his breechclout, leggings, shirt, and moccasins lay. For a moment, he stood in the sunlight, appreciating the little warmth it offered on this cool spring day. He adjusted the leather cord he wore around his waist, then paused.

It felt as if the sun had gone behind a cloud, but, as he looked around, he saw no shifting shadow. Instead of his breechclout, he took up his old knife. He listened . . . and heard the wind in the trees, the song of the river, the nearby chattering of a flock of field sparrows. He sniffed . . . and caught the scent of pine, of winter-dead grasses, of coming rain—or late-spring snow. He watched . . . and saw nothing out of the ordinary.

Yet something—or someone—was there. Or had been.

Perhaps some part of Black Moon's spirit had accompanied her brother on his visit to the sweat lodge, for Grey Eagle felt the same sense of strange heaviness in the air that he felt in Black Moon's presence. He dressed quickly, then tucked the long-bladed knife into the belt he wore over his buckskin shirt. After a quick stop at the fire pit to cover the coals with dirt, Grey Eagle started down the path toward the village, still on guard. He tried to hold on to some of the peace that had come to him in the sage-scented steam, tried to believe that his Spirit Woman had been on her way to him when Two Bears interrupted, but the teasing sense of peace drifted away as surely as did an early-morning mist before the strength of the rising sun. Not even the eagle cried again.

Grey Eagle felt very alone.

From her position behind a tumbled cluster of boulders, Black Moon watched Grey Eagle until he disappeared from sight. Anger warred with desire, and she didn't know which to give in to.

The sight of Grey Eagle coming from the sweat lodge to stand proudly naked in the sunlight, of him coming from the river like some god of ancient times, had set primal forces to play in Black Moon's belly with a ferocity she had never known. The desire had grown to a driving need that pounded in her until she thought she would die if she did not again touch his glistening chest as she had done yesterday, if she did not touch his broad shoulders, his flat belly, narrow hips, and long legs, if she did not pull the power of his fascinating manhood into her aching depths. It had taken all of her self-restraint to stay behind the sheltering rocks, and, in the end, only his insulting words kept her in her place.

She is not the woman for me.

Now her anger grew, drowning the desire. Soon, all in the village would know of her interest in Grey Eagle, if they didn't know already. She, who could have her choice of men, would be humiliated beyond redemption if the man she chose did not choose her. His rejection of her today only strengthened her own resolve.

"I *am* the woman for you, Grey Eagle Beaudine," Black Moon vowed, to herself and to any spirits who might be listening. "You will know it. No man can stand against me." Especially not when she enlisted the aid of Buffalo Woman, an aged medicine woman who knew the secrets of herbs and love. With a grim smile, Black Moon rose from her cramped position in the rock formation, brushed the dirt and dead pine needles from her deerskin dress, and hurried back to the village by a route different from the one Grey Eagle had taken.

After all, he was a Beaudine, and, like his brothers, famous for his tracking skills. It would not be wise to allow him—or her brother—to discover that she had been spying on Grey Eagle's naked beauty.

And what beauty he had so unknowingly offered. The memory of him thus would warm her for a long time to come.

From a distance, a man watched Black Moon approach, his forehead puckered in a frown. Hidden in a thick stand of trees, Calls the Wind had heard the exchange between Grey Eagle and Two Bears, had been filled with a fierce gladness to learn at last and for certain that Grey Eagle would not stand in his way. Although he didn't want to, he would have killed the youngest son of Jedediah Beaudine had that man been foolish enough to take Black Moon as wife.

Grey Eagle was no longer a problem. But, from the angry, determined expression on Black Moon's face as she passed within a few feet of his hiding place on her way back to the village, she had not yet given up on Grey Eagle.

Calls the Wind's mouth tightened with his own renewed determination.

Black Moon belonged to him, even if she didn't know it yet. The spirits of the Old Ones had told him. Oh, they had made him do penance for his unworthiness by allowing her to marry once before, but now that was finished. Just as a man suffered in the Sun Dance, he had suffered through the long months of her marriage, thinking sometimes—perhaps hoping—that he would die from the pain of it. Not even the pain of the Sun Dance—which he had finally danced in a desperate attempt to appease the Old Ones—had eased that other terrible hurt.

Now the penance was paid. The scars on his chest proved his worthiness.

So patiently Calls the Wind had waited, watching with dark, silent humor as Black Moon sent all the horses away, as he had known she would. He would bide his time, and when the Old Ones told him to, he would take his horses to the lodge of Two Bears.

Black Moon would not send his horses away. She would take him as husband, or she would die the widow she was now.

Chapter Five

Gideon Murdoch died on a cool April morning, resting in the shade of a budding cottonwood that overlooked the Laramie River, with Diana holding his hand. As he had requested, a few soldiers had carried him and his bed outside to the low bluff, and there he and his daughter spent their final hour together.

That hour was a peaceful one. Diana was grateful that, because of the close relationship she had always shared with her father, there was nothing left unsaid between them—which was just as well, for Gideon could speak only with great diffi- culty, and Diana feared she would not be able to speak at all around the huge lump of grief that lodged in her throat and kept threatening tears. She did not want her father's last image of her to be such a sad one, and so she struggled to keep her composure.

The loyal Sparrow stayed beside them, reaching out every now and then to gently brush the hair off Gideon's forehead, which the breeze would promptly blow back.

When it became clear the end was not far off, Diana sent Sparrow for Aunt Phoebe and the Reverend and Clara Steed. Soon after their arrival, with the murmured prayers of the reverend floating on the breeze, Gideon slipped from one life to the next.

Diana felt his hand go limp, heard the rasping struggles for air stop for the last time, and she realized in some part of her numbed mind that dying—an event so feared by most people—was actually quite simple. One breathed; then, one did not breathe.

In an instant, her beloved father was gone. Diana bowed her head and let the tears come. At her side, Phoebe sobbed quietly, and Sparrow started moaning in a singsong way that was heart-breaking in its sorrow.

Phoebe eventually drifted away, as did Clara and the reverend when Diana would not allow them to send for the soldiers who would carry Gideon's body back to the house to be prepared for burial.

For a long time, she sat with her father and watched the day grow, listened to Sparrow's mourning wails—which somehow seemed appropriate—and periodically gazed upon her father's still countenance. Gideon appeared to be sleeping, and looked more at peace than she had ever seen him. She stroked his lifeless hand, torn with grief that he was gone, grateful that he was free and no longer ill and suffering.

There had been no word from her mother or sister, and Diana wondered if Gideon had taken the pain of that with him to wherever he was now. Were some kinds of pain powerful enough to carry over to the next life? If so, she knew she'd carry the pain of losing Gideon with her when her time came. But then again, he would be waiting for her, and so, perhaps, at that time, the pain that tore at her now would ease. All she could do was hope that was the case.

She finally allowed two soldiers to carry her father back to the house she had shared with him. They tended to Gideon's body, and when he was laid out in the parlor, his hair neatly combed and wearing his best clothes, the two privates quietly left. Diana spent a sleepless night keeping her father company in the parlor, with candles lit and Sparrow at her side.

Gideon was buried the next day, in the tiny cemetery that so far held the remains of only one other person—a young soldier Gideon had been unable to save from pneumonia. Most of the population of Fort Laramie was present, including several Indians from various tribes, who stood at the outer edge of the crowd. As Diana followed her father's coffin to the gravesite, she recognized the elderly Sioux who had come to Gideon for the sake of his wife. The old man was alone, and she could not help but wonder if his stoic, suffering old wife had also died, and was now with Gideon.

Did the Sioux and the white man share the same heaven if their beliefs were different?

Diana insisted that Gideon's grave and plain pine coffin be situated so that he was facing west, toward California. The reverend read a simple service, which was followed by the bugler's almost perfect rendition of taps. Diana had heard the traditional military song played every evening since she and her father had arrived at Fort Laramie over seven months earlier, so she was very familiar with the compelling tune. But never had she heard a more haunting sound than that of the sad bugle notes echoing over her father's coffin and the windswept prairies. The equally traditional twenty-one-gun salute followed, which caused a nearby flock of field sparrows to take flight, and the coffin was lowered into the dark earth. Diana bent to gather a handful of that earth, and straightened. As she allowed the dirt to trickle through her gloved fingers, she said quietly, "You can go to California now, Papa. You can go wherever you want to."

At her side, Sparrow—who had been respectfully silent throughout the service—started her mourning wail again, shuffling her feet in the still-dead prairie grasses. Some of the Indians on the outskirts of the crowd joined in. The wails had the same haunting effect on Diana as taps had, and she closed her eyes. In its own way, Sparrow's heartfelt grieving song was beautiful, and it seemed fitting that she sing it now.

"Stop that at once!"

At the harsh command, Diana's eyes flew open, and she saw Belinda Mullen give Sparrow a hard shake. Sparrow's mouth clamped shut, and her pretty face lost all expression. A sudden stillness descended upon the gathering, broken by one strident voice.

"That caterwauling is vexatious to the Lord," Belinda continued, her fair features twisted with outrage.

"Leave her alone, Belinda," Diana snapped as she pried the woman's fingers from Sparrow's arm. "She loved my father, and has the right to mourn him in her own way." She waved to indicate the other mourners. "They all do."

"That heathen screeching is disrespectful to your father." Belinda glared at Diana. "Shame on you for not stopping it yourself, Diana Murdoch."

A hot rage roared through Diana, fueled in no little way by the force of her grief. Her voice came out low and dangerous. "No. The shame is on you, Belinda Mullen, for disrupting my father's service with your narrow-minded self-righteousness. I will thank you to leave his gravesite at once."

Belinda's face flushed red, and her lips flapped as she struggled for words. "Well . . . well . . . I . . . never . . ."

"Belinda, please," pleaded Clara. "Come along with me. We'll see to the refreshments back at the mess hall." She hooked her arm with Belinda's.

With an apologetic glance at Diana, and with a little more force than his wife exhibited, Reverend Steed took Belinda's other arm and led both women away. The gathering broke up, and most of the people followed the reverend down the small incline that led to the fort. Colonel Mackay and Captain Adam Rutledge expressed their sympathy and left, as did Miles Breen, the fort's sutler. Soon, only the two soldiers who would fill the grave, two other mourners, and the small group of Indians remained with Diana and Sparrow. At Diana's nod, the soldiers—who she recognized as those who had tended to her father's body the day before—took up their shovels and began the sad work of filling in Gideon's grave. The sound of the dirt hitting the coffin seemed to echo across the prairies and bounce off the faraway mountains to return and reverberate all the way to Diana's very bones. She shook off the strange, terrible feeling and turned to the old man and the young man who stood on the other side of the grave.

"Mr. Jensen, it's not necessary for you and Thomas to stay," she said.

"*Ja*, it is," Knute Jensen responded, his voice accented with the lilt that had come with him from his native Norway. His long wavy hair, which was as white as his thick mustache, blew in the wind. "Your father, he took good care of me and my troublesome old heart. No doubt he is the reason I'm still here. Him I liked and respected, Miss Diana, and the least my grandson and I can do is escort you and your young friend home when you have finished saying your good-byes."

Diana smiled at him, then at Thomas. The boy was thirteen and on the verge of manhood, as tall as his grandfather, his hair as golden blond as Knute's probably once was, as golden blond as his sister's—Annie Rose Beaudine—still was. "Thank you both," she said.

Knute Jensen might appear to be a thin, frail, elderly man, but Diana knew the story of his life, how he had rescued his grandchildren from unhappy situations back East and brought them to the wild land he had come to love. He was a wily, tough, fair-minded man, and Diana knew that he would not tolerate any of Belinda Mullen's nonsense, even if that woman should decide to pursue the unpleasantness she herself had instigated. With Knute at her side, Diana would have the strength to stop in at the funeral reception Clara Steed had arranged at the mess hall, for she felt she must at least make an appearance.

She turned to Sparrow. "I'm sorry for what Mrs. Mullen did, Sparrow."

Sparrow shrugged. "Not your fault. Thank you . . . for protecting me."

"It wasn't protection. I meant what I said to her. You have the right to mourn as you see fit."

One of the soldiers cleared his throat.

Diana turned to face him.

He snatched his hat off and squashed it against his chest. "Miss Murdoch, me—uh, I'm Private Dawson, miss—me and Private Ross, here"—he motioned toward his friend—"well, we're just as sorry as hell about your pa dyin' . . ."

Private Ross swatted Dawson with his hat and glared at him.

Her father lay newly buried at her feet, but Diana still had to fight a smile as the red-faced Dawson continued.

"Sorry, miss, for my cussin'," he muttered.

Then he met her gaze, and the sincerity Diana saw in the man's eyes tore at her heart.

"Yore pa was a fine man, Miss Murdoch, and you do him proud. We—me'n Ross, here—we offer our true condolences."

"Yes, miss, we do," Ross added.

Deeply touched, Diana looked from Dawson to Ross. "Thank you, gentlemen. And thank you for your kind care of my father's . . . body. Your gentleness with him comforted me." Again, tears welled in her eyes.

Private Dawson blinked rapidly, and Private Ross looked away, toward the far-off mountains.

"Yes, miss," said Dawson. "You're surely welcome, miss."

"We was proud to tend to him," Private Ross added.

"Thank you, gentlemen," Diana said quietly. "There is no way I can repay you for your kindness to both me and my father during this difficult time, but if I can ever offer my assistance, please do not hesitate to ask."

"Yes, miss." Private Dawson slapped his hat back on his head. "Thank you, miss."

"Yeah, thank you, miss," added Private Ross. He brushed a hand across his eyes before he also replaced his hat.

The two men shouldered their shovels and walked away, in the direction of the fort. Suddenly, Ross stopped. Dawson halted also, with a questioning glance at his friend. Still holding his shovel, Ross clicked his heels together and spun around in true military fashion. Instantly, Dawson followed suit, and, in perfect unison, the two soldiers gave Diana a crisp salute.

Her eyes watered anew, and Diana offered the men a tremulous smile.

Their backs ramrod stiff, their heels clicking again, Privates Dawson and Ross turned and marched away, their burial shovels held as proudly as any rifle or sword.

"Now we sing?" Sparrow asked.

Diana nodded. "Yes. Please sing." She turned again to the

grave as Sparrow's haunting song rose into the sky. The other Indians moved closer and joined her, shuffling their feet in time with some ancient pulse of the earth, the wind, and the sky. Knute and Thomas Jensen stood respectfully with their hats in hand, content to wait.

The cool wind blew against Diana's black skirts, causing the modest hoops underneath to sway, while the long ribbons of her black bonnet rode that same wind. The mournful keening of the Indians comforted her, perhaps because she, too, felt like wailing, and would not allow herself to do so. Instead, she let her tears slide silently down her cheeks as she looked out over the prairie that stretched away to the mountains in the west.

She heard the eagle before she saw it, heard the unmistakable call. Had Franklin come to bid her father farewell? Had he come to take Gideon with him?

Eagerly, Diana searched the sky, at last finding the dark vee shape highlighted against the wispy clouds. Closer and closer the eagle circled, but he still remained high. If it was Franklin, he would not come to her today, not with so many people in such close proximity.

As she fought a stunning sense of disappointment, Diana became aware of an approaching rider. She shaded her eyes against the sun and waited. When she recognized the buckskin-clad man, her lips curved in welcome. "Mr. Sage," she called, attempting to be heard over the Indians. "How good of you to come."

A tall, lanky man slid the long-barrelled Hawken he held into its scabbard, then eased himself from saddle to ground with careless grace. He snatched his battered hat from his head, revealing a head of long bushy hair as grey as his equally long and bushy beard.

"Miss Diana. Howdy, Knute. Thomas. I just rode in from the Cheyenne encampment and saw the gatherin' up here. I didn't know who was bein' buried until I saw you, miss." He glanced at the unadorned wooden cross that stood at the head of the grave. "Your pa was doin' poorly the last time I saw him; I reckon it's him who's passed on."

Diana nodded. She, too, looked at the cross. "We're having a headstone made. He died only yesterday, so there wasn't time for more." Her voice trailed away.

"I sure am sorry." Jubal stepped to her side and, in a surprising gesture, put an arm around Diana's shoulders. He simply stood with her, encircling her with his concern and compassion.

How strange, Diana mused as she willingly and gratefully leaned against Jubal's strength. Two aging frontiersmen, a boy, a Cheyenne girl, and a few Indians she didn't even know offered her more comfort than did her own family. Her mother and sister hadn't come from St. Louis, Uncle Angus hadn't bothered to come from his trading post, and Aunt Phoebe had been one of the first to follow the reverend back to the fort. Diana looked at the small, odd group of people surrounding her, and felt blessed.

The song of the Indians faded away, the eagle cried one last time and disappeared into the heavens, and Diana knew it was time to go. She found it surprisingly difficult to leave her father. In a strange way, she was glad that the unfortunate soldier rested near Gideon. At least neither would be alone on the lonely, windswept hilltop. She turned to Sparrow. "Are you ready, Sparrow?"

"Sparrow?" Jubal repeated.

Diana nodded as Sparrow stepped to her side. "I believe you two know each other, for Sparrow asked about you." She moved to put an arm around Sparrow's shoulders, then frowned, for Sparrow and Jubal seemed frozen. Each stared at the other, each with a curious expression of joy. Then Sparrow launched herself into Jubal's welcoming arms, and the mountain man danced around with the happy girl.

"Lordy, lordy, girl!" Jubal cried, his eyes suspiciously moist. "I plumb didn't recognize you there. You're all growed up now, and so pretty!" He set her on her feet. "How did you come to be here? How did you escape the Crow? We went after you, your pa and your uncles and me; we searched for weeks. Then the snow came, and even the Hunter couldn't pick up the trail. How'd you get here? Talk to me, girl."

"Maybe she could, if you'd hush up, Jubal," Knute put in,

his tone quiet but touched with an unmistakable note of joy. "And, as happy as you two are to have found one another, let's not forget that Miss Diana has just buried her pa."

Stricken, Jubal faced Diana. "Oh, I *am* sorry. I meant no disrespect."

"I know," Diana said soothingly. "No doubt my father is smiling over this reunion himself. Let's go back to the fort, and you two can catch up along the way."

At her words, the entire group moved away. Diana hung back, and at last was left alone.

She glanced down at the dark mound of earth at her feet and found it difficult to comprehend that her father lay under there, that he would lay there forever. Never again would Gideon smile at her, or teach her more about the medical mysteries of the human body; never again would he offer his wise, loving counsel in times of doubt or confusion.

Once, she had feared that when the time came, she would prostrate herself on her father's grave and sob embarrassingly and uncontrollably until all of her grief was spent, or until she died herself—whichever came first.

Instead, now that the dreaded time was upon her, Diana felt numb and empty, and her new fear was that no amount of sobbing would ease the terrible grief that tore at her heart. Perhaps she was beyond tears.

"I don't know what to do without you, Papa," she whispered. "I don't know where I belong; I'm not even certain of who I am." Mercilessly, she twisted a handkerchief between her hands. "You are gone, and Sparrow will soon leave, too, for Mr. Sage will take her home to her people, where she belongs." Like a woolen mantle, a thick depression settled over her, and, for a moment, Diana wished that she could sink into the earth and follow her father to wherever he had gone. She did not want to stay here alone.

The eagle called.

Thankful that he had returned, Diana lifted heavy, squinting eyes to the sky, and finally made out the form of the eagle. As she watched, the magnificent creature drew closer and closer, then seemed to move in slow motion as it fanned its mighty wings and settled daintily onto the cross that stood at the head of Gideon's grave.

"Franklin?" She whispered the name.

The eagle turned its head to one side and blinked.

Slowly, Diana inched closer, one gloved hand reaching, in desperation, in hope. Franklin had been gone for so long; would he still allow her touch? Other than shifting its feet, the eagle did not move. Her fingers touched its dark head, and the bird made a strange cooing sound.

"Franklin." Tears welled in Diana's eyes and spilled down her cheeks. "Thank you for coming." She jerked the glove from her hand, then stroked the narrow space between the eagle's eyes with a bare finger. "You've grown so much; you're so tall now." Her hand travelled down the raptor's neck to his back, and Diana marvelled at the shiny feathers and striking coloring of the young eagle she had once cuddled to her breast. "You are beautiful, Franklin."

Diana sank to the ground, her hooped skirts making a black pool around her folded legs, the wind lifting a wayward strand of her hair as well as the silk ribbons of her bonnet. She sat next to the cross that marked her father's grave, with the shadow of the eagle falling over her, and although the terrible grief remained, she knew the first inkling of peace.

All would be well.

She didn't know how, but all would be well. Diana had the sudden, powerful sense that forces were at play—forces she did not understand, forces that would change her life. Again.

Was that force the Christian God with whom she had been raised? Or perhaps the Great Spirit of Sparrow's people? Or perhaps even some other power or force as yet undiscovered?

Diana didn't know, and didn't care.

Her father's death had already changed her life, in an unhappy way. The change she now sensed coming was different, and Diana took comfort from that.

All would be well.

Franklin told her so.

Chapter Six

Diana glanced at the pale face of the young soldier on whose bloody calf she worked. "How are you holding up, Private?"

"Just fine, ma'am."

How she admired his courage! The sheen of sweat on Private Dawson's forehead, along with his clenched jaw, told Diana that he was not fine, but there was nothing to be done for his pain—which caused her a different kind of pain. How had her father coped with the frustrating truth that medical science could offer only so much aid? Aid that all too often was not enough?

Minutes earlier, Dawson had been brought to her by his friend, Private Ross, and neither of them seemed to feel that her aid was lacking. Diana had immediately recognized the two as the compassionate soldiers who'd been assigned to her father's burial detail, and she was glad that Dawson had taken her up on her graveside offer to help him if she ever could.

As she gently and methodically cleaned the gash in Dawson's leg, Diana thought back on how her life had changed in the month since Gideon's death. Regardless of what Franklin told her at her father's grave, none of the changes had been for the better.

Sparrow, too, was gone now; ten days earlier, Jubal Sage had taken her away, to return her at last to her family and her people. The departure of her beloved sister-friend, following so soon on the heels of her father's death, left Diana with a loneliness more devastating than any she had imagined could exist. She waited and hoped for the return of the Beaudine brothers and their families—and the honest friendship they all so freely offered her. Surely they would arrive any day.

Because of Army regulations, Diana had been forced to move from the surgeon's modest house, even though no surgeon had yet arrived to take her father's place. The terse letter from her mother demanding that she immediately return to St. Louis *when the proprieties concerning your father's death have been observed* had been burned upon receipt and so far went unanswered. By the reluctant and resentful grace of her uncle, softened somewhat by the pitiably eager welcome of her aunt, Diana now lived in a small, unheated, windowless room attached to the side of Angus MacDonald's trading post store, a room for which she was truly grateful. At least she had a roof over her head.

There, the few brave people who felt comfortable entrusting the care of their health to a woman sought her out for her healing skills. Her patients consisted of enlisted men, laundry women, Indians of various tribes, and frontiersmen, all of whom responded with heart-touching gratitude to her sincere if imperfect efforts. Others believed it unseemly, if not downright illegal, for Diana to practice her medical skills—after all, she was a *female,* and certainly was no schooled and licensed physician. Those self-righteous people were quite vocal in expressing their views, most following the spiteful example of Belinda Mullen.

The two soldiers now with Diana apparently had no such reservations. On the contrary, Dawson had delivered himself into her hands with a confidence so innocent and touching that Diana hoped she would prove worthy of his trust.

The unfortunate man, while working with a wood detail, had fallen victim to a loose ax head. The wound was serious, but not grievously so. However, because the accident had occurred a few miles away, he'd lost enough blood to cause Diana

concern, just as the less-than-ideal surgical conditions caused
her concern.

Private Ross stood at her side, holding a lighted oil lamp—
much needed in the dim interior of Angus's store—while Dawson lay on a rough table, one she had hurriedly cleared of cast-
iron pots and various other trade goods. Those dusty goods
now lay in a heap on the dirt floor, and, not for the first time
that day, Diana offered silent thanks that her unpleasant uncle
had gone to confer with Miles Breen about a lost shipment of
whiskey.

She smiled down at Dawson in what she hoped was an
encouraging way. "You are very brave, sir. I know my work
on your leg is painful to you, and I won't be much longer. You
were lucky that the ax head hit where it did."

Dawson's brow wrinkled in a confused frown. "Ma'am?"

Good, Diana thought. She hoped she could distract him long
enough to perform her next procedure, which was certain to
cause the poor man even more pain. "One end of the ax blade
hit the top of your boot." She poured a generous amount of
her father's brandy over the wound. "The toughness of that
leather kept the blade from going deeper."

Private Dawson gasped. "Yes, ma'am," he whispered
hoarsely. "I sure am lucky."

Again, Diana smiled at him. "That was the worst." And
again, she cleansed the wound and the surrounding area with
a clean cloth that still steamed from the hot water in which she
had first soaked it. Then she reached for a cotton cloth that had
been folded to form a pad. As she pressed the pad against
the wound, she said, "You must listen to me very carefully,
Private." With a nod of thanks, she accepted a rolled bandage
from the observant and capable Private Ross. "It is absolutely
essential that this wound be kept clean until it forms a scab."

"Disgraceful!" A shrill voice echoed from the direction of
the front door.

Without looking, Diana knew that Belinda Mullen had
uttered the scathing word. She ignored the woman, and noticed
that both soldiers did as well. Calmly, she continued her instructions. "There will be some seepage as the wound drains, and

perhaps a little blood—both are to be expected.'' She made a lengthwise tear in the bandage and tied it in place. "Are you familiar with infection, Private?"

Before Dawson could answer, Belinda spoke again, her tone frigid. "Diana Murdoch, you will exhibit enough manners to acknowledge my presence, even though I have discovered you engaged in the clandestine and improper activity of tending that man's exposed leg—activity for which your qualifications raise serious doubts." She sniffed in outrage. "And without a chaperone's proper supervision," she finished triumphantly.

Diana fought for control of her tongue. Until the unpleasant scene at Gideon's gravesite, she had managed to tolerate Belinda, but since then—and even more so following an uglier scene a few days later, when Diana found Belinda forcing Sparrow's head under the surface of the Laramie River and calling it a 'Christian baptism'—she could not, no matter how hard she tried, be civil to the woman.

"Diana!"

The witch was not going to leave.

Resigned to yet another disagreeable scene, Diana was about to turn when she caught a glimpse of Dawson's face. He rolled his eyes, then winked at her. Because Belinda's husband was their master sergeant, neither Dawson nor Ross could safely say or do anything in Diana's defense, and she understood that. But Dawson's subtle sign of support—coming from a man who had to be in terrible pain—caused her to throw all caution to the wind, and she turned to face her adversary.

"How dare you interfere with my treatment of a seriously wounded man?" Her hands found her hips, and Diana took grim pleasure in the startled expression on Belinda's face. "Would you have me leave him outside, bleeding in the dirt, until someone you deem a proper chaperone could be found? Are you willing to help me, Belinda? Will you stain your hands with this brave man's blood and tend to his hurts?"

Belinda stared as if Diana had sprouted horns. Then she straightened and lifted her chin. "Your father, God rest his soul, was a good Christian man, and a proper gentleman. He would be ashamed were he to see and hear you now."

Diana took a deep breath. Her rage was a thing alive in her chest, struggling to claw its way out. If that rage broke free, she feared for Belinda's safety. She forced her hands, now clenched into fists, to her sides. "You are not worthy of mentioning my father's name, let alone telling me how he would feel," she ground out, her voice sounding deadly even to her own ears. "You call yourself a servant of the Lord, Belinda Mullen. Yet, with your rigid, judgmental twisting of the teachings found in the Bible, you do far more damage than good for the sake of your precious Master."

Belinda gaped at her, her pretty face sheet white under her flowered bonnet, one gloved hand at the dainty froth of lace that decorated the neckline of her stylish hooped gown.

Diana could not help but be very aware of her own unadorned black mourning gown—which she wore with no hoops—and the bloodstains on her white apron, and the nagging tendrils of hair that curled down the sides of her face and along her neck. She felt dowdy and disheveled, which did nothing to help her mood. She advanced on Belinda, who had not yet found her tongue.

"No doubt you came to call upon my aunt, who is foolish enough to take you seriously," Diana snapped. "She is having tea with Clara Steed, and it is my sincere hope that Clara's gentle influence will undo some of the harm you have caused poor, weak-minded Phoebe." She stabbed her forefinger in the direction of the door. "Go. Get away from me, and from my patient. He does not need your poisonous presence when he is already badly injured."

Belinda's mouth worked silently, like that of a recently landed fish, but only a strangled cry emerged. She whirled about and hurried out the door without closing it behind her, her hooped skirts swaying gracefully.

Relieved and shaken, Diana stared at the empty doorway. Never in her life had she spoken in such a manner to anyone other than Belinda Mullen, and that had happened only once before—the day she rescued Sparrow at the river. Then she had railed at the woman for the insufferable arrogance of forcing her beliefs on other people, especially young, innocent children who were physically incapable of defending themselves.

"Sorta makes you feel sorry for the master sergeant, don't it?"

Ross's calm voice echoed in the room, drawing Diana from her morbid reverie, dispelling in an instant the anger and frustration that engulfed her. With a smile, she turned to face the two men.

"If she was my woman, I'd choke her," Dawson announced as he sat up on the table. "No court in the world would convict me, neither. The verdict would be justifiable homicide."

"You're right," Diana said, her smile broadening. Then she sobered. "Thank you, both of you, for your support."

"You were wonderful, Miss Murdoch."

The sincerity in Dawson's words made Diana blush.

"You were," Ross added. "I ain't never seen anyone stand up to Mrs. Starchy Drawers like that."

Diana fought another smile as she watched Dawson smack Ross's arm. "Mrs. Starchy Drawers?" she repeated.

Ross shrugged. "We figure it has to be something like that. What else would make a pretty young woman like her so crotchety?"

"I don't know why it is so important to her that everyone act and believe as she sees fit," said Diana. And she didn't care, either. She just wanted Belinda Mullen to stay away from her. After today's incident, maybe the woman would. In an effort to get back to more pressing matters, she said, "You must watch out for infection, Private Dawson, for it can lead to gangrene, which can lead to amputation. Cleanliness is the best weapon you have, so I urge you to follow my instructions. I'll come by the barracks tonight—with a proper chaperone— and check on you, and again tomorrow. If all looks well, I may take a few stitches at the deepest part of the wound, but not until I know there's no infection."

"Yes, ma'am. I'll do exactly as you say. Ain't no way I'll lose my leg—might as well shoot me if it comes to that." He swung his legs over the edge of the table.

"It shouldn't come to that," Diana assured him. She looked at Ross. "You probably have to report back to Captain Rutledge." At his nod, she continued. "Please tell him that Private

Dawson is to stay off that leg for a day or two—bed rest, and no riding, either—and after that he will need a crutch for a few more days. The wound will heal faster if he rests the leg as much as possible. If the captain has any questions, ask him to see me."

"Yes, ma'am." Ross settled his hat back on his head. "Thank you for your help, Miss Murdoch. We sure are lucky you haven't headed back to St. Louis yet."

"There's no danger of that, at least not for a while."

"Good." Ross wrapped an arm around Dawson's waist and helped him off the table, while Dawson draped his arm over Ross's shoulders. The two men made their awkward way to the door.

"Thank you again, Miss Murdoch," Dawson called.

"You're welcome, Private. I'll see you tonight."

The door closed behind them, and Diana set to work scrubbing the blood from the table. If her luck held, she would have the table and the room put to rights before Angus returned.

She finished with the table and cleaned her arms and hands, then carried the basin of used water outside. Just as she was about to reenter the store, an Indian with long greasy hair and wearing dirty buckskins rode up at a fast trot.

"Missy Mur-doch! Missy Mur-doch!"

Diana paused at the door and shaded her eyes with one hand for a better look at the man. She did not recognize him. "Yes?"

"Jubal Sage hurt bad. Bear mauling. Need you come, Missy Di-an-ah Mur-doch. He need your . . . medicine."

"Mr. Sage is hurt?" Diana stared up at him, her heart in her throat. "Where is he?"

"Bridger cabin. Go now." He turned his horse's head away.

"Wait!" She took a few steps. "Take me to him!"

The man nudged his horse to a walk, then a trot. "Bridger cabin!" he shouted over his shoulder. "Go now! Hurry!"

In despair, Diana watched as the man rode away.

Jubal needed her—if he was still alive.

But where on earth was the Bridger cabin, and how was she supposed to find it?

Chapter Seven

Diana repositioned the reins in her gloved hand and looked back over her shoulder at the two soldiers who followed her on horseback. Privates Sedley and Grimes seemed alert and competent, and so far there had been no sign of any kind of trouble, but she had met both men only hours ago, and could not shake a feeling of foreboding. Then her gaze returned to the man who led the way, and her stomach knotted with renewed intensity.

Lieutenant Ransom Thatcher had been assigned as leader of the little expedition, and Diana wished that it had been anyone else. But most of the soldiers were away from the fort on this cool May day—either on patrol or wood detail—and few had been available to accompany her on her mission of mercy. Captain Rutledge was with the wood detail; Ross was on his way to rejoin the captain; Colonel MacKay led the routine patrol; and Dawson was injured and in bed. The acting commander, Captain Winslow, had assured her that Thatcher was the only soldier who knew the exact location of the old Bridger cabin, a derelict structure rumored to have been built years earlier by the famed Jim Bridger himself. Jubal's urgent need of her medical skills was the only reason Diana agreed to go with Thatcher and two soldiers she did not know. The knot in her stomach came as much from her concern regarding her escorts as it did from worry over her dear friend.

She shifted in the saddle and pressed her feet against the stirrups in an attempt to give her aching legs a good stretch. There had been little opportunity to ride in the past month, and already her legs were stiffening. She thought longingly of the sidesaddle she had been forced to leave behind in St. Louis and wondered if she would ever become accustomed to riding astride. Her mother would be appalled to see her in such an unladylike position, with her skirts hiked up almost to her knees and her stockings and lace-trimmed drawers exposed.

"How much farther do you think it is, Lieutenant?" she called.

"My guess is an hour, Miss Murdoch, at the most." Thatcher pointed to the north, where a bank of clouds hung low on the horizon. "Beyond that ridge a good-sized creek runs toward the Platte. The cabin sits on the bank of that creek." There was no hint of anything but professional politeness in Thatcher's tone, much to Diana's relief.

Since the beginning of the journey several hours earlier, Thatcher had been composed, efficient, and respectful. Not so much as a single leering glance did he send her way, exposed drawers or no. Diana wanted very much to believe that the lieutenant had lost all personal interest in her, for he was certainly acting that way. But she could not forget the uncomfortable meeting in Colonel Mackay's office some months earlier, and later, on the porch, when she discovered that the professional demeanor Thatcher had displayed before the colonel had been just that—a display.

Thatcher pulled his mount to a stop and looked back at her. "Are you doing all right, Miss Murdoch? You've been in the saddle for hours now. We can rest if you need to."

Again, there was nothing but professional concern in his voice. If Thatcher was putting on an act for the benefit of the two privates behind her, the act was very convincing. Diana tried to relax. "Thank you for your consideration, Lieutenant, but it isn't necessary to stop." Her aching leg muscles seemed to tighten even more in protest at her words. "I'd like to get to the cabin as quickly as we can. I'm very worried about Mr. Sage." She also dreaded seeing the injuries Jubal must have suffered. Most run-ins with a bear ended with the bear the victor, and Diana hoped it was not too late for her to help him.

"As you wish, miss." Thatcher nudged his horse's sides, and they continued on toward the ridge.

The call of an eagle echoed through the still air. Diana looked about eagerly and spotted a bird some distance to the west. Whether or not it was Franklin, she did not know. The tiny, faraway figure rode the air currents, and she was reminded of the sad day when Jubal Sage left Fort Laramie for the Cheyenne encampment, accompanied by Sparrow and a packhorse laden with the supplies and gifts she had sent along with the girl. Diana had ridden out with them, to a hill perhaps a mile from the fort.

"Di-an-ah, you come with us," Sparrow begged. "You will be happy with my people."

Jubal Sage offered her a place to stay, in the tipi he shared with his wife, Sweet Water. "It would be good to have you there, Diana, what with the little one comin' and all."

Because of her love for Sparrow, Jubal, and Sweet Water, Diana was sorely tempted. She had no desire to obey her mother's written command and return to St. Louis, nor did she want to live with her aunt and uncle, but the idea of leaving Fort Laramie to stay with the Cheyenne was simply too far-fetched. White men lived with various tribes, but Diana had never heard of a white woman doing so, unless the woman was a captive. "Thank you both," she said. "A part of me wants to ride off with you now, today, so that I never have to go back to Angus's house. But, for now, my home is there, if for no other reason than the fact that my presence offers Aunt Phoebe some comfort." She would not be swayed from her position.

Then Franklin came for a visit. He settled on the ground near Diana's skirts and remained still when she crouched down next to him. Jubal knew the story of the eagle, and had seen her with Franklin before, so he showed no surprise at the eagle's calm acceptance of her touch. Sparrow, however, was *speechless, her dark eves wide and staring, her skin several shades more pale than usual. Diana's gentle explanations— as she stroked the favored spot between Franklin's eyes—that the eagle was sort of a pet did no good.*

"You have been touched by the Spirit of the Eagle, Di-an-ah, in more ways than one. You belong with my people. One day you will know this as surely as I do."

Then, after sad embraces, Sparrow and Jubal left, headed northwest along the Platte, and took a part of Diana's heart with them.

The memory of that painful day faded as Diana again focused on the eagle in the sky, and she took comfort from the knowledge that there had been no other choice but to send the now-healed Sparrow back to her people. There had been serious trouble, both with Belinda Mullen and her relentless attempts to convert Sparrow to Christianity, and with Uncle Angus and his constant cruelty toward the girl. The man had even gone so far as to suggest that Sparrow be put to work as a whore.

At least she no longer had to worry about Sparrow's safety.

A strong gust of wind rushed down the ridge, and Diana noticed that the clouds on the western horizon had taken on an ominous darkness. She sighed. No doubt they were in for another spring storm, which would only hinder their return trip to Fort Laramie, and, judging by the position of the sun, it was already past noon. For the first time, it occurred to Diana that she and her companions might be forced to spend the night in Jubal's rough sanctuary. Thunder rumbled across the sky, followed by a flash of lightning. Her mare sidestepped nervously, and Diana saw that the eagle was gone, no doubt seeking refuge from the coming storm. Would she and the rest of her little party reach whatever shelter the old cabin offered before the storm hit?

As if he read her mind, Lieutenant Thatcher nudged his mount to a trot, calling back over his shoulder, "We'd better get moving!"

For the next half hour, Diana had no opportunity to think about anything except controlling her mount as they hurried up the steep face of the ridge as quickly as the rough terrain would allow. When they came out on the top, the wind struck them with ferocious zeal, and Diana was grateful for the strings that tied under her chin and kept her wide-brimmed hat from blowing away.

The grass-covered ridge dropped down in a gentle slope that made for much easier and faster riding, and Lieutenant Thatcher led the way through small batches of fir trees and scattered rock outcroppings. The slope ended in a narrow valley, at the bottom of which Diana could see a creek peeking through the stands of willow and box elder trees. Drops of cold rain stung her cheeks, and she hoped the cabin was not far, for her sake as well as for Jubal's.

Without hesitation, Lieutenant Thatcher led them on, seeming to know exactly where he was headed. Diana wondered how he had first found the cabin, especially when no one else at the fort knew where it was. They followed the path of the wide creek to the north, and eventually rounded a sharp bend. Just ahead, through the increasing rainfall, Diana could make out a rough log structure, which supported a clinging, open-faced shelter on the near side, a shelter she assumed was meant for horses. Behind that, the remains of a corral could be seen; several of the fence rails were missing and two of the posts were knocked over.

Puzzled by the fact that there was no sign of Jubal's horse, Diana pulled her mount to a stop and, as uncomfortable as she was with Lieutenant Thatcher's nearness, allowed him to help her down from the saddle. Her legs wobbled when her feet touched the ground, and she was forced to hold on to the lieutenant's arms longer than she wanted to.

"Steady there, miss," Thatcher said, his hands tightening at her waist. "Take a minute to get your bearings."

Diana glanced up at him. Again, there was no sign of any emotion on his face other than polite concern. "Thank you, Lieutenant." She released him. "I'm fine now. I'd best see to Mr. Sage."

Instantly, his hands fell away from her waist, and Thatcher nodded. "You go on and get out of this rain. I'll bring your medical bag."

Diana turned and hurried to the door of the run-down cabin. The higher of the two leather hinges had ripped through, causing the heavy door to hang at an angle, and it took all of her strength to lift and push the door inward. "Jubal?" She peered into the dim interior and was able to make out a fireplace along the back wall, in front of which stood a sadly leaning table. "Jubal, it's Diana." She pushed again at the door.

"Allow me to help, Miss Murdoch." Lieutenant Thatcher handed her the leather satchel that held clean bandages, a small bottle of laudanum, and her father's surgical instruments, then applied his strength to opening the door wide enough for entry. He stepped inside, and Diana followed him. Squinting in the poor light, she looked about the single room. A rough pallet lay on the dirt floor in a far corner, the only furnishing other than the dusty table. A small pile of various-sized sticks rested next to the fireplace built of smooth riverbed stones, and the remains of a candle formed a pale lump of wax on one of the more protruding stones. That was all the cabin held.

"He's not here," Diana said unnecessarily. Her heart grabbed with renewed worry for Jubal. Where could he be? There was no evidence—such as blood—that he had been there. "I don't think anyone has visited this cabin for quite some time."

"It sure looks that way," said Thatcher in agreement.

Diana faced him. "You're certain this is the Bridger cabin?"

"Yes, miss."

She frowned and once more surveyed the cabin, as if she could have missed Jubal's form. "I'm certain the man said the Bridger cabin."

"I'll see to the horses, Miss Murdoch, then we'll figure out what to do. Under any circumstances, I think it best that we wait here until the weather clears. Maybe we can get a fire going." The lieutenant moved toward the door.

"Yes, that would be nice," Diana murmured absentmindedly. She was aware that Thatcher left. "Where are you, Jubal?" she asked the empty room. She moved to the table and set the satchel down, then pulled off her damp gloves.

Worry for Jubal sat like a rock in her stomach, but another emotion simmered warningly.

Something was wrong.

Diana paced the small room, her bottom lip caught in her teeth, and replayed the incidents of the day in her mind. All seemed straightforward and free of intrigue.

Where could Jubal be?

A shiver raced through her body. The cabin was damp and cold, and the rainwater that dripped steadily from one damaged corner of the roof did little to dispel the strange sense of gloom and danger. Diana loosened the string under her chin and removed her hat, then blew some of the dust off a corner of the table before she set the hat down. She took up the largest of the sticks from the pathetically small wood pile and poked at the ash in the fireplace. As Lieutenant Thatcher had suggested, a fire would be nice. So would a pot of tea, and Diana was glad that she had thought to bring along a tin of the fragrant leaves. Because she knew that no soldier ventured into the wilderness without his basic mess kit, she had no doubt that it would be possible to soon have a small pot or pan of tea steeping. She would be able to think better once she'd enjoyed a fortifying cup of tea. Then perhaps she could put her finger on whatever was niggling at the back of her mind.

But the tea leaves were in her saddlebag, which was still with her horse. She pulled her cloak more tightly around her and moved to the partially opened door.

"Lieutenant!" she called out into the storm. The rain was falling heavily now, accompanied by occasional rounds of thunder. Diana blinked at the drops that hit her face. "Lieutenant Thatcher!"

There was no answer, which did not surprise her, for surely the soldiers could not hear her over the noise of the storm. The thought that a badly injured Jubal might be out in such weather troubled her greatly. Diana pulled the obstinate door open farther and prepared to dash out to the horse shelter.

Then it struck her.

Why would Jubal have travelled so far from the Cheyenne

encampment—and Sweet Water's side—when his child could come at any time?

Without a very good reason, he wouldn't have. Diana knew the man well enough to know that. Jubal was fiercely devoted to his young wife.

Was it possible that Jubal was not here because he never had been? That he was not injured at all, but instead was safe with Sweet Water and her people?

Diana staggered against the stout door frame. Had the whole thing been a ruse?

If so, why?

What reason could there be to lure her out into the wilderness? And who would have such a reason?

Was Lieutenant Ransom Thatcher behind it?

Diana gnawed on her lower lip. The thought that Thatcher planned the whole episode made her blood run cold. Was the man capable of such patient, devious plotting? After months of following MacKay's orders to the letter, of keeping his distance, of not so much as looking at her, would he have planned this, now that everyone's guard was down?

If so, how could he have planned it to go so smoothly? There were too many variables. Even if he had hired the Indian messenger, Thatcher would have had no way to ensure that all of Diana's soldier-allies would be gone or incapacitated at the same time. Nor could he have ensured that Captain Winslow, who was no friend to the lieutenant, would assign him the duty of escorting her, especially in light of their past difficulties, which were common knowledge. He would not have been able to prevent the additional escort of the two privates without arousing great suspicion, and because of wood detail and patrol, he could not have guaranteed that any of his cohorts would be available. She would have refused to go with Thatcher alone, and she was certain that even if she had been willing, Captain Winslow would not have allowed it. Diana was more grateful than ever for the presence of the two privates.

Thatcher could not have planned this. There had to be some other explanation.

She needed her tea.

With a quick prayer that Jubal truly was all right, Diana pulled her cloak tight and darted out into the rain, before any additional crazy fears assailed her. She rounded the corner of the cabin and approached the lean-to. The sounds of horses nickering and men talking reached her ears. Just as she was about to call out, the words of one of the privates stopped her.

"You mean we have to stay out here with the horses?" She recognized the young, whiny voice of Private Sedley. "Sir," he hastily added.

"Yes," Lieutenant Thatcher snapped.

"Even if we're here all night?"

"Yes, damn you. If either of you so much as poke your ugly face around that door, I'll shoot you dead and claim I thought you were a goddamned Injun."

Diana flattened her back against the side of the lean-to, thankful that she had not barged into the gathering on the other side of the flimsy wall. The cold rain pelted her face and soaked her hair.

"But why, sir?" Sedley asked.

"Because he's gonna have the woman, you idiot," snapped the other private, Grimes. "Isn't that right, sir?"

Even from where she stood, Diana could hear the sneer in the man's last word.

Thatcher's voice was angry and gloating at the same time. "Unmarried white women are too rare out here, and sooner or later, some officer is going to get her. I aim to make sure it's me, that's all. I'm tired of using Injun whores all the time. I want a wife, and I intend to have Diana Murdoch as such. The arrogant bitch will have no choice but to marry me when I'm finished with her today. If she tries to refuse, I'll make her a pariah. I'll destroy her reputation to the point that no other man will have her and no decent woman will so much as speak to her." He paused, and Diana held her breath, irrationally afraid that he could hear her pounding heart. Then Thatcher continued. "You both will stay out of that cabin, no matter what you hear, and that is an order. Understood?"

"Yes, sir."

"Yes, sir."

"Was that a privy out back on the far side of the corral?" the lieutenant asked.

"Yes, sir," Sedley answered.

"Find some dry matches," Thatcher ordered. "I'll get them on my way back. The bitch wants a fire."

"Yes, sir."

Diana heard the sound of splashing footsteps, loud at first, then fading away. Her heart hammered and her breath came in little gasps. What was she to do? The question slammed around in her head, and no answer came.

Thatcher *had* planned it, had planned everything. She had to get away, now, before Thatcher cornered her in that cabin. Would either of the two soldiers on the other side of the wall help her? Before she could summon the courage to make her presence known and ask, Sedley spoke again, in a low tone.

"It ain't right for the lieutenant to force the doctor's daughter, Grimes. She's a nice lady."

"It's none of our business," Grimes answered. "Thatcher can make our lives a living hell if we piss him off, and I got no intention of doing that. He's determined to have the woman, and we can't stop him."

"We could try."

"You don't have to make it so obvious that you're an idiot, Sedley. Thatcher's meaner'n a snake. If we cross him, we could end up dead, and I'm not gonna die over some stupid woman. He's willing to marry her after he's ruined her, so what's the problem? Now get out your gawddamned matches. The lieutenant'll be back any second."

"It ain't right, I'm tellin' you. She oughta have some say."

"Shut up, will you? It's gonna happen. I just wish I could watch."

"That ain't right, neither."

"Shut the hell up, Sedley."

Both men fell silent.

Diana had her answer. There would be no help there. She had to get away, and there was no possibility she could get one of the horses. There was no time to even retrieve her hat and medical satchel. Her gaze darted about the area. Which way to go? The forest appeared to be thicker on the other side of the creek. The dense jumble of trees seemed to call to her, inviting, beckoning.

Run, Diana. Run.

Or was it her father who called?

Diana picked up her skirts and ran.

Chapter Eight

Across the clearing Diana ran, to the creek and into the water, the cold, cold water. Several times she almost fell on the slippery, underwater rocks, but managed to work her way across the creek, grateful that the water came no higher than her knees. The weight of her rain-soaked cloak pulled on the tie at her throat, making it more difficult to breathe. She fought on, and scrambled up the bank on the far side.

A curse echoed across the clearing. Diana glanced back and saw Thatcher racing toward her, the two privates following close behind him. A fear like nothing she had ever known flooded through her, leaving a bitter, metallic taste in her mouth and sending a shock of vibrant strength to her legs. Again, she ran.

The knotted ties of the cloak pressed tighter against her throat, and Diana released her skirts to claw at the strings. Hampered now by sodden skirts and the stubborn knot, she lost some of her lead, and knew it. Still, desperation drove her on. Her breath rasped in her chest, tearing and burning, until that and her hammering heart were all she could hear. The knot gave a little. A fresh burst of hope gave her renewed strength. At last, the strings loosened. Diana tore the cloak away from her neck at the same instant the garment was caught from behind. The cloak flew free. She stumbled, and Thatcher grabbed her skirts.

"Bitch!" he snarled as he jerked her backward into his arms. "You thought you could get away from me?"

Like a cornered mountain lion, Diana fought him. She twisted and kicked and clawed and bit. And could not escape. The air rang with his curses as Thatcher dragged her back toward the creek, each of his determined steps forcing her closer to the dismal little cabin, the stained, dirty pallet, and his evil plans for her. She *had* to get away.

She could not get away.

Thatcher dragged her down the bank into the creek.

"Help me," she begged the two privates who stood on the opposite bank, waiting. "You know what he intends to do."

Grimes's face was expressionless, while Sedley seemed upset. Neither man moved.

"They are under orders and will not interfere," Thatcher said, panting. "Stop fighting me, damn you!"

"Never!" Diana vowed. Somehow she managed to find his shin with the heel of her boot, and Thatcher cursed again.

"Please, sir, stop!" Sedley splashed into the water. "This ain't right, sir!" He pulled at Thatcher's arm.

"God damn it!" Thatcher roared. He came to a halt and jerked Diana around to face him. With a vicious backhand, he slapped her across the face so hard that she was knocked sideways into the water.

She cried out as she fell. Submerged rocks scraped the palms of her hands, but she managed to catch herself before her face went under the surface. Stunned and gasping, she lay in the water, braced on her arms, pain pounding through her head and down her body like a hammer ringing on an anvil.

"Ah, you shouldn't've hit her, sir. She's a woman, for Christ's sake, and it ain't right for a man to hit a—"

Whatever Sedley was going to say was silenced by the lieutenant's fist connecting with his jaw. The private's boots slipped on the rocks, and he went down backward, hard.

Horrified, Diana watched as the man's head hit a large rock

that thrust out of the water. A terrible cracking sound echoed up and down the creek. The current carried his limp body a short distance until it lodged against a fallen tree trunk. One leg jerked, then Private Sedley went still, his head at an odd angle, his unseeing eyes half open, a trickle of blood at a corner of his slack mouth, one outflung arm floating on the water.

Oh, God. Tears formed in Diana's eyes.

After a moment of silence, Thatcher faced Grimes. "Do you have anything to say about what's not right, Private?"

"No, sir. Not a thing. I tried to tell him to let it be, but he wouldn't listen, sir."

"Well, he'll listen now, won't he?"

"Yes, sir."

"Get back to the horses."

"Yes, sir."

Diana struggled to a sitting position and watched Grimes go, knowing it would do no good to appeal to him. The rain continued to pour down.

Thatcher turned on her. "Damn you, Diana." The cold fury in his voice was somehow more disturbing, more threatening than his earlier screams and shouts. "I had this all planned so carefully. It took weeks, months, but the opportunity finally presented itself. Everything went fine until now."

The crazed gleam in his eyes frightened Diana, and she felt a frantic need to keep him talking, to buy time enough to come up with a plan. "It would not have worked," she said. "No matter what you did to me, I would never marry you."

"Oh, you would have. Your uncle would have seen to that."

Angus was involved? The shock she felt must have shown on her face, because Thatcher continued. "Yes, your beloved uncle Angus knows everything. We planned this together. All we had to do was wait until your Army friends were away, and that happened this morning, thanks to wood detail and patrol. Angus sent your aunt to have tea with Mrs. Steed, and he arranged a meeting with Miles Breen—so that you would be alone, with no one to turn to save me when you received the false message about Sage. Not even Dawson's unexpected accident interferred. It would have worked except for you."

His hands closed into fists, then opened, then closed again, and Diana knew he wanted to use those fists on her. Thatcher glanced at Sedley. "It's your fault he's dead, Diana. If you hadn't fought me, none of this would have happened."

"You dare to blame me?" Diana got to her knees, determined to stand. Stand she did, swaying. Her battered face throbbed and chills wracked her body, but she felt as if she were on fire from her rage. "Whether you intended to kill him or not, the man is dead by your hand. How do you intend to explain that to Colonel MacKay?" She backed up the bank of the creek, edging toward the beckoning forest, her frozen fingers tightening on the fist-sized rock she held in one hand. "Will you tell the truth? That you struck Sedley, and inadvertently killed him, when he attempted to save me from being raped by you?" She gave a harsh laugh. "I doubt it, as you are not a truthful man. Are you foolish enough to think that neither Grimes nor I will tell what happened here today?"

Somewhere during their struggle, Thatcher's hat had fallen off, so it was easy for Diana to see the fury that flushed his face red. She also saw the flash of fear in his eyes. Her grasp on the rock tightened even more.

"That's right, Lieutenant," she taunted. "You made a big mistake, one you can't escape from. You, an officer, assaulted an enlisted man and killed him. Maybe you should be the one running." She took another step backward.

"Why, you . . ." Thatcher started toward her as he spoke. Just as hers—and Sedley's—had, his boots slipped on the smooth, underwater rocks, giving Diana the opportunity she had been waiting for. With all her strength, she threw the rock at his head.

". . . little bitch—"

The rock struck a glancing blow to Thatcher's forehead, not enough to do real damage, but enough to throw him further off balance. With a shout, he went down, and landed right on top of Sedley's body.

Again, Diana gathered her skirts and ran, this time for her life as well as for her virtue.

Thatcher's curses rent the air, but the sound of his furious voice gradually grew more faint.

On she went, dodging trees and bushes, ducking branches, leaping over rocks and scrambling over fallen logs. As before, her breath tore through her chest, her throat burned, the muscles in her legs screamed—and she ignored it all. Her mind was numb to everything except the desperate, feral need to escape.

Finally, her spent body forced her to slow to a trot. Diana gasped for breath as she went on, and fought to get her frozen fingers to release their death-grip on her skirts. Her ears strained to hear any sounds of pursuit, but she heard nothing save the falling rain as it pummelled the trees, bushes, and rocks all around her. A clap of thunder jolted through the leaden sky, so loud that she knew the following lightning strike would be nearby. She slowed to a walk, and, sure enough, saw the bolt shoot down from the angry clouds. The loud crashing sound as well as the repercussions of the hit and the tingling of the fine hair on her forearms told her the strike had been close.

For some reason, rather than frightening her, the lightning comforted her. The crazy thought came that perhaps a divine power—or perhaps her father—was stepping in to protect her.

Did Thatcher still pursue her? If he did, would the lightning strike put the fear of God into him?

Diana slowed to a walk and looked back over her shoulder. She could see nothing, hear nothing, except the forest caught in a storm. Her shoulders sagged and a sigh of relief escaped her lips. She faced forward.

And stopped.

Not ten feet in front of her stood an Indian warrior.

Tall and imposing, he stared at her. His face was chiseled as if from stone, his long, long hair as black as night. The rain ran off the fringe on his beaded buckskin shirt and leggings, and he held a very large knife in one hand.

For what seemed an eternity, he stared at her, and she at him. Then, in two long strides, he was in front of her. Diana could not breathe, could not have moved if her life depended on it, which it probably did, considering that wicked-looking knife.

The man grabbed her arm, in a firm but not painful grip, and motioned with his head that she should go with him. His touch galvanized her, and for the second time that day, she fought to escape a man far more powerful than she was.

But this one put a knife to her throat. Diana froze. Terrified, she stared up at him, into his strangely colored eyes. Why was he familiar to her? Had she met this man before, she would not have forgotten him—of that she was certain. He motioned again with his head, pulled on her arm. She had the strange sense that the knife at her throat was meant more as an attempt to get her attention than as a threat. Then the man's head came up. His gaze darted all about, he sniffed the air, he cocked his head as if listening.

Now Diana heard it—the angry sounds of pursuit. Thatcher, crashing through the forest, screaming her name, screaming foul words.

Run, Diana.

Gideon's voice echoed in her head. Again, she looked up at the Indian. His grip on her arm tightened, and he pulled more powerfully, more urgently now.

Thatcher or the warrior?

Diana chose the warrior.

Chapter Nine

Deeper into the forest the warrior led her. Diana labored to keep up with him, which was difficult with her heavy, sodden skirts and her exhausted body. She felt that she had been running for hours, and wondered how much longer she could go on.

But the sounds of pursuit dogged her, drawing ever closer, and somewhere deep inside she found a hidden reservoir of strength that allowed her to keep pace with the warrior. She suspected he was holding himself back for her sake, and was grateful.

"Diana!" Thatcher's furious voice echoed through the forest. "You can't escape me!"

Over the falling rain she heard a new sound—that of horses' hooves. The other soldier—Grimes—must have joined Thatcher and brought the horses with him. Fresh panic rose up in her. Diana had no doubt that the warrior knew how to use both the knife he held so confidently and the rifle in its beaded case, which was slung over one shoulder and angled across his back. But how could she and her imposing rescuer hope to escape two armed soldiers on horseback?

The warrior raced up a small incline and around a large jumbled tangle of long-ago downed trees now heavily overgrown with budding vines. Diana rounded the obstacle a moment later, and was astonished to find the warrior on his knees, his knife clenched in his teeth, pulling clumps and mats of dead leaves and broken pine branches from under the largest of the fallen logs. His efforts revealed a cave of sorts, formed by the slant of the earth and the tangled logs.

Diana lurched to a stop beside him, her chest heaving as her lungs fought for air. "What are you doing?" she demanded in a tense whisper. "We must run. They are gaining on us."

Without a word, the warrior grabbed her hand and yanked her to her knees beside him. Then he lay down and backed into the dark, dank cavity underneath the log. With a jerk of his hand, he motioned for her to join him.

Terrified, Diana realized that he meant to hide from the pursuing soldiers. "No! We'll be trapped! We must run!" Then it occurred to her that the man probably did not understand or speak English.

He snatched the knife from his teeth and motioned again, more forcefully this time.

"Diana!" Thatcher's voice sounded hoarse, and very near. The horses could easily be heard, and, to Diana, it seemed as if they were just on the other side of the log tangle.

There was no time to run.

She gathered her skirts more closely around her hips and legs and, following the example of the warrior, dropped to a prone position and backed under the log.

The warrior's arms snaked around her and jerked her against the hard length of his powerful body. His leg draped over hers and one firm hand travelled down her hip and thigh. A new kind of fear rose up in her, and, for an instant, Diana wondered if she had made a terrible mistake in trusting the man before she realized that he was tucking her skirts under her. He grabbed handfuls of the leaves and small branches and pulled them in on her. Diana instantly understood what he was trying to do and offered her assistance. Then the man's arm tightened around her, pressing against her breasts, and she saw the knife blade just centimeters from her face.

Thatcher was upon them.

Diana could see the hooves of the two horses as they danced close to the log. The man who held her so tightly against his body may as well have been made from wood, just as the protective log was, for he was so motionless that she could neither hear nor feel his breathing. She closed her eyes and stilled her own breathing.

"God damn it!" Thatcher roared. *"Diana!"*

"I don't see her, sir," Grimes said. He sounded nervous. "It's as if she disappeared."

"She didn't disappear, Private Grimes," Thatcher barked. "She's here somewhere."

Diana fought the urge to draw a deep breath into her tortured lungs, which Thatcher would surely hear, and instead breathed in through her nose. Something crawled over her forearm. Something else caused a maddening itch on her ankle. The man hiding with her held her much too tightly. The knowledge that she could not move only added to her torment.

By the time the two soldiers guided their horses away from the log tangle, Diana was ready to scream. Her body was wracked with uncontrollable shivers, no doubt from her soaked clothing, yet the heat of the man's body beside her warmed her in unfamiliar and unsettling ways. Never had she been so close to a man physically. Their bodies were stuck together like two wet spoons, his chest to her back, her bottom cradled against his groin, one of his legs over both of hers. One of his arms curved under and around her waist, while his other arm lay across her breasts, pressing against her with disturbing intimacy. His warm breath tickled her ear and neck, which gave her shivers for a different reason.

She was as much at the warrior's mercy as she had been at Thatcher's. The knowledge made Diana even more uncomfortable, yet she dared not move. She could only guess at what the warrior had in mind for her; there was no question what Thatcher intended.

After what seemed an eternity, the man relaxed his hold on her. When she did not move, he gently pushed her. Stiff and cold, Diana scooted out from under the log. She stayed in a crouched position and looked around. There was no sign of

Thatcher or Grimes, no sound of the horses, no sound of anything except the incessant rain landing on pine needles, leaves, logs, and earth. Diana heaved a small sigh of relief as she tried to brush some of the dirt from her skirts. The task was hopeless.

The warrior scrambled out of the shelter and also stayed low, balanced on the balls of his feet, the knife held in one hand. He perused the area with sharp and knowing eyes, cocked his head to one side as if he listened intently to a far-off whispered conversation, sniffed the air as a wolf would. Gracefully, he straightened his long, tall body and stood over her, his stance somehow protective as he continued his surveillance.

Diana stared up at him, mesmerized. The rainwater dripped off the fringes of his buckskin shirt and leggings and plastered his waist-length black hair to his shirt. An eagle feather hung dispiritedly from the end of a narrow braid that kept his hair out of his face. His was a noble face—high forehead, prominent cheekbones, firm jaw, aquiline nose, well-shaped mouth—and his remarkable eyes were surrounded with black lashes that seemed ridiculously long on a man.

As she studied him, Diana felt as if she could hear his heartbeat; she knew his raw strength and power; she sensed his intelligence and cunning; she recognized his fierce pride in the way he stood, in the way he carried himself. Like a moth drawn to a flame, she could not look away. Even rain-soaked and somewhat dirty, her warrior was majestic and beautiful.

He turned to her and held out a hand. Shyly, she took it, and allowed him to pull her to her feet. He slid the knife into a beaded buckskin sheath at his waist, then examined her, his gaze piercing and perceptive. His hands travelled down her arms and over her back and sides. He lifted the long, tangled locks of her hair, which had come loose from their pins, and inspected her neck, then, with gentle fingers, her head.

By the time he took her chin in one hand, Diana could not breathe—again. But not because of fear this time.

She knew she should protest the liberties he took, but she did not feel threatened. He was checking her for injuries; she knew it instinctively, even before he so lightly laid a finger on the swelling below her right eye, where Thatcher's brutal blow had landed. For an instant, his jaw tightened, and anger flashed in his odd-colored eyes. Again, Diana had the sense that she knew the warrior. But from where?

Perhaps from a dream? Or from another life?

The strange words came unbidden, and only added to her confusion.

Suddenly, the warrior stepped away from her, and the spell was broken. Diana fought an odd sense of disappointment and loss, and shook her head, wondering if Thatcher's blow had addled her mind as much as it had injured her face. The warrior looked at her questioningly for a moment, then reached for her hand. He turned and led her deeper into the forest, farther away from the cabin. For reasons she could not explain even to herself, Diana clung to his hand and followed him willingly.

For the next fifteen or twenty minutes, neither of them spoke. The terrain grew more rough, and although he didn't want to, Grey Eagle was forced to release the woman's small, cold hand. He was surprised at her docility, especially after having seen the way she fought Thatcher. Like a wildcat she had been. Not so now. He glanced back at her, wondering if she was in a state of shock. She certainly had cause to be, after what she had endured and witnessed today.

Diana.

Her name was Diana, if that bastard Thatcher was to be believed. A lovely name, Grey Eagle thought. The Goddess of the Hunt. Another mythological name, like that of his brother, Orion, the Hunter. Again, he looked back at her. Diana plodded along behind him, determined and uncomplaining, holding her mud-stained skirts high, revealing filthy, ankle-high boots, dark stockings, and a peek of lace-trimmed drawers. It was hard to tell for certain, with her long hair wet and flat against her head, and the infuriating, darkening bruise on her pale cheek, and her equally infuriating swollen lip, but he had the sense that she was a beautiful woman.

Perhaps it was her courageous soul that he sensed; perhaps that was what was beautiful about the woman called Diana.

He hoped so, because physical beauty meant nothing if the heart and soul inside were unkind or unhappy or twisted—Black Moon gave evidence of that.

The rain had slowed to a drizzle by the time he spotted his horses. Relieved, Grey Eagle slowed his step to match Diana's. She looked up at him questioningly, her dark-lashed hazel eyes wide and trusting. Grey Eagle's breath caught. If he came to learn that nothing else about her was beautiful, Diana's eyes most certainly were. He blinked, and mentally shook himself as he pointed toward his horses. Before he could speak, she did.

"Your horses." She was out of breath, and he felt a stab of guilt for the pace he had set. "I wondered . . . where you were . . . taking me."

Grey Eagle now chose not to speak. Why, he could not say. His two horses nickered their welcome. George Washington, his great and beloved Appaloosa stallion, went further and stamped his foreleg and whinnied. Unable to contain a smile, Grey Eagle moved to the saddled stallion's side. "You pussycat," he chided affectionately—in Cheyenne—as he scratched the horse's forehead. With one hand still caressing George Washington's neck, he turned to Diana. And paused.

She watched him with those beautiful eyes, intently, assessingly. Grey Eagle had the feeling he was on a stage, under an unforgiving light, being put to some kind of test. He did not like the feeling at all.

"*Hamestoo'estse!*" he commanded, with an imperious pointing of his finger toward the ground. *Sit down.*

Obviously startled, Diana's eyes widened even more. Again, he stabbed his hand downward.

As she hesitantly moved to obey him, Grey Eagle remembered what had brought him to this place, at this time.

His mission was to fetch the healer named Diana Murdoch from Fort Laramie and take her to the Cheyenne encampment. Sparrow, his beloved niece so recently and joyously restored to him, had told him of the dark-haired medicine woman with the mark of the Eagle on her shoulder, a woman who could call the Eagle to her side. A good and brave woman, Sparrow said, now lonely and unhappy because she had lost her father and so had lost herself. Sweet Water, the wife of his beloved friend, Jubal Sage, and beloved in her own right, wanted Diana, the doctor's daughter, with her when she delivered her firstborn and soon-to-come child.

So Grey Eagle had promised to bring Diana. Was his unexpected guest the very woman he was obliged to take to the encampment? Had the Great Ones led him to her here in the wilderness rather than at Fort Laramie? For her sake as well as his?

He did not know. It would be a remarkable coincidence indeed if this was the woman he sought. Finding her here would save a full day of travel, and with Sweet Water's coming babe, that saved day could become crucial.

Under any circumstances, this Diana needed his help, now, today.

Without speaking, he draped a buffalo robe over the woman's shoulders, handed her his knife with hand signals that she should use it for protection, rechecked the position of the rifle in its case slung across his back, and vaulted into the saddle. His eyes met hers for a long, powerful moment, then he guided George Washington into the forest. As he rode, he was very aware of her gaze upon his back, for it warmed him like no fire could.

Unbelieving, Diana watched him ride into the forest. He was just going to leave her? Why? For how long? She shivered and drew the buffalo robe more tightly around her shoulders. The warm protection of the robe was welcome, but nothing could stop the shivers that shook her to her very bones.

It wasn't only the cold. In the last hour, she had been physically assaulted, threatened with rape and death, had seen a young man give his life because he had come to her aid, and she had chosen to follow an unknown warrior into the wilderness in order to escape soldiers of her own kind.

The side of her face throbbed, and Diana laid a cold hand against her cheek, as if that could ease the pain. With weary eyes, she looked about the small clearing where the patient packhorse waited with her. What had drawn the warrior into the forest on foot, away from his horses, toward the cabin, so that he was there to find her in her hour of need?

Whatever it had been, Diana was grateful for it. She was safely away from Thatcher's reach—for now—but what were the warrior's intentions toward her? Even though she'd had good reason to, she'd been foolish to trust Thatcher. Did she dare trust her rescuer any more than she already had? If she did, how could she make it clear to him that she needed to return to Fort Laramie? Was it possible that he was headed there himself?

The need to return to the safety of the fort grew powerful. Diana decided that she would leave at once. Surely she could find her way back. She eyed the warrior's packhorse and instantly discarded the idea of taking the animal. Not only did she find the thought of stealing from her rescuer repugnant, but the warrior would surely come after her, and Diana had no doubt that he and his beautiful stallion would catch her long before she reached the fort. On foot, the journey would take hours, but she could make it.

She threw off the buffalo robe and struggled to her feet, and it suddenly became very clear that her shaking, aching legs would not carry her far. Every muscle in her body hurt, and a sick, dizzy feeling of exhaustion rolled over her like a wave. Numbly, Diana sank back to the ground and reached for the robe.

Whatever happened, her lot had been thrown in with the warrior's, at least for now.

The rain had stopped falling from the sky, but it still steadily dripped from the trees. The woman's discarded cloak, which he had found at the scene of one of her battles, was tied behind his saddle, and Grey Eagle held his rifle across his thighs as he rode, the weapon secure in its case in an attempt to keep the powder dry. It would take only a second to free the rifle, should the need arise—which it very well might, because he was headed for the Bridger cabin.

He whispered a prayer of thanks to the Spirit of the Eagle for the inspired idea to seek shelter under the log tangle. Alone, he could have easily lost the two soldiers, but not with the woman. If he had not found the cramped shelter, more blood would have been spilled.

Now he was headed to the cabin with the hope that Diana's horse was still there—and the hope that the two soldiers were not. He did not want to force a confrontation with them, but he would oblige them if they insisted on it. His jaw tightened. There was no doubt in his mind as to what the lieutenant had intended for the woman. If that unfortunate young soldier had not stepped in—and given his life—when he did, Grey Eagle would have had to take them all on.

The odds were more in his favor now.

Although he would not have hesitated to kill the soldiers in order to save the woman, he did not want to, no matter how much that lieutenant needed killing. Grey Eagle was a Beaudine, as much as his brothers Joseph and Orion were, but there were those who would never forgive him his Cheyenne blood, just as some Cheyenne would never forgive him his white blood. There were those at the fort who would not believe his word over that of a bastard like Thatcher, simply because of race and parentage. Grey Eagle had learned that it was better to avoid trouble with the U.S. Army.

He pulled George Washington to a halt and slid to the ground. The Bridger cabin was just over the little rise in front of him. On silent moccasinned feet, Grey Eagle darted through the trees that covered the rise, and paused at the top. He could see the cabin on the other side of the creek. Two horses waited in the makeshift stable. He was about to start in that direction when he heard voices.

The soldiers had returned.

With great care, Grey Eagle backed down the rise a short distance and made for a large boulder that offered some protection. He dropped to a prone position and peered around the boulder. The two mounted soldiers splashed across the creek without so much as a glance at the body of the young soldier, and pulled to a halt in front of the cabin.

"There's no way she could've got back here before us, sir," the private said, his tone argumentative.

"I told you to shut up, Grimes." Thatcher jumped down from the saddle and forced the stubborn cabin door open. After a quick look, he ran to the stable, then rejoined Grimes.

"Her horse is still here." Thatcher scrutinized the area, his eyes almost closed in a squint. "She can't be far, God damn it. Come nightfall, she'll be cold and hungry; that'll bring her crawling back here."

Grimes sent him a mocking look. "Nothing's gonna bring her back here, Lieutenant, not even her bag—not if she knows you're here. That woman isn't gonna let you touch her again. She'll die first."

"Shut up, damn you!"

For a moment, Grimes obeyed. Then he spoke again, with exaggerated patience in his tone. "The woman isn't coming back, and we aren't gonna be able to find her. We have to get our stories straight, sir. How are we going to explain to the colonel the disappearance of the doctor's daughter and the fact that Sedley is dead?"

So the Diana he'd found *was* the woman he sought. Grey Eagle smiled, a small, grim smile. A full day of travel had been saved. Then his fingers tightened on his rifle. If Grimes didn't quit pushing the lieutenant, he could pay for it as the other soldier had. The cold, furious expression that came over the lieutenant's face only reinforced Grey Eagle's feeling. He slid his rifle from its case.

"*We* aren't going to explain anything, Private," Thatcher snapped. He grabbed the butt of his holstered pistol.

Unwilling to let the lieutenant kill another soldier, Grey Eagle took aim at Thatcher. Before he could squeeze the trigger, Grimes fired, then again. Both shots hit the lieutenant.

Thatcher's single shot went wild. His pistol flew out of his hand as he fell to the ground, his arms wrapped around his middle. The horses jumped and neighed.

Grey Eagle lowered his rifle. Justice had been served, although somewhat crudely.

Grimes stayed in the saddle. He guided his horse to stand near the wounded man. "I've been waiting for you to try something, Thatcher, ever since the woman pointed out that we witnessed what you did. There wasn't anything else for you to do but kill us. If I ever run across her again, I'll be sure to thank her for warning me. And I'll tell her she doesn't need to worry about you anymore." He leaned out of the saddle. "Looks like I gut-shot you." He shook his head, mocking again. "Pity. You'll die now, painful and slow. Serves you right for trying to kill me."

On the ground, Thatcher curled up, his moans loud enough for Grey Eagle to hear.

"I been thinking about deserting, maybe heading toward Mexico," Grimes said conversationally. "Or maybe California—get some of that gold for myself. Now seems like a good time." He reached for the reins of Thatcher's horse and rode to the stable, where he took up the reins of the horses Diana and Sedley had ridden.

"You can't leave me like this!" Thatcher shouted.

Grimes laughed. "Sure I can." Leading the three horses, he rode off to the north, apparently decided on California.

Thatcher's curses rang in the rain-cooled air.

Grey Eagle rose to his feet and descended the small hill. He crossed the creek, snatched up the lieutenant's pistol from the ground, tucked it in his belt, and came to a stop at Thatcher's side. The lieutenant's eyes widened with fear, then he gave a strange little laugh.

"It's too late to kill me, Injun. I'm already dead." Thatcher laughed again, and spoke more to himself. "I'm talking to a stupid Injun who can't understand a word I'm saying." His words ended on a moan, and his eyes closed. He rocked back and forth in agony.

No close examination was needed for Grey Eagle to know that the lieutenant was mortally wounded. Grimes was right—Thatcher was going to die, and painfully; it was only a matter of time. Assured that the lieutenant presented no danger, Grey

Eagle leaned his rifle against a tree, then made his way to the body in the creek. He had seen death before, had been forced to kill when the circumstances called for it, and still, he found the staring, unseeing eyes and the frozen expression of awful surprise on the soldier's young face disturbing. He pulled the man from the freezing waters and dragged him up the bank to the base of a pine tree. There he laid the body out, straightened the arms, and gently placed the soldier's hat over his face. Because of his concern for the woman, Grey Eagle felt there was no time to bury the man. He also knew that Colonel MacKay would send out a search patrol when the lieutenant and his party failed to return to Fort Laramie. The soldiers would see to burying their own.

He checked the rough stable for anything of use that might have been left. All he found was a tin of matchsticks, half hidden in the old, dirty straw. He took the tin and made his way to the cabin. Inside on the rickety table he found a woman's wide-brimmed hat, a pair of damp, small gloves, and a leather satchel, which no doubt was Diana's medical bag. He placed the gloves and the match tin in the satchel, grabbed the hat, and went back outside.

"Now, isn't that like an Injun?" Thatcher called out derisively. He grimaced, as if the effort of speaking was painful, but he managed to add, "To steal anything he can."

Grey Eagle said nothing as he retrieved his rifle. He started toward the creek.

"Don't leave me!" Thatcher screamed. "Put me out of my misery, or at least give me my pistol so I can do it myself!" He started sobbing. "Damn you. You don't understand me."

After a moment's hesitation, Grey Eagle retraced his steps to Thatcher's side. He pulled the lieutenant's pistol from his belt and, because he didn't want a bullet in the back for his trouble, laid it on the ground about two feet from the man's reach. "I understand you very well, Lieutenant," he said in English. "May you find relief in death."

Thatcher gaped up at him.

Grey Eagle turned and walked away. He forded the creek, then paused to look back. Thatcher was inching toward the pistol. With a heavy sigh, Grey Eagle continued on his way. Just as he reached George Washington's side, the expected shot echoed through the wet forest. Two men had died this day, for no reason other than one man's unholy lust for an innocent young woman. It seemed such a waste.

Now, that young woman waited for him, if she hadn't been foolish and run off into the forest. Maybe he should have introduced himself before he left, to set her mind at rest. Suddenly anxious that he had unexpectedly found Diana Murdoch only to lose her, Grey Eagle quickly secured the medical satchel, his rifle case, and Diana's hat over the saddle horn, climbed into the saddle, and set off. Although Diana needed tending, he wanted to put a few miles between them and the cabin before nightfall—before Colonel MacKay came looking for her.

Grey Eagle did not want the Army to find them. If that happened, there would be trouble, because not even the Army would stop him from keeping his promises to Sparrow and Sweet Water.

Whether she wanted to or not, Diana Murdoch was going with him to the Cheyenne encampment.

Chapter Ten

He found Diana where he had left her. Although she huddled under the buffalo robe, he could see the powerful shudders that wracked her body. More than anything, Grey Eagle wanted to stay right there, to build her a roaring fire and get her warm again. But the urgency he felt about getting farther away from the cabin had not lessened. With a silent promise to make it up to her later, he stepped down from the saddle.

She raised weary eyes to him. "I heard the shots," she said, her voice dull and lifeless. "Did you kill them?" Before he could answer, she laughed mirthlessly, much like Thatcher had. "Why am I asking? You don't speak English."

Grey Eagle stiffened. It irritated him that many white people assumed that all Indians were thieves and killers, and it also irritated him that many white people assumed no Indian could speak English. Of course, very few Indians of any tribe *could* speak English, but the condescending assumption still bothered him. He could state just as derisively that she did not speak Cheyenne. But he did not. Instead, he pulled the buffalo robe from her shoulders.

"Please don't take that!" She pointed toward the robe, then

wrapped her arms around herself and deliberately shook, as if to tell him she was cold.

"I speak English, Miss Murdoch," Grey Eagle snapped as he tied the robe behind his saddle. He faced her, and was not surprised to see her mouth open in astonishment.

"D-do I know you?" she asked, then shook her head. "You are familiar somehow, but I'm certain I would remember meeting you." She put a hand to her forehead and rubbed, as if her head ached. "I would remember."

Grey Eagle took pity on her. "We have not met, although you know most of my family. I am told that I greatly resemble my brother, Orion."

Recognition dawned on Diana Murdoch's bruised face. "You are Grey Eagle Beaudine."

"I am."

"You could have told me sooner," she said peevishly. "I would not have been so frightened. How did you know who I am?"

"I figured it out from the soldiers calling you 'Diana' and 'the doctor's daughter.'" He bent down and grabbed her elbows, then helped her stand. "We must go."

She gave a weary nod. "Yes, or we will not reach Fort Laramie before nightfall."

"We are not going to Fort Laramie." He led her toward George Washington.

Diana pulled away from his grasp. "I am returning to the fort. If you do not wish to accompany me, I will go alone." She snatched her hat from the saddle horn and plopped it on her head. "I see you found my cloak and my medical satchel. If I may have those, I will be on my way."

Grey Eagle crossed his arms over his chest and studied her. Her hat was perched at an odd angle on her head, her wild, matted hair hung about her shoulders and down over her breasts—soft, full breasts, as he recalled from their contact under the log—her black skirts were muddy, one sleeve had been partially torn from her bodice at the shoulder, and her face was deathly pale where it wasn't bruised. She swayed from exhaustion, yet she held her chin high and dared to defy him. He felt a surge of admiration for the stubborn Miss Murdoch, as well as a strange touch of affection. All the same, she was going with him.

"I am not going to the fort, and I will not leave you to attempt the journey alone and on foot." He pulled her to George Washington's side. "Put your foot in the stirrup."

"I will not." Diana struggled against him. "I am most grateful for your earlier assistance, Mr. Beaudine, but, unless you are headed to Fort Laramie, I will not go with you. And you cannot force me."

Grey Eagle turned her to face him, his hands firm on her upper arms. "Yes, Miss Murdoch, I *can* force you, with superior physical strength if nothing else. You will come with me if I have to tie you in the saddle." Her mutinous expression did not fade. He leaned a little closer. "You will not win this battle."

Her jaw tightened and her eyes flashed fury, but she said nothing. She shrugged away from him and turned to lift her booted foot to the stirrup. Her capitulation surprised Grey Eagle, and made him wary. He grabbed her about the waist and helped her into the saddle, a part of his mind registering the fact that no whalebone stays contributed to the narrowness of that waist. When she reached for the reins with too much eagerness, Grey Eagle caught her hands in a firm grip and threw the reins forward over George Washington's head.

"Release my hands at once, Mr. Beaudine," she snapped.

Grey Eagle did as she asked. "Even if you had succeeded in securing the reins," he said calmly, "George Washington will not obey your commands without my permission to do so." Diana looked away from him, her lips pressed in a tight, furious line.

Moving quickly, Grey Eagle freed the packhorse from its hobble rope, tied the lead rope to a ring on the saddle, repositioned the reins, and climbed into the saddle behind Diana. Her hat poked his eye, and, in exasperation, he pulled it from her head and again looped the hat string over the saddle horn.

"Mr. Beaudine, I ask that you release me at once." A note of fear had crept into Diana's voice.

"You will come to no harm." He put an arm around her waist to pull her closer. She resisted, but could not help being pressed back against his chest. If nothing else, perhaps the warmth of his body would warm her a little and ease her violent shivers. He took up the reins.

"Please release me."

Grey Eagle could tell that she hated to beg. "No," he said, and urged George Washington to a walk. For a few more minutes she held herself stiffly, then she slumped back against him in surrender. Her shoulders shook, and he could not tell if it was from cold or tears.

He hoped he hadn't made her cry. Her tears would only add to the nagging guilt he already felt toward Diana Murdoch— guilt for not tending to her hurts at once, guilt for not giving her a choice about going with him. But he was determined to follow through with his plan.

They had gone perhaps a mile through fairly thick forest when they came out on top of a hill. George Washington nickered, and Grey Eagle instantly drew him to a halt. Down the hill and across a little clearing rode a man on horseback, leading three saddled horses. The man also stopped, and Grey Eagle recognized Private Grimes. He'd told Thatcher he was going to California, and the Oregon Trail lay several miles to the north, the same direction as the Cheyenne encampment.

Grimes stared at them, his eyes wide, his face pale.

Diana stirred in his arms, turned her head, cleared her throat, as if she were about to call out.

"He will not help you now any more than he did earlier, Miss Murdoch," Grey Eagle said. "He has stolen the horses and intends to desert."

Even as he spoke, Grimes turned his horses back in the direction from which he had come and rode at a lope from view. Perhaps Mexico seemed a better choice to the private now.

Again, Diana slumped back against him. "At least he's not dead."

"Did you think he was?"

A pause. "There were several shots."

Grey Eagle heard the question in her statement, and it bothered him. "Would it matter if I fired some of those shots?"

Another pause. "I don't know. If you did, it was probably necessary."

"Thank you for that." He nudged George Washington to a walk. "None of the shots were fired by me, Miss Murdoch. The lieutenant intended to leave no witnesses. Thatcher missed when he shot at Grimes; Grimes acted in self-defense, and did not miss."

"He killed Thatcher?"

"No. He gut-shot him and left him to die."

Diana sighed, then spoke, her tone reluctant. "Can the lieutenant be helped?"

Grey Eagle shook his head in amazement. After all the lieutenant had done to her, had tried to do to her, had intended to do to her, still the healer inside Diana came out, willing to do what she could for the man. "He could not be helped. His wounds were mortal, and agonizing." He paused. "I put his pistol within his reach. The last shot you heard was his own."

Diana shuddered. After a moment, she said quietly, "Well, I guess I don't have to worry about him anymore."

"No, you don't."

"I only have to worry about you."

She didn't, but Grey Eagle knew she would not believe his assurances. At least not right now. Both he and Diana lapsed into silence.

An hour later, Grey Eagle pulled George Washington to a halt, this time for the night, even though a few hours of daylight remained. Diana's shivers had not abated, and he was becoming worried. She needed to get warm, and to rest. He stepped down from the saddle and reached for her. After a moment's hesitation, she placed her hands on his shoulders and allowed him to help her to the ground. Her knees buckled, and Grey Eagle swung her up into his arms.

"Mr. Beaudine," she protested.

He did not respond, but carried her to a position near a stand of pine trees and carefully set her down.

"Thank you," she murmured.

"You are welcome." Grey Eagle untied the buffalo robe from behind his saddle and tested its wetness. The damp side would go down on the ground. He selected a place and spread the robe there, then smoothed it, pulling out the worst of the rocks and branches beneath it.

"May I please have the robe again?" Diana asked.

"Not until you take off your clothes."

After a moment of silence, she said in an incredulous tone, "I beg your pardon?"

Grey Eagle straightened and turned to face her. "Miss Murdoch, your clothes are soaked through and you are shaking with cold. The robe will do no good unless you get those wet clothes away from your skin." He marched over to the pack-horse and pulled another buffalo robe from under the protective oilskin tarp.

"But it will take hours for these clothes to dry," Diana protested. "And I have no others with me."

"That is beside the point. Take off your clothes—and I mean all of them—and get between these two robes." He tossed the folded robe onto the spread one. "I will keep my back turned."

Diana scrambled to her feet. "Mr. Beaudine, I will not take orders from you. And I most certainly will not disrobe at your command."

At least there was some life in her voice again. "Miss Murdoch," Grey Eagle said gently. "You are battered and exhausted. You need warmth, and rest, and food. Please do as I say. Take off your clothes and get between the robes." She opened her mouth to protest, and he held up a forefinger. "Do not argue. If you will not undress yourself, I will do it for you."

Diana's eyes widened with shock. "You wouldn't."

"I would. You will not win this battle, either, so give it up." He turned again to his stallion. "It won't take me long to finish with him," he said pointedly over his shoulder.

"You may be a Beaudine, but you are no gentleman, sir." Her frosty tone struck him like a thrown snowball.

"Perhaps because I am half Cheyenne," Grey Eagle mildly suggested.

"That has nothing to do with it."

Grey Eagle fought a smile. Her response pleased him, because it told him that she did not have a prejudice against his mother's people, as so many in his life had. He heard the rustle of her clothing, and a few minutes later she spoke in that same chilling tone.

"I am between the robes."

He turned. She lay on her back and had pulled the top robe up to her chin, yet he could see that shivers still tormented her body. Her face was turned away from him, as if she did not want to look at him. Suspiciously, Grey Eagle eyed the neat pile of her clothing. He saw no evidence of underclothes. In two strides he was at her side, where he crouched down. Without a word, he thrust his hand between the robes and touched her shoulder.

Diana looked at him now. "How dare you?" she cried.

"I told you to take *everything* off, and I meant it." He spoke through clenched teeth. Quickly, his hand ran down the side of her body from shoulder to knee. Sure enough, she still wore her damp chemise and drawers.

"Mr. Beaudine!"

Grey Eagle pulled his hand free of the robes and held it out toward her, his fingers bending toward his palm, then straightening. He did not have to say a word. He did, however, have to keep his eyes focused on a point above Diana Murdoch's furious, intriguing, wiggling movements under the robe. Her face flaming with embarrassment, she thrust her wadded drawers into his hand. He added the garment to the pile, then held his hand out again. Her jaw set in a stubborn line.

"I will take it off myself," he softly warned.

She glared at him, her anger making her hazel eyes appear to be more green than brown. But she obeyed him, finally placing the chemise in his hand.

"Are you satisfied now?" she snapped.

Grey Eagle again slipped his hand between the robes. A hurried brush down her disturbingly cold body assured him she was naked, and he pulled his hand free. "Yes. Thank you for your cooperation, Miss Murdoch. I am acting in your best interests, whether you believe me or not."

Her mouth set in a tight, angry line, Diana still glared at him. One pale arm snaked out from under the top robe as she tried to tuck it under her body. Her right shoulder was bare, and Grey Eagle froze at the sight.

He felt as if he could not breathe. Wonderingly, he reached out with a shaking hand. Diana's expression softened from one of anger to one of confusion.

"*Netse,*" he whispered as his finger touched the small dark mark on her shoulder. Sparrow was right—the mark resembled the symbol used by the Cheyenne to represent the eagle. Diana flinched, but she did not pull away from his touch. Wide-eyed, she stared up at him, and Grey Eagle had the sense that her heart was pounding as furiously as his was. His gaze met hers, and now he truly could not breathe.

Now he recognized her.

The sad eyes, the dark hair, the pale skin.

His Spirit Woman had come to him in the flesh, at last.

His hand jerked away from her shoulder as if he had touched a hot coal. Diana watched in amazement as the arrogant and domineering Grey Eagle Beaudine lurched to his feet and stumbled away from her side. Did he think her birthmark the mark of the devil, as some did?

Oh, God. With all her heart, she hoped not, and that in itself surprised her. Ten minutes ago, she would have welcomed anything that would have sent him away from her. She did not feel that way now.

"It is only a birthmark," she said, hoping that her casual tone would ease any fears he might have. She pulled her arm back under the robe.

"It is more than that."

Diana found the contrast between the warrior's fierce appearance and his cultured voice and flawless English to be startling. As she watched, he grabbed a short-handled ax and began to dig out what she assumed would be a fire pit. "The devil didn't put the mark there, if that is what you mean." She sounded defensive even to her own ears.

At that, he looked at her. "Of course not. Do some think the mark is a sign of evil?"

Wondering if she would ever be warm again, Diana turned on her side facing him and curled into a fetal position, uncomfortable with her naked body. "The suggestion has been made, by a few of the more superstitious. Others find it disfiguring." She did not mention that the most vocal 'other' was her own mother, who had refused to allow Diana to wear off-shoulder ball gowns for fear the mark would be exposed.

"The words of the foolish and the vain should be ignored." Grey Eagle arranged a few rocks around the edge of the shallow pit, then gathered a handful of twigs and leaves.

"I do ignore them."

"Good." Grey Eagle faced her again. "What do you think of the mark?"

No one had ever asked her that. Diana pondered his question for a minute, then said, "Truthfully, I don't think about it often. I am used to it."

"Do you find it ugly or disfiguring?"

"No. I rather like it, although I'm glad it's not bigger. As my father used to say, the mark is part of me, and he assured me that since I am not evil or ugly, the mark cannot be evil or ugly, either." Her throat grabbed at the mention of her father.

"Your father was a wise man. I have heard many good things about him, and am sorry I did not have the opportunity to meet him." Hungry flames devoured the tinder and licked at the larger branches Grey Eagle had arranged in the pit.

Diana turned her face into the soft robe, fearful that she would cry. A faint wave of warmth from the growing fire touched her now, and, suddenly, so did Grey Eagle's strong hands, through the robe that covered her back. She started and jerked her head up to look at him.

Before she could scold him for again taking liberties, he gently said, "You must get warm, Miss Murdoch. Please don't fight me."

She searched his eyes—his green eyes so like those of Orion, the Hunter—and found nothing there but concern. No leering, no lust, no evil. Just concern. Diana relaxed and gave in to his kindness. She straightened her legs and rolled onto her stomach. Grey Eagle's hands rubbed down her body, and she found that his brisk ministrations did indeed warm her, in more ways than one. A sharp longing flashed through her, a longing to pull away the buffalo robe that lay between his hands and her bare skin. Mortified, Diana again buried her face in the robe. Where did such a thought come from? She had known this man for little more than an hour, and she was having carnal thoughts about him, thoughts she had never had about any other man. What was wrong with her?

Mercifully, Grey Eagle moved away from her.

"Thank you," she said in a small voice.

"You are welcome, Miss Murdoch."

A moment later, he was at her side again, this time the side away from the fire. With gentle hands, he pulled her wet hair from under the robe and applied a length of cloth to it. Diana sighed with contentment, for she was reminded of the ritual she and Sparrow had shared of tending each other's hair.

"Thank you," she said again, this time in a whisper.

"Sleep, Diana. Sleep."

Diana was aware that he called her by her Christian name, but she could not find the strength to correct him. She stared at the flames of the comforting fire, until her eyes could stay open no longer, and she fell into an exhausted sleep.

With the length of cloth, Grey Eagle blotted as much water from Diana's long hair as he could without waking her. He would brush out the tangles later. Now he sat back on his heels and observed her sleeping form.

His Spirit Woman. He could not quite believe he had found her at last, yet he knew he had. He had always known that he would recognize her when he met her.

How much would she fight him when she discovered he was taking her to the Cheyenne encampment? It didn't matter, he decided, his jaw set. If he had to tie her to the horse, he would, just as he had threatened.

He remembered a time, almost two years earlier, when he had suggested that Orion kidnap his beloved Sarah, who, at the time, was promised to another man. In the end, the kidnapping of Hunter's bride was not necessary, for Sarah had followed her heart. Then, Grey Eagle had been only half serious about stealing Sarah away.

This time, he was deadly serious about taking Diana away. Whether she wanted to or not, she would accompany him to the Cheyenne encampment. She would stay with his mother's people at least until Sweet Water's babe was born, and longer than that, if he could persuade her.

Grey Eagle looked down at her and brushed a strand of dark hair away from her cheek. His jaw tightened at the sight of a forming bruise on her forehead, and he was certain that her slender body bore many other bruises as reminders of her desperate fight with the Army officer. For a moment, he was sorry the lieutenant was dead, because he was filled with the powerful urge to kill the man himself for what the bastard had done—and intended to do—to Diana.

A gust of cool wind swirled through the camp, causing Grey Eagle to look up at the sky. The dark clouds were giving way to more and larger patches of blue. He guessed that the rain would not trouble them again today. Still, he would not leave for the Cheyenne village until the following morning. By then, Diana's clothes would be dry, and she would be a little more rested.

Because he had planned to be in Fort Laramie tonight, he had little to offer his guest for supper. Diana would need hot, filling, and nourishing food, the fire would need a great deal of relatively dry wood, and the horses needed tending. Grey Eagle stood, newly energized. There was much to be done.

Chapter Eleven

Diana stirred, slowly awakening. The air on her face was cool, and she was grateful for the warmth of the blankets covering her. She rolled onto her back, wondering why she felt so sore and stiff, and luxuriated in the feel of the soft covering against her naked skin. Then she froze.

She was naked?

The events of the day came rushing back. She was not covered with blankets, but with a buffalo robe that belonged to Grey Eagle Beaudine. Now fully awake, she rose to lean on one elbow, careful to keep the robe tucked under her chin, and looked around the tidy campsite.

Grey Eagle was nowhere to be seen.

The sun had dropped low enough in the western sky to leave long shadows on the ground, which told Diana that she had slept for a couple of hours. The fire still burned cheerfully, and a small cast-iron pot rested on an iron grate that had been placed over one section of the flames. Her clothes and what looked like a buckskin shirt were neatly draped over lengths of rope strung between a few trees, and Grey Eagle's two horses could be seen a short distance away, diligently nibbling at the fresh young grass that grew in scattered patches of sunlight.

Diana stared longingly at her chemise and wondered if it was dry enough for her to wear now. Naked, she felt very vulnerable, even though she was covered by the sturdy robe. Her movements were restricted to the point that she did not want to even sit up, for fear of which expanse of skin she might unwittingly expose. Wearing that thin cotton garment would be better than wearing nothing at all.

Determined to retrieve the chemise, Diana studied her surroundings, and, as Grey Eagle had done earlier after they crawled out from under the log, she listened carefully, and even sniffed the air. She saw no sign of him, heard no sound of him, and smelled nothing but campfire smoke.

Where had he gone?

More importantly, how soon would he return?

Surely she had time to get the chemise. Diana pushed herself to a sitting position and groaned. Every muscle in her body screamed at that small movement, and she was astonished that her body refused to move any farther. She braced her weight on her palms and rested, hoping that the worst of the pain would pass quickly. It didn't. Her head dropped forward, causing her unkempt hair to fall around her face, and the robe slipped down to her waist.

At that moment, she didn't care that her breasts were covered only by her hair. She didn't care if Grey Eagle—and his brothers, and all the soldiers posted to Fort Laramie, for that matter—suddenly marched into the camp and found her thus. All she could focus on was the pain that washed over her in waves, because its depth and intensity confused and frightened her. How had she come to be so injured?

With another moan, she fell onto her side and lay there, clutching the robe over her breasts with shaking fingers. The pain didn't seem as bad when she lay still.

A few minutes later, Diana opened her eyes to see that Grey Eagle had appeared beside the fire, with a string of fish held in one hand. She stared at him, not in surprise, but in wonder.

Diana had not heard him coming—not even the slightest sound—yet she had known before she opened her eyes that he was there. It wasn't his noiseless approach that amazed her; it was the picture he presented, standing before her, touched by the dying rays of the afternoon sun.

The buckskin shirt that hung with her clothes was evidently the one he had been wearing, because now he wore no shirt at all. She had thought him handsome when he was rain-drenched and a little dirty. Now that he was dry, clean, and half naked, she felt that 'handsome' did not do him justice.

His black hair had obviously been brushed, and a refreshed eagle feather was tied to one of two narrow braids that kept the hair back from the sides of his face. The rest of his hair fell free almost to his waist, and, to Diana, his was the most glorious hair she had ever seen. Her fingers itched to touch the shining strands, to sift through them and to finally brush them away from the majesty of his naked chest.

Through her work with her father, Diana had seen the naked chests of many males, all shapes and sizes and ages, but she had never seen one like Grey Eagle's—broad, bronze, and muscular. He stood there, tall and proud, wearing nothing but fringed leggings, a breechclout, moccasins, and his magnificent hair, and she was reminded of the old Celtic tales of ancient gods, gods of the earth and the sky and the forest, gods who could choose to become men. Surely Grey Eagle was one of them.

She was painfully aware of her nakedness under the buffalo robe, painfully aware of herself as a woman in a way she never before had been. The force of the primal instincts and female needs that at long last burst to life inside her twenty-three-year-old body was shocking. Diana closed her eyes, unable to bear the glorious sight of him—and the pulsing rhythm of life and desire within her—any longer.

At once he was on one knee beside her, one gentle hand brushing her hair back from her face. "What is it? Are you ill?"

She shook her head against the robe, astonished again, this time by the deep sense of comfort he gave her just by stroking her aching head. "Not ill. Just sore. But I'm so sore that I cannot move, and I don't understand why. I feel as if I've been beaten."

"I'm not surprised, Miss Murdoch. In a way, you were beaten. At the least, you were involved in a desperate fight."

His tone became harsh, and Diana peeked up at him. His jaw was clenched, his eyes as hard as stones. When he realized she was watching him, his stern features relaxed, a little.

"No woman should ever have to go through what you did this day," he said. "I wish I could have stopped it."

Diana frowned. "But you did. You saved my life, Mr. Beaudine. Once he killed Private Sedley, I knew Thatcher would kill me, too, when he was finished with me." She could not suppress a shudder. "Thank you for saving me from all of that. The bruises will heal. I'm not certain rape would heal, and death most certainly would not. I shall recover from these little injuries."

"Yes, you will." He picked up her left hand and drew her arm out from under the robe. For some reason, she did not protest or pull away from him. "You are probably covered with bruises like these," he said as he ran a gentle finger down the length of her arm. Diana shivered, and he tucked her arm back under the robe. "I brought willow branches from the creek." He straightened and moved to the fire. "I'll use them to make you a tea; it should help with the pain, at least a little. Do you like fish?"

"Yes."

"Good, because that's what we have for supper." He crouched down next to the fire, laid out the string of fish, then, with his knife, began to strip the bark from one of the willow branches he had collected. "What were you doing out here with the soldiers?"

"Word came through a messenger that Jubal Sage was wounded and needed my help, that he waited for me at the Bridger cabin."

Grey Eagle swivelled on the balls of his feet to stare at her. "Jubal is healthy and uninjured, at the Cheyenne encampment with his wife, awaiting the birth of their child."

"I suspected as much; I'm happy to know for certain. Is Sparrow safely returned to her parents?"

"Yes. There was great rejoicing in the village when Jubal

brought my niece home. There are many who wish to thank you for rescuing her from Sikes and Horton, myself included.''

"There is no need for thanks. It was a delight having Sparrow live with us for a time. I miss her very much.''

"She longs to see you, also." Grey Eagle resumed work on the willow branch. "So Thatcher and the two privates were your escort on your mission of mercy.''

"Yes. I was uncomfortable about it, because there had been trouble between the lieutenant and me a few months ago." Diana shifted, trying to find a more comfortable position. "But he was a model of respect and professionalism on this journey, until I overheard him order the two privates to stay out of the cabin, no matter what. I knew then that the whole episode had been a ruse to get me alone with him." She watched Grey Eagle's face, saw his jaw tighten again. A piece of willow bark flew from the slashing blade of his knife. She continued. "He and my uncle agreed that when my father died, I should marry the lieutenant. Because I refused, Thatcher came up with the plan to force me into marriage.''

"I know of your uncle. Angus MacDonald cheats on his trades and sells poison to the Indians and calls it whiskey." Grey Eagle's harsh tone gave Diana pause.

"He is an unscrupulous man," she finally admitted.

"And he is a bastard without conscience for attempting to give his niece to a man like Lieutenant Thatcher.''

Diana could think of nothing to say to that. Evidently, she and Grey Eagle shared the same opinion of her uncle. She looked up at the sky and could tell that dusk was not far off. Without asking, she knew that Grey Eagle intended to spend the night here. She would spend the night in the wilderness, alone with a man. A sigh escaped her. When she returned to Fort Laramie, tongues would wag—especially Belinda Mullen's— but, given her condition and how miserable she felt, Diana was grateful that there would be no more riding today. Just the thought of getting on a horse made her ache even more.

But what were Grey Eagle's intentions for tomorrow? Where did he intend to take her? Was there any hope that she would be able to talk him out of his plan, to persuade him to return her to the fort? Their recent conversation had been quite companionable. Perhaps he would be more reasonable now.

She decided to find out. "I would like to ask you to reconsider your decision, Mr. Beaudine, and return me to the fort tomorrow. You'll lose only one day of travel."

"That is out of the question, Miss Murdoch." Grey Eagle spoke so casually, he might as well have been discussing the weather.

Determined to keep rein on her rising temper, Diana forced her tone to remain calm. "Then I must insist, sir."

Grey Eagle looked up from the willow stick. His penetrating gaze seared her like a flame. "I will not take you to the fort. Do not ask me again."

A chill came over Diana that had nothing to do with the lowering temperature. She stared at Grey Eagle's stonelike face, fighting the dread that knotted her stomach. "So, just as Thatcher did, you also have a plan for me?"

"My plan is nothing like his," he answered harshly. "No harm will come to you."

Although she had known Grey Eagle for only a matter of hours, Diana believed him. The knot of dread dissolved and blossomed into anger. "Are you going to tell me this plan?"

"You will go with me to the Cheyenne encampment."

Her response was immediate and firm. "I will not. I wish to return to Fort Laramie. As I told you earlier today, if you won't take me, I'll go alone."

"You will go to the encampment with me. There will be no more discussion about it." Grey Eagle placed the pieces of willow bark in the small pot and moved it over the flames.

For a moment, Diana was speechless. *There will be no more discussion?* "Why, you arrogant . . ." She searched for just the right word and the best she could come up with was "cad!" Again, she sat up, holding the robe to her breasts, ignoring her screaming muscles. "Mr. Beaudine, I realize that I owe you a great deal for your assistance today, and I am truly grateful to you, but you will *not* dictate where I shall or shall not go and what I may or may not discuss!"

Grey Eagle did not respond. His expression was the same

closed one Sparrow wore when she was angry or upset. As if
Diana had not spoken, he pulled a cast-iron frying pan from a
pack on the ground and set it near the flames.

Exasperated now, Diana tried again. "Please be reasonable.
You cannot think that you have the right to order me about."

"I did not order. I made a statement of fact."

"You cannot force me to accompany you!"

Grey Eagle straightened and came to stand over her. Diana
looked up at him, hating the weak and subservient physical
position she was in. If only she had her chemise! She would
stand and face him, no matter the price her aching body would
demand. She was not frightened of him, but she dared not risk
exposing her nakedness, so all she could do was glare up at
Grey Eagle Beaudine. And what she saw gave her pause, for
a different reason than his beauty.

The face she had earlier found handsome was now fierce
and forbidding. The fringe on his leggings and the blue cloth
of his breechclout moved in the wind, as did the eagle feather
and long strands of his hair. Dressed thusly, with the backdrop
of forest behind him, there was no evidence of Grey Eagle's
white blood in his appearance or stance; he was every inch a
Cheyenne warrior. A dangerous Cheyenne warrior.

"You will go with me to the Cheyenne encampment, Miss
Murdoch. I do not wish to force you, but I will if I have to. I
gave my word that I would bring you back with me, and my
word will not be broken. There will be no more discussion."
He stared down at her, his green eyes seeming to flash with
the force of his words.

"This is another battle I won't win, isn't it?" she asked
bitterly.

"Yes."

He would do whatever was necessary to keep his promise
of returning her to the Cheyenne camp; that Diana knew, just
as she knew that, like a lesser dog in a wild pack, she was
backing down when she finally looked away from his intimidat-
ing eyes. She was as furious as Grey Eagle clearly was, but he
had her at a distinct disadvantage—on the ground, injured,
weakened, naked. That would not always be the case, she

vowed. One day Grey Eagle Beaudine would regret the high-handed manner he took with Diana Murdoch this day. "May I have something to wear?" she asked.

If her complete change of subject surprised him, he did not show it. Without a word, Grey Eagle turned and crossed the campsite to where her clothing hung. Apparently not satisfied with the dryness of her chemise, he returned to the pack by the fire and drew out a shirt. "It's wrinkled, but clean," he said as he tossed it to her.

"Thank you." She forced as much cold politeness into her tone as she could.

"You are welcome," he responded, just as coldly and politely, then turned his attention to their supper.

Diana gathered the large muslin shirt close. It smelled of soap and sage—a pleasant smell, one that brought unexpected memories of being pressed close to Grey Eagle's powerful and oh-so-male body in the claustrophobic closeness of the sanctuary under the log.

She forced those memories away.

With one hand holding the robe in place, Diana managed with the other to get the shirt over her head, then, one at a time, inserted her arms into the voluminous sleeves. She pulled the garment down to her hips and—painfully—under her bottom, relieved that the material reached to her mid-thighs. In order to free her hands from the sleeves, she had to roll the narrow cuffs back several times, and even though she drew tight the lacing at the deep vee down the front of the shirt, the neckline that would probably reach just below Grey Eagle's collarbone plunged to between her breasts. Unless she was very careful in her movements, her breasts would be as exposed while wearing the shirt as when not. Still, it was better than being stark naked.

Exhausted by the effort of that simple task and by the emotion of the argument just past, Diana collapsed back on the buffalo robe. The last of the day's light faded from the sky, and neither she nor Grey Eagle spoke. From the wonderful smells that came from the direction of the campfire, she knew he was frying the fish in bacon grease, and her mouth watered.

Suddenly, Diana was ravenous. The unhappy and unappetizing breakfast of old potatoes and bitter coffee she had shared so many hours ago with her unhappy and bitter aunt and uncle seemed like another lifetime. When Grey Eagle came to her side with the offer of a plate, she accepted eagerly and with sincere thanks. He put his saddle behind her to use as a backrest, and Diana ate with relish, certain that she had never in her life tasted anything as delicious as those Indian meal-dusted fried trout and bacon grease-soaked corn dodgers.

Later, he insisted on helping her walk a short distance away from the campsite so she could, as he so delicately put it, see to certain bodily necessities. He left her for a time, then escorted her back. Grey Eagle acted very nonchalant about the whole thing, but Diana thought she might die from embarrassment, due as much to the exposure of her legs from mid-thigh on down as to his ungentlemanly—although practical, she had to admit—mention of those 'necessities.' He tucked her back into the makeshift bed of buffalo robes and handed her a battered enamel cup filled with bitter willow bark tea, along with the stern admonition to drink all of it.

As she forced the vile brew down, Diana reflected on the different sides of Grey Eagle Beaudine she had witnessed this long, unbelievable day.

Heroic Rescuer. Fearless Warrior. God of the Forest. Compassionate—if forceful—Nurse. Good Cook.

Arrogant Overlord.

Drowsily, Diana watched him as he cleared the last remnants of their meal and straightened the drying clothing one more time, and she wondered which of those personas was the true Grey Eagle.

Perhaps they all were.

No matter the answer, he was, without question, the most fascinating man she had ever met.

The most irritating.

The most beautiful.

Diana blinked. Either the willow bark tea was taking effect or the events of the day had left her addled.

Grey Eagle approached, silently checked to ensure that the

cup was empty before he took it from her unprotesting grasp, and moved away to bank the coals in the fire pit. When he approached her again, he wore only his breechclout, and carried a length of rope in his hands. She watched with weary eyes as he bent those long, muscular, naked legs to kneel at her side and tie one end of the rope around her right wrist.

Deep inside, some fight still remained, and she demanded, "What is this?"

"A compliment, in a way." He sat back on his heels and calmly tied the other end of the rope around his waist, leaving perhaps three feet of rope between them. Then he rested his palms on his thighs and looked into her eyes. "You are an intelligent woman, Diana Murdoch, and a fighter. Given the opportunity, you could devise a method of escape, even from me."

She glared at him. "Thank you so much."

Grey Eagle shrugged. "I need a restful night's sleep, and I'll have a better chance of getting one if I know you can't sneak away."

"If I were so inclined, Mr. Beaudine, how could I hope to sneak away when I can't get my battered body to move?" She picked at the rope with stiff and awkward fingers. "Remove this at once."

"Good night, Miss Murdoch." Grey Eagle lifted the top buffalo robe and slipped in beside her. He turned on his side and faced the glowing fire coals.

The rope snaked between them, connecting his waist with her wrist, although they didn't touch. Diana stared at the rope, then at Grey Eagle's back. His naked back. His hair pooled on the bottom robe near his head, only inches from her fingers. How desperately she wanted to reach out and touch those raven locks, to bring a strand to her nose and see if it smelled of sage, as did his shirt. He would never know if she did.

She curled her traitorous fingers into a fist and pressed it against her mouth.

He would know.

Stiff and straight Diana lay, her tethered right arm rigid at her side, unable to believe that the first time she shared a bed with a man was under such ridiculous circumstances. Determinedly, she kept her eyes on the stars, until she could keep them open no longer.

Grey Eagle knew the minute Diana fell asleep. He heard the change in the rhythm of her breathing, sensed the relaxing of her tension-filled body, and breathed a sigh of relief himself.

Had it been necessary, he would have died for Diana Murdoch today, even before he realized she was the woman of his visions. Instead, he had lived, and she had lived, and now he could not get the memory of her indomitable spirit, her full breasts, and her soft skin out of his mind.

He had always believed he would recognize the Woman if and when he met her in the flesh. He'd never dreamed that he would want to caress that woman's flesh with a passion that shook him to his very core.

Until today, his feelings for his Woman of the Clouds had bordered on worship. How could he be so sorely tempted to debase that worship with mere carnal desire?

The rope tugged at his waist. He glanced over his shoulder to see that Diana, in her sleep, had turned on her side, toward him, her hands clasped at her breast. A frown puckered her bruised forehead—a frown of pain, of anger, of confusion, he did not know. Still, that small frown troubled him.

He wanted to wash away the scrapes and bruises from her skin, brush away the ache in her head, smooth that frown with his touch, ease the haunting sadness that had always been in her eyes, even before today.

Then he wanted to touch her again, with love, and with passion—touch not only her body, but her heart and her spirit.

All those things, he wanted. Now. Tonight. Tomorrow. Someday. All the days. Forever.

Tonight, at last, he shared his buffalo robes with his Woman of the Clouds, and she had no wish to be there. She was in his bed only because she was roped to him, too injured and too weak to fight him, to escape.

That was not how he wanted it, not how it should have been.

Still, he had found her.

And he would gratefully accept her, however she came to him.

Even unwillingly?

The accusing question echoed in his weary mind. The weary answer sounded just as clear: *for tonight—yes.*

Chapter Twelve

Early the next morning, Diana awakened to find herself alone in the buffalo robe bed. The rope had been removed from her arm and lay neatly coiled near the fire. Absentmindedly, she rubbed her wrist. Although the sun had not yet cleared the eastern horizon to burn away the chill of the night, the sky above the trees was pale blue and clear, the air brisk and pine-scented. It promised to be a lovely morning.

The robes—and the nearness of Grey Eagle's body, she admitted to herself with a blush—had kept her warm through the night, but had not offered much padding. The ground on which she lay felt as hard as solid rock. Diana stifled a moan as she carefully stretched, and was dismayed to discover that little in her physical condition had improved over last night.

Disappointed, she rubbed her eyes, and was startled to feel a painful swelling around her right eye. No doubt her face was as bruised as the rest of her was. Diana moaned aloud this time. Not only did she feel bad, but surely she looked bad, as well.

The unexpected and unfamiliar surge of feminine vanity surprised and irritated her. Why did she care what sort of picture she presented to Grey Eagle Beaudine? She'd met the man only yesterday, under trying and dangerous circumstances, and since then, he'd made it clear that her wishes mattered little to him. He had saved her, only to abduct her. And she was concerned about how she looked? Diana shook her head. She *was* addled.

There was no sign of her rescuer-turned-abductor in the campsite. The fire burned high, radiating welcome warmth. Her clothing, folded and neatly stacked, lay where Grey Eagle's head had, and even her boots, cleaned of yesterday's mud, were close by. A steaming enamel pot gave off the enticing scent of coffee, and Diana's stomach growled in a most unladylike fashion. She wondered what Grey Eagle had planned for breakfast.

But first, she took the opportunity to dress. She struggled to a sitting position and threw the top robe back off her legs. During the night, Grey Eagle's shirt had hitched up around her hips, offering her a clear view of her aching legs. Diana was shocked, because both legs were spotted with purpling blotches of varying sizes. She jerked one long shirtsleeve back, then the other, and found her arms to be the same. *The badges of battle,* she thought grimly. At least she'd won that particular battle— thanks to Grey Eagle.

With a last quick glance about the area, she whipped the oversized shirt off over her head and hurried into her chemise. She shivered as the night-chilled material whispered down her body, and reached for her drawers, pushing away the embarrassing thought that Grey Eagle had seen and handled her most intimate apparel.

By the time he appeared a few minutes later, Diana was struggling with the back hooks of her damaged bodice, and only her boots remained to be donned. He again wore leggings and moccasins in addition to his breechclout, but no shirt— which secretly pleased her—and drops of water could be seen on the bronze expanse of his chest. He must have been washing at a nearby creek or pond. How Diana would love a bath herself, but a warm one rather than one drawn from the icy waters of a creek.

"Good morning, Miss Murdoch," Grey Eagle said as he

dropped to one knee beside the fire. His voice struck her anew—masculine and low, with a faint, intriguing accent to it.

Diana decided that she liked the sound of his voice. "Good morning," she replied, suddenly feeling shy. After all, she had shared a bed with the man last night.

He stirred the fire and added a few more sticks of wood. "How do you feel?"

"Fine."

Grey Eagle arched a disbelieving eyebrow.

Diana sighed. "Awful," she admitted. "I've never been so sore." She raised one hand to gingerly touch her swollen eye. "I'm a sight, aren't I?"

"Be proud. You look like a warrior."

As if in response to his command, a strange thrill of pride went through her. Diana fought another accursed blush and watched him pour what she could tell was more of the nasty willow bark tea into a cup. "I'd rather have coffee, Mr. Beaudine," she said, even as she accepted the cup from his hand.

"Drink this first. It will help with the pain." Grey Eagle moved behind her and sat down.

Diana froze when his long, long legs stretched out on either side of her own skirt-covered legs. Without asking permission, he closed the rest of the bodice hooks for her. She lost the battle with the blush, and could do no more than force herself to murmur, "Thank you."

"You are welcome. Now drink the tea."

Yes, sir! Somehow, Diana managed to stop the sarcastic words before they escaped her lips. Holding the warm cup with both hands, she obeyed him and took a sip, then nearly choked on the tea when his hands smoothed over her head and pulled her tangled and matted hair back behind her shoulders. Self-conscious and a little embarrassed at the unkempt condition of her hair, she cleared her throat. "I could use a brush."

"I will use the brush. You drink the tea."

Lordy, the man was bossy! Diana rolled her eyes, then gave in to the comforting feeling of being ministered to. She sipped the bitter tea, and was not surprised that Grey Eagle knew what he was doing with a brush, perhaps because of his own long hair. He managed to work out each tangle without pulling, and soon her hair lay smooth against her back. Sparrow had often brushed her hair for her, but this felt different. Grey Eagle's gentle actions were somehow intimate. And stirring.

"Your hair is lovely," he said, his voice husky, his hands stroking the long strands. "The sunlight brings flashes of red fire to its rich darkness."

The feeling of intimacy grew, and Diana's eyes closed. Her hands trembled around the cup. No one had ever told her that her hair was lovely; certainly no man had.

With swift fingers, Grey Eagle wove her hair into one thick braid and secured the end with a piece of fringe he tore from his legging. Lightly, his hands rested on her shoulders for a long moment, then he pulled away from her and stood.

"Again, thank you," Diana said quietly, both relieved and sorry that the spell had been broken. She didn't dare look up at him, not until the unfamiliar and unwelcome feelings in the pit of her stomach settled down. "I have much to thank you for, Mr. Beaudine. I did notice that you got most of the dirt and mud off my skirt, and that you cleaned my boots. You have doctored me, cooked for me, and tended to me. I owe you a great deal, including my life."

"You owe me nothing." He took the empty cup from her hand and moved toward the fire.

"I do," she insisted.

Grey Eagle turned to face her. "Then come with me to the encampment peacefully."

To Diana, his words sounded like a challenge. Angry now, she glared up at him. "You have a great deal of nerve. You've made it very clear that I have no choice about going to the encampment, yet you dare to ask me to go peacefully, to meekly give in to your demands."

"You will go one way or the other, Miss Murdoch." He shrugged. "Peacefully would be easier for both of us."

Her anger turned to fury. Not trusting herself to speak, Diana reached for one of her boots, drew it on, and laced it. The odious man! She grabbed her other boot. The infuriating, confusing man! She thrust her foot into the boot and laced it with jerky movements. One moment he was kind and gentle, tending to her hair, the next he was arrogant and imperious, as if he were a chief or something!

Diana froze.

Maybe he *was* a chief.

She wrapped her arms around her shins and rested her chin on her knees as she wracked her brain to remember all that she had heard about Grey Eagle, the third of the famous Beaudine brothers. Joseph and Orion, the two older brothers, were respected and well liked in the close-knit little community that encompassed Fort Laramie and outlying areas. They had always treated both her and her father—and everyone else, including the Indians, as far as she knew—with courtesy and fairness. Much of the trust Diana had instinctively placed in Grey Eagle came from the fact that she trusted and admired his brothers, considered them, as well as their wives, her friends.

But neither Joseph nor Orion were half Cheyenne. Neither was a chief.

Was Grey Eagle? Diana knew from discussions with Jubal Sage that there were different levels of 'chiefhood' in an Indian tribe. Was Grey Eagle a high chief? A war chief? A medicine man of some kind? Being a chief did not excuse his arrogance, but if he was one, Diana could better understand him.

Just like an Army officer, no doubt he was used to giving orders and having them obeyed, without question. She'd fought him on several things, and—no doubt—would fight him on several more. No wonder there was contention between them.

Well, he would learn that she was not Cheyenne, and did not have to blindly obey him, as others in his tribe might. Then she bit her bottom lip to keep from smiling.

Grey Eagle already knew that.

Diana lifted her head to look at him. His jaw was set, his face expressionless in the proud way of the Cheyenne. The fire he had so recently built up he now worked to extinguish by emptying the coffeepot on the flames.

At first disappointed and a little hurt that he didn't save any of the brew for her, Diana then discovered that he had set a cup of steaming coffee near the edge of the buffalo robe on which she sat. Touched and confused by that simple act of kindness—extended to her in the middle of an argument—Diana watched him for a moment longer, then spoke.

"I will no longer oppose the journey to the Cheyenne village."

He paused in his movements, then looked at her. "You will go peacefully?"

Diana got to her knees, then, with gritted teeth, pushed her protesting body to stand. At once, Grey Eagle was at her side, his hand at her elbow, offering her his other arm. Humiliated by her weakness, Diana nonetheless was forced to choose between clutching his offered forearm for support or collapsing into his arms. She chose his forearm, and clung to him. Her hand looked very small and very pale compared to his tan, muscular arm. She would not look at his face when she spoke.

"I'm not certain there can ever be peace between us, Mr. Beaudine. I said I will not oppose the journey. There will be no need to bind me to you in the night for fear I will escape."

"That will do."

Now she did glance up at him, and instantly regretted it. The concern in his eyes was genuine, and only added to her confusion. Obeying the demands of her aching body, she forced herself to ask, "Will we eat before we go?"

"We will eat on the trail."

Relieved that there would be some sort of nourishment, Diana said, "I'd like to wash my face."

Grey Eagle nodded. "There is a small creek through those trees." He pointed. "I will take you there, and return for you when the horses are ready."

"Thank you."

Grey Eagle left her at the creek, returned a moment later with the cup of coffee and a length of cloth to use for washing, and disappeared again.

When she finished washing and had seen to other needs, Diana sat on a sun-warmed rock and, deep in thought, sipped the hot, hearty coffee. A month ago, Sparrow had suggested—had begged—that Diana return with her to the Cheyenne village. At the time, the idea seemed so ludicrous that Diana, as much as she loved Sparrow, did not even consider it. Now, she was on her way there.

Her aunt came to mind, and Diana wondered if Phoebe was worried about her. If she were to be honest with herself, she had to admit that she felt no sorrow at being away from her uncle's trading post—her current home, sorry though it was— or even being separated from her sweet-natured, weak-willed aunt. If not Phoebe, who at the fort did Diana really miss? Especially since the rest of the Beaudine family—Joseph, Annie Rose, Orion, Sarah, Florrie, Juliet, Cora—had not yet returned from St. Louis? Why had it seemed so urgent last night that she get back?

No one now there really cared about her, in the way of families or genuine friendship, as her father had cared, as Sparrow cared, as the rest of the Beaudine family cared. Then she corrected herself. Knute Jensen and his grandson, Thomas, cared, but they were very busy, running both the Beaudine trading business and their own horse training business. She did not feel comfortable turning to them.

Right now, there was no good reason to return to the fort.

But what awaited her at the Cheyenne village? A warm welcome? Danger? Would she be treated as a guest? Or, would she be enslaved by the Cheyenne, as Sparrow had been by her Crow captors? Diana doubted it, but there was no way she could know for certain until she arrived there. Only the knowledge that Jubal Sage, Sweet Water, and Sparrow would be there had given her the courage to agree to go with Grey Eagle. *As if I'd had any other choice,* she thought bitterly.

Because of her experiences with Sparrow, Sweet Water, and other Indians she had met at the fort, Diana wasn't frightened of the Cheyenne people as much as she was apprehensive about being in their midst, and about being so far from the fort. It would be much like visiting a foreign country, she decided, and that was how she would treat her forced visit—with open-minded curiosity and a willingness to get along with her hosts.

Whether or not she could get along with her escort was another matter.

Grey Eagle came for her, and the time for speculation was over. Within a matter of minutes, they were on their way.

Again and again, he glanced back at her, careful to keep his face expressionless. Grey Eagle was impressed with her Cheyenne-like uncomplaining fortitude, but he was also concerned—deeply so. Diana had to be in pain. He'd heard the distressed gasp when he lifted her into his saddle, could see even in the shadows made by her hat brim that her lips were pressed tightly together and her face, where it wasn't bruised, was very pale. Her gloved hands clung determinedly to the saddle horn, and she had not so much as whimpered since they left the camp over two hours ago.

She rode the saddled packhorse, while he rode George Washington bareback. The supplies and equipment were split between the two horses, tied in packs over their rumps, and Grey Eagle kept the pace steady, but, due to Diana's battered condition, they moved slower than he would have liked. Evidently, George Washington didn't like the slow pace any more than he did, because the stallion chafed at the bit and made clear his desire to run.

The black material of Diana's bodice and skirt—both of which seemed too big for her slender body—was dusty and ripped in places, most notably on her right shoulder where part of the sleeve had torn free of the bodice. He could not help but wonder if the eagle birthmark showed through the tear. The fact that the Great Ones had marked her so clearly for him still astonished him.

Grey Eagle did not mention to Diana that a patrol from the fort was probably already on its way to the Bridger cabin, nor did he mention that he wanted to be as far away as possible from that cabin by the time darkness fell. He wanted to give her no opportunity to change her mind about going with him willingly—an encounter with a patrol would definitely offer an opportunity—and he had no desire to engage in a battle with the Army, especially with Diana as the prize. The Army would have questions about how two of their soldiers died, about where the third soldier was, about where Diana Murdoch was, and Grey Eagle wasn't certain that his answers to those questions would be believed. He preferred to avoid the whole situation. When they reached the safety of the Cheyenne encampment, he would send word to his brothers—or, if Joseph and Orion were not yet returned from St. Louis, to the Norseman, Knute Jensen—that Diana Murdoch was safe and with him.

So Grey Eagle kept the pace as steady as he dared, although he stopped periodically for Diana's sake. The noon meal consisted of more of the chokecherry and buffalo pemmican he had offered her for breakfast, and they were on their way again.

Diana did not speak, whether because she was in a great deal of pain, or because she was still angry with him, he did not know. For the first part of the day, she sat rigidly straight in the saddle, but by mid-afternoon, her shoulders slumped and her head dropped down on her chest. He could not tell if she slept or not. He did know that she could not go on in this condition. Although a few more hours of daylight remained, they had to stop.

The campsite he chose was one familiar to him, and only minutes away. Once there, Grey Eagle quickly set up a bed for Diana, and carried her from the horse and laid her down. She was asleep within seconds, it seemed. He awakened her later to force down more of the willow bark tea, and urged her to take small pieces of the unlucky rabbit he had caught and roasted for supper. Then he allowed her to sleep again. He lay next to her that night, without the rope, and studied her face. Even though he'd known it in his heart from the beginning, in the dim light of the dying fire there was no question that Diana Murdoch was his Woman of the Clouds. Grey Eagle fell asleep wondering what was in store for both of them.

She slept on a bed made of stone. Diana was certain of it. How her thin pallet on the dirt floor of the dark, windowless room at her uncle's trading post had turned to stone, she didn't know. But it had.

A soft moan escaped her lips as she stretched. Why was she so cold? Why did her body ache so badly? She sensed more than felt a source of heat nearby, and instinctively reached for it. Her fingers touched warmth—naked warmth.

Instantly, Diana was wide awake . . . and remembered.

The early-morning sky had lightened a little, enough to show that she was nestled under a buffalo robe, and, even now, her traitorous body inched closer to the inviting warmth of Grey Eagle's naked back. Diana snatched her tingling hand back as if it had touched a live coal.

At least her wrist was not bound by rope.

Silently, she took stock. She was fully clothed, except for her boots; her body protested her movements, but not quite as loudly as it had yesterday; she was hungry; she missed her father. That last feeling Diana pushed away, and her eyes closed in despair at the thought of another endless day in Grey Eagle's uncomfortable saddle, travelling toward a place she did not want to go.

"Good morning, Miss Murdoch."

His quiet, sultry voice washed over her as his hand brushed the hair back from her forehead.

"Good morning," she whispered, and opened her eyes.

And froze.

He had rolled over to face her. Although their bodies did not touch, he was very close. If she so chose, she could, with only a slight forward movement of her head, place a kiss on Grey Eagle's gloriously naked chest. The desire to do so blossomed within her so powerfully that Diana's own chest tightened, from deep inside all the way to her nipples, and she felt that she could not breathe. Seemingly of its own accord, her hand moved closer to that tempting expanse of bronze male skin, and she closed her wayward hand into a tight fist, fighting the urge to press that fist to her lips so they could not also betray her.

"Is something wrong?" There was a genuine note of worry in Grey Eagle's voice.

"No," Diana managed to get out. She dared not say more.

"Are you better today?"

"Yes." A pause. "A little." She saw the doubt on his face. "Truthfully, Mr. Beaudine. I feel a little better."

"Good." He threw back the covering buffalo robe and gracefully rose to his feet. With his back to her, he stretched his arms wide.

Diana gaped up at him. Grey Eagle wore nothing save his blue breechclout, which covered vital things—and didn't cover nearly enough. His long hair reached past his waist when he arched his back in more of a stretch, and each muscle in his arms and legs was clearly and exquisitely defined.

She had never seen a more magnificent sight. For the first time, Diana considered the concept of male beauty, and she knew that for the rest of her life, Grey Eagle Beaudine would be her definition of it.

He moved, breaking the spell, and Diana forced herself to breathe again.

"We will leave at once," he announced as he pulled on one legging.

So fascinated by his actions that she did not protest the lack of hot coffee if they left immediately, Diana watched as he secured the buckskin legging to the rawhide cord tied around his waist—the same cord that held the material of his breechclout in place. Even when wearing the leggings, his hips and the smooth sides of his muscled buttocks were exposed. He reached for the other legging, then paused, his eyebrows raised in question.

"Are you certain nothing is wrong, Miss Murdoch?" he asked.

"Believe me, not a thing is wrong," Diana answered hoarsely. She sat up and reached for her boots, struck by the intimacy of their dressing in front of each other. Desperate to change the subject, she asked, "When will we reach the encampment?"

"If there is no trouble, we should be there by nightfall tomorrow." He pulled his buckskin shirt over his head and secured a beaded belt around his waist.

Diana frowned as she fought with a knotted bootlace. "What kind of trouble could we possibly encounter?"

"Violent weather. A bear or a cougar, a hunting party or

war party from a hostile tribe. Perhaps villainous mountain men who would do anything to have a white woman. Then there's the U.S. Army." Grey Eagle's eyes locked on hers.

She was taken aback. He spoke so nonchalantly about such terrible things, almost as if he were trying to frighten her. Then the last thing he said struck her and she asked, "Why would an encounter with the Army present a problem?"

"You might change your mind about going with me. The Army would support your decision, and"—he positioned his sheathed knife in his belt and a cold expression came over his handsome face—"I would be forced to abduct you again." He shrugged. "The soldiers would try to stop me. I will not be stopped. There would be trouble."

Diana stared at him, wanting to make some retort but not daring to open her mouth. Grey Eagle's features were fierce and immobile, his body tall and rigid, his hands clasping the long rifle he no doubt knew how to use. Again, no sign of his white blood showed, except in the striking green of his eyes. An aura of danger emanated from him, one that Diana could feel as surely as if he had reached out and touched her. A shiver of fear raced down her spine. Grey Eagle was not a man to cross. She would be wise to remember that.

"Let us go." His words came out as an order, setting Diana's teeth on edge, but she kept quiet as she stood and folded one of the buffalo robes.

Because Diana wanted no one else injured or killed on her account—including Grey Eagle, she had to admit—she would meekly accompany the warrior to the encampment, even if they did encounter an Army patrol. Once there, she would enjoy a short visit with Sparrow and Sweet Water. After the baby was born, she would prevail upon Jubal Sage to take her back to the fort.

Having decided that, Diana felt a sense of relief. It was always better to have a plan. Grey Eagle could be as arrogant and Cheyenne-like as he wished. She would endure his company for the next two days, then be finished with him. Jubal would protect her, even from a Beaudine—she knew that instinctively. The loyal frontiersman would take her home.

Home. The word gave Diana pause. She had places to stay, to live, but she no longer had a home—not at the fort with her uncle and aunt, not in St. Louis with her mother and sister, not anywhere in the world. Her home had died with her father. A deep loneliness grabbed her heart and held on tight.

She might as well go joyfully to the Cheyenne village. There was nowhere else to go.

Chapter Thirteen

Grey Eagle kept a faster pace that morning. Diana followed him without complaint, although every inch of her body ached. As much as she disliked the annoying tingly feeling, she was almost thankful when her legs fell asleep. At least then they didn't hurt so badly.

The realization that there was no pressing reason to return to the fort had sobered and disturbed her, prompting a thorough soul-searching. Since her father's death, she had been adrift on a sea of grief, with no direction or even real concern for her life and her future. Gideon would not want to see her like that, Diana knew. He would want her to be strong, to pick up the pieces of her life and go on, to find a good man and marry, settle down and have children. He would want her to return to her mother's home in St. Louis.

"I'm sorry, Papa," Diana murmured, blinking away tears. "That I cannot do. I don't know yet what I will do, but I will do something. Just not that."

Grey Eagle looked back over his shoulder at her and held George Washington up until Diana's horse came alongside. "Were you speaking to me?" he asked.

The sun shone full on his handsome face and caused his

eyes to glitter like dark green jewels. Diana saw sincerity in those eyes and, without thinking about how crazy it might sound, answered him truthfully.

"No, to my father. I told him that I can't go back to St. Louis to live with my mother and sister, as he wanted me to do after his death."

If Grey Eagle thought her odd for speaking to the dead, he did not show it; he only nodded. "You can't go back because I have forced you to accompany me." A statement, not a question.

She shook her head. "No, Mr. Beaudine. My father died a month ago. Had I planned to leave, I would have by now. I will not go to St. Louis even when you have finished with me. There is nothing for me there."

"Your mother and sister are there."

Diana repositioned her hat on her head and shrugged, looking away from him. "I would like to see my sister," she admitted.

"But not your mother."

Again, he made a statement rather than asked a question.

"No" was Diana's terse response. She did not want to talk about her mother, and was relieved when Grey Eagle did not press the issue.

Instead, he changed the subject. "Perhaps a half an hour ahead we will come to a creek. We will stop there to rest the horses and eat."

Diana nodded her agreement, and he nudged George Washington to a lope. She fell in behind him, remembering his instructions to follow in his horse's track as much as possible so that anyone who might happen upon their trail would not know for certain how many were in the party.

The land through which Grey Eagle led her was beautiful. Hills and valleys lined up, one after the other, covered with various prairie grasses and dotted with stands of lodgepole pine and outcroppings of tumbled boulders and rocks. Numerous narrow creeks meandered along the floors of the valleys, and while she spotted the foliage of several different kinds of wild-flowers, it was still too early in the season to see many blossoms. They passed one good-sized herd of buffalo and a few scattered bands of mule deer. It was a land of plenty, with the air clean and clear, and the sky heartbreakingly blue. As much as her body ached, Diana found the scenery lovely, and that loveliness had a calming effect on her.

Watching the man before her, however, was not calming. Grey Eagle rode George Washington with only a blanket between them, and the Appaloosa was feisty this morning. The stallion tossed his head and pranced, as if he challenged the man who so effortlessly and patiently held him in check, yet Grey Eagle rode with such grace that it seemed he was truly one with the stallion.

It struck her like a lightning bolt.

In a sense, the man and the horse *were* one with each other, and, in turn, they were one with the wild and beautiful land around them. They knew their place in the world, knew where they belonged, and Diana felt a poignant stab of envy, as well as a strange sense of longing. As if she were an orphaned street urchin, with her nose pressed against a frosted window, watching through the glass as a close-knit family gathered together in front of the fireplace on a cold winter's eve, Diana craved to belong somewhere, to belong to someone.

The powerful feeling of being lost, of being adrift in the world, was unsettling. Diana was grateful when Grey Eagle led her into a shady glen and dismounted. For a while at least, while they ate and refreshed themselves, she would have respite from her nagging and troubling thoughts.

Grey Eagle returned to the site of the noon meal and found Diana resting on a buffalo robe in the shade, her eyes closed. His little jog up a nearby hill and a thorough scrutiny of the wide valley they would soon cross had revealed no sign of danger, but once out in that basin, they would be visible to any who lurked in the surrounding forest-covered hills. The thought bothered him, and he wondered if it would be wiser to circle the valley, always staying near the protection of the trees, rather than save at least an hour by travelling straight across.

Because of his concern for Diana, he was truly torn. She'd

held up fairly well through the first part of the day, had not once complained, but her fatigue was evident, and they still had miles to cover today. *Safety or time?* He again perused the valley, as if he could find an answer out there.

"What is it?" Diana asked.

Grey Eagle focused on her. She sat up now, and brushed a hand over the side of her head in a futile attempt to tame several loose strands of dark hair. The bruise that spread over her cheekbone and under her right eye stood out with angering vividness against her pale skin, and Grey Eagle wished it was possible to exact punishment from a dead man.

"I cannot decide whether to cross the valley, which will save time, or circle it, which will be safer," he explained.

Diana frowned. "Safer from what? Have you seen something?"

"No. But that doesn't mean nothing is out there."

She studied him and, after a moment, said softly, "Which route would you choose if you were alone?"

"If I were alone with George Washington, I would cross the valley, for he can outrun anything. The packhorse cannot. If I were alone with both horses, I would circle the valley."

"Then it seems to me that we should take the longer route."

"Are you up to it, Miss Murdoch? It will add an hour of travel to today's journey."

Diana held a hand up to him, and he pulled her to her feet. Her hand felt small and cold in his, and he held it longer than he should have.

She pulled away from him. "I appreciate your concern for me, Mr. Beaudine, but it isn't necessary. Lead the way, and I will follow. I have no choice but to trust your judgment." She looked up at him, and, in the soft light of the sun-dappled shade, her hazel eyes looked very green. "And I do," she added.

Her words of confidence warmed him. "Then let us go."

Within minutes, they were on their way. The position of the sun in the still cloudless sky told Grey Eagle that it was about an hour past noon. If they kept a brisk pace, they would reach his next planned campsite a little after dark. Then again, barring any trouble, all that remained was one last long day of riding. If all went well, he and Diana would eat supper tomorrow night in the lodge of Jubal Sage.

With luck, Sweet Water's child would wait to make its appearance at least until then.

Grey Eagle glanced back at the woman who so gamely trailed him. He could, without having to exert force or explain himself, keep Diana Murdoch in the Cheyenne village until the Sages' child was born. He knew her well enough to know that she herself would not want to leave until she had seen the babe safely into the world. After that, what?

Yes. What then? his own mind taunted. *How will you keep her then, when you have no intention of ever letting her go?*

He shifted on George Washington's back, as if that small movement would ease the prodding guilt that tormented him. Diana Murdoch had said it herself—she had nowhere to go. Why would she not stay with him?

Then again, why would she? Why would she give up her own people, her culture, her way of life, for him?

Because they were fated to be together. Grey Eagle knew it as certainly as he breathed. Surely Diana knew it, too. The Great Ones would not have told him and not told her.

Would They have?

He looked at her again, plagued with doubt—an unusual and extremely uncomfortable feeling for him. Did he have the right to keep her with him against her will? It was one thing to declare one's intention to abduct and detain another person; it was quite another to actually follow through with the plan.

But he would not let her go.

Of that, he had no doubt.

Grey Eagle pulled his mind from the confusing thoughts of Diana and studied the area. He could not shake the feeling that something was wrong.

"What is it?" Diana called.

"I don't know." He pulled George Washington up until she reached his side. "Stay close to me, Miss Murdoch." He lifted his head and closed his eyes, his ears and nose on full alert. What was out there?

From a distance came the sound of a horse neighing a greeting. George Washington responded with an answering neigh. Grey Eagle dropped the reins, then pulled his shirt from under the belt at his waist and whipped the garment off over his head. With quick fingers, he untied his leggings at the waist and, first one then the other, pulled them off over his moccasins. He tucked the buckskin garments under the rope that held the supplies in place on George Washington's rump and slid his rifle from its case. All the while, his gaze darted about the area.

"What are you doing?" Diana asked, a note of worry in her voice.

"Preparing for battle. Can you use a pistol?"

"Yes, but with little hope that I'll hit what I aim for."

"Do the best you can." Grey Eagle pulled a pistol from the pack behind him and handed it to Diana. Her hand shook slightly when she accepted it, but she made no protest, expressed no fear. She shoved the weapon into the pocket of her skirt and looked at him. He reached out and grabbed the packhorse's halter. "Listen carefully, Miss Murdoch. A horse called, and where there are horses, there are usually men. Red or white, friend or foe, I don't know. Chances are they are not friendly. If we come under attack, you must do exactly as I tell you. Is that understood?"

There was no sign of fatigue in Diana's posture or eyes now, although her skin was very pale. "Yes."

"Until whoever or whatever is out there makes their move, we will keep on as we have been, with the forest close on our left. Stay with me unless I tell you otherwise." He released the packhorse and nudged George Washington to a walk, all the while cursing himself for bringing Diana Murdoch into danger.

They had not travelled far when a group of Indians rode out of the protection of the trees some distance in front of them. The group faced them and stopped, waiting. Grey Eagle heard Diana's sharp intake of breath and resisted looking back at her. He kept George Washington at a slow walk and spoke in a low voice. "There are five—Ute, I believe—and none wear war paint, so I assume they are a hunting party. However, one never knows how the Ute will react to the Cheyenne. They are often hostile. We must be very careful.''

"I shall follow your lead," Diana responded calmly.

A surge of admiration for her filled him, then he focused on the danger at hand. When he had closed the distance between them to perhaps twenty yards, he pulled George Washington to a halt. Diana kept the packhorse back a few feet.

With his rifle balanced across his lap, Grey Eagle made the sign for *Good day.*

One of the Utes nudged his horse forward a few paces and, also using sign language, answered with a similar greeting, then asked who he was and where he was going with a white captive.

Grey Eagle fought the desire to answer *None of your business* and instead signed, *I am Grey Eagle, of the Cheyenne, and we go to my village. She is a medicine woman, and her skills are needed.*

His reply apparently caused great interest among the Utes, for they drew close together for a discussion.

"What is happening?" Diana asked in a low tone.

"I don't know. They're conferring about something, though."

"They don't seem hostile. Can't we just move on?"

Without taking his eyes from the Utes, Grey Eagle answered, "Not yet. If we did, it would be seen as a challenge. All hell could break loose." He didn't add that the odds of five warriors to one were not good.

The leader of the Utes again nudged his horse forward a few paces, then stopped and signed.

Grey Eagle's jaw tightened. He stabbed his right index finger toward the palm of his left hand and jerked it back. *No!* Then he went on, his hands moving fast. *Woman not for trade.*

The Ute warrior frowned and rejoined his fellows.

"What do they want?" Diana asked.

He glanced at her. "You."

Diana's face paled even more, but she said nothing.

The Ute leader again came forward. His hands moved in a flurry of gestures.

Jessica Wulf

"They've raised their offer," Grey Eagle said to Diana, even as he repeated his answer to the Utes. His signals were abrupt and forceful. *Woman not for trade.* Then he added, *We go now,* and the sign for *Good-bye.*

"If you value your life, Miss Murdoch, stay with me." He spoke in a low tone as he turned George Washington's head to the right and nudged him to a walk. He headed toward the open valley. Diana urged the packhorse to follow. "Don't look back at them," he instructed. "They will have more respect for us if we show no concern or fear."

"What happens now?" she whispered.

"Either they let us go, or they don't. We'll know in a minute."

"And if they don't let us go?"

"We will fight." Grey Eagle looked at her then, full in the eyes, and a sadness washed over him. "Perhaps we will die."

Diana met his gaze, and swallowed. "Perhaps we won't."

Grey Eagle managed a small, encouraging smile, and kicked George Washington to a trot. He was pleased that Diana stayed right with him. Now he did hazard a glance at the Utes. They were making their move.

"Run, Diana!" he shouted as he kicked George Washington to a gallop.

The Utes screamed their war cries and Grey Eagle could hear the pounding of their horses' hooves. Desperately he searched for some place to take refuge, or to make a stand, for the packhorse could not keep the galloping pace for long. Up ahead he saw a tumble of good-sized rocks and boulders. Perhaps they could make it there.

He looked over his shoulder and was dismayed by how far back the packhorse had fallen already. The Utes were gaining on Diana. He dropped back to her side and pointed to the boulders. She nodded in understanding and leaned low over the packhorse's neck. Grey Eagle stayed right behind her.

Suddenly, George Washington stumbled. Grey Eagle fought to keep his seat. Then an arrow found its mark and buried itself in his left thigh. The stallion lost his footing and went down. Grey Eagle threw himself clear of the horse, hit the ground hard, and rolled. He heard Diana cry out. Instantly, he gained his feet and took aim with his rifle. He fired. One of the Utes jerked in the saddle, but kept on coming.

Grey Eagle spun around, saw that Diana had slowed, was turning her horse around. "Get to the rocks!" Grey Eagle shouted. He saw the indecision in her eyes. "Do as I say!" he roared. "Go!"

With an anguished expression, she pulled the horse's head around again and kicked the packhorse to a gallop. George Washington struggled to his feet and raced after Diana. An arrow protruded from the stallion's rump.

A glance at his left thigh showed that a steady stream of blood coursed down his leg to soak his moccasin. Grey Eagle felt a dull throbbing, but no pain. He would remove the arrow later, if he was still alive to do it. Fleetingly, he thought of the loaded pistol he had given Diana, and prayed that she could use it successfully. Then he faced his oncoming attackers, filled with a fierce determination. If nothing else, he would even the odds for her at least a little.

Grey Eagle stood tall in the prairie grasses, his now useless single-shot rifle poised as a club, his knife ready at his waist, and prepared himself for death. The May wind felt cool against his face and caused strands of his long hair to tickle his naked back. The valley was beautiful, the day was beautiful. It was a good place and a good day to die, although he could not deny a gripping sadness that he had found his Woman of the Clouds at last, only to be forced to leave her so soon.

Perhaps she would not survive this day, either, and they would be together forever. Perhaps that was what the Great Ones had intended all along.

Grey Eagle tightened his grip on the rifle barrel. If death came knocking on his door, he would answer. His battle cry echoed across the pristine valley.

Chapter Fourteen

She couldn't do it.

She couldn't leave him out there in the middle of the valley to face the Utes and certain death alone, even though he wanted it that way. As courageous and noble as a fabled knight of old, Grey Eagle had met the Utes without fear, sitting tall and proud on George Washington's back, and now he stood tall and proud, alone and greatly outnumbered, prepared to die for her.

If he—and she—were to die this day, then they would die together.

Diana pulled the packhorse to a walk while she fought with the ropes that held the supplies on behind the saddle. What she wouldn't give for Grey Eagle's wicked-looking knife right now!

Her hat hung against her back; its string pulled at her throat, and, with a muttered curse, she tore it off and flung it away. The packhorse sidestepped, confused and nervous as the pack on his rump began to shift. In the end, he helped get rid of it by further loosening the ropes with his kicking. Somehow, Diana managed to stay in the saddle. The pack fell away, and she headed the horse back toward Grey Eagle, pulling his pistol from her pocket as she rode.

When she drew near, he turned. Expressions of anger and

dismay raced across his face, and he motioned her back toward the rocks. With a determined shake of her head, she guided the running horse past him, then slowed and turned so that she and the packhorse were positioned between Grey Eagle and the approaching band of Utes. She took careful aim with the pistol and shot at the Ute leader—once, then again.

There was no evidence that she hit anyone or anything with her shots, yet the Utes pulled to a halt; none returned her fire. Diana found that odd, but wasted no time in trying to figure it out. She guided the horse back toward Grey Eagle, slowed the animal to a walk, and, as she suspected he could, Grey Eagle threw himself up behind her. He held his rifle in one hand, while his other arm whipped around her waist and he molded his chest to her back.

A feeling of relief flooded through her, so powerfully that she gasped. Then she looked down. The sight of the arrow protruding from Grey Eagle's bloody thigh horrified her, as did the quick glance that told her the Utes were again after them. She urged the tiring horse toward the boulders, painfully aware of the target presented by Grey Eagle's broad back.

After a run that to Diana lasted forever, the plucky packhorse leapt over a small creek and brought them to the dubious shelter offered by the rock formation. Grey Eagle slid off the gelding's rump, leaned the rifle against a rock, then pulled Diana from the saddle and into his arms. For a moment, he held her tightly. She still carried the pistol, but that did not keep her arms from circling his waist, and she clung to him. Her cheek rested against the warm, naked skin of his shoulder; against her breast she could feel the pounding of his heart. Her own heart lurched, with a powerful, unidentifiable emotion. Then he set her back.

The Utes were upon them.

The wheezing packhorse moved off. Grey Eagle took the pistol from Diana's hand and thrust her behind him. Determined not to cower like a frightened child, Diana snatched up the heavy rifle and stepped to the side, a little behind him. She modelled her stance after Grey Eagle's—tall and immobile. This was her battle, too. By God, those Utes would know they faced two warriors.

The five Utes drew up a short distance from the rock formation. The leader again moved forward and began to sign.

"Translate for me," Diana commanded in a whisper.

Without looking back at her, Grey Eagle said, "Because they are impressed with our courage—me, for standing alone, you, for coming after me—they will not kill me if I give you to them."

Her heart hammering with fear, Diana stepped forward to Grey Eagle's side. She looked up at him, found his green eyes burning into her. If going with the Utes would save his life, she would go. "I will go," she said quietly.

His eyes widened in surprise, then grew hard. "Do you think I will let them have you?" he demanded.

"If it will save your life—"

He cut her off with a single word. "Diana."

For the second time that day, he used her Christian name, and Diana found that she liked it.

"I will not give you up." The fierce determination in Grey Eagle's voice both warmed and strengthened her.

"Then we will fight together," she said. Something new flashed in his eyes—approval?—as he nodded once. His hands spoke. At the same time, Diana stared right at the Ute leader and defiantly shook her head.

The man's mouth tightened, and his hands motioned furiously.

Grey Eagle spoke even as his hands moved in reply. "He wants to know why I let a captive dictate terms. I tell him that you are not a captive."

Diana raised her chin another notch and kept her gaze pinned on the leader, whose hands moved again. From the corner of her eye, she could tell that Grey Eagle did not answer. "What did he say?" she asked.

"He asked if you are my woman."

At that, Diana turned to Grey Eagle. Now his hands moved in elegant motion. "What is your reply?" she asked.

"I tell him that you are indeed my woman, and a powerful medicine woman, whose skills are needed at the Cheyenne encampment. I warn him not to start a war with the Cheyenne over you.''

Diana watched Grey Eagle's strong yet graceful hands as their flowing movements spoke. She was strangely touched by his declaration that she was his woman. It wasn't true, of course, but the thought made her feel protected.

A sneer crossed the Ute leader's face as he signed with angry motions.

Now Grey Eagle's jaw also tightened with anger.

"What did he say?" Diana demanded.

"He asks how much respect the Cheyenne have for their medicine women if we beat them."

Diana self-consciously touched the bruise on her cheek.

Grey Eagle's hands moved, in motions as threatening as his tone. "I tell him that the soldier who put the bruise on your face is dead, as they will be if they try to take you from me."

After a moment of glaring at Grey Eagle, the Ute leader pulled back to confer with his companions.

"Do they want me because I'm a white woman?" she asked.

His fierce gaze did not leave the Ute as he answered. "Not entirely. They risk involvement with the Army if they take a white woman captive, and word always gets around. Even if I am killed, the Army would eventually learn that the Utes have you. They want you more because you are a medicine woman. That is why they did not shoot back at you. They think or hope that your powers will help them and their people."

"But I have no special powers," Diana protested. "I studied at my father's side, Mr. Beaudine; that is all. I am not a medicine woman, nor am I a physician."

"The official title means nothing. You are a healer." Grey Eagle's firm tone brooked no argument.

Diana offered none; it didn't matter any longer. Numbly, she looked around the pretty valley, wondering if she and Grey Eagle would die here today. If so, she would soon be with her father again, and that made the idea of death not quite so frightening. A part of her would welcome it—would welcome an end to the grief and confusion and loneliness. But she could not bear the thought that Grey Eagle would also die. He was so powerful, so beautiful, so *alive*. The loss of his life would be a terrible waste.

A short distance away, Diana saw George Washington and the packhorse—one injured, one winded, both waiting—and she was grateful that both horses still lived. It struck her as odd that she would welcome death for herself, yet rejoice in life for others. As dire and hopeless as the situation was, a part of her—a strong part of her—desperately wanted to live.

A distant call whispered on the wind, so faint that Diana was certain she imagined it. *Franklin.*

The Utes appeared to have reached a decision, for their tight group dispersed. Diana held her breath, hoping, praying, that the five men would ride away. But they did not. Each removed his shirt. They lined up side by side, facing the rock formation.

"They will attack," Grey Eagle said quietly. He held the pistol—with its three remaining shots—in his right hand, his knife in his left. "Stay behind me, Diana. Find cover in the rocks. I will take as many with me as I can."

"It is better that we present a united front," she argued. "You said they don't want to hurt me. Let me stand with you." She still held the heavy rifle, useful for nothing now except a club because the powder and shot needed to reload it were tied in the pack on George Washington's wounded rump. However, all around lay rocks of varying sizes. If necessary, she would resort to those as weapons. One had come in handy enough during her battle with Lieutenant Thatcher.

"Get back!" Grey Eagle ordered her.

"We are in this together, Mr. Beaudine, to the end." Now it was her tone that allowed no argument. Diana glared at him, every bit as determined as he was.

Again, something flashed in his eyes—approval, pride, she didn't know what for certain, except that it was favorable.

"As you wish, Diana Murdoch. You are a worthy comrade-in-arms. May the Spirit of the Eagle watch over us."

Diana stared up at him, deeply moved by his words. Then she heard it again, from faraway. The familiar call. She shivered—and not from fear. Had Grey Eagle's innocent prayer to the Spirit of the Eagle been heard?

The Utes began their war songs.

Grey Eagle lifted his head. His battle cry echoed off the encircling rocks, and sent another shiver down Diana's spine. To the very gates of hell, Grey Eagle would fight for her. She knew it, as surely as she knew Franklin was coming.

The Eagle was coming.

The line of Utes surged forward.

Grey Eagle roared his fierce battle cry once more.

Diana clutched the barrel of the rifle and searched the skies. *Come to me, Franklin,* she pleaded. *Come now.*

Perhaps her unusual friendship with an eagle would convince the Utes she was a medicine woman with extraordinary powers, as it had convinced Sparrow.

Perhaps the five determined warriors would be afraid of her supposed powers, and she could use that fear to her advantage.

Perhaps no one need die today.

The eagle called, closer now. And again.

She saw him and cried his name. *"Franklin!"*

He came toward her, slowly and with great majesty. Without taking her eyes from him, Diana set the rifle aside and fumbled with the buttons at the waist of her skirt. When they came free, she stepped out of the skirt and hurriedly wrapped the material around her right wrist and forearm. She stepped forward, toward a boulder which stood about three feet high.

"Diana!" Grey Eagle's concerned voice touched her, as did his hand, reaching for hers. "What are you doing?"

Diana glanced back at him. She realized that the Ute war cries had stopped, that Grey Eagle's face seemed pale, his eyes wide—in fear, in amazement, she didn't know. She tightened her hold on his hand. "Trust me," she whispered.

He stared at her, searchingly, a moment longer, then released her hand. Diana turned from him and looked to the sky. Franklin circled the rock formation now, with a lazy grace. A quick glance at the party of Utes showed her that they were as dumbfounded and as motionless as Grey Eagle was. Hope surged in her chest, as well as a rush of confidence. She stepped forward, her aching right arm held out to the side at shoulder height, her eyes on the eagle.

"Come here, Franklin," she called.

The great bird came in for his landing, his flapping, wide-spread wings sending gusts of wind that blew strands of her tousled hair away from her face. With a smile, Diana closed her eyes and felt the power of Franklin's spirit. She felt as if she were embracing a long-lost friend, and she opened her heart and her eyes to welcome him. Franklin landed on her arm, as he had done so many times before. She tilted her head away from his long wing as his talons found purchase in the cloth of her skirt. Then he folded his wings at his sides and became still, except for the constant slight movements of his head and the blinking of his eyes.

"Hello, Franklin," Diana whispered, her eyes tearing in joy. "How good it is to see you." She reached up to smooth the feathers of his chest. "You look wonderful—so strong and healthy." He made a cooing sound deep in his throat and shuffled his feet. Diana realized that the material of her skirt shifted and slid in a way her leather wrist guard did not, and that Franklin might not be confident about his perch on her arm. She took a few steps toward a large boulder that stood perhaps four feet tall, and put her arm close to it. Franklin moved from her arm to the boulder, his sharp talons making scraping noises as he shuffled his feet. They were separated by only inches. Diana ran a caressing hand down the sleek feathers on the eagle's back, then calmly turned to face Grey Eagle.

He stared at her with a look of awe and pride on his handsome face. She nodded reassuringly at him before turning to the Ute warriors. They gaped at her, both in reverence and in fear.

"Please translate my words, Mr. Beaudine," she said, without taking her eyes from the Utes.

Grey Eagle moved to her side. He slipped the pistol into the belt around his waist and held up his hands.

She spoke, and his graceful hands signed. "I belong with Grey Eagle and the Cheyenne. If you take me from them, the Eagle will be displeased. Do not bring the wrath of the Eagle upon you and your people." She pointed across the valley, in the direction from which the Ute had come, and her voice took on a more commanding tone. "Go now. Leave us in peace."

Franklin again shuffled his feet and made a strange squeaking sound, as if backing up her words.

After several moments of silence, the leader of the band of Utes made several signs.

"He asks forgiveness, from you, the medicine woman, and from the Eagle," Grey Eagle said.

Diana's shoulders slumped with relief as she looked at him. "He has it. They all do."

"Do this." Grey Eagle held his hands palms up in front of his chest, then lowered them slightly and moved them toward Diana, as if he were handing her something. "It means you give them your blessing."

She straightened her weary shoulders and faced the Utes, then moved her hands as Grey Eagle had shown her. The movement was simple, but it had a powerful effect on the five anxious men toward whom she directed it. All of them appeared to be consoled; one raised his bow toward the sky and yipped. As if that action were a cue, all pulled their horses around and rode off at a gallop, yelling and shrieking.

Such a powerful feeling of gratitude flowed through Diana that her knees felt weak, and she braced her hands against the strength of the sun-warmed boulder. Franklin spread his wings once, as if stretching, then folded them against his body and shuffled closer to Diana. She reached out with a shaking hand and stroked the place between Franklin's eyes. "Thank you for coming, sweetheart," she whispered. "Your timing was perfect."

"You know and understand the Spirit of the Eagle, as my niece told me you did." The solemn, almost reverent tone of Grey Eagle's voice bothered Diana. Wearily, she turned to him.

"I know how this must look to you—how it must have looked to the Utes—but there is nothing mystical about the friendship Franklin and I share, Mr. Beaudine. When he was very young and much smaller, I found him injured on the prairie. Together, my father and I tended him and nursed him back to health. It is not that I know the Spirit of the Eagle, it is that this particular eagle knows me."

"You do not give yourself credit where it is due, Diana."

His voice rolled over her, offering her warmth as well as a compliment, neither of which she could accept. "There is no mystery to Franklin's presence here today," she insisted.

After a long, uncomfortable minute of silence, Grey Eagle spoke quietly. "You are wrong, Diana Murdoch, but I will not argue with you." He paused, then asked, "Will he let me near?"

"I don't know," Diana answered, relieved by the change of subject. "He always let my father near, and eventually Mr. Sage, but we released him to the wild several months ago. I wasn't certain he would come to me today." She stepped back. "You are welcome to try. Make no sudden moves."

Grey Eagle limped the few steps to the rock, and Diana remembered that he was seriously wounded. "He likes to have the place between his eyes stroked," she offered, her hands clasped tightly together. A fold of the skirt fell forward over her hands, reminding Diana that she stood in her petticoats. She could not make herself care as she watched the man and the eagle.

With infinite caution and ever so slowly, Grey Eagle extended a hand toward the eagle. Franklin shuffled his feet, but did not pull back. Grey Eagle laid a gentle finger on the eagle's head and stroked down the feathered neck, once, then again, then he stroked the place Diana had mentioned to him and whispered words in Cheyenne. Franklin made odd cooing sounds.

A strange feeling rose up in Diana at the sight of the man caressing her eagle. They shared a connection of some kind, the warrior and the eagle, the same kind of connection that Diana shared with Franklin. In her heart, she knew it. Did that mean that the three of them were connected? Was she connected to Grey Eagle in some mystical, spiritual way?

"You called him Franklin." Grey Eagle spoke quietly as he stroked the eagle's back.

"We named him after Benjamin Franklin."

"I thought Mr. Franklin was more enamored of the wild turkey than of the eagle."

Diana was impressed with Grey Eagle's knowledge, and it struck her again how odd it seemed that such perfect English and such obvious education came from an almost naked Cheyenne warrior out in the middle of the wilderness. "Yes. I fear we were poking fun at Mr. Franklin, God rest his patriotic soul."

"It is a good name for your eagle." Grey Eagle whispered again to Franklin in Cheyenne, then stepped back.

Diana caressed the eagle's head a few more times, then also stepped back. "Fare you well, Franklin, until we meet again," she said. "Thank you for your assistance today."

As if he understood her words, Franklin flapped his mighty wings and rose into the air. His call echoed down to them as he circled higher and higher. Diana shaded her eyes against the sun and fought threatening tears as she watched the eagle fly from sight.

"Once I soared with him." She put her thoughts into spoken words without fully realizing it. "I danced through clouds, felt the kiss of snowflakes on my face before they fell to the earth, saw the world from an incredible height. Many times since then I've wished I could fly away with him and never come back." She lowered her hand and brushed it across her eyes. "I think that, after he died, my father flew with Franklin. He would have enjoyed that." Then she heard her own words, and blushed. How could she have said such things to Grey Eagle Beaudine? To anyone? Any who heard her speak thusly would think her mad. She gave a shaky little laugh as she unwrapped the skirt from her arm and hurriedly stepped into it. "No doubt I sound like a foolish schoolgirl." She secured the buttons at her waist, then straightened her shoulders and turned to Grey Eagle. "I must see to your leg."

He stared at her, his green eyes warm with understanding. "You are not foolish, Diana Murdoch. You are one of the wisest people I have ever known. And you are wrong about not having special powers. You do not yet know your own strength."

Diana waved his words away. "I think the loss of blood has left you addled, Mr. Beaudine. Please let me tend you before you say something that will later cause you embarrassment."

Grey Eagle caught her hand in his. "I know what I say."

The intensity in his eyes, in his expression, the gentle strength in the hand that held hers, made Diana uncomfortable at the same time they beckoned her closer. *Like a moth to the flame.* She pulled away. "You cannot ride until I doctor your leg, and George Washington is wounded, as well. Even when I am finished with the both of you, it would be best if you rested until tomorrow." She put her hands on her hips and perused the area. "This is a good place to camp. The rocks offer some protection."

"The Utes know we are here. We must move on."

"They are frightened of me," Diana argued. "And they won't tell anyone else."

"Perhaps not, but they might gather their courage and come back. They might decide that it will be more beneficial to their tribe to have you as their medicine woman, no matter the cost." He pointed toward the far side of the valley. "Not far beyond that forested hill is a good campsite."

Diana pushed away the fear that the Ute warriors might return and stubbornly said, "You can't ride until I remove that arrow, Mr. Beaudine."

"I can and I will." He pursed his lips and emitted a sharp whistle. To Diana's astonishment, George Washington—who was a good two hundred yards away—pricked his ears, then obediently trotted to Grey Eagle's side. The man stroked the stallion's neck and said to Diana, "I need you to gather the pack you threw off your horse."

"I did that to help you," Diana snapped.

"I know, and I am very grateful. I meant no criticism. I owe you my life, Miss Murdoch. However, I need your help for a while longer."

"I am *trying* to help you by insisting that you allow me to see to your wound! And his!" Diana pointed to the arrow that protruded from George Washington's rump.

Grey Eagle straightened the blanket on George Washington's back, then examined the stallion's wound. "He will have no trouble reaching the campsite I have chosen," he announced. "His injury is more annoying than serious."

Diana glared at Grey Eagle's broad, bare back. "This is yet another battle I will not win, isn't it?"

"Yes."

It was all she could do not to stamp her foot in anger and frustration. "You are the most infuriating man I have ever met, Grey Eagle Beaudine. Not thirty minutes ago, I feared you would die. Now, I almost hope you do. Go ahead and bleed to death—it would serve you right. And don't expect me to waste any tears crying over your grave." She marched to where the pack and several items that had come free of the oilskin cover lay strewn about. "See if I care, you arrogant . . . *chief,*" she muttered as she grabbed the coffeepot and reached for the iron fire grate.

She did care.

Grey Eagle's wound was serious, whether he believed so or not, and the tight knot of worry in her stomach would not ease until she removed that blasted arrow and thoroughly cleansed the injured area. The same with George Washington's wound. She cared about the warrior, and about his magnificent stallion.

How had she come to care so deeply in two short days?

With a troubled sigh, Diana carried the coffeepot and grate to the boulder, then retraced her steps to drag the pack to Grey Eagle's side. "What about the packhorse?" she asked, gazing at the unconcerned horse who contentedly grazed on the spring meadow grasses several yards away.

"You must get him."

Diana jerked her head around to glare at Grey Eagle, and her snippy retort died on her tongue. He leaned against George Washington's back only briefly before he straightened, but it was long enough to remind Diana that she cared. There was no question that his face was pale now, and that paleness wasn't caused by awe at meeting a somewhat tame eagle at a most fortuitous time, any more than the fine beading of sweat on his forehead was. Grey Eagle was suffering.

"Is there a secret to catching him?" she asked.

Grey Eagle shook his head. "Just approach him slowly. He knows you; he shouldn't bolt."

With a silent prayer that the horse would behave as Grey Eagle predicted, Diana hiked her skirts and set off across the meadow.

Chapter Fifteen

Grey Eagle fought a smile as he watched Diana go after the packhorse. He liked that she wasn't afraid of him, wasn't afraid to speak her mind, wasn't afraid to stand at his side against a formidable enemy, wasn't afraid to face death. Diana Murdoch was a courageous woman, honorable and intelligent.

She understood the Power of the Eagle.

His faint smile faded, and he stared at her intently as she captured the horse, then started back toward him.

She could deny it all she wished, but the truth remained—Diana had been blessed with a precious gift from the Great Ones. The Spirit of the Eagle had touched her heart, had come to her in the physical form of Franklin, had taken her on a flight most could not hope for until death. She was a true medicine woman, and that title did not refer only to her healing skills.

And she had come back for him. A warm feeling engulfed him and he saw her again in his mind as she clung to the saddle, pulled out the pistol, and defied him in order to confront the Utes. She had risked death, had taken a foolish chance, and had saved his life. Two days ago, he saved her life, and today she saved his. Now he and she were bound together even more intimately. Bound together with the Eagle.

Never would he let her go.

"You were right," Diana called when she had closed the distance between them to perhaps thirty yards. "He let me take up the halter rope with no troub—" A frown furrowed her brow. "Mr. Beaudine, are you all right?" She hurried to his side, pulling the horse along. "You don't look well."

Her words tore Grey Eagle from his pleasant reverie and reminded him that he had an arrow buried in his thigh. For the first time, he was fully aware of how painful his wound was. And there was no time to tend it now. He spoke more brusquely than he intended. "We must go."

Diana's mouth pressed into a tight line, and her eyes shot daggers. "If you won't care for yourself, then I won't care, either," she snapped.

She marched to the large pack that lay on the ground near his feet and picked up one end of it. Grey Eagle stooped and lifted the other end, biting down hard on his lip at the spasms of pain that rolled through his entire body. Together, they managed to secure the unwieldy pack behind the saddle on the patient packhorse. Diana stuffed into the pack the few items that had escaped, then faced him. "Are we ready?" she asked. Her voice fairly dripped icicles.

Grey Eagle handed her the hat she had thrown off before coming to his rescue. It had been trampled, but was still serviceable.

"Thank you," she said as she took it from him, then she looked at him fully. The anger drained from her face and was replaced by a concern so obviously genuine that he was touched. "Shouldn't we at least break off the feathered end of the arrow before you ride?" she asked.

"To do so would jar the arrowhead and perhaps do more damage. We will wait." He fought to keep his face expressionless as he carefully climbed onto a good-sized rock. It had been a long time since he'd been so seriously wounded, and he'd forgotten how excruciating the pain could be. "The best thing to do now is get to a safe camp as quickly as possible." He eased himself onto George Washington's blanketed back, taking great care not to bump the arrow shaft or move his injured leg too much. "There I shall place myself in your competent hands, and you may do with me as you wish."

Diana plopped the battered hat on her head and drew the string tight under her chin, then clambered into the saddle. Her dusty skirts hiked up to her knees, revealing a torn stocking and the lacy edge of her drawers. Her bodice was ripped, her face bruised, and her hair, crowned with the disreputable hat, hung down her back in an untidy braid, yet she held herself with pride. "You will regret giving me such liberty, Mr. Beaudine, because the first thing I'm going to do when we are settled in our 'safe' camp is hit you upside the head for being so blasted obstinate. I think your frying pan will serve nicely."

"If hitting me in the head will take my mind off the pain in my leg, I shall welcome it." In the face of her humorless, unrelenting glare, he managed an impertinent grin, then turned George Washington's head and led the way from the scant protection of the rock formation into the open valley. All traces of humor left him. "Keep your eyes and ears open, Miss Murdoch. There's no telling who else might be in those hills, watching us even now. We are headed for that hill to the north, the one cut down the middle by a gully. Once there, we will turn to the west and travel a distance in the protection of the trees, then cross over the top into the safety of the hills beyond."

"How long do you think it will take?"

"An hour, maybe a little longer."

"I shall stay right behind you, sir." Diana's voice was subdued and somber.

"Good." Grey Eagle gritted his teeth against the fresh waves of pain he knew were coming and nudged George Washington to an easy lope. Then he said a silent prayer to the Spirit of the Eagle that both he and his weary, wounded horse had the stamina to follow through with his plan.

Grey Eagle had estimated an hour to reach the campsite upon which he was so intent, but, due to the terrible worry that ate at Diana, the journey seemed to take much longer. At any moment, she expected him to pitch off the stallion's back, overcome at last with pain and loss of blood. But he did not.

Patiently, she followed him across the valley floor, praying with each step her horse took that no more trouble came from the forested hills surrounding them. A great relief filled her when they reached the comforting shadows of the forest, and she assumed that they did not have far to go.

But then he led her into a narrow, tumbling creek and, in a low voice—whether from caution or from weakness, she could not tell—ordered her to keep the packhorse in the water as they moved up the hill. Diana understood that he was trying to hide their tracks, and she found it very troubling that Grey Eagle felt there was a reason to cover their trail. It seemed that she had been surrounded by danger for weeks rather than the mere three days it had actually been.

When the increasing slant of the hill made travel in the creek risky, he led her back into the trees and through a pass of sorts between two hills. At last, the beautiful, treacherous valley was gone from sight.

Now, Diana looked about the campsite, satisfied that Grey Eagle had chosen a good place to stop. A half-moon of jumbled boulders created a sheltered hollow against the side of the hill, and she could hear in the distance the gurgle of yet another creek. Plenty of branches and fallen trees lay about the area, providing firewood, and enough light remained in the afternoon sky to ensure that she would be able to closely examine the wounds of both Grey Eagle and George Washington. She climbed down from the saddle, filled with determination. Grey Eagle himself had said it: she was in charge now.

She removed her hat and tossed it aside as she marched over to where he and George Washington waited. The pallor on Grey Eagle's face scared her, but she kept her voice firm as she ordered, "Allow me to help you down, Mr. Beaudine."

"Yes, ma'am. Please stand right there. I'll brace myself on your shoulder."

Diana followed his instructions. She watched as he brought his uninjured right leg over the stallion's neck. He leaned forward, grasped her shoulder in a tight grip, and slid off the horse, careful to take the brunt of his weight on his right leg. Upon landing, he made no sound, but his face paled even more.

"I want you over there by that boulder, in the sunlight, so I can see what I'm doing." Diana slipped an arm around Grey Eagle's waist, and he draped his arm over her shoulders. Lordy, but the man was tall, and solid. He was also, with the exception of his breechclout and moccasins, naked, and his long black hair caressed the side of her face.

Diana blushed and took firm control of her thoughts and her annoyingly female senses. She simply *had* to think of Grey Eagle as her patient, and nothing more. He was not a warrior, nor a chief, nor a beautiful, nearly naked man. He was a fellow human—granted, a very male human—in need of her medical skills. And that was all he was.

For now, that was all she could allow him to be.

Together, they made their way to the sunny spot she had in mind. Grey Eagle eased himself to the ground and leaned against the boulder at his back. He did not complain, but his furrowed brow and the lines of tension around his tight mouth told her of the terrible pain he had to be suffering.

She hurried to get the canteen and returned to his side. "Drink," she urged. "Then I want to examine that leg."

Grey Eagle accepted the canteen and drew up his injured leg, the knee bent, his foot flat against the earth. Diana drew a deep breath and fought a sudden, paralyzing fear. She had seen worse injuries than the one she now faced, but never had she worked on so serious a wound without her father at her side. What if she did something wrong?

As if he read her mind, Grey Eagle grasped her hand, just for a moment, and gave it a reassuring squeeze. That little gesture was of great help. Diana gathered her courage and slipped into the role of physician, forcing her mind to a scientific bent, trying to forget that the bloody, injured thigh she examined belonged to a special man.

The arrow had entered the outside of his thigh at a downward angle, but had not broken through the skin on the inside of the leg. She estimated the trajectory angle and, with the hope that she did not hurt him further, gently pressed on the inside of

Grey Eagle's thigh. Finally, her searching fingers found the hard bump which she believed to be the arrowhead. Because of the angle of the shaft, she was fairly certain that the arrow had missed the bone. She looked up at him. "It is my understanding that to pull an arrow back out the way it went in will cause greater damage to the wound."

"If it is a war arrow," Grey Eagle responded.

"There is a difference between arrows?"

He nodded. "Hunting arrows are designed to be withdrawn with ease, to be used again. War arrows are designed to inflict as much damage as possible going in, and even more coming out. The rear shoulders of the war arrowhead are barbed for that reason."

Diana stared at him, horrified by the fiendish ingenuity of weapons of war, even in the wilderness among supposedly primitive peoples. A study of history had taught her that mankind in general was very adept at inventing terrible and clever ways to injure and kill fellow men; she had not known that particular talent extended to the natives of the North American continent.

Grey Eagle went on. "I believe the Ute party was a hunting party; therefore, it is most likely that my particular arrow is a hunting arrow. However, since we can't be certain until we see the arrowhead ourselves, I suggest that we assume it is a war arrow, and proceed accordingly."

For several moments, Diana continued to stare at him. Grey Eagle's cultured mode of speech might well have come from the mouth of a West Point-educated Army officer, yet his physical appearance was so clearly Cheyenne. And she found his calm discussion of his own painful wound disconcerting. How could he be so composed? So dispassionate?

"Miss Murdoch?"

Diana blinked, and drew herself together. "I agree, Mr. Beaudine." She realized that her hands still held his naked thigh, and she lightly pressed with the fingertips of her left hand. "The arrowhead is here, perhaps a half an inch down. I will make a small incision, break off the feathered end of the shaft, and force the arrow the rest of the way through your leg.''

Again, he nodded.

Diana looked at him, determined to do whatever she could for him, and terrified of what that entailed. ''What I'm going to do will cause you a great deal of pain, Mr. Beaudine, and I hate that. If you think it will help, I have some laudanum in my father's case.''

''I thought you were going to hit me with the frying pan. It seems that would be simpler.''

Startled, Diana looked more closely into his eyes, saw the spark of humor there, and could not stop a small smile from curving her lips. ''I should, if for no other reason than to force you to heed my threats,'' she retorted. Then she sobered. ''Do you want the laudanum?''

''No, but thank you. You're going to need my help pushing the arrow through.''

She frowned. ''Will it be that difficult?''

''Yes. I have done this before.''

''You've been shot with an arrow before today?'' she asked incredulously.

He shook his head. ''I have helped dig them out and push them through. Over the years, many of us—my brother Orion, my father, Jubal, Raven's Heart, who is Sparrow's father—have stopped enemy arrows. My brother Joseph and I have both been shot with firearms.'' He touched a place on his side, and Diana saw a scar she had not noticed before. Her shock must have shown on her face, for he said, ''The frontier is a dangerous place, Miss Murdoch. Even if he seeks peace, a man has many enemies out here—the land itself, the weather, some of the creatures who live here, as well as other men who are armed with bow and arrow, rifle, pistol, or disease.''

''Disease?''

Grey Eagle leaned his head back against the rock and closed his eyes. ''White man's diseases have killed far more Indians of all tribes than have white man's weapons.''

Stricken, Diana looked down at her hands, clasped tightly in her lap. She knew he spoke the truth, and she hoped that she and her doctoring would not eventually play a part in Grey Eagle's death. "I must build a fire," she murmured as she scrambled to her feet. "Stay here and rest."

Other than a slight nod, Grey Eagle did not respond.

The weakness of that simple movement—which told her that the loss of blood and the unremitting pain were sapping the warrior's strength—galvanized Diana to frantic action. In twenty minutes, a small fire burned within a circle of rocks she had formed under a pine tree so that the smoke would disperse as it rose through the branches. The pot in which Grey Eagle had brewed her willow bark tea now held fresh water from the nearby creek, water that was close to boiling. A few flowering stems of the common and plentiful yarrow plant—which offered excellent cleansing and clotting properties—had been harvested and lay near the fire. The saddle and packs had been removed from the horses and the buffalo robes laid out in a bed under the intertwined branches of two other pine trees. A quick examination of George Washington's wounded rump assured Diana that the stallion would be all right for a while longer. Both horses had been watered at the creek, and they now grazed on the young spring grasses that grew on the side of the hill.

Diana returned to Grey Eagle's side and crouched down to place a hand on his brow. He instantly opened pain-clouded eyes.

"I'm sterilizing my scalpel in the flames," she told him. "I'll see to your leg in just a few minutes." At his nod, she returned to the fire and checked on the scalpel. Many times over the last several years she had watched Gideon use that very instrument, his graceful, long-fingered hands steady and confident. It seemed strange to think of the scalpel as hers, yet it was. The scalpel itself and the knowledge of how to use it— at least in this case—were part of her legacy from her father. At that moment, Diana was very grateful for that legacy.

With a shy glance over her shoulder to make certain Grey Eagle did not watch—which was ridiculous, she admitted to herself, since the man had seen her wearing nothing but his shirt and had shared a bed with her, let alone the fact that little more than an hour ago she had removed her skirt in front of him and five Ute warriors—she lifted her skirt and untied one of her two petticoats, then stepped out of the garment. After locating the cleanest part, she grabbed the surgical scissors from the medical bag and cut the white cotton into wide strips for use as bandages and a few smaller pieces to serve as washing cloths. Returning to Grey Eagle's side, she arranged her 'surgery,' such as it was: the small pot of boiled water in which the blade of the heat-sterilized scalpel waited, the bandages, the yarrow stems, her father's medical bag open and at hand.

"I wish to God we were in my father's surgery," she said fervently, "but we are not. I will do the best I can with what I have."

His eyes, alert and filled with an unsettling faith, bored into hers. "You will do well, Diana Murdoch. The Spirit of the Eagle is with you, and with me."

Diana did not share his confidence, but she did whisper a quick prayer to her father's loving spirit. If anyone was watching over her, guiding her hand, she preferred it to be Gideon. She took a deep breath and again forced herself into an unemotional, scientific frame of mind.

The first discovery she made was that the best position for her was to sit cross-legged between Grey Eagle's bare calves, facing him. He seemed to think nothing of it, and moved to accommodate her.

Bearing in mind his earlier comment about jarring the arrowhead while it was still imbedded in his leg, she changed her mind and made the incision first, then pushed the arrow through enough to free the arrowhead. Grey Eagle snapped off the feathered end, and she tried to pull the remainder of the shaft through. He had been correct about the shaft not moving easily through tissue and muscle, but, with him pushing, Diana was able to at last pull the hated arrow free. She stared at the bloody thing in her shaking hand, noticed with gratitude that it was indeed a hunting arrow rather than a war arrow, and threw it as far as she could.

Blood flowed freely from both entrance and exit wounds, but not enough to worry her that a major vein had been hit.

Diana wet two of the smaller pieces of the petticoat in the still hot pot of water, then pulled them out and pressed one to each wound. She noticed that most of Grey Eagle's leg was covered with blood, as were her hands. For the first time since taking up the scalpel, she looked at his face.

Grey Eagle had not made a sound through the whole ordeal. His head rested against the boulder, a fine sheen of sweat glistened on his forehead, and his striking green eyes were on her. "Well done, Dr. Murdoch."

Those simple words released a tightly coiled spring of tension and fear inside her, and Diana's eyes filled with tears. "I'm so sorry I had to hurt you," she whispered. "There was no other way."

"You did not hurt me." He reached out and gently touched her cheek, then let his arm fall back to his side. "The arrow did."

At that, she managed a small smile, and blinked the tears away. A quick check under the pieces of cloth she held to the wounds showed that the bleeding had slowed, much to her relief. In another few minutes, she would wash his leg and properly bandage it. "Please hold these in place, like this." She nodded toward the coverings she held over the wounds. Grey Eagle obeyed her, and Diana dug the mortar and pestle out of the medical bag. She shrugged her shoulders in an effort to release some of the pent-up tension in the muscles there, then went to work mashing yarrow flowers and leaves. "Why did you take off your shirt and your leggings to prepare for battle? Why did the Utes also remove their shirts?"

"Exactly for this reason." He indicated his wounded leg. "The risk of infection in a battle wound is far greater if pieces of the warrior's clothing are carried inside the body by the bullet or arrow that strikes him. If I'd had time to properly prepare for battle, both I and George Washington would have been covered with war paint."

Diana shuddered at his casual discussion of something as terrible as war, of preparing for wounds one expected to receive. Still, she was curious about the customs of the Cheyenne, even the war customs. "Paint cannot stop a bullet or an arrow. What is the purpose of war paint?"

"To invoke the protection of the Great Ones, to help the leader of an expedition identify his men from a distance, to build up one's confidence, to instill fear in one's opponent. There are several reasons, all of them important to the Cheyenne—important to all of the Plains tribes, actually."

Feeling that she had much to learn about the ways of the Cheyenne—wondering why she wanted to learn—Diana set the mortar aside, rewet one of the cloths, and thoroughly cleansed the areas around his wounds. She then took up two clean pieces of her petticoat, folded them into thick pads, and placed a good amount of mashed yarrow on each.

"Please hold these in place while I wrap the bandage around your leg." He did as she instructed. Diana could feel his intense gaze on her face as she worked, felt a blush heat her cheeks. When Grey Eagle's hands were no longer needed to hold the pads, one of those hands brushed strands of her hair away from her face and eyes, and his gentle touch sparked a fire deep inside her.

How could she be singed by the heat of his gaze and feel shivery at the same time? Diana had never known the kinds of feelings Grey Eagle Beaudine awakened in her, and she did not know how to respond to them. Wishing she was anywhere but trapped between his long, muscular, naked legs, she rinsed most of the blood from her hands, then snatched up a fresh cloth, wet it, and began to scrub the dried blood from his leg. For fear of what she might see there, she would not look at his face.

After several long moments of silence, Grey Eagle spoke, his voice warm and low. "Why did you come back for me?"

Caught off guard by his question, Diana hesitated to answer, just as her hands paused in their movements. "I couldn't leave you out there to face them alone."

"Why not?"

"I just couldn't. They would have killed you."

"And taken you captive."

"Perhaps; I didn't think about that."

He said nothing.

Now she looked at him. "I didn't," she insisted.

"I know, Diana." The enticing warmth in his voice settled over her like a soft, comfortable blanket. She fought against letting her heart melt into that warmth, because Grey Eagle was already too close, and she didn't mean physically, although he was that also. He continued. "Had you been concerned for your own safety, you would have ridden away as fast as the packhorse would carry you, with the hope that I could buy you enough time to escape. Instead, you came back for me."

Very aware that he had again used her first name, annoyed at the surge of pleasure that went through her because he did, Diana scrubbed at a stubborn spot of blood near his foot, frowned at the bloodstained moccasin in her way, then finally pulled his moccasin off. His topic of conversation was making her very uncomfortable, and she didn't understand why. "If the situation had been reversed, you would have come back for me," she finally said, her voice sharp with the irritation she felt.

"Of course."

"Then why is it so difficult to understand why I returned for you? What difference does the 'why' make, anyway?" She finished with his leg and tossed the piece of cloth into the pot. "I came back; that is all that matters." Then she made the mistake of looking at his face, at his chest, at *him*.

Grey Eagle leaned back against the boulder, his spread legs bent, his hands resting on his knees. The sunlight highlighted his green eyes and kissed his skin with a golden sheen. A slight breeze stirred strands of his long hair and the eagle feather tied to the end of one narrow braid. His flat stomach disappeared under the dull blue breechclout secured at his hips, and Diana forced her gaze back up to the well-defined muscles of his chest and arms.

How she ached to have those strong arms close around her, and the recognition of that powerful ache stunned her. Diana was so close to him that she feared he could hear the accelerated beat of her heart, that he knew how she longed to kiss his mouth, to touch him, to let her fingers play with his long hair as she pushed the strands back so that the expanse of his chest was revealed to her in its entirety, free for her fingers to explore, free for her lips to explore.

Oh, God.

Diana buried her face in her hands, shamed to her soul by the unfamiliar longings that tore at her. Where had such wanton needs come from? How could her traitorous body feel even the stirrings of desire when the man was wounded and in pain? Why was she drawn to this man like she had never been to any other?

"Diana."

He whispered her name. Her hands fell to her lap, where they clasped each other tightly; her eyes remained downcast. Grey Eagle leaned forward until his forehead rested against hers. His hair fell over her hands, caressing her, tormenting her.

For a long time, he did not move.

She could not move.

Then he turned his head slightly, and pressed his mouth to her cheek. Her eyes drifted closed. She could not breathe.

His mouth moved closer to hers, kissed her cheek again. Her lips parted, and Diana could not stop herself from turning her head just enough to meet his mouth.

Her heart slammed against her ribs as his warm lips moved over hers. His tongue teased the corner of her mouth, then lightly stroked her bottom lip, and she moaned.

Only their mouths touched—her hands remained clasped in her lap, his held on to his knees. Somehow, the effect of not touching anywhere else made the kiss they shared very erotic to Diana. Her fingers hurt, she squeezed them so tightly, desperate to keep from throwing her arms around him and drawing him close.

Finally, mercifully, Grey Eagle pulled his mouth from hers and kissed her forehead. "Thank you for tending to me, Diana Murdoch," he whispered.

"You're welcome, Grey Eagle Beaudine." She whispered, too. His full name had slipped out, and Diana was too shaken from the effects of his devastatingly gentle kiss to care. After another long minute, she gathered herself together enough to say, "I need to get things cleaned up, and you need to rest." Suddenly very shy, she pulled back from him without looking at his face, taking great care not to touch his legs, and managed to get to her feet.

"I will rest when George Washington has been seen to."

The familiar annoyance rushed through her, and she was about to point out that he had put her in charge, but one look at the stubborn, Cheyenne expression on Grey Eagle's face told Diana that she would be wasting her breath. Anyway, could she blame him for wanting to care for his wounded horse? His concern was admirable, if she looked at it in the right light. "Very well, Mr. Beaudine. But after that, you will not argue with me again, not until we leave this camp. By your own words, you have put yourself in my hands. I am the closest thing you have to a physician, and you will do as I say. Is that understood?"

"Yes, ma'am," he said, with such brisk seriousness that Diana was certain he mocked her.

She drew herself up to her full height. "Take care with your tone, sir. I still have access to that frying pan."

"Yes, ma'am," he repeated. This time, the spark of laughter in his eyes told her that he teased rather than mocked.

Diana shook her head and leaned down to offer her assistance as he stood. "You are the most exasperating man I have ever met, Mr. Beaudine."

"I take that as a compliment, Miss Murdoch."

"Of course you do," she muttered, more exasperated than ever. "Of course you do."

Chapter Sixteen

Orion Beaudine and his stallion, Thunder, approached Fort Laramie at a lope. He had not been back one full day from a two-month-long trip to St. Louis before Colonel MacKay sent him out on an emergency scouting mission. Once he learned the nature of that mission, Orion had gone without question or complaint.

Two days earlier, Diana Murdoch and an escort of three soldiers set out for the old Bridger cabin after receiving word that Jubal Sage was injured and waited there for assistance.

Yesterday morning, upon learning that the little party had not returned and that Lieutenant Ransom Thatcher had accompanied Diana, Colonel MacKay set out with a patrol. They came upon Private Grimes with three extra horses, and, after hearing the tale Grimes told of being attacked by Indians, made their way to the cabin to discover Thatcher and Private Sedley dead and Diana gone. The patrol returned to the fort with Grimes and the two bodies; MacKay discovered that the Beaudine party had arrived from St. Louis; and Orion had gone to the Bridger cabin today. What he discovered there troubled him deeply.

He and Thunder entered the unenclosed grounds of Fort Laramie. Rather than stop at the headquarters building to report in to the colonel, as he normally would have done, Orion directed Thunder to the crumbling white adobe structure on the south side of the compound and circled around to the back. There, snuggled against the reinforced south wall of old Fort John—the predecessor to Fort Laramie—he and his brothers had constructed comfortable homes for themselves and the rest of their extended family. There, he hoped to find his older brother, Joseph.

He jumped down from the saddle and hurried into the largest of the rooms, one shared by all members of the family as a kitchen, dining room, and parlor. As he hoped, Joseph was there with most of the rest of the clan, who were beginning to gather for the evening meal. Delicious aromas filled the room and reminded Orion that he'd eaten nothing since breakfast, and that had been before first light.

"Joe, we have to talk," he announced without preamble. "Hello, all." A chorus of greetings sounded as he took his seven-month-old son, Henry Jedediah, from the arms of his beloved wife, Sarah.

"Did you find any sign of Diana?" Orion's stepmother, Florence, asked. She stood at the scarred work table, her long skirt covered with an apron, her dark hair pulled up and twisted into a chignon. With her trim figure and laughing brown eyes, few would guess that the two pretty young women assisting her were her grown daughters and that she was approaching her fortieth birthday.

"Yes, but sign is all I found. Still, I think she's alive, and is being cared for. I'll tell you more later." He gave Sarah an absentminded kiss on the cheek.

"You call that a kiss?" Sarah demanded with a low, musical laugh. "You'll have to do better than that, Orion Beaudine, especially after you've been gone all day. But it can wait until later." Her blue eyes were full of promise, and Orion wondered if he would always feel like he was the luckiest man in the world. He suspected that he would, although he knew that Joseph would argue that *he* was the luckiest man in the world, because of his marriage to the lovely, golden-haired Annie Rose Jensen. Either way, both brothers had married happily.

Orion brought his attention back to what Sarah was saying. "You have something important on your mind. Leave Henry with me and go talk to your brother."

With a grateful grin, he returned his son to Sarah's arms, kissed the boy's head, then kissed Sarah again, full on the mouth. "That is a promise for later," he whispered, and was delighted to see a delicate blush touch her cheeks.

"I'll hold you to it," Sarah whispered back. "Now go."

Joseph waited by the door, his brown eyes filled with curiosity. He let Orion pass him, then followed outside.

"Where's Annie Rose?" Orion asked.

"With her grandfather at the corral. That bay mare is getting ready to foal and they want to keep an eye on her."

His answer didn't surprise Orion. Both Annie Rose and her grandfather, Knute, shared with Joseph a special gift of understanding and communicating with horses. Orion had no doubt that Joseph would soon be at the corral himself, out of concern for both the mare and his wife, because Annie Rose had announced just last week that Henry Jedediah would have a cousin in about six months.

Joseph eyed the sweaty Thunder as they passed the stallion, and he glared back at Orion, one eyebrow raised in question. "You came to chat without seeing to Thunder first?" he demanded.

"I know, I know. But this is serious, Joe. It won't take long. I have to run it by you before I report to Colonel MacKay." He led the way along a path to a bench that had been cut out of the low bluff below the house, and sat down.

"You didn't report in yet?" Joseph frowned as he took a seat next to Orion. "That *is* serious. Talk to me, little brother."

Orion took off his hat and ran a hand over his hair, pulling the long lengths to the back of his neck. "I found plenty of sign around the Bridger cabin. I didn't have too much trouble reading it, either. Something doesn't wash with what that soldier said happened up there, but right now that isn't important. What's important is figuring out what happened to Diana Murdoch."

"Do you have any idea?"

"She ran into the woods, that much is certain. Grimes claims they got to the cabin and shortly thereafter were attacked by Indians, and she panicked and ran off, but I don't believe him. There was no sign at all that the cabin had come under attack—no arrows, no bullet casings, no bullet holes in the walls, no large numbers of outlying horse tracks. The only signs of shooting were the bullets in Thatcher's gut and head, and the one in his head he put there himself."

Joseph frowned. "What the hell happened up there?"

"I don't know everything, but this is what I do know: Somehow, Private Sedley's neck got broken while he was in the creek, because it was as plain as day that someone pulled his body out of the water. Did he slip on the rocks? Was he pushed or hit? I don't know. Someone gut-shot Thatcher and left him to die a bad, slow death, which is why, I assume, he shot himself in the head. Grimes took off with the horses—I'm guessing with intentions of deserting, although he didn't say so, of course."

"What makes you think that?" Joseph asked, smoothing his mustache.

"Grimes could have easily reached the fort that first night if he'd wanted to, and the colonel caught up with him south of where he should have been if he'd been heading back here."

Joseph nodded. "That does sound suspicious. What else?"

"Something or someone forced Diana to run into the woods, not once but twice. She ran, was caught and dragged back to the creek, then got away and ran again. And someone else—an Indian, Grimes says—found her and took her away." Orion rested his elbows on his knees and held his hat between his hands as he stared out in front of him. The Laramie River flowed silently by the foot of the bluff, looking like a large, dark snake in the fading light. After a moment, he faced Joseph and gave him the most troubling news of all. "I found George Washington's track, Joe. I think Grey Eagle took Diana Murdoch."

"*Grey Eagle?*" Joseph stared at him. "He kidnapped her? But why? They've never met, Orion. What possible reason could he have? Where would he take her?"

Orion shrugged. "My guess is the Cheyenne encampment. The tracks headed in that direction, which, of course, doesn't mean anything when the encampment is probably two, maybe three days away—he could change direction at any time. But I can't think of any other place he would go. For some reason, he wouldn't or couldn't bring her back here."

"Damn." Now Joseph leaned forward and rested his elbows on his knees. "If Eagle took her, he had good reason."

"That's what I figured. That's why I don't want to make my report until you and I decide how much to tell. I'm thinking the best thing to do is tell the colonel that I don't know for certain what happened—which is the truth—and that you and I will go back up to the site. You know the old adage that two heads are better than one."

"And Colonel MacKay is going to believe that the Hunter needs help tracking," Joseph retorted, rolling his eyes.

"Do you have a better idea?" Orion demanded. At Joseph's negative shake of the head, he continued. "We'll leave at first light. I'll show you all I found and we'll follow the trail as best we can. If we lose the trail, we'll go straight to the encampment."

Joseph nodded his agreement. "We sure as hell don't want the Army blundering into Cheyenne territory looking for Diana, not until we know what's going on. I hate leaving Knute and Thomas and the women to organize all the supplies we brought back from St. Louis, but there's no help for it. They'll understand when we explain what's going on." He stood up and hooked his thumbs in his belt. "You know, Sweet Water's time is near," he said thoughtfully. "If Grey Eagle knew or found out that Diana is Doc Murdoch's daughter, he may have asked her to go with him, you know, to help with the birthing. Maybe he didn't force her at all."

"Grimes swears the warrior held her in front of him on the same horse and that her hands were tied. If he was telling the truth about that, it sure sounds like force." Orion also stood.

"Yes, it does." Joseph gave a troubled sigh. "So much happened while we were gone, Orion. Sparrow found, Gideon lost, kind-hearted Diana forced to move into that bastard Mac-

Donald's filthy place, and now this. Two Army soldiers dead—one an officer, and a bastard, too, but that's beside the point—a white woman missing and feared to be a captive of one of the tribes, and our brother a possible if not probable suspect of murder and kidnapping. I sure hope Grey Eagle knows what he's doing.''

Orion clapped a hand on Joseph's shoulder. ''So do I, big brother. So do I.''

Grey Eagle rested on the bed Diana had made of the buffalo robes and watched as she went about setting up the campsite. His back was supported by the saddle and he held a cooling cup of willow bark tea in one hand. The memory of her perverse pleasure in informing him that it was his turn to drink the foul stuff brought a smile to his lips.

The treatment of George Washington's wound had gone as smoothly as could be expected, and Diana had admitted that she could not have done it without his help. Because of the location and position of George Washington's arrow, it didn't matter whether it was a hunting arrow or a war arrow—the only way to get the blasted thing out was to pull it back out. Diana held the stallion's head and spoke to him soothingly while Grey Eagle carefully removed the arrow, and they both were relieved when that arrow also proved to be a hunting arrow. Diana had insisted upon mashing more of the yarrow leaves and flower heads, which she mixed with a little of the cooking fat. Since utilizing a bandage was out of the question, the combination of fat and yarrow would stick to the stallion's wound. Both George Washington and the packhorse now rested comfortably in the shade of the nearby trees.

Grey Eagle forced down another swallow of the willow bark tea. He agreed with Diana's assessment that the brew was nasty, but he had no doubt of the benefits it offered in terms of relieving some of his pain. A wave of fatigue washed over him, and he wondered how long he would be able to resist the powerful temptation to sleep for a while.

Diana looked at him from her position near the fire, where

she sat on her heels and arranged cooking utensils. ''Did you have anything in mind for supper?'' she asked.

''I had planned to hunt something this afternoon.'' He grimaced as a spasm grabbed his injured thigh. ''I apologize for not being better prepared, Miss Murdoch. I thought I would have a chance to restock my supplies at the fort, which I never reached. I also did not plan on being wounded.''

''It's your own fault that you didn't get to the fort, Mr. Beaudine.'' She stood up and brushed off her skirt, to no noticeable avail. The black material still looked grey. ''Perhaps if we had gone there, as I asked, you would not be wounded now. However, that's water under the bridge, isn't it?'' She looked at him and did not give him a chance to respond before she spoke again. ''I hope you aren't counting on me to bring in our supper. As you no doubt saw when I fired at the Utes, I am a poor shot at best, and I also fear that my courage would be found lacking were I to take aim at a rabbit or a deer. Clean them and cook them, I can do; kill them, I cannot. I would not be able to pull the trigger.'' She spread her hands in the age-old gesture of question. ''Any ideas? I can go without supper, but you cannot. You must keep your body strong.''

''Neither of us will go without supper. You will find a beaded bag in that canvas pack.'' He pointed to the pack that had been taken from George Washington's back. ''The bag holds buffalo jerky. Broken into smaller pieces and cooked in water with wild onions and whatever else we can find, it will make a filling soup.''

''Sounds good to me.'' Diana moved to and searched the pack, then triumphantly held up a bag. ''Is this it?''

''Yes.''

She examined the beadwork on the bag. ''This is truly lovely. Where did you get it?''

''It was a gift.'' Grey Eagle was having a difficult time keeping his eyes open.

As she looked a moment longer at the bag, a tiny frown marred Diana's forehead, then was gone. She came to his side, dropped to her knees, and sat back on her heels, letting the bag of jerky fall to her lap. ''You should try to get some sleep, Mr. Beaudine.'' She laid a gentle hand on his forehead. ''No fever yet. That is good." After a quick examination of the bandages on his leg, she nodded in satisfaction. "All seems well; excellent, actually. I am pleased."

"I'm certainly glad to hear that you are pleased."

"Don't get sarcastic with me, sir. Given proper provocation, I can become quite a martinet, and there is no question that you can provoke me." The concern in her eyes belied the sting of her words.

Grey Eagle stared at her face, fascinated. The sunlight made her eyes appear to be golden, soft wisps of dark hair teased her forehead and cheeks, her lips were moist and rosy and seemed to call out for his touch. He dared not kiss her again, although he wanted to more than he could remember wanting anything in a very long time. Instead, he reached out and brushed the fullness of her bottom lip with the pad of his thumb. "I shall be on my best behavior," he said, surprised by the huskiness of his own voice. "What would you have me do?"

Diana stared at him. Her lip trembled under his touch, and her breath came in shallow gasps. She blinked, as if awakening from a dream, and turned her head just enough to break the contact with his thumb. He let his arm fall to his side.

"I would have you sleep," she said, her voice no more than a whisper. "If you hope to travel tomorrow, you must rest as much as possible today and tonight."

It took tremendous willpower for Grey Eagle not to invite her to sleep next to him, for she was tired, too. He could see the weariness in her eyes, in the slight slump of her shoulders. But, as if she were a skittish colt, he had to move with infinite care and patience. So all he did now was nod.

"I'll see to supper," Diana said as she stood, dodging the branches of one of the pine trees under which she had spread the robes.

"You will find a small bag containing wild onion bulbs in that pack, too," Grey Eagle said as he shifted farther down on the buffalo robes. "Make use of whatever you find in either pack. Don't go far from camp. And waken me at once if you hear or see anything unusual."

"Don't worry about anything," Diana said. "George Wash-

ington will alert me if anything—man or beast—comes our
way. And I shall stay close by.''

Grey Eagle had to be satisfied with that, even though there
was a hint of rebellion in Diana's tone. He closed his eyes,
determined to do no more than rest, and perhaps doze. Without
a doubt, his painful, throbbing leg would keep him from any
real sleep.

Diana strode purposefully through the forest, back toward
the valley they had so painstakingly left. Grey Eagle's pistol
was once more nestled in her pocket, she clutched his knife in
one hand, her battered hat again covered the top of her head,
and her temper again—still—simmered. Lordy, but the man
was bossy! Was he always like that? she wondered. If so, it
was no mystery why Grey Eagle alone of the Beaudine brothers
was not yet wed. No woman would put up with him.

She certainly wouldn't.

Then she remembered the compassion in his eyes and the
gentleness of his touch as he helped her move about that first
terrible, painful day after Thatcher's attack. She thought of how
safe she felt when she was with him, of how he had saved her
from Thatcher and later stood against five Ute warriors, fully
prepared to die for her. She remembered how he looked wearing
nothing but his breechclout and his glorious hair, stretching in
the early-morning light.

Diana came to an abrupt halt. Her breathing was ragged, and
she couldn't blame that entirely on the exertion of her walk.
She had never seen a man more beautiful than Grey Eagle, and
it would do no good to deny it. He fascinated her in ways no
one ever had in her life. ''It's just because he's different,'' she
muttered as she perused the wide meadow she had come upon.
Surely it was here that she had seen the flowers of the prairie
turnip, which, among other wild herbs and foods, Sparrow had
taught her to look for, and to harvest. If she had passed the
place she sought, or if she had succeeded in getting lost, she
could blame no one but herself, and her senseless preoccupation
with an arrogant, aggravating man.

Luck was with her. She spotted several of the plants in bloom, and with Grey Eagle's knife, dug some of the bulbous roots from the soil. They would make a welcome addition to the watery soup she would serve for supper. And if she could find just one poppy mallow plant, she would harvest a few of those leaves to use as a flavorful thickener for her soup. Depending on how much Indian meal he had left, she might even be able to make up another batch of corn dodgers. Perhaps this would turn out to be a decent supper after all. She hoped so; for all her annoyance with Grey Eagle's imperious manner, she had meant it when she said he needed to eat in order to keep up his strength.

It would also do Diana good to show Grey Eagle that she could contribute to their survival, could carry her own weight, especially now that her bruises and sore muscles were healing.

A short distance away, she spotted what looked like a poppy mallow and, after taking a moment to again peruse the area, to listen and sniff and study, to ensure that she was still alone, she headed toward the plant, wishing she'd brought something in which to put her foraged food items other than the pockets of her skirt. An image of the beautifully beaded bag that held the buffalo jerky flashed in her mind. Grey Eagle had received it as a gift, he'd said. From some gorgeous Cheyenne woman, no doubt, who had labored long and lovingly over it. She'd never before considered that he might have a sweetheart waiting for him at the encampment.

The thought poked at Diana with little jabs of jealousy, and the jealousy irritated her. Why on earth would she care if he had a sweetheart who gave him gifts?

"Because I like him," she muttered unhappily. "The insufferable man—I actually like him, and I hope he likes me. And I'll never let him know, for he would become unbearable." As Diana bent to retrieve a few leafed stems of the poppy mallow, she could only wonder how such a thing had come to pass.

For the first time in her life, she found a man to be attractive and special, a man whose single kiss had left her emotionally shaken and trembling with need, and, rather than bring her joy, as she had always believed it would, the discovery of her deepening feelings for Grey Eagle only saddened her and made her determined to hide those feelings.

If, by the grace of God, Grey Eagle returned her feelings—and he had given no indication that he felt anything special for her—what possible future could they have together? Part white though he be, Grey Eagle was a warrior, proud and free. Diana could not imagine him settling down as his brothers had done, living in a little house scavenged from the crumbling adobe of old Fort John, trading with passing emigrants, frontiersmen, and the Indian tribes. He needed to be free, to roam the prairies as did his nomadic Cheyenne kin.

And she could not live with the Cheyenne. A visit was one thing; her presence in the village might be tolerated for a while, but she doubted she would be welcomed and embraced by the entire tribe. Then there was the question of giving up her family—such as it was—her language, her culture, and her way of life. Could she do that for a man, even such a man as Grey Eagle Beaudine?

She didn't know. With more force than was necessary, Diana hacked off a stem of the poppy mallow with Grey Eagle's knife. How foolish she was! The man had done nothing but kiss her—one little devastating kiss—and she considered plans for a future with him!

Perhaps the sun was getting to her, or maybe she was more hungry than she thought. No matter the reason, she determined to put all thoughts of Grey Eagle out of her mind. As she headed back in the direction of the camp, she sighed in discouragement.

There was no getting the man out of her mind, not now, perhaps not ever. The thought that he—a Cheyenne warrior who had basically abducted her—had that much control over her feelings and emotions frightened and confused her.

"Oh, Papa," she whispered. "I wish you were here to talk to me. I'm in uncharted waters and have no idea what to do, other than to keep my guard up and not lose my heart."

Perhaps there was nothing more that could be done, at least for now.

"Except make soup," she muttered, and hastened her pace so she could do exactly that. Domestic activity usually made her feel better. She hoped it would do so today.

Chapter Seventeen

When Grey Eagle awoke, dusk had fallen. He heard the soothing crackling of a fire, and the aroma of something wonderful wafted on the considerably cooled air, yet he felt warm and comfortable. The discovery a moment later that Diana had laid her cloak over him warmed him inside, as well. He searched for her in the fading light, and found her sitting cross-legged by the fire, bent intently over something in her lap. The white cotton of her chemise glowed in the firelight, and he realized that she had removed her bodice. The small mark of the Eagle on her right shoulder stood out against her pale skin.

She straightened her shoulders then, and leaned her head back, rubbing her neck as if it ached. The action caused the white cotton to stretch across her breasts, and showed off the soft mounds and the darker tips.

Grey Eagle suddenly felt hot under the cloak. He licked his lips, longing to place those ready lips on the tips of her breasts and tease them into tight, feminine buds. Diana might be a spirit woman of the Eagle, but she was also tantalizingly human. He remembered the feel of her soft skin that first night when he checked to ensure that she had taken everything off, and now he wished her naked again, and beside him, sharing the

cover of her cloak. As passionate as she was about so many
things, as passionate as her very spirit was, surely Diana would
prove to be passionate in his bed as well.

The fierce desire to find out was at once pleasurable and
agonizing. Grey Eagle squeezed his eyes shut and fought his
growing male hardness. *Patience,* he counseled himself. The
day would come when Diana Murdoch shared his bed as a
lover; of that, he had no doubt. His ability to wait, however,
he did doubt, and gravely. No vision quest had required a more
tortuous path than the one that demanded he keep his hands
off Diana Murdoch when they shared the same bed, as they
would again tonight. He would rather go without food and
water. Such a sacrifice would be easy compared to the one he
now faced.

He forced himself to lie still, to listen to other parts of his
body rather than the currently most bothersome one. His thigh
ached, which was to be expected, and a careful probing of the
bandages indicated a slight swelling at each wound site, also
to be expected. Other than that, he felt remarkably refreshed,
although hungry. The sleep he'd been so determined to avoid
had done him good.

Finally, Grey Eagle dared to open his eyes. Again, Diana
was bent over her project, and from the movements of her right
arm, he deduced that she was sewing.

"Diana." Her name slipped out, soft and whispered.

She started and looked at him, her eyes wide, then clutched
the item in her hands to her breasts, as if to cover herself.
"Oh," she breathed. "You're awake."

"Only just now." He shifted his position and leaned against
the saddle. "What are you sewing?"

"My bodice, where the sleeve was torn from the shoulder.
The sun has burned my exposed skin there." As if she felt a
need to explain further, she added, "I used the stitching thread
and needle from my father's medical bag. I hoped, uh, thought,
you'd ... sleep ... longer." Her voice trailed off and she
looked away from him.

He realized she was embarrassed to be caught so unclothed.
"Finish your task." He draped a forearm over his eyes, as if

he was weary. "Then we shall eat whatever it is you have cooking. It smells wonderful."

"I'll hurry."

Grey Eagle peeked under his arm and found her hard at work again, her hand flying as she stitched. He smiled and closed his eyes, imagining that they were in his lodge, at his fire, that she was his woman, his wife, sewing for him, cooking for him. The dream was a very pleasurable one.

A few minutes later, her voice touched him and drew him from his reverie. "I took you at your word and made use of what I found. We will dine tonight on buffalo jerky soup, corn dodgers, and coffee."

"Sounds great." Grey Eagle sat up. None of the enthusiasm in his voice was feigned. He was ravenous, and her mere description of the menu made his mouth water.

Diana knelt next to the fire, now wearing her bodice, he noted with a sense of disappointment. She said, "I've wondered since that first night when you fixed meal-battered fish—how is it that you have Indian meal, when the Cheyenne do not grow their own corn and have been isolated in their winter encampment for months?"

"Actually, you have yourself to thank for it," he answered. At her puzzled glance, he continued. "You sent Sparrow home to her people laden with many gifts. The meal I have is from the barrel you gave her. She shared it with all."

A slight smile curved Diana's lips, in a way Grey Eagle was coming to treasure, for she rarely smiled. "Sparrow is very kindhearted and generous. I have missed her terribly, and am most anxious to see her again."

"My niece will welcome you with great joy. And I will welcome my supper the same way."

Diana's smile broadened just a little. "You sound like a hungry man, Mr. Beaudine."

He made his voice low and suggestive. "Indeed, I am *very* hungry, Miss Murdoch."

The blush that flamed her cheeks told him that she had not missed his deliberate double entendre. "Then I'd better give you something to eat," she retorted. "If nothing else, it should

keep you quiet for a time." Diana stood up, bearing a bowl
and spoon, and approached him. "The bowl is hot," she warned
as she gave it to him. "I'll be right back with coffee and corn
dodgers."

After serving him, Diana filled a bowl for herself and joined
him, sitting demurely on the top buffalo robe, her legs curled
to one side. They ate in companionable silence for several
minutes. To Grey Eagle, the soup—which he instantly knew
consisted of more than jerky, onions, and water—was delicious.
He recognized chunks of prairie turnips, and another flavor
teased his memory.

"This is wonderful, Miss Murdoch," he said. "What did
you put in it?"

"Turnips—that is, prairie turnips—and I used some poppy
mallow for seasoning and as a thickener."

Grey Eagle stared at her, amazed. "Where did you get
them?"

"I hunted and found them."

"But how did you know to look for them?"

Diana shrugged. "Sparrow taught me. In the two months we
spent together, we taught each other many things about the
different ways of our respective peoples."

"I am impressed."

"It was not difficult." She shrugged again, as if to shrug
off his praise, yet a small, pleased smile teased the corners of
her mouth.

Grey Eagle wished he knew the secret to get Diana to fully
smile. He was certain that she would become radiant, and he
would be even more lost. The teasing smile fled and her face
took on a somber expression.

"To whom did you give your word that you would bring
me back to the encampment?"

Her complete change of subject startled him. He'd forgotten
that he'd told her the basis of his mission. "To Sweet Water,"
he answered. "Her child comes soon. She is fearful, and wishes
you to be with her." He paused and looked down at his nearly
empty bowl. "And to Sparrow. She is certain that if you remain
at Fort Laramie in the miserable home of your uncle, or, if you

return to your mother in St. Louis, your spirit will die. She does not wish that.'' He hesitated again, then looked her directly in the eyes. "Nor do I.''

At his last words, Diana's eyes widened, and again, a blush touched her cheeks. "At one time, I feared the same thing. I know now that my spirit will not die simply because I'm in an unhappy situation. I am made of stronger stuff than that."

"Yes, you are, Diana Murdoch. But I do not want to see your spirit even wounded."

She broke eye contact and looked down. When she spoke, her voice was little more than a whisper. "But my spirit is already wounded, Mr. Beaudine, deeply so."

She did not need to explain further; Grey Eagle knew what it was to lose one's father. He longed to take her into his arms, to offer what meager comfort he could to her inconsolably wounded spirit. "The pain of losing your father will ease, in time."

"But the wound will never completely heal, will it?" Diana leaned forward and watched him intently, as if his answer was terribly important to her.

He chose his words with care. "I have come to believe that one never completely recovers from what one views as a great loss, no matter what that loss is. The pain eases, and one accepts the loss here''—he touched his chest, over his heart—"but complete healing?" He shook his head. "I don't think so."

"The pain eases, but a scar is left."

"Scars are evidence of the trials we endure and survive. Is that a bad thing?"

After a moment, Diana answered, "No. I suppose it is the way of life."

Grey Eagle nodded his agreement, then scraped his spoon on the bottom of his bowl.

"Would you like more soup?" she asked.

"Yes, please."

Diana took the bowl from him and moved to the fire. "Will we reach the encampment tomorrow?" she asked as she stirred the pot.

"No. We lost too much time today. We should get there

around noon the day after tomorrow.'' He watched her ladle soup into his bowl. ''Are you nervous about arriving there?''

''Yes.'' She straightened and carried the bowl to him, for which he nodded his thanks. Diana continued. ''Your brother Joseph once showed me sketches he made of a Cheyenne village, so I have an idea of what the village will look like. But, with the exceptions of Sparrow and the Sages, I'm uncertain of my reception by the rest of the tribe.''

There was at least one person who would not welcome Diana at all, Grey Eagle knew. But he would not mention Black Moon yet. Much too quickly, his time alone with Diana was coming to an end. He did not want to mar that precious time with even the thought of Black Moon. ''You will be made welcome. There are many who wish to reward you for the care you took of Sparrow and for seeing that she was safely returned to her family.''

''I want no reward,'' Diana protested. ''I did nothing out of the ordinary. It was my father who fixed her leg, and Jubal who brought her home.''

''It was you who rescued her from the clutches of Painted Davy Sikes and Conway Horton. It was you who kept the fanatical Mrs. Mullen from drowning her during a baptism she did not need or want. It was you who kept your uncle from making her a whore for the soldiers.'' As he recited the litany of Diana's accomplishments, Grey Eagle's anger against her opponents flared to new heights. She and Sparrow should never have been in the situations they'd had to face and overcome. ''Sparrow told us all,'' he said in conclusion.

Diana shifted uncomfortably. ''Many would have done the same in my place.''

''Most would not have. Perhaps you do not realize how unusual it is for a white person—especially a white woman— to stand up for an Indian.''

''She is only a child.''

''Which made her even more helpless and vulnerable. Whether you are willing to admit it or not, Miss Murdoch, you saved my niece's spirit and her virtue, if not her life. You must allow those who love Sparrow to express their gratitude, especially her parents. Raven's Heart and Little Leaf are most anxious to meet you.''

A frown formed between Diana's eyebrows. ''Then you mustn't leave my side, Mr. Beaudine, once we are in the village. You must translate their words to me, and mine to them, and tell me how to behave so that I don't unintentionally embarrass myself or offer insult to them.''

I assure you, Diana Murdoch, I will never leave your side. ''I will guide you,'' he promised.

She nodded and reached for a corn dodger that rested on the plate between them. The troubled expression did not leave her face, nor did she seem to be inclined to talk anymore. Grey Eagle was content to leave her alone with her thoughts for a while, because he found fulfillment just in watching her.

The full darkness of night had settled around them when Diana announced, in a most dictatorial tone, that it was time he got more sleep. After a short argument about him walking unassisted the distance to check on the horses—an argument that ended abruptly when he asked if she intended to also support him while he saw to certain bodily necessities—she cleaned up the supper dishes, and allowed Grey Eagle to check on the horses by himself. Satisfied that George Washington was doing as well as could be expected and grateful that both horses had survived the day—indeed, that they all had—Grey Eagle returned to the welcoming bed and was settled between the buffalo robes when Diana approached with a torchlike piece of wood aflame at the top.

''Please hold this while I check the bandages,'' she said formally.

He pulled the top robe away from his injured leg, then accepted the torch and watched the light play on her face. The same serious frown that had earlier marred the smooth skin of her forehead was present as she studied her handiwork on his thigh, and the golden light showed the bruise under her eye in sharp relief, but still Grey Eagle found her beautiful. More than physical beauty, though, it was her spirit he so admired, he decided. Her kind and gentle yet indomitable spirit, the integrity of her character—those were what called to him, and were far more important than whatever beauty the outside package presented. Of course, there was nothing wrong with Diana's outside package, either.

"In the morning I will cleanse the injury sites and apply fresh bandages." She pulled the robe back over his leg, then placed a small, cool hand on his forehead and nodded, as if satisfied with what she felt. "I want you to drink more of the willow bark tea before you sleep. As of yet, there is no indication of a fever, but I don't want to take chances." She raised an eyebrow in question. "You *did* tell me that willow bark helps fight fever?"

"Yes. And pain."

"Good. I'll be right back." She took the torch with her and tossed it in the fire.

Grey Eagle tried not to grimace when she knelt at his side a moment later and handed him a cup almost filled with the healing tea. He raised up on one elbow and drank. It amused him that she watched carefully to ensure that he swallowed every nasty, bitter drop. She took her role as physician very seriously, utilizing to full advantage the freedom he had given her to tell him what to do. When he lay down, she took the empty cup from him and sat back on her heels. Without a word, she again touched his forehead, her hand first lying still for a long time, then gently stroking. Then her hand moved to his hair, brushed long locks away from the side of his face and off his shoulder. The lingering touch of her fingers on his naked skin sent a shudder through him, and he wished that she would touch him all over.

"Are you chilled?" Diana asked, her concern immediate and obvious.

He closed his eyes and shook his head. *No, Diana. I am on fire.*

"You must rest." Her hand moved over his shoulder again, like the caress of a butterfly's wing, then was gone. He heard her stand and move away. "Sleep well, Mr. Beaudine."

He was certain she meant to offer comfort, but that was not what he felt. Grey Eagle clenched his hands into fists and resolved to be asleep before Diana returned to lie beside him.

* * *

His long, long hair had called to her from the first day she met him, and finally, to her shame, she had given in. A blush heated Diana's cheeks, although none but the two horses, whom she had also—needlessly—come to check, could see her. She shook her head with disgust. Not only had she stroked his hair, but she had caressed his naked shoulder, and it had taken every bit of self-control she possessed not to let her fingers wander down over Grey Eagle's chest, to feel his powerful heart beat against her palm.

Lordy.

Diana covered her face with both hands. What was happening to her? What was *wrong* with her? Ever since yesterday morning, when he stood nearly naked and stretched in the morning sun, tormenting images had popped into her head with disturbing regularity—images of his fingers in her hair, as they had been this morning when he wove her tresses into a braid, images of her fingers evening the score by playing with his long, seductive hair. Images of his mouth on her mouth . . . and on other . . . places. Images of Grey Eagle's naked chest, pressed against her . . . naked breasts. Images of . . . other . . . things.

She wanted him.

For the first time in her life, Diana felt the raw power of honest physical desire—the ancient, primal desire Woman was meant to feel for Man—and she felt that power so strongly that it frightened her. Not only did she long to touch Grey Eagle everywhere, but her inexperienced and traitorous body also cried out for *his* touch—her lips tingled, her breasts ached, her legs shook, a blaze roared through her belly, deep down inside, and somehow she knew that internal flame could be extinguished only by him, and only with him inside her.

With a frustrated moan, Diana leaned her forehead against George Washington's warm, horsey-smelling shoulder. The stallion nickered and tossed his head.

Why hadn't it been enough to simply *like* the warrior? Why did she have to *want* him as well?

She would not—could not—continue to want him.

Those feelings of desire had to be stopped, nipped in the bud, now, tonight, before she made a fool of herself, or Grey Eagle discovered her shameful vulnerability where he was concerned. If he knew how she felt about him, he would press his advantage, as she suspected—knew—most men would. Wouldn't he?

But Grey Eagle was not like most men, just as his brothers were not. They were a special breed, the Beaudines.

Special, but not perfect.

Gentlemen, but still *men,* in the purest sense of the word.

Grey Eagle was a *man.* If he knew of her feelings for him, if, as most men would, he chose to press his advantage, Diana doubted her ability to resist him. Therefore, her incredible, wondrous, appalling, inappropriate feelings for him had to be squashed, stomped out, before they created embarrassing problems for both of them.

A wild, beautiful, and free Son of the Wilderness would not tether himself to a staid, dependable, rather plain Daughter of Civilization.

"And he shouldn't," Diana whispered to the patient and understanding George Washington. "He shouldn't."

Confident that both horses rested comfortably, Diana made her way to the fire circle, where she banked the coals in order to save them for the morning fire. Then, with slow, reluctant steps, she approached the inviting, terrifying bed she shared with Grey Eagle.

Why had she not, after that first night when the Warrior part of him was in charge, insisted upon each of them taking one of the two buffalo robes? Sandwiched between the folded halves, the thickness of the coverings would offer the same shelter as would the joined bed. Of course, she and Grey Eagle would not enjoy the appealing warmth of shared body heat, but both would survive the night—and she with far less torment than that which threatened her tonight.

Focus on his injured leg. He is but a patient.

Impatiently, instantly, Diana discarded those thoughts. Grey Eagle's injured leg did not appear to be bothering him overmuch, and, no matter what she tried to tell herself, he was far more than a patient.

He was a *man*.

Fortunately, the irksome man appeared to be asleep. Even in the now almost total darkness, she could tell that from his deep, easy breathing patterns.

With a troubled sigh, Diana sank down on the bed of buffalo robes. A shiver raced through her as the cool night wind blew, stirring the fragrant boughs of the pine above her into soft whispers.

Grey Eagle's comforting heat, his reassuring strength, beckoned her as surely as any Siren's call to the sailors of ancient times.

She could not crawl under that buffalo robe with him.

Blindly, Diana searched for her cloak, the one with which she had covered Grey Eagle that afternoon. When her desperate fingers found the woolen garment, she laid back on the top robe and pulled the cloak over her. Compared to the weight and warmth of a buffalo robe, however, the cloak offered meager protection against the chilly night air. It also carried the pleasant scents of campfire smoke and sage—scents of him.

Through the boughs, Diana could make out tiny, winking stars in the impossibly clear night sky she had come to associate with the western wilderness. She watched their nocturnal journey with weary eyes, grateful for anything, no matter how small, that offered her distraction from the man asleep beside her.

Chapter Eighteen

Diana awoke stiff and cold, and, keeping her back to Grey Eagle, looked about the campsite with bleary, gritty eyes. The day was still very young—the sky unclouded but grey, the sun not yet risen over the eastern horizon. She stretched, then stifled a moan of pain, unable to tell if the aches that tormented her entire body were the old, familiar ones from her struggle with Thatcher and too many hours in the saddle, or if they were new ones, from the miserable night she had spent huddled under the woolen cloak.

"Did you sleep well?" Grey Eagle's solicitous voice rolled over her, and irritated her mightily. She glared over her shoulder at him, then regretted the movement, which sent spasms through her stiff neck.

"Very well, thank you," she snapped. She sat up, determined to keep her expression neutral. Surely she would feel better when she started moving about.

"I don't believe you. Why did you not sleep under the robe?"

"It isn't proper that we share the same bed." Again, Diana glared at him, and again, she regretted it, for an entirely different reason. Grey Eagle was raised up on one elbow, facing her, the buffalo robe pushed down to his waist, his sleep-tousled hair laying about his shoulders and over his chest. His green eyes seemed to shine in the growing light, and the expression on his painfully handsome face was one of concern. She fought the absurd desire to lean closer and brush his hair back over his shoulders.

"We shared these robes for two nights before last night. What is not proper all of a sudden?"

"We shared the robes the first night because you tied me to you," Diana retorted. "The next night I was too weary and sore to fight you. Last night, I could choose." Her sharp words hung heavy in the air, and she wondered why she was angry with him.

He stared at her, right into her eyes, as if he searched for something. "What are you afraid of, Diana Murdoch?" he asked quietly.

The instinctive words of denial almost came out, just as she almost looked away from his unsettling, understanding eyes. But she refused to be dishonest with him. "You, Grey Eagle Beaudine. I am afraid of you." She stood up, rather slowly, surprised to discover that even her feet hurt, and limped away from him.

Grey Eagle watched Diana as she built up the fire and prepared coffee. He didn't know why, but he was surprised by how efficient she was around a campsite. Perhaps he had expected the educated daughter of a gentleman physician and a socialite from the East to know little about life in the wilderness; in that respect, he had underestimated her.

He had also never expected her to confess that she was frightened of him, because he knew that she was not, at least not in a physical sense. She knew that he would not harm her; she trusted him with her life, as she had proven many times over the past few days. She stood up to him, argued with him, ordered him about, risked her life for him, returned his kiss—no, Diana was not afraid of him. Yet, he would swear she had spoken the truth when she said so. He'd read the aching honesty in her eyes.

Could she feel the fire inside him that burned for her? Was that what frightened her? His passion for her? Perhaps he had not done as good a job of hiding the intensity of his feelings as he'd thought.

Grey Eagle sat up and ran his hands through his tangled hair. He would have to be more careful.

His Spirit Woman could not be afraid of him, not on any level. She simply could not be, for that would ruin everything.

Diana poked at the fire, annoyed that the coffee had not yet boiled, grateful that Grey Eagle did not try to draw her into any kind of conversation. He seemed to understand that she needed some room—to breathe, to think, to sort out her feelings. It had been easy last night, under the cover of darkness, when she was alone but for the horses, to swear to herself that she would no longer want him. That foolish determination had disappeared the instant she'd looked at him, and saw his soul in his beautiful eyes.

The wanting would not go away.

She knew that now, and wondered again what was wrong with her. It was almost as if she were a mare in heat, desperate for her mate. The analogy embarrassed her, even though she only thought the words, but they were true words. A wall had to go up around her heart, and at once. *Only a day and a half longer,* she silently intoned, again and again. Then she would be with Jubal and Sweet Water and Sparrow. Then she would have other things to think about, other people to tend to. And when the baby was born, she would go home. Or back to the fort, anyway.

In silence, they ate a modest breakfast of cold corn dodgers and hot coffee, then broke down the camp and readied the horses for the day's journey. True to her word of last night, Diana changed the dressing on Grey Eagle's leg, and she was pleased with the look of his wounds—just slightly swollen, pink but not red around the edges, a little seepage of pus and blood. Grey Eagle seemed to be in only moderate pain, and his limp was hardly noticeable, but whether his behavior was

some kind of stubborn Cheyenne stoicism or a genuine indication of how he felt, she did not know, and she refused to worry
about it.

Although Diana had never ridden bareback—a fact she did
not mention to Grey Eagle—she insisted that he use the saddle
so that his injured leg would have the support of the stirrup.
The issue was one on which she would not budge, and he
finally gave in, with the muttered complaint that they lost too
much time in arguing.

At last, they were on their way. Diana felt strangely vulnerable riding with no saddle, as if she would slide off the packhorse's back at any moment, and so clung to the horse with
all of the strength in her legs. Eventually, she figured out that
if she relaxed and let her body move with the horse's, she—
and the horse—was much more comfortable. Except when
absolutely necessary, neither she nor Grey Eagle spoke. As she
rode behind him, Diana was grateful that he wore his shirt and
leggings today. She found it much easier to be strong when he
wasn't almost naked.

They argued again around noon, when Grey Eagle wanted
to stop only long enough to water the horses and eat a few
pieces of buffalo jerky, and Diana insisted that they stop long
enough to give the horses a real rest and allow her the time to
examine his injured leg.

In the end, she won.

The wounds had bled enough to seep through the bandages,
which Diana had expected to happen when Grey Eagle rode.
Because there was still no sign of infection, she felt it safe to
close the wounds. She did so with a few neat stitches and
offered a sincere apology to Grey Eagle for the pain she caused
him, although he gave no indication that the needle passing
through his flesh gave him even the least bit of discomfort.

The afternoon was spent as quietly as the morning, as was
the evening, and, to Diana, it seemed that the long, somehow
lonely day would never end. Finally, thankfully, there was
nothing left to do but sleep. She knelt to check Grey Eagle's
leg one last time, and, pleased with what she found under the
bandages, pulled the buffalo robe back over his now naked leg.

"The wounds are healing well," she commented, deliberately keeping her gaze from his also-naked chest. She wished he didn't insist upon sleeping in nothing but his breechclout. "Very well, in fact."

"You sound surprised." Grey Eagle sat up straight and reached for her hand.

"I am, a little. Most wounds develop at least a touch of infec— What are you doing, Mr. Beaudine?" Diana pulled her hand back just as he slipped a rope around her wrist.

"You appeared to have no problem with the logic of sharing these robes when I tied you to me that first night." He knotted the other end of the rope around his waist. "So I will tie you to me again tonight. I won't allow you to make yourself miserable over a misplaced sense of propriety."

"How dare you?" Diana stared at him, unable to believe that he was serious. "Untie me at once." She picked at the rope encircling her wrist.

"No. Tonight you will sleep under this robe, with me, and be warm and comfortable. You are ill-tempered in the morning when you don't sleep well." He moved over, making room for her. "Come now. Let us sleep."

Diana fought a growing sense of panic. "You can't tether me like a dog who might run off in the night. I promised to accompany you to the encampment, and I will keep my word."

"I did not tie you to keep you from leaving; I tied you so that you will be warm." He lay down.

"But—"

He reached up to place a forefinger across her mouth, only for an instant. "You will not win this one," he said quietly. "Lie down."

Diana stayed as she was, sitting on her heels, her hands resting in her lap. In desperation, she looked up to the tops of the pine trees that swayed in the cool night wind, then to the tiny, sparkling stars beyond, as if they would offer advice. What to do? She could not lie next to him, yet she knew from the tone of his voice—no, she knew because she knew *him*— that he would not release her until morning.

"What do you think will happen if you share the warmth of

these robes with me tonight?" he asked, his tone as soft as the darkness.

She thought for a moment, and answered him honestly. "I think we will both sleep."

"Then lie down."

Because she had no choice, because she trusted him, Diana obeyed him. As far from him as the hated rope would allow, she curled into a fetal position, her back to him, and clutched the edge of the buffalo robe to pull it over her shoulder. Her breath came in shallow gasps as she willed herself to sleep.

Moments later, his arm snaked around her waist and pulled her against his body. Instantly, she stiffened, unable to breathe at all. "Release me," she ordered, her voice rasping painfully in her constricted throat.

As if he soothed a distressed child, Grey Eagle held her, the one arm still around her waist, his other hand smoothing the hair back from her forehead, his body solid and warm at her back. "Shh, Diana. Shh."

"Release me." Her whispered words were now more a plea than an order.

"He'kotoo'estse."

He felt so warm against her. She felt so safe. "What did you say?"

"Be quiet."

Again, Diana obeyed him.

She was relieved to find herself alone in the makeshift bed when she awoke the next morning. Grey Eagle's tenderness toward her—and his arms around her for most of the night—had introduced a new level of intimacy between them, one which Diana feared would cause awkwardness and embarrassment in the light of day. But there was no such trouble when Grey Eagle appeared from behind the horses, other than a shyness on Diana's part which quickly faded at his cheerful friendliness. As if an unspoken truce existed between them, Diana found that she and Grey Eagle got along much better while they ate a quick breakfast, broke camp, and started the day's journey.

Perhaps it was because she felt truly rested for the first time in days, and so was able to be more patient with his occasional displays of arrogance—an arrogance she had come to believe was a totally unconscious aspect of his personality.

Perhaps, now that they had safely passed into Cheyenne territory, he was more relaxed, although still vigilant.

Perhaps it was that a camaraderie had developed between them, if not a more intimate friendship. Sharing life-and-death experiences—and a pair of buffalo robes, Diana admitted to herself with a slight blush—could forge such a friendship. Now, rested, healing, pleasantly filled from the noon meal and following Grey Eagle and George Washington through absolutely beautiful country on an absolutely beautiful afternoon, she felt a contentment she had not known in a long time.

"How did you come to name George Washington?" she called out, giving voice to a question that had plagued her since Grey Eagle first told her his stallion's name.

Grey Eagle pulled up until Diana and the packhorse came alongside him, then they proceeded, side by side, at a leisurely walk. "There is no great mystery to it," he answered. "When he lived in the wild, with his own herd, this fellow"—he gave the stallion an affectionate pat on the neck—"was a great leader and a fearless fighter, traits he shares with the man for whom he was named. And his mane is long and white, as was the man's hair. From a study of history, I'd come to admire George Washington—how he was able to unite the rebelling colonists behind him; how he led a vastly outnumbered and outgunned army against the greatest army in the world and defeated them; how in the difficult first years of peace in the new republic, he helped forge colonists from thirteen different states into relatively united Americans. He was a truly remarkable man—no president since has been so universally accepted and loved by the American people. I honored this great horse by giving him a great man's name." He patted George Washington again, then looked at her, his expression sheepish. "That sounds strange, doesn't it?"

Diana attempted to keep her amazement at his knowledge and interpretation of American history from showing on her face. "No. It sounds fascinating. I must ask, though; how do you know so much about George Washington, the statesman?"

"That is no mystery, either," Grey Eagle answered with a shrug. "My father was an educated man from a wealthy Virginia family. Between them, his three wives gave him five children, and he insisted upon treating all of his children the same, regardless of race or gender. He taught us himself." A smile touched the corner of his mouth. "I remember the nights of my childhood, all of us gathered near the fire—either in the St. Louis house or a tipi somewhere on the Plains, listening to him as he read aloud history books on the United States, England, and Europe, stories of the Greek and Roman civilizations and their mythologies, the works of Shakespeare, the novels of James Fenimore Cooper, and, to please my stepmother and my sisters, even those of Jane Austen."

"Your father was an amazing man," Diana commented, seeing in her mind Grey Eagle as a boy, eagerly devouring the words of the ages.

"In many ways." Grey Eagle eyed Diana. "In keeping with his personality and beliefs, my father also included all of his children in the Cheyenne way of life. My brothers and sisters are as fluent as I in the language of the Cheyenne, and in the sign language of the Plains tribes, just as they are familiar with Cheyenne customs and way of life."

Diana gaped at him. "Your sisters, too?"

"Yes. I am—we all are—very grateful for the way our father raised us. We Beaudines are a very close family."

"That has always been obvious to any who would look. You are very fortunate." Diana felt a powerful pang of loss and loneliness—a mourning, almost—for a childhood she never had, one with a united family that embraced all members of that family within a circle of love and brotherhood. A moment later, she was startled by Grey Eagle's hand covering hers in a gesture of comfort.

"You look so sad," he said quietly.

She managed a small smile. "I'm fine." She looked away

from the concern in his eyes, desperate to find a topic of discussion to take his attention off her. "Have you ever read Alexandre Dumas?"

He pulled his hand away. "Yes, *The Three Musketeers.* I enjoyed it very much." He paused. "Diana, I know your family is not as close as mine, that you lost your best friend and mentor as well as your father when Gideon Murdoch died, and I am sorry for that. I didn't mean to cause you pain by telling you of my family."

"You didn't. The pain has been there for a long time. All children should be so welcomed, so loved and accepted, so fairly and equally treated, as you and your siblings were." She shook her head once. "But that is not the way of it for many children; it certainly wasn't for me, at least as far as my mother was concerned. Still, I was lucky. My father truly loved me, and made certain I knew it. Now, as an adult, it is up to me to do the best I can with what was given to me."

"You have done well."

Surprised by his compliment, even more surprised that she felt comfortable talking to him about things she had never discussed with anyone, Diana looked at him. "Thank you, Mr. Beaudine, but I don't feel that I have done very well at all. For as long as I can remember, my life revolved around my father. Now that he is gone, I am lost. I am twenty-three years old, and have not found my place in the world, not even a place to call home."

"Perhaps you are on your way home now."

She frowned in confusion. "Surely you cannot mean that the Cheyenne village is my home."

Grey Eagle shrugged, keeping his gaze forward. "With some people, perhaps their soul belongs in a place their mind does not yet know. For them, the journey home takes longer. And, I would say that it is possible that some people never find the true home of their soul."

Diana stared at him. Even though he rode with a white man's saddle, Grey Eagle looked every inch a Cheyenne warrior, with his beaded buckskin shirt and leggings, his long black hair blowing in the warm spring wind, his body held tall and proud, keeping an easy natural rhythm in time with George Washington's movements. How strange it was—how fascinating—to hear thought-provoking, philosophical words come from his mouth. She enjoyed talking with him like this as much as she enjoyed looking at him. "Have you found the home of your soul?" she asked quietly.

At that, he turned his head and met her gaze, his green eyes intense and burning. "I have now."

Her heart thudded in her chest, making it difficult for Diana to breathe. What did he mean by that? She could not take her gaze from his.

"All things happen in their own time, Diana Murdoch," Grey Eagle said. "You will find your home, as surely as I have found mine."

His voice was calm, but Diana sensed a conviction in his words, a strength she did not understand. She gave a nervous little laugh. "You sound as if you know what my future holds."

He did not respond except to stare at her, into her eyes. Even though they did not touch, the power between them, the connection, was a living thing. Diana felt its pulsing, its warmth. It called to her; *he* called to her, without saying a word. She could see nothing but him, feel nothing but him, hear nothing but the whisper of the wind and the faint call of the eagle.

The Eagle.

Diana could not tear her gaze away from Grey Eagle's eyes, not even to look for Franklin, to ensure that she had not imagined the call. At that moment, somehow, they were all connected—Franklin, Grey Eagle, and she. The very air seemed to shimmer with a holy light. Perhaps her father was giving his blessing.

His blessing for what? Diana wondered dreamily. Where had that thought come from?

The packhorse stumbled, and the spell was broken. Diana clutched the horse's mane as the animal found his footing.

"Are you all right?" Grey Eagle asked.

She nodded, feeling shaken for more reasons than almost losing her seat.

"He stepped in a critter hole—nothing serious." Grey Eagle

looked to the north and pointed. "There's a small lake about
an hour ahead. We'll camp there tonight. Tomorrow, we should
reach the encampment by noon."

Numbly, Diana nodded again. Grey Eagle did not act like
it, but something had just happened between them—something
powerful and important. Surely he had felt it, too; had heard
it, too. She searched the sky for sign of an eagle, but found
none.

Perhaps she had imagined everything.

Troubled by the thought, Diana pulled the packhorse into
place behind George Washington and kept silent until they
arrived at the campsite.

"Miss Murdoch."

Grey Eagle's voice reached her, as if from a far distance.
Diana shook her head and looked up at him over the comforting
fire. Her eyes took a moment to focus on his features after
staring so long at the flames. "Forgive me, Mr. Beaudine. I
was wool-gathering. Did you ask me something?"

"Not yet. I was about to ask if you are all right. You've
been very quiet tonight."

"Again, I apologize. I have been a poor dinner companion,
and after you went to such trouble to hunt these delicious sage
grouse." She managed a smile. "Thank you for your concern.
I guess I'm a little apprehensive about going into the village
tomorrow. I just don't know what to expect." That was part
of the truth, anyway, Diana guiltily admitted to herself. Honest
though she usually was with him, now she could not be. She
did not want to tell him all that weighed so heavily on her
mind. She did not want to ask Grey Eagle if he had felt the
strange connection between them that had been so powerful to
her, because she was afraid the answer would be 'no.' She did
not want to tell him that, despite her best efforts, special feelings
for him were growing within her.

"You have nothing to fear from the Cheyenne people, Miss
Murdoch. They will welcome you and come to love you."

"I know you are only trying to comfort me, and I appreciate

your efforts. I will be glad of their welcome, but I won't be there long enough for them to learn to love me. When the babe has been born, I will ask Mr. Sage to return me to Fort Laramie." Was the flickering firelight playing a trick on her eyes, or did Grey Eagle's jaw tighten?

"Should the day come when you wish to return to the fort, I will take you there myself. It is only right, since it is I who took you so far away." He rose from his cross-legged sitting position and stalked off toward the horses, his limp more pronounced now after a day of riding.

Diana stared after him in confusion. Surely he wasn't angry because of anything she'd said. As she gathered the supper dishes for washing, she thought back over her words, and decided that something else had to be troubling him; no doubt his leg caused him pain. They would both feel better after another good night's sleep. She refused to think about the fact that this would be the last night they would share a bed.

She had not even arrived at the Cheyenne village, and already Diana was planning to leave!

Grey Eagle ignored the dull throb in his leg and poured all of his frustration into the brushing he gave George Washington.

"Didn't she hear me today?" he whispered to the stallion, who merely nickered in response. "I practically told her outright that she's on her way home. Didn't she feel the Spirit of the Eagle connecting us, as it has always connected us?" Grey Eagle didn't want to admit it, but he was worried. He'd felt the connection so strongly that he'd not been able to breathe, and he'd been certain she felt it, too. But she said nothing, gave no sign, no indication. Instead, she had withdrawn from him into silence, putting a distance between them that reached farther than any number of miles could.

Had she felt the connection and rejected it—and him?

If she hadn't felt it today, would she ever? What if Diana never felt the connection?

What if the Great Ones did not tell her, as they had told him, that she and he were one?

"Then I'll tell her myself," Grey Eagle muttered.

What if Diana does not believe you?

The question came from his own mind, his own heart, yet it seemed that the words had been shouted and even now echoed from the surrounding hills.

At last, his greatest fear had been put to words.

Perhaps she would not return his feelings for her . . . ever.

"I'll see that she does, no matter what it takes," Grey Eagle informed George Washington, but the confident words did not ease the gnawing fear in his gut. Suddenly anxious to see her, to be near her, he hurriedly brushed down the packhorse, checked both horses' hobbles, and made his way back to the fire.

The campsite was neat and orderly, the cleaned plates stacked near the fire, waiting for the morning meal, the kindling pile replenished, the water bucket filled with fresh water. Diana sat near the fire with her cloak about her shoulders. She raised questioning eyes to him. "Now it is my turn to ask, Mr. Beaudine; are *you* all right?"

"Yes, thank you. I think we should get to bed."

Diana's eyes widened in surprise, no doubt at his curt manner, and Grey Eagle tried again to keep his voice calm. "Today was a long day. We both need some rest."

"I agree." Diana took up a stick and began to bank the coals.

As the firelight faded from her face, Grey Eagle eyed her suspiciously, and with weariness, dreading her answer to the question he had to ask. "Will I have to tie you to me again tonight, Miss Murdoch?"

"No. I have no wish to cause you concern over my comfort. We will share your robes one last time, Mr. Beaudine."

Grateful though Grey Eagle was that she would join him willingly, her solemn tone and quiet words troubled him.

This will not be the last time we share my robes, Diana, he vowed as he followed her to the makeshift bed. *It will not be the last time.*

It cannot be the last time.

Chapter Nineteen

Any hopes Diana had for a refreshing night's sleep were dashed by restless, persistent dreams and the knowledge that morning would come too soon. After all her protests to the contrary, and for all her wishing it otherwise, the thought of never again sharing Grey Eagle's robes distressed her. All night, she tossed and turned, trying not to wake him with her movements, longing to but not daring to move closer to the warmth of his beautiful body for fear of touching him—and not being able to stop.

After one of many bouts of fitful dozing, Diana gave up any attempt to sleep. When she opened her eyes, she found that the sky had lightened and that she lay on her side facing Grey Eagle. He, too, lay on his side, facing her. Not more than a few inches separated them, but nowhere did they touch. Diana was content to watch him sleep, to explore his handsome face with hungry eyes, to memorize his features for the time in the future when he would not be with her.

An unbearable sadness assailed her at the thought, and she pressed a hand to her lips, fearful that a moan would escape and perhaps wake him.

In four days—and nights—her feelings for Grey Eagle Beaudine had run the gamut from fear and annoyance to tolerance and respect to tentative friendship and undeniable longing. How had such a thing happened in so little time? Why had she allowed it to happen?

A thick strand of his long hair fell over his shoulder and lay in a tempting coil on the robe between them. Of its own accord, Diana's hand moved toward that coil. Her fingers accidentally brushed Grey Eagle's naked chest, sending a shiver through her as she picked up the strand and brought it to her lips. At the faint scent of sage and smoke, her eyes closed.

Wild, erotic visions filled Diana's mind, so vivid that her heart rate accelerated—visions of throwing the top robe back and away to expose Grey Eagle's beauty, of running her hands over and through all of his hair, of kissing his mouth with joyous abandon, of caressing his chest and feeling his heart beat against her eager hand, of removing that accursed breechclout to see and touch all of him, of holding him at last in the way a woman held her man.

Shaken and ashamed, Diana brushed the lock of his hair against her cheek and struggled to calm her breathing. Only then did she realize that his hand stroked her upper arm. Her eyes flew open and her face heated with a blush. As if dropping a hot coal, she released his hair and pulled back from him.

His hand tightened on her arm, kept her from rising. Grey Eagle said nothing—only stared at her, right into her eyes, into her heart, and her soul. Diana stopped struggling. His grip loosened and his hand again stroked her arm. His touch soothed her.

"You felt it yesterday, didn't you?" he asked, his voice barely above a whisper.

Diana did not need to ask what he was talking about. A tremulous, hopeful joy welled up in her heart; if he knew to ask about it, he must have also felt it. She nodded. "You did, too."

"Yes." Grey Eagle inched closer to her, his intention clear. Diana did not attempt to escape his mouth. His lips touched hers, and she laid her palm against his chest at last.

It seemed that his heart leapt under her hand. His skin was

warm and smooth, with no trace of the masculine hair that most men had on their chests, and Diana found that she liked that. She also liked what Grey Eagle's mouth did to hers, with its nibbles and kisses, and that his tongue teased for entry into her mouth. She granted him access, and discovered a whole new world of feeling. Now a moan did escape her, one she was helpless to stop. That little sound had an odd effect on Grey Eagle, for he became very still.

"We must stop," he whispered. "Now, before I cannot stop." He kissed her lips one last time, then rested his forehead against hers, stroked her arm and her back, pulled her hair away from her neck. "Let us go home, Diana Murdoch."

Diana nodded, and allowed him to pull her to her feet. She returned his smile, determined that his use of the word 'home'—which meant his home, not hers—would not destroy for her the fragile happiness they had somehow stumbled upon.

Several hours later, Grey Eagle drew George Washington to a halt on the top of a low rise. He turned back and watched as Diana closed the distance between them.

"The encampment of my mother's band of the Cheyenne," he said proudly, one arm outflung.

Diana stopped the packhorse and looked at the sight before her, apprehensive and, at the same time, fascinated.

The village was much larger than she had expected, spread out over a wide valley. A river curled along the bottom of the rise on which they stood, the clear waters sparkling in the sunlight. There had to be fifty, maybe even sixty tipis, some nestled among the scattered trees, some nearly encircled by brush wind breaks, all with their entry portals facing east. A large herd of horses grazed on the far side of the valley. People moved about, and the sounds of laughing, shouting children and barking dogs floated on the wind.

"How many people live here?" Diana asked.

"Approximately two hundred," Grey Eagle answered. "Soon the camp will break, though, for the summer hunt. Smaller groups will go their own ways, searching for buffalo.

All summer we hunt and gather, to prepare for the coming winter, then we assemble together again. The cycle of life goes on, dictated by the four seasons.''

Struck by the unconscious poetry of his words, Diana could only stare at him. He was beautiful to her, sitting so tall and proud on George Washington's back, his long hair moving in the wind. He wore his leggings today, but instead of his buckskin shirt, he covered his chest with only a breastplate made of hair-pipe bone and decorated with brass beads, elk teeth, and an eagle talon. All morning long, she'd had trouble taking her eyes off him. A poignant sadness touched her; her time alone with Grey Eagle had come to an end.

He did not seem to notice her overlong perusal, for he merely said, "Let us go down. There are those who are anxious to see you."

At that, Diana frowned. "How do I look?" she asked, and before he could speak, answered her own question. "Awful, I know." She pulled off her hat and smoothed her hopelessly tangled hair, then tried in vain to brush some of the dust from her torn skirts.

"Miss Murdoch, you look fine."

"I do not," she said hotly. Her eyes narrowed into a glare when she realized he was fighting a smile. "*You* look fine, Mr. Beaudine, in your buckskin leggings that don't show dust so badly, and your nice breastplate and your hair blowing in the wind." Actually, he looked magnificent, which made Diana feel even more self-conscious as she continued. "I look dirty and disheveled, and no doubt my face is still discolored with bruises. I do not wish my friends to see me like this."

She did not mention that she also did not want the rest of the Cheyenne tribe to see her in such shabby condition, and that she was sorry Grey Eagle had seen her thus. For some confusing and unidentified reason, Diana wanted to make a good impression on the people she was about to meet, both for her sake and, even more puzzling, for Grey Eagle's sake. Why did she care so much what the Cheyenne would think of her?

Grey Eagle's expression sobered, even if the look in his eyes didn't. "I can understand that," he conceded. He stepped down from the saddle and limped to her side. "Come." He reached for her waist, and Diana allowed him to help her to the ground. Grey Eagle retrieved the hairbrush from his pack. He turned her away from him, then pulled the leather tie from the end of her unravelling braid and handed it to her. "At least we can brush your hair. And your cloak is not as dusty or as torn as your skirt and bodice are. Put that around you. I fear that little can be done with your hat, and I told you before that your bruises—which are fading, by the way—are the mark of a warrior. Wear them with pride."

Diana eyed the battered hat she held in one hand, then gingerly touched her cheek. "I really look better?"

"You really look fine." Grey Eagle turned her to face him.

"Aren't you going to braid my hair?" Diana ran a hand down the long, loose lengths.

"Rather than a straightlaced and proper white man's village where only young girls and whores wear their hair down, you are about to enter a Cheyenne village, where beautiful hair like yours is appreciated and admired. Leave it down."

Still not used to the idea that he found her hair to be beautiful, Diana dropped her gaze. The sunlight teased fingers of red fire from the dark depths of the strands that slid forward over her shoulders and now fell to her waist. The effect *was* pretty, she had to admit. But she'd been taught all her life that ladies did not wear their hair down in public, and she felt uncomfortable about doing so now. All the same, she slipped the leather tie into the pocket of her skirt.

Grey Eagle draped her cloak around her shoulders and pulled her hair from under the material. "Later, Sparrow and Sweet Water will take you to a heated pool where you can bathe, and we will find fresh clothes for you. You will feel better about everything, including how you look, after a bath and something to eat."

"A warm bath would be wonderful," Diana confessed. "Is the pool one of the hot springs I've heard about?"

"Yes. There are many such pools throughout this entire territory, some so hot they will boil any creature foolish or unlucky enough to go in. There is a truly fantastic land far to the northwest of here, a land of boiling mud and exploding waters and indescribable beauty.'' He helped Diana back onto her horse, then arranged her skirts so that her drawers and stockings were covered.

"Thank you," she murmured, embarrassed by and grateful for his intimate attentions at the same time. She certainly did not want to ride into the Cheyenne village with her drawers exposed. "I should like to see such a land."

"It is the land of the Shoshoni. We would not be welcome there.'' Grey Eagle climbed back into the saddle, taking care with his injured leg.

"Yet you were once.''

"Not I. My father is the one who saw that land, and I'm not certain how welcome he was. He went up there with Jim Bridger, and always told us they were lucky to escape with their lives.''

Grey Eagle led the way along the top of the rise until he reached a wide, rocky gorge that cut the face of the hill below them. As they started down a rough trail that would eventually bring them to the floor of the valley, a series of excited shouts and yips came from the direction of the village. Diana looked up from the treacherous terrain on which her horse struggled for footing to find that several warriors raced toward them on horseback, waving what appeared to be weapons. With her heart in her throat, she managed to ask, "Why are they attacking us?''

"They are not attacking.'' An equally blood-chilling cry issued from Grey Eagle's throat. "They are greeting us!'' He yipped and pumped his clenched fist in the air over his head, seemingly unconcerned that George Washington scrambled with difficulty down the steep trail. Grey Eagle had no trouble keeping his seat, and Diana could not help but admire the power and grace of his splendid body.

They reached the bottom of the gorge and splashed across a shallow ford in the lazy river. As they urged the horses out of the water, the yelling warriors surrounded them, then fell into step as they rode into the village. Shouting children and barking dogs added to the noise and confusion. Diana held herself straight and kept the packhorse close to George Washington. Children ran alongside her horse fearlessly, several of them little more than toddlers, all staring up at her with blatant curiosity, some brave enough to touch her boot. The smile she offered the children belied her fear that one of them might fall under her horse's hooves and be injured.

Grey Eagle pulled George Washington to a stop in front of a tipi, and Diana was overjoyed to see that Jubal Sage and a very pregnant Sweet Water waited there, both dressed in buckskin and wearing broad grins.

"Howdy, Diana!" Jubal called as he stepped to her side and lifted her down from the packhorse. "It sure is good to see you." He startled her by drawing her into a hug, which Diana returned with equal feeling, then turned her to face Sweet Water. "I told you Eagle'd get her here in time, honey, and he did."

Diana hugged Sweet Water, as close as the woman's extended belly would allow, then stepped back, keeping her hands on Sweet Water's shoulders. "How are you feeling?"

"Big," Sweet Water answered with a smile. "I very glad you here, Di-an-ah. Now little one can come." She rested her hands on the shelf made by her belly.

"Di-an-ah! *Na-mahane!*" Sparrow's young voice echoed through the village.

"She calls you 'older sister,' " Grey Eagle said.

"I know." Diana turned, searching. She made out Sparrow's form as the girl raced toward her, braids flying. Tears formed in Diana's eyes and she held out her arms. *"Na-semahe!* My little sister."

Sparrow hurled herself into Diana's arms and the two clung together.

"Di-an-ah. *E-peva'e tsexe-ho'ehneto.* It is good you came." Sparrow stepped back. Her big dark eyes searched Diana's face, and she frowned. With a gentle finger, she traced Diana's bruised cheek. "You are hurt."

"No, I am healing." She met Grey Eagle's warm gaze over Sparrow's head. He said something in Cheyenne, to which Sparrow responded, then he nodded at her and, with Jubal at his side, led the two horses away. A panicky feeling rose in

Diana's chest. He had promised not to leave her! A large crowd
of people milled about in front of Jubal's tipi, all of them
staring at her. Some wore expressions that bordered on the
hostile, but most seemed merely curious. One old woman
approached and without preamble grabbed a lock of Diana's
hair, examined it closely, turning it this way and that, and
chattered in Cheyenne.

"Grandmother says you have fire in your hair," Sparrow
explained.

Diana winced as the old woman tugged on the lock. "Is that
good?"

"Heehe'e. Yes."

The elderly woman released Diana's hair and smiled, revealing the fact that she'd lost a few teeth, then tottered away.

"She is your grandmother, then?" Diana asked.

"Not in white man's meaning." Sparrow took Diana's hand
and led her away from the tipi. "All elders are called Grandmother and Grandfather, in respect." Sweet Water waddled up
to join them, carrying a bundle.

"Where are we going?" Diana asked.

"Grey Eagle say to take you to bath," Sweet Water informed
her.

"Oh, good. I have soap in my medical bag. Where is it?"

Sparrow darted back to the tipi, and returned a moment later
with the bag. Diana glanced back over her shoulder, dismayed
to see that several women and girls followed them. Surely they
would have the courtesy to allow her to bathe in private.

They didn't. When Sparrow stopped next to a clear pool that
smelled of sulphur, the crowd stopped as well. Sweet Water
untied the cloak string at Diana's throat and pulled the garment
away, while Sparrow worked on the row of hooks down the
back of Diana's bodice.

Diana was glad to remove the dirty bodice, which she had
not taken off except when she washed herself since Grey Eagle
had forced her to remove it that first night. Sweet Water frowned
and lightly touched a bruise on Diana's upper arm.

"What happen, Di-an-ah?" she asked. "Grey Eagle not do
this."

"No. He wouldn't hurt me in such a way." Diana was surprised to hear herself defending him, just as she was surprised that she knew she spoke the truth. "An Army officer attacked me. It was he who caused the bruises. Grey Eagle rescued me from him."

Sparrow peered around her arm, now working on the buttons of Diana's skirt. "That lieutenant who wanted you, it was he." She made a statement rather than asked a question, and Diana wondered how the girl knew the truth.

"Yes."

"He should die." Sparrow emphasized her harsh comment with a spit of disgust. She worked the skirt down to the ground, and Diana stepped out of it.

"He did die, Sparrow." Diana wondered how she could report Thatcher's death so calmly, why she felt no real emotion. That terrifying day in the rainy forest seemed like another lifetime rather than just four days earlier.

"Grey Eagle kill him," Sweet Water declared triumphantly.

"No. The lieutenant killed himself, after he was badly wounded. Mr. Beaudine killed no one."

Sweet Water appeared to be disappointed, and Diana remembered that the Indians prided themselves on the killing of their enemies.

Sparrow said something in Cheyenne and pointed to Diana's shoulder. Sweet Water's eyes opened wide, and Diana heard the word *"Netse."* The word circulated among the women and girls, spoken with reverence and awe. The crowd pressed closer, and some women craned their necks for a better view, which caused Diana a great deal of discomfort.

Eagle. She remembered the word that both Sparrow and Grey Eagle had spoken. The new interest was over her birthmark, and Diana fought the urge to cover the small mark with her hand. Then she realized that Sparrow was pulling her petticoat down her legs, leaving her with only her chemise, drawers, stockings, and boots to protect her from the curious and intrusive looks of the crowd around her.

"Will you ask them to leave so that I may bathe in private?" she asked Sparrow, unable to keep the tension out of her voice.

Sparrow looked at her strangely. "I cannot do that. The pool belongs to all."

"Then I shall come back later, when no one is here." Diana reached for her clothes, which Sparrow had thrown in a heap on the ground.

Sweet Water and Sparrow carried on a hurried conversation in Cheyenne, both speaking in whispers, then Sweet Water turned to the crowd and addressed them. With disappointed murmurs and mutterings, the women and girls turned away and left the three alone.

Diana stared after them. "What did you say?"

"I say that it is not the way of your people to bathe together, that you are hurt and tired. I ask them to honor your wish this one time, since you are a great medicine woman."

"You told them that?" Diana demanded in dismay. "Sweet Water, I'm not a great medicine woman. Now they will have expectations of me that I cannot possibly meet."

Sweet Water merely shrugged, not apologetic in the least. "You need your bath, Di-an-ah. Get in water."

Her shoulders slumped in resignation, Diana obeyed. After removing her boots, stockings, drawers, and, with a last shy, uncomfortable look around, her chemise, she took a bar of soap from the medical bag and waded into the water, marvelling at its warmth, welcoming its comfort. Sparrow undressed and followed her in, carrying a small crock.

"Soap for your hair," she explained at Diana's curious look. "Made of bear grass and love vine, and scented with wild rose, all boiled down together." She held the crock out.

Diana took a cautious sniff, which proved that the gel-like substance smelled sweet and clean. She smiled her approval, and allowed Sparrow to wash her hair for her, while she cleansed her body with the strong soap from her bag. Then she asked Sweet Water to toss her soiled clothes into the water, and Diana scrubbed those worn garments as best she could. Sweet Water took them from her and draped the garments over nearby bushes to dry.

When the chores of cleaning were done, Diana floated in the warm water, sleepy and relaxed. She had never bathed in an outside pool like the one she now luxuriated in. To be naked and clean while out in nature gave her an incredible sense of freedom.

Uninvited, Grey Eagle popped into her mind, and Diana wondered if he would later bathe in these very same waters, rinsing the dust and the sweat from his body as she had done. What would it be like to share this pool with him, to wash his hair for him, as Sparrow had for her? The sudden heat that now coursed through Diana's veins had nothing to do with the temperature of the water. She deliberately ducked her entire body under the surface, as if that could wash the blush from her cheeks and the aching need from her breasts and lower belly.

When she came up, she lifted her face so that her hair was washed back over her shoulders. "Did you bring something I can wear until my clothes dry?" she called to Sweet Water.

From her sitting position in the sun, Sweet Water nodded and handed a bundle to Sparrow, who was now dried and dressed again.

"The drying cloth is there," Sparrow said, and pointed to a long piece of muslin that lay folded on a rock near the pool.

Diana made her way toward the rock, hating to leave the warmth of the water. Goose bumps rose on her skin and her nipples puckered in the cool breeze. Taking care with her footing, she climbed out of the pool and reached for the drying cloth. Just as her hand touched the cloth, the material was snatched from her grasp. Startled, she looked up.

Before her stood the most beautiful woman Diana had ever seen, of any race. She wore a fringed and beaded dress, the soft-looking doeskin bleached almost white, and her shining black hair was tamed in two long braids that fell past her hips. Her large dark eyes were lovely, as were her features—or as they would have been if the woman's face wasn't twisted into an expression of loathing. Her hostile gaze roamed over Diana's naked and bruised form.

As cold and as vulnerable as she felt with no clothes on, as puzzled as she was by the hatred in the woman's expression, Diana would not back down into the water, nor would she

reach for the drying cloth. Grey Eagle had told her she was a
warrior and should be proud; his words helped her now. She
straightened her spine and raised her chin, small actions that
seemed to anger the woman even further.

Sparrow grabbed the drying cloth from the woman's hand
and draped it around Diana. She glared at the beautiful woman
and pointed toward the village. *"Ta-naestse!"*

Instead of leaving, which was what Diana assumed Sparrow
had ordered, the woman stepped closer. She pulled the cloth
away from Diana's right shoulder and stared at the birthmark
there. Her eyes widened, and her lovely face paled. Then her
mouth twisted and she caught Diana's flesh—and the birthmark—in a vicious pinch.

Diana grabbed the woman's hand and jerked it away from
her shoulder. "Do not touch me!"

Sparrow spoke in Cheyenne, apparently translating.

The woman glared at Diana. *"Ne-saa-netse."* she said, her
voice heavy with disgust. She turned and stormed away.

Relieved, Diana watched her go, and rubbed her aching
shoulder. "What did she say?"

"She say you are no eagle," Sweet Water supplied as she
struggled to her feet.

"Of course I'm not." She looked at Sparrow. "Who was
that?"

"In English, her name is Black Moon. She is prettiest, most
wanted woman in the village." Sparrow's sullen tone indicated
that she did not hold Black Moon in the esteem others apparently
did.

Diana rubbed the muslin drying cloth briskly over her skin.
"Does she hate all white people in general, or is it just me?"

Sparrow shrugged and shook out a folded deerskin garment.

"She not hate white people so much," Sweet Water
announced. "She like Grey Eagle well enough, and he half
white."

Those few words explained everything. Diana's heart sank.
Grey Eagle did have a sweetheart in the village, and a lovely
one at that. No wonder the woman was so hostile toward her—
she had just spent several days alone in the wilderness with

Black Moon's man. An acute disappointment that bordered on despair gripped Diana, stunning her with its intensity.

"But Grey Eagle doesn't like her well enough," Sparrow said as she took the drying cloth from Diana and handed her the deerskin garment.

"What?" Diana asked dully.

"He not like her back," Sweet Water said.

Hope was rekindled. "Why not?" Diana asked. "She is lovely."

"Not in here." Sweet Water laid her fist over her heart. "Grey Eagle smart man, not like many others. You stay away from Black Moon, Di-an-ah. She hurt you."

"Oh, I'll stay away from her." A new happiness sang through Diana's veins, and she looked down at the garment whose softness surprised her. "Where are the underclothes?"

"The Cheyenne wear no underclothes," Sparrow answered. "Not like the whites."

"But I need some," Diana protested. "I can't wear this by itself."

"You can." Sparrow flashed her a mischievous grin. "You will grow to like the freedom of Cheyenne clothes."

Determined to retrieve her chemise and drawers as soon as they dried, Diana pulled the deerskin dress over her head. The material felt feather-soft as it slid down her body. The fringed sleeves fell to her elbows, while the fringed hem reached to mid-calf. Two rows of tiny colored beads and small shells had been sewn along the yoke. She stroked the softness of the dress. "It's very nice."

Sweet Water beamed. "I make for you."

Diana stared at her. "But how did you know for certain that I was coming, and that I would need to borrow a dress?"

"Grey Eagle promise you come." She did not elaborate further. Evidently, Grey Eagle's word was all Sweet Water needed.

"I made these for you, Di-an-ah." Shyly, Sparrow held out a pair of moccasins and a matching pair of knee-high leggings, each decorated with modest beading.

Deeply touched, Diana accepted the articles. "Thank you,

both of you. Your kindness warms my heart." She leaned
against a large rock and pulled one moccasin on, then the other.
Amazingly, they fit. She looked at Sparrow. "How did you
know my size?"

"I measure your boot at the fort. If you did not come, I
would send them back to you with Jubal Sage. White man's
shoes and boots hurt the feet."

Diana remembered that when Sparrow lived at the fort, she
would not be persuaded to wear the shoes Gideon had purchased
for her at Angus's trading post. The girl had cleaned her old
moccasins as best she could for cold weather use, had worn
only stockings when inside the house, and went barefoot when
it was warm enough to do so.

Sparrow showed Diana how to secure the leggings at her
knees with leather garters, then stood back and surveyed the
end result. "You look like Cheyenne," she announced happily.

With an answering smile, Diana asked, "How do you say
'thank you' in Cheyenne?"

"Ne-a'eshe," Sparrow answered.

"Ne-a'eshe," Diana repeated carefully. *"Ne-a'eshe."*

Both Sparrow and Sweet Water favored her with wide smiles.

"It is so good to see you both," Diana said sincerely as she
hugged first Sparrow, then Sweet Water.

"Heehe'e!" Sweet Water took Diana's hand and tugged her
in the direction of the village. *"Ne-ta-mesehe-ma!* Let us eat!"

With a laugh, Diana grabbed Sparrow's hand and allowed
herself to be pulled along toward the lodges. In the company
of her friends, she felt comfortable and safe.

But the memory of Black Moon's viciousness did not fade.
Diana made a silent vow to be on her guard whenever the
beautiful Cheyenne woman was near—which, since it was clear
that neither Sparrow nor Sweet Water liked Black Moon, she
hoped would not be often.

Still, Diana knew that Grey Eagle, of all men, was a man
worth fighting for. On some deeply intuitive female level, she
understood Black Moon's hatred of her perfectly.

Chapter Twenty

Sweet Water led Diana and Sparrow back to the buffalo hide lodge she shared with Jubal, and, Diana learned, much to her surprise, Grey Eagle. *So this is his home,* she thought as she moved toward the place Sweet Water indicated at the back of the lodge. There she sat down on a comfortable bed of buffalo robes, her legs curled to one side, the hem of her deerskin dress tugged down as far as it would go, which was not far enough, in Diana's opinion. An oblong fire pit in the center of the tipi boasted a cheery fire which added its dancing light to the soft daylight that came through the hide walls. A flat stone approximately the size of Grey Eagle's frying pan rested between the fire and Diana's seat, and on it a twisted rope of some kind of grass smoked, sending up a distinctive and unfamiliar scent.

The interior of Sweet Water's lodge was neat and orderly, and, Diana felt, very welcoming. She found it difficult to refrain from asking many, many questions about the fascinating contents of the simple home, but she feared that would be viewed as rude, and so determined to ply Grey Eagle or Jubal with her questions when she next saw either man.

Sweet Water explained that she would keep Diana inside the

lodge with her that afternoon, to give her respite from the open
curiosity of the other villagers and allow her to rest after the
long and difficult days of travel. So, Diana spent a relaxing
afternoon with Sparrow and Sweet Water, and later, Sparrow's
shy mother, Little Leaf, joined them. The Cheyenne women
cooked a pot of elk stew for the evening meal, marvelled
over the contents of Diana's medical bag, took turns brushing
Diana's hair as it dried, and chattered companionably in Cheyenne, with Sparrow and Sweet Water translating.

By late afternoon, Diana could no longer keep her eyes open,
and lay down for a nap. When she awakened, she was alone
in the tipi. By the reduced light inside and by the color of the
sky she could see through the open door flap, she knew the
sun had set and that darkness would soon descend. The sounds
of a happy community reached her—chattering voices, both
male and female; laughing children; barking dogs—as did the
wonderful smells of food being prepared. She stretched lazily,
luxuriating in the incredible comfort of the bed on which she
rested, and, for the first time in longer than she could remember,
Diana felt safe and welcome.

The realization startled her. She had been in the village for
only a matter of hours, but in those few hours she had been
greeted with love—and protected and defended—by dear
friends, she had been given treasured gifts of new clothing,
had enjoyed a wonderful bath, had eaten and rested. Not since
her father's death had she felt welcome anywhere, and the
months before his death had been fraught with worry and grief.
How strange that she should find such warmth and welcome
in a Cheyenne village.

She stretched again, then sat up and gave her curiosity free
rein as she looked about the lodge. The bed on which she sat
was wide enough for two, and long—perhaps seven to eight
feet. She assumed it was the bed Jubal and Sweet Water shared.
Another bed lay along the wall to her left, and one along the
wall to her right. The three beds were laid out on an earthen
shelf perhaps six inches high and five feet wide which encircled
the rim of the tipi and were separated by two double-sided
backrests, which offered support to any who rested on any bed.

Curious as to what made the beds so comfortable, Diana lifted one corner of Jubal's bed and saw that next to the earth lay a mattress of sorts, constructed of what looked like willow rods strung on long lines of string or thin rope. On top of that lay a mat of loosely woven rushes, and on top of that, several thick buffalo robes. No wonder the bed was so comfortable.

As she looked at the other two beds, Diana wondered which belonged to Grey Eagle. Did the robes on his bed carry his light scent of sage and smoke? To whom did the other bed belong? She resisted the urge to examine each bed in search of his and instead continued her perusal of the tipi.

A lining tied halfway up the support poles reached to the ground and was tucked under the beds, ensuring that no drafts crept under the outside cover, and a stack of firewood patiently awaited its fate on one side of the oval entry. Cooking utensils surrounded the low-burning fire. Bundles wrapped in hides and furs were stacked in an orderly fashion in various places, and she saw that her apparently dry clothes were folded in a neat pile by the door. Diana was struck by the ingenuity and the coziness of the lodge. It offered far more comfort and warmth than many cabins and log structures she had seen.

Jubal stuck his grey head in the open doorway. "So you're awake." He easily clambered through the opening and sat on one of the side beds. "How do you feel?"

"Well, thank you." Diana smiled at him. "Sweet Water and Sparrow have spoiled me." She smoothed the soft deerskin dress. "I'm touched by their gifts, Mr. Sage, I truly am. They've made me very welcome." To her surprise, her eyes teared with emotion.

Jubal leaned forward and patted her hand. "Well, we're just as glad as can be that you're finally here, girl. And since you'll be sharin' this lodge with us for a while, I sure wish you'd drop that 'Mr. Sage' stuff and call me 'Jubal,' like ever'body else does."

Diana brushed a hand over her eyes and managed another smile. "All right, Jubal." Then his other words struck her. "I'll be staying here?" *With Grey Eagle?*

"We figured it best, at least until the baby comes—if you

don't mind, that is. Sparrow wanted you to stay with her and her folks, though, and maybe you'd rather. It's your choice. But we made this here bed up for you.'' He patted the bed on which he sat. ''Sweet Water would sure like you to stay.'' He eyed her thoughtfully. '' 'Course, Grey Eagle stays with us when he's here, too. Since it's the womenfolk who own the tipis, an unmarried or widowed man with no woman of his own has to stay in the lodge of family or friend. It don't cause a problem, Grey Eagle stayin' here, too, does it?''

As hard as she tried to stop it, a blush heated Diana's face, and she looked down at her hands, desperate to avoid Jubal's perceptive gaze, afraid of what he might see in her eyes. ''No, that isn't a problem. I'm happy to stay with you, especially with the baby coming, and I appreciate the invitation. You'd asked me earlier, if you remember, when I wouldn't come with you and Sparrow.''

''I remember. You shoulda just come then.'' A scowl darkened his bearded face. ''Grey Eagle told me what that bastard Thatcher did to you, what he and your no-good uncle had planned.'' Jubal ran a light finger across her bruised cheek, then spat angrily in the fire. ''That lieutenant's lucky he's dead, or him and me woulda had some unpleasant words. And I never did like that scoundrel Angus MacDonald, even if he is your kin, though poor Phoebe ain't so bad. One has to pity her, bein' wed to a man like that. Anyways, if'n you'da come with me and Sparrow when we asked, you'da been saved from all that.''

''The time wasn't right, Jubal.''

''Well, it is now.''

''It had better be—I'm here.'' She smiled at him again, and realized that Jubal often made her smile. A rush of affection for the aging mountain man filled her.

Jubal returned her smile with a wink, then clapped his hands on his buckskin-covered knees and said, ''Little Leaf and Raven's Heart have put together sort of a supper feast to welcome you and show their thanks for savin' their daughter. I'm to fetch you over to their lodge. Are you ready to go?''

Suddenly nervous, Diana ran a hand down her unbound hair. ''I'd like to wash my face, and I could use a brush.'

With an understanding nod, Jubal reached for a skin bag that hung from a lodge pole, poured water from it into a wooden bowl, and handed it to her. "I don't reckon Grey Eagle would mind if you used his brush. It's right here." He pulled the familiar brush from a pack near the door.

"Probably not," Diana shyly assured him. "He brushed my hair with it himself." She splashed cool water on her suddenly warm face and allowed the drops to run down her neck. Refreshed, she took up the brush. "Mis—uh, Jubal, shouldn't I put my hair up? I feel like I should dress up in some way." As she pulled the brush through her hair, a faint scent of roses wafted to her nose, and she was grateful again for Sparrow's hair soap.

"You can braid it if you want to, but there ain't no need. The Cheyenne are proud of their hair, and it ain't impolite or shocking for a woman to leave hers unbound, like it is for white women." He studied her. "You got real pretty hair, girl. Leave it down."

"All right." Uncommon as it was to have her hair flowing down her body to her waist as it did, Diana felt that the long, shining locks acted as a shield, something behind which she could hide if she had to.

"Let's go, Diana, or Sweet Water'll have my hide for holdin' things up." Jubal exited the tipi, then held down his hand to assist Diana through the low opening.

She clung to his hand for dear life, refusing to release him as they walked. Her free hand stroked down the skirt of her dress in a futile attempt to make it longer. Although her Cheyenne dress was comfortable to wear and easy to walk in, Diana felt exposed in an unseemly manner with her calves and ankles showing, even if they were covered with leggings. Finally, she could no longer keep inside the question she longed to ask. "Will Grey Eagle be at the feast?"

"Yep. He wanted to get cleaned up first, but I reckon he's there by now. You did a fine job doctorin' his leg. He'll be back to dancin' before you know it." Jubal pierced her with his sharp gaze. "By the way, how do you like the youngest of the Beaudine brothers?"

Taken by surprise, Diana stumbled over her words. "Um, fine, he's . . . ah . . . fine." She took a deep breath, feeling like an idiot. "He saved my life, you know."

"And you saved his. That makes for a powerful bond between two people." He paused. "He likes you just fine, too, in case you was wonderin'."

Something in Jubal's tone made Diana look up at his face. There was an obvious teasing light in the man's eyes.

Oh, Lord. The last thing Diana needed was Jubal Sage teasing her about Grey Eagle Beaudine. Then a horrifying thought struck her. What if he teased Grey Eagle about *her?* Would he do that?

Diana stifled a groan as she looked away from him. Of course he would, if Jubal's easygoing relationship with both Joseph and Orion Beaudine was anything to judge by. He and the Beaudine brothers were very close; an affectionate camaraderie existed among all of them, which included the occasional pulling of pranks and sometimes merciless teasing, all good-natured, of course. If Jubal ever got any idea of the special and confusing feelings she had for Grey Eagle, she did not doubt that he would tease both of them. The realization made Diana more determined than ever to keep her feelings for Grey Eagle hidden from everyone.

They approached a lodge around which were gathered many laughing, talking people. Diana's grip on Jubal's hand tightened.

"You'll do fine, girl," he said in a low tone.

"Because I'm ignorant of their customs, I'm afraid I'll do something wrong, insult or offend someone without knowing it." Diana pulled on Jubal's hand until he stopped, then released him, as if he might drag her on when she wasn't ready to go. "Grey Eagle said he wouldn't leave my side, yet he did. Please guide me if he's not around, Jubal. Sparrow and Sweet Water helped me today, but they may not be as forthright with me as you and Grey Eagle will be if I really mess up."

"I'll watch out for you, but I'm a tellin' you, Diana, if you remember your manners, you'll do fine. No matter what customs they follow, ever'body the world over likes to be treated with courtesy. Now, I'm gonna give you a lesson in dealin' with the Cheyenne. They are a proud people, and they respect pride in others.'' A note of scolding came into his voice. ''Straighten your shoulders and lift your chin. You are the daughter of Gideon Murdoch, and a gifted healer in your own right, and a good-hearted, beautiful woman. Present yourself as such.''

Jubal's words calmed her and gave Diana some badly needed confidence. She obeyed him and held her head high. She even managed a small smile.

''That's my girl.'' Jubal brushed her hair back over her shoulders, much as her father had done when she was little, then grabbed her hand again. ''Let's go get this over with. You'll feel better in a few minutes, when you see that there ain't nobody here gonna hurt you.''

As they walked on, Diana did not tell him that one woman had already hurt her, thinking of the fresh bruise on her shoulder caused by Black Moon's vicious fingers. She fervently hoped that woman would not be present at the feast, and, just as fervently, she hoped Grey Eagle was.

One of Diana's wishes came true. Black Moon was not among the many Cheyenne who greeted her, welcomed her, shared in the generous feast provided by Raven's Heart and Little Leaf. Sparrow stuck by her on one side, pretty, proud, and happy, and the jovial, very pregnant Sweet Water remained at her other side. Between them, the two introduced her to countless people, translated for her, and saw to her every comfort—a backrest against which to lean, hide cups filled with water and various herbal teas, more food than she could eat in a week.

And, as Grey Eagle had warned, the Cheyenne brought her gifts—an overwhelming number of them, including an exquisite pair of shell earrings from Sparrow's true grandmother on her mother's side; another deerskin dress from Little Leaf's sister; several feathered and beaded hair ornaments from some of Sparrow's young girlfriends; various hides and tools from different families; a lush buffalo robe beautifully embroidered with dyed porcupine quills from Little Leaf; and, most astonishing of all, from Raven's Heart a lovely chestnut mare with a long mane and tail, complete with a Cheyenne-style saddle, constructed with a high wooden cantle in back and a high pommel in front, the whole covered with padded buffalo hide, and decorated with beaded flaps.

Jubal quietly explained that the lavish outpouring of gifts to Diana was a tremendous honor for Sparrow, for it clearly demonstrated how well loved the girl was, how joyous her people were at her safe return to them. Based on the depth of love Diana herself felt for Sparrow, she had no trouble believing him. Still, she felt uncomfortable with the generosity of the village.

"How can I ever repay them?" she asked Jubal in a whisper.

"Ain't no need to. They're tellin' you thanks for savin' their Sparrow—they felt they was in your debt. The best thing to do is accept their heartfelt gifts graciously."

Knowing it would do no good to protest that no one had ever been in her debt, Diana could only nod and smile, and thank them with her newly learned Cheyenne word, *ne-a'eshe*—and wonder where Grey Eagle was.

At last the parade of people and gifts ended, as did the parade of wooden bowls and plates—each containing something to eat—that were pushed at her from all sides. Jubal and Raven's Heart wandered off to speak to some of the men and smoke, while Little Leaf and several of the women checked the numerous bowls and platters and pots of food, leaving Diana alone with Sparrow and Sweet Water. Content in every way except one—Grey Eagle had not yet appeared—she relaxed against the backrest and watched the gathering.

Now that the last of the daylight had vanished from the western sky, several fires had been lit in the immediate area, providing light and warmth against the chilly night. All around the blazes sat families on robes and skins, eating, drinking, sharing, talking, laughing—just like a Sunday church picnic back in St. Louis, Diana thought, except that the people dressed in a different manner and spoke a different language.

Then he was there, directly in front of her. Diana knew it

was him before she raised her gaze to meet his, even though she had never before seen the beaded dress leggings he wore, the red breechclout, the elaborately decorated war shirt. Strands of his clean, brushed hair danced on the cool breeze, and he did not break eye contact as he hunkered down in front of her. His gaze roamed over her. Diana self-consciously touched the feather ornament Sparrow had tied in her hair, then the shell earring that dangled from her ear.

Unable to stand his silent, intense perusal one moment longer, she snapped, "Well?"

"You are beautiful, Diana Murdoch." He reached out and lifted her chin so that he could again look into her eyes. "Beautiful."

"Thank you, Mr. Beaudine," she murmured shyly. "So are you."

Sparrow giggled, as did Sweet Water, and Diana pulled away from Grey Eagle's hand. How could she have said something so stupid? Surely he would think her unattractively forward. Surely he would become only more arrogant.

"Thank you, Miss Murdoch." There was no hint of teasing or cockiness in Grey Eagle's voice—only warmth. He settled down cross-legged in front of her, and she worked up the courage to look at him.

"How are you enjoying your evening?" Grey Eagle asked her.

Grateful for the casual question, Diana responded, "Everyone has been very kind. And overly generous." She waved a hand at the pile of gifts, around which a fat black-and-white puppy sniffed, and at the mare tied beyond.

"I told you Sparrow's people would want to reward you."

"I know, and I'm grateful, but it wasn't necessary."

"It was to them." He accepted the filled bowl Sparrow handed him with a smile of thanks and set it aside. The puppy immediately lost interest in the pile of Diana's gifts and nosed its way closer to the bowl. "I have gifts for you, as well," Grey Eagle said as he gently pushed the puppy away from his bowl.

Suddenly uncomfortable again, Diana shook her head.

"Please don't. There is no need." Nor was it appropriate, she thought woefully. An unmarried woman did not accept gifts from an unmarried man unless there was an understanding between them—a much deeper and more intimate understanding than that which existed between her and Grey Eagle, an understanding which both parties assumed would lead to marriage.

As if he'd read her thoughts, Grey Eagle said, "You are with the Cheyenne now, Miss Murdoch. You must follow their ways. It would be considered very poor manners on my part not to reward the person who saved the life of my beloved niece." He held out to her something wrapped in a soft pelt.

Her heart pounding, Diana whispered miserably, "I can't." The gift hovered between them, balanced on his hand.

Grey Eagle's expression became shuttered and frozen.

Sparrow grabbed her arm. "You offer great insult to my uncle, in front of the entire village, if you do not accept his gifts," she whispered anxiously.

Stricken, Diana instantly took the offered package, glancing around as she did. Sparrow was correct about one thing—the eyes of the village were indeed upon her, and the comfortable sounds of talk had disappeared. "*Ne-a'eshe,* Mr. Beaudine," she said loud enough for those on the closest robes to hear. The murmurs of talk rose again. She leaned forward, fighting the urge to grab his forearm. "Forgive me," she pleaded in a whisper. "I come from a different world, one where my accepting your gift is most inappropriate. You must understand that this is very difficult for me."

His harsh expression softened a little as he pointed to the pile of other gifts. "You accepted those with no hesitation. My gift is no different."

"You're wrong." Diana straightened her spine. "I accepted those gifts most reluctantly, first of all, and second, your gift is indeed different."

He frowned in bewilderment. "Why? I thank you for saving my niece, as they did."

How was she to explain that his gift was different from the others because her feelings for him were different? How was she to explain that he was special to her, which made accepting his gift even more inappropriate? She could not.

With a sigh, Diana gave up. "I accept your thanks, Mr. Beaudine. You are most welcome." She stroked the pelt that covered something hard and rather heavy, amazed at the incredible softness of the fur, then pulled it away from Grey Eagle's gift. A book rested in her hands. She turned the leather-bound cover to the firelight and read the gold-embossed title. *The Three Musketeers, by Alexandre Dumas, translated from the French, 1848.* Wonderingly, she looked at him. "You would give this up?"

Grey Eagle shrugged. "I treasure the book, but I treasure my niece far more. It is a fitting gift—one treasure for another."

Deeply touched, Diana caressed the soft leather cover. "I shall treasure the book now, although I, too, treasure your niece more." She smiled at Sparrow, who in turn beamed at both her and at Grey Eagle.

"There is one more thing I would give you," Grey Eagle said, snatching the pup away from his bowl once more. He held the squirming puppy out to Diana. "She is yours, to watch over you and protect you."

With a glad cry, Diana accepted the puppy and cuddled it against her chest. "She's beautiful."

"You *do* like dogs," Grey Eagle stated in an uncertain tone.

"Oh, yes." Diana buried her face in the puppy's soft fur. "I love dogs, but have never been able to have one of my own, not even as a child. My mother wouldn't allow dogs in the house, and when I moved with my father to Fort Laramie, he felt it best not to have one in the surgery." She held the puppy up and examined her in the firelight. "She really is a pretty girl. Thank you, Mr. Beaudine." Then a thought occurred to her, and she turned to Sweet Water. "How do you and Jubal feel about a puppy in your lodge?"

Sweet Water smiled. "It all right. Grey Eagle ask first."

Grey Eagle reached out to scratch the puppy's ears. "She's a mongrel, a camp dog. But she's smart. If you work with her, I think she'll make you a real good dog."

"I'm certain we'll get along very well." Diana touched her

nose to the puppy's cold, wet one, and was rewarded with a warm lick. She giggled. "What shall I name you, you little scamp?"

"Wait few days," Sweet Water suggested. "Little one's name come to you." She shifted as if trying to get comfortable.

"Are you all right?" Diana asked.

"Oh, yes. But I will be happy when baby is born."

Out of the darkness suddenly came the pounding of a drum. Other drums joined in and many voices raised in chanting songs. People moved back from the fires, while several men formed circles around the flames.

"Now the dancing begins," Grey Eagle explained. He picked up his bowl, and the puppy squirmed from Diana's grasp to sit expectantly at Grey Eagle's side.

"You eat, then dance, Grey Eagle," Sweet Water urged.

"Not until his leg is more healed," Diana said firmly. She turned her gaze to him. "I want to check the wounds tonight before you sleep."

"Yes, Doctor," he said around a mouthful of meat.

Diana touched the book in her lap and smiled, feeling blessed by the good friends who surrounded her. Surely her sad existence at Fort Laramie had been in another life.

From the shadows of a nearby tipi, Black Moon stared at the group on the robe with hate-filled eyes. She did not like the friendly manner between Grey Eagle and the white woman. The white woman brought trouble, of that Black Moon was certain.

At first, when she saw the bruises on the woman's face, she'd assumed Grey Eagle caused them, that he'd captured her, perhaps as a slave. Hope had flared high—perhaps he meant to present the slave to her as his wedding gift, so that she wouldn't have to work so hard after they married and set up their own lodge.

Then she saw Jubal Sage and his wife greet the woman with joy, saw Sparrow hug her, and Black Moon had known instantly who the woman was. Di-an-ah, Sparrow's rescuer, the doctor's daughter, the Eagle Woman.

The white woman had stood up to her, had held her pale, bruised body with pride, which had angered Black Moon greatly. And the mark on the woman's shoulder had spooked her, but only for a moment. The mark meant nothing. Even if it did, the mark would not stop Black Moon. Grey Eagle would be her mate before the summer's end. She whirled about and stalked away.

Calls the Wind watched her go, then followed at a safe distance. He was profoundly disappointed when Black Moon entered the lodge of her brother, Two Bears, and closed the skin flap. He would not be able to dance for her tonight, nor watch her dance.

He slapped his thigh in frustration, then instantly forced himself to be calm. He had waited a long time for her. He could wait a little longer.

Still, he was growing impatient. The love charms he'd purchased from Buffalo Woman had not yet taken effect, but the medicine woman assured him they would work, given time.

Although he had already given years, Calls the Wind would give a little more time—but only until the end of the summer. If Black Moon was not more receptive to his cautious overtures by then, he would act with greater force, with charms or without. She was meant to be his; the Old Ones had told him. And the Old Ones never lied.

Chapter Twenty-One

Dying firelight flickered on the hide walls of Jubal's lodge as Diana lay wide awake and stared upward. The feast had ended well over an hour ago, and all in the encampment—except those guarding the horse herd, Grey Eagle explained—had been in their beds since soon after that, but she could not sleep, weary though she was. Even the energetic puppy was asleep, curled up near her feet.

Jubal and Grey Eagle had helped her carry her gifts back to the lodge, then Grey Eagle had left to see to her new mare while Sweet Water helped her store her things in various nooks and crannies. Later, an examination of Grey Eagle's leg showed that his wounds were healing with astonishing speed and seemed to cause him but little discomfort. He'd insisted upon taking the feathered ornament from her hair, then once more brushed her hair, which had the effect of lulling her to the brink of sleep. She'd removed her moccasins and leggings and gladly crawled under her new buffalo robe—and then she'd learned that the Cheyenne generally slept in the nude, as was evidenced by her companions calmly stripping off all they wore before they entered their own beds. Remembering how she'd wished that Grey Eagle would wear more to bed those nights in the wilderness, Diana now knew that he had made a concession for her when he'd worn his breechclout.

She simply did not feel comfortable sleeping naked in such small quarters shared with three other people—one of whom was a father figure, another, a man for whom she felt a shameful carnal interest. Indeed, she would never forget the sight of Grey Eagle's gloriously naked backside, which she had earlier glimpsed before she realized what was happening and turned her flaming face to the wall. Now she knew what his breechclout hid, at least on one side, and it was as magnificent as the rest of his body.

Preserving her modesty as best she could under the cover of the robe, Diana had reluctantly struggled out of the deerskin dress, neatly folded it, and laid the garment near her head, as Sweet Water had done with her dress. Then she had smuggled her clean chemise and drawers under the robe and squirmed into them, causing the puppy to shift its position until the tiny creature yipped in frustration. Now afraid to move for fear of further disturbing the puppy—and so her companions—Diana lay still, watching the shadows on the hide walls, listening to the wind blow through the trees outside, thinking over her incredible day.

She wished that her father could have been with her. Gideon would have been as fascinated by the Cheyenne village as she was. It had been her father who had instilled in her the basic regard with which she held the Plains Indians. He had explained that, while different from white civilization, the Indian cultures were very developed in their own way, and worked quite successfully, providing their people with a comfortable living from the world around them, and giving them a spiritual belief system that deserved respect even if one did not embrace it.

The sounds of shifting came from Jubal's bed, followed by a low moan of discomfort. Sweet Water whispered a response to Jubal's concerned question. They spoke in Cheyenne, so Diana did not understand what they said, but she suspected that Sweet Water was very uncomfortable, if not in the beginning stages of labor. The child would come soon.

Diana took the risk of turning on her side and faced the fire.

The puppy did not protest, much to her relief. She rested her cheek on one hand and stared at the coals, marvelling at how snug and warm the interior of the lodge was. Then she felt a heat of a different kind, and raised her gaze to see that Grey Eagle also faced the fire, and watched her intently over the coals.

The look in his eyes took her breath away and seared her to her soul. He brought a forefinger to his mouth and kissed the tip, then pointed the finger at her. As if his mouth itself had touched her with the soft, enticing warmth she remembered so well, her heart leapt against her breast and the familiar fire ignited deep in her belly.

Oh, Lord.

Diana pressed her fist to her mouth to stifle a moan of her own. She didn't need Jubal asking if she was all right, for there was no way to explain to him why she was not. She'd known it would be a mistake to stay in the same lodge as Grey Eagle. Determined to sleep, she turned onto her stomach and buried her face in the soft buffalo robe, her hands clasped together under her chin. But the image of his eyes would not leave her; the fire from his airborne kiss would not die. Before she could consider the wisdom of such an action, Diana pressed a forefinger to her own lips and, without looking, thrust her hand out from under the robe, her finger pointed in Grey Eagle's direction. Then she again clasped her hands together and turned her face to the wall, her eyes squeezed shut, not knowing—and not caring, she insisted to herself—whether or not he still watched, and so received her 'kiss.'

Grey Eagle smiled when she pointed her finger at him, knowing that she 'kissed' him in return. Whether she wanted to admit it or not, Diana Murdoch was drawn to him. And to his mother's people.

He'd been proud of her today.

She had responded with courage and grace to situations that many—most—white people would have quaked at.

Sparrow told him of the incident at the bathing pool, and he knew he'd have to explain the situation with Black Moon as soon as possible. Would Diana care that another woman wanted him? He hoped she cared.

Hell.

He hoped she cared about him, period.

She had looked so beautiful to him tonight, in her deerskin dress, with her lovely hair down, Cheyenne ornaments in her ears and in her hair. He'd watched her from the shadows for a long time, saw that she treated those to whom she had been introduced with courtesy and kindness. She hugged small children, and thanked people for their gifts in their own language.

Yes, he was very proud of her—inappropriately so, he knew, because she was not really his woman. Not yet.

Diana's only stumble had been with him, when she would not at first accept his gift. Why had she hesitated? He was familiar with the customs of the white man, knew that an unmarried woman could not accept a gift from an unmarried man unless they were officially courting. But Jubal had explained to her the custom of the Cheyenne regarding gifts. She knew the custom, yet hesitated only over his gifts. She'd said his gifts were different from the rest.

They were different because she had special feelings for him.

Grey Eagle turned on his back, his hands under his head, a smile tugging at his mouth, and changed his mind about one thing.

Diana Murdoch *was* his woman, although she didn't know it.

By the end of the summer, she would be his wife.

Diana's first full day in the Cheyenne village started very early, when the morning was rent with yips and calls. She was instantly awake, her eyes wide, and she hurriedly turned over to see Grey Eagle's backside—now thankfully covered with his breechclout—disappear through the entry flap. The puppy scrambled after him, barking excitedly. A quick look around showed her that Jubal was also gone. Sweet Water sat on the edge of her bed, the buffalo robe at her waist, her heavy breasts resting on her big belly. Shouts echoed outside.

"Are we under attack?" Diana asked, her heart in her throat. Sweet Water looked at her, puzzled. "No."

"Where did the men go?" Diana sat up and pushed her tangled hair back over her shoulders.

"To bath, in the river. Each morning, the men and boys of the village take bath."

"Why don't they use the warm pool?"

"They do. But river water cold, make them strong." Sweet Water grimaced and put a hand at her lower back, as if it ached.

Diana was at her side in an instant. "What is it?"

"Back hurt. Belly tight." Fear flashed in Sweet Water's large brown eyes.

"That's nothing to worry about," Diana said soothingly. "You are in the first stages of labor, Sweet Water. Your child is on its way." She pushed long black hair away from the sides of Sweet Water's face. "You're in for a painful day, dear friend."

"I not care about pain, Di-an-ah." An incredible sadness came over Sweet Water's round face. "My mother die when I born. I want not to die." She patted her belly. "Baby need mother."

That explained Sweet Water's fear of childbirth, Diana thought. The Cheyenne woman was usually so stoic and strong about everything she faced that Diana had been puzzled when Grey Eagle told her that Sweet Water needed her, especially when she knew there were midwives in the tribe. Now she more fully understood his determination to bring her to the village, and any lingering resentment she may have felt toward him for virtually abducting her disappeared in the face of Sweet Water's understandable terror.

"You will not die, Sweet Water," Diana assured her, with the silent hope that she spoke the truth. "It's true that childbirth can be dangerous, for both mother and baby, but you are young and healthy and strong. You will be fine."

Sweet Water gasped and grabbed her belly. Diana placed her hand on the stretched brown skin; the muscles underneath were rock hard. "You're having a contraction," she explained. "It will pass soon, and in a few minutes you'll have another. As the day goes on, the contractions will occur closer and closer together, until the child is pushed out of your body."

Jubal stuck his head in the opening, then eased himself inside. He wore nothing but a breechclout, and water dripped from his beard and hair. Diana was extremely thankful that she wore her drawers and chemise from the night before, because she would not have taken the time to dress when she saw that Sweet Water was in distress.

"How is she?" Jubal asked as he came to take his wife's hand.

"Your child is coming, Jubal."

"Oh, lordy, oh, lordy." Jubal kissed the back of Sweet Water's hand. "You'll be fine, honey. Diana's here, and she ain't gonna let nothin' happen to you." He stroked her hair and leaned his forehead against hers.

Diana was shocked to hear genuine fear in Jubal's voice, and she was relieved when Grey Eagle came in a moment later, also dripping, also wearing only a breechclout. "The baby is coming," she told him in a soft voice. He nodded.

"I want to walk," Sweet Water announced.

"Then you shall walk," said Diana. "The best thing is to follow the dictates of your body. It knows what to do."

She and Jubal helped Sweet Water pull her dress over her head, then guided her to the opening, where Grey Eagle waited to offer his aid. He assisted Sweet Water out and to stand, while Jubal hurriedly pulled on leggings, moccasins, and a plain buckskin shirt. He looked at Diana, and, without warning, pulled her into his arms for a fierce hug.

"I'm so damned glad you're here, girl. Her mama died birthin' her, and we're both scared the same'll happen to her."

Full of sympathy, Diana patted his shoulder. "Everything will be all right."

"God, I hope so. I don't know what I'd do without her, Diana." He released her and hurried to the opening. " 'Scuse my swearin'," he called as he slipped outside.

Grey Eagle returned. "Jubal will walk with her." He added a few sticks to the fire coals. "What can I do?"

Diana pulled her tangled hair to the back of her neck, again very glad that she at least wore her underclothes. "Most likely she will be in labor for several hours, which will give us time to prepare." She looked at him. "Surely the Cheyenne have their birthing traditions. I'd like to know what they are."

"I don't know much," Grey Eagle answered, "and certainly not the details, but usually the mother's women relatives come to help, and I know they use a post of some kind for the mother to cling to, and they spread straw about."

"Are the priests or medicine men in attendance?"

"No. Birthing a baby is strictly in the women's domain."

"Is the father present?"

"Not that I know of."

"Very well." Diana reached for her folded deerskin dress and pulled it over her head. "Will you please ask Sweet Water's female relatives to come?"

"She doesn't have any." Grey Eagle tied one of his leggings at his waist. "That's another reason why she and Jubal are so scared. Except for each other, they are both alone in the world." He pulled on his other legging and secured it.

Diana frowned. "Are there midwives we can call?"

"I'll ask Little Leaf what she suggests." He straightened the buffalo robes on his bed, then, with an encouraging smile, ducked back through the door, leaving Diana alone.

She pulled her dress down over her hips, straightened Jubal's bed, then her own, and took up Grey Eagle's brush. As she worked the tangles from her hair, Diana thought about the coming child and offered a silent, heartfelt prayer for the well-being of both mother and baby, then added a prayer for herself. "Watch over me, Papa," she whispered. "Guide my hands; help me know what to do if anything goes wrong."

Little Leaf and her sister, Blue Corn Woman, came with Sparrow to help with the birthing. The Cheyenne women cleared away Diana's bed, then set up a curious, waist-high framework of thick poles and spread armfuls of fresh meadow grasses around it. Little Leaf explained, with Sparrow translating, that Sweet Water would kneel on the grasses, hold on to the poles for support, and in that position deliver her baby into Diana's waiting hands.

To Diana, the position seemed an uncomfortable one for Sweet Water, but she did not argue. Little Leaf and Blue Corn Woman would assist and offer encouragement, Sparrow would be available to run errands, and Jubal would be kept busy outside, tending the fire and helping the women who would cook for the delivery team.

When Jubal brought Sweet Water back to the lodge with the nervous announcement that her water had broken, Little Leaf took over with the calm authority of a commanding general and gave everyone their instructions. There were no complications, and, late that afternoon, Sweet Water was delivered of a healthy daughter.

Diana looked down at the squirming infant, who cried so angrily that her tiny face turned red, and felt the same surge of love and wonder she'd always felt when helping Gideon with a delivery. She and Sparrow followed Little Leaf's instructions and cleaned the baby, then gently greased and powdered her before wrapping her in small, soft robes. Sweet Water delivered the placenta, was cleaned and praised, then helped into her own bed, where Diana laid the infant next to her.

An exhausted smile curved Sweet Water's mouth as she smoothed the thatch of black hair on her daughter's head. "*Nahtona,*" she whispered. "My daughter."

Little Leaf called out to Jubal, who hurried to his wife's side. After a tender reunion that brought tears to Diana's eyes, he carefully picked up his daughter and eased back out the entry with her. Curious, Diana watched through the opening as Jubal proudly held the bundle of baby and robes high in the air. A series of cheers and shouts rang throughout the village, and, a minute later, Jubal handed his daughter through the door to Diana, clambered through himself, and took the baby back to Sweet Water, where he settled on the bed next to his wife and daughter.

In no time at all, it seemed to Diana, she, Little Leaf, Blue
Corn Woman, and Sparrow had Sweet Water's lodge put to
rights. They all left to give the Sage family some time alone
together, and found that a small feast had been laid out in front
of the lodge for them and for their families. Diana realized that
she was ravenous. But before she ate, she wanted to wash up,
and so made her way to the creek.

The cold water felt good on her face, neck, and arms. She
sat on the grassy bank and redid the single long braid that held
her hair back, then tied it with the piece of fringe Grey Eagle
had given her. The late May afternoon was cool and breezy,
the sky dotted with fluffy white clouds, the river making its
lazy way along the bottom of the rise. The beauty and peace
of the place crept into her heart, where they mingled with the
deep love and satisfaction Diana felt over the birth of Sweet
Water's daughter. She sighed in contentment.

"Why the sigh?"

Diana started as Grey Eagle dropped to sit beside her, then
giggled when an energetic ball of black-and-white fur barrelled
into her lap. "It was a happy sigh," she explained, picking up
the puppy for a quick hug. "A new life has come into the
world, this particular spot is as beautiful as the afternoon is,
and a delicious meal awaits me. What more could I want?"
She looked at Grey Eagle and could not help but notice that
his eyes appeared very green, that his expression was relaxed,
that his face was very handsome. *I could want you!* her mind
shouted. Would she ever get to the point where *his* beauty did
not take her breath away?

"Thank you for helping with the baby," he said.

"Truthfully, Mr. Beaudine, I did little, and then only when
instructed by Little Leaf. There were no complications, thank
God, and I certainly cannot take credit for that."

"Your presence offered great comfort to both Sweet Water
and Jubal. For their sake, it is good that you were here."

"It's you who got me here, and just in time, too." She set
the puppy down, and the little one promptly stuck her nose to
the ground and wandered off, exploring some fascinating scent.
Suddenly shy, Diana plucked at the grasses near her hip. "I

did not know until this morning that Sweet Water had an unusual fear of childbirth. I'm glad now that you would not allow me to return to the fort.''

"Ah. So I am forgiven for abducting you."

The teasing note in his voice annoyed Diana, but it was hard to hold on to her self-righteous irritation when he was correct in what he said. "Yes, although I wish you had not been quite so forceful and arrogant about it.''

"You would not have taken me seriously had I not been forceful.''

"That's probably true," she allowed.

"Then I would have had to tie you to the horse.''

"I know I really had no choice but to go with you, Mr. Beaudine," Diana said crossly. "There is no need to belabor the point.''

"You're right." Grey Eagle leaned closer and placed a light kiss on her cheek.

Thrilled and hopeful, Diana turned to him, her lips parted, her heart hammering, when a series of yips and howls echoed off the rise across the creek. She jumped and looked about with wild eyes. "This time are we being attacked?''

"No. We have visitors. They are being welcomed, as we were yesterday." Grey Eagle got to his feet and held down a hand to her.

Diana allowed him to pull her up, loving the feel of her hand in his, but he released her at once. She hid her disappointment by brushing the grass and dead leaves from her skirt. "Does the tribe often have visitors?''

"Not often. But these visitors I expected.''

With a hand shielding her eyes from the sun, Diana searched the area. "I still don't see them.''

Grey Eagle put one hand on her shoulder and pointed with the other. Now Diana made out two men on horseback—both wearing hats, which indicated they were most likely white men—surrounded by shouting Cheyenne warriors. "Who are they?''

"My brothers.''

Puzzled by his solemn, almost angry tone, Diana turned to

look at him. "Joseph and Orion? Aren't you happy to see them?"

Grey Eagle strode off toward the new arrivals. She stared after him as he said over his shoulder, "Not if they've come with the intention of taking you back to the fort."

Chapter Twenty-Two

Diana caught up to Grey Eagle. As she walked beside him, one glance at his dark expression convinced her that it was best to keep quiet for a while.

What if Joseph and Orion had come with the intention Grey Eagle feared? What would she do? Sweet Water's baby was safely born. There was no reason for her to remain longer in the village. She'd always said that she'd leave as soon as the babe came. Now she could, and without asking Jubal to leave his wife's side. Of course, Grey Eagle had insisted that he would return her to the fort when the time came, but Diana doubted the wisdom of subjecting herself to perhaps irresistible temptation by spending another several days alone in the wilderness with him. Travelling back to Fort Laramie with Joseph and Orion was the perfect solution.

So why did she not feel happy?

They approached the excited group surrounding the brothers.

''Grey Eagle!'' Joseph raised one hand in the air in greeting, then stepped down from the saddle. Orion did likewise.

''I figured to find you here, Diana,'' Orion said as he drew her into his arms for a friendly hug. ''It's good to know for certain that you're safe.'' He pulled back and looked at her face. For an instant he frowned, then smiled again.

"Hello, Orion," Diana said warmly. "Don't worry about this.'' She touched the fading bruise on her cheek. "I have been well cared for.'' She turned to Joseph and held out a hand. "Joseph. How good it is to see you both again. When did you get back to the fort?"

Joseph grabbed her hand and kissed it, his mustache tickling her skin, then released her. If either he or Orion found it odd that she wore the clothes of the Cheyenne, neither indicated so.

"Later that same day you left, Diana." Joseph took off his hat and ran a hand through his shoulder-length hair. "We were sure sorry to hear about your father. We all knew the time was coming, and our women feel bad that they couldn't be with you.''

"I would have welcomed their company. Thank God I had Sparrow.''

"Now, this is a story I want to hear—how Sparrow came to be with you." Keeping his arm around Diana's shoulders, Orion pinned his gaze on Grey Eagle. "You don't seem surprised to see us, little brother."

"I'm not."

"You don't seem to be all that happy to see us, either," commented Joseph.

"I'm always glad to see my family, Joseph. However, I may not be glad to know the reason you have come."

Grey Eagle stood a little apart, his face expressionless in the closed Cheyenne way Diana had come to know so well. It struck her how much the brothers looked alike—especially Orion and Grey Eagle, with their black hair and green eyes. Joseph's brown hair, brown eyes, and thick mustache set him apart from his brothers, but there was no question he was a Beaudine. All three wore buckskin shirts and leggings, all three were tall, proud, and handsome.

All three were on edge.

"A feast is spread out at Jubal's lodge to celebrate the birth of his daughter this afternoon," Diana said. "We will talk when you have eaten and rested."

"Good idea," Joseph said, and set his hat back on his head. "So Jubal has a little girl. I'll bet he's as proud and as happy as can be. How is Sweet Water?"

"Also happy, and tired. Everything went well."

Raven's Heart gathered the reins of the weary horses and took the animals away, while Diana led the brothers toward Jubal's lodge, wondering what could possibly be wrong between the usually close-knit Beaudines.

Grey Eagle trailed his brothers and Diana. He watched her walk, the tail of her long dark braid and the fringe on her dress moving in time with her swaying hips and graceful step. From the back, she looked like a Cheyenne.

Cheyenne or white, she was beautiful.

His heart lurched and his stomach grabbed, and, for just a moment, his eyes closed against the onslaught of feeling that engulfed him.

How he wanted her.

Then he opened his eyes and his gaze fell upon his brothers. He loved them to the depths of his soul, as he did his sisters and his stepmother, and all the other members of the extended and growing Beaudine family. But he knew that Joseph and Orion had come today on the Army's business, as well as for Diana's sake—and his.

He had no doubt that his brothers would believe his side of the story, would defend him against any accusations the Army might make, would defend him to the death if necessary. He was not so certain that they would not insist upon taking Diana back to the fort with them.

In fairness to Joseph and Orion, Grey Eagle granted that he had no idea what the Army thought happened that day at Bridger's cabin. His brothers knew and understood the aftermath of that day—in the eyes of the Army—far better than he did.

But he would not give up Diana.

Not even to his beloved and trusted brothers.

Not even if she wanted to go with them.

"We need to know what happened at the Bridger cabin," Joseph said quietly, breaking the congenial mood among the group surrounding the fire in front of Jubal's lodge. Food had been shared, as had the general news: Everyone who made the trip to St. Louis was back at Fort Laramie and doing well, Henry Jedediah thrived, Annie Rose and Joseph expected a baby in about six months, Sweet Water's sleepy daughter was welcomed and exclaimed over, heartfelt congratulations were offered to the practically strutting Jubal, Sparrow was tearfully and lovingly embraced by her newly arrived uncles.

Now, all had returned to their lodges except Jubal, the three Beaudine brothers, and Diana. Darkness had fallen and a cool wind blew, making Diana wish for the protective cover of her new buffalo robe, which was inside on her bed. Grey Eagle sat cross-legged at her side, but no warmth was to be found in his somber, guarded demeanor.

Diana knew that Joseph had been a captain in the Army and was familiar with military procedures, so it was only natural that he ask the questions, since the two men who died that fateful day at the Bridger cabin were soldiers. "We need to know," he repeated, his voice still calm.

Jubal touched a firebrand to his pipe and drew deeply. "I wouldn't mind hearin' the story from start to finish myself," he said around the stem as smoke puffed from his mouth.

The camp was quiet around them, and Diana idly wondered if everyone was still recovering from the late and exuberant festivities of the night before. But there was no putting off the necessary unpleasantness any longer. "It all started with me," she said, "so I'll start the story. Several days ago—" She stopped and looked blankly at Joseph. "What day is this?"

"Friday, May twenty-third," he supplied.

"Thank you." Diana shook her head. "I've lost all track of the days. It seems like last week was a lifetime ago." She took a deep breath. "A week ago—Friday morning, it was—an

Indian messenger came to my uncle's trading post with the message that you"—she nodded at Jubal—"had been mauled by a bear and awaited my help at the Bridger cabin."

"Eagle told me that part of the story. I wanna get my hands around the throat of that lyin' cur," Jubal said darkly.

"Did you recognize the man?" Joseph asked.

"No. That bothered me, but I wouldn't take the chance that he wasn't telling the truth." Her gaze fell on Jubal, and her throat thightened. "I'd just lost my father. But even if I hadn't, I couldn't lose you, too. I would have gone through hell itself to help you."

Jubal reached over to pat her hand. "From what I hear, you about did, girl."

Diana shrugged and took another steadying breath. "As it turned out, the only person at the fort that morning who knew the location of the Bridger cabin was Lieutenant Ransom Thatcher. There had been trouble between him and me in the past—"

Joseph interrupted her. "What kind of trouble?"

"I refused his suit." Diana felt Grey Eagle's gaze on her, but did not look up at him. "The lieutenant did not respond favorably to my request that he leave me alone until my father asked Colonel MacKay to intervene."

"So the man harbored a grudge against you." Joseph thoughtfully stroked his mustache.

"Apparently. He hid it well, for months. I had misgivings about going with him to the cabin, but that day there was no other choice. I later learned that it was all a carefully planned ruse, devised by Thatcher and my uncle. They waited until a time when none of my allies was around, then sent the false message." She nodded at Orion and Joseph. "You two, Captain Rutledge, Colonel MacKay, even Privates Dawson and Ross—none were available. I did not know Privates Sedley and Grimes before that morning."

"So the three of you went to the cabin," said Joseph.

"Yes. Of course, Jubal was not there, nor was there any indication that he ever had been. A storm came upon us and we decided to wait it out." Diana gave a humorless laugh. "I have the desire for a cup of tea to thank for my first escape."

At Joseph's questioning look, she continued. "The men were outside with the horses, and my tin of tea was in my saddlebag. I went to get it, and overheard Thatcher order the two soldiers to stay out of the cabin, no matter what they heard."

"Such as your cries for help," Joseph put in, his jaw tight.

Diana nodded grimly. "He told them he'd marry me, even if he had to ruin me and my reputation to do it. I waited to hear no more, and ran into the forest."

Beside her, Grey Eagle stiffened. His hands, which rested on his spread knees, closed into fists, but he said nothing.

"You were caught and dragged back to the creek," said Orion.

"Yes." Diana stared at him. "How did you know?"

"I read the sign."

Orion Beaudine was known as the Hunter for a good reason, Diana thought admiringly.

"What happened next?" Joseph prompted.

"Private Sedley came to my aid, or rather, he tried to. Thatcher struck him and he fell into the water. He hit his head hard, and broke his neck." Diana swallowed the lump that had grown in her throat. It was difficult to relive that horrible day, that poor young soldier's death.

"So Sedley's death was an accident."

"Yes. But Thatcher felt no remorse for it. He blamed me, said I had ruined all his careful plans because I fought him. I got away from him again, and that's when your brother found me. Grey Eagle hid me from Thatcher and Grimes, then brought me here." Diana heaved a sigh, relieved that the story was told.

"Was your party attacked by hostile Indians?" Orion asked.

Diana frowned. "Grey Eagle and I had some trouble with a Ute hunting party, but that was a few days later."

"Were you attacked at the cabin?"

"By Indians, no. Where would you get such an idea?"

"Private Grimes told the colonel that you were attacked, that the Indians killed Thatcher and Sedley, and kidnapped you," Orion explained. "He saw you being taken away, on an Appaloosa stallion, with your hands tied."

"My hands were not tied!" Diana insisted. "Nor were we attacked. There was no one else there but those I've mentioned. Private Grimes is lying."

"We figured he was," said Joseph. "We just don't know why."

For the first time since the questioning had begun, Grey Eagle spoke. "Because he shot his lieutenant and left the man for dead."

Joseph stared at him. "Grimes shot Thatcher?"

Grey Eagle nodded once, curtly. "In self-defense. Thatcher intended to leave no witnesses, even though his killing Sedley was an accident. He assaulted Miss Murdoch with intent to rape, and both soldiers knew it."

"It appeared that Thatcher shot himself in the head."

"He did. His wounds were agonizing, and mortal. Nothing could be done for him. It was I who put the pistol within his reach." Grey Eagle paused. "Grimes told Thatcher he was going to take the horses and desert. How did you find him?"

Joseph shrugged. "I guess he didn't have time to get far. He was discovered heading south rather than back toward the fort. He claimed he got lost." He fixed his stern gaze on Grey Eagle. "Why didn't you take Diana to the fort?"

Grey Eagle's jaw tightened and his back stiffened. A long moment passed before he answered. "Because I'd promised Sweet Water and Sparrow I would bring her here. I was on my way to the fort to get her when I came upon the cabin."

"Sweet Water's baby was coming," Diana hastily added. She felt very protective of Grey Eagle, for it seemed to her that Joseph was badgering him.

Joseph kept his eyes on Grey Eagle. "Two soldiers were dead, and, judging by the bruises on her face, Diana was battered. She needed medical attention, and you needed to report to Colonel MacKay."

"No," Grey Eagle snapped. "I saw to Diana's hurts, and I needed to get her here in time for the birth of Sweet Water's baby. I am not in the Army, Joseph. I did not need to report to the colonel."

Joseph ran his hands through his hair in frustration. "It would have helped the situation if you'd gone to the fort right away, Eagle.''

Grey Eagle rose to his feet and stood stiff and forbidding. ''I've told you what happened. Do with the information what you will.'' He strode off into the night.

Confused and troubled, Diana watched him go, then turned back to Joseph. ''Surely no one suspects that Grey Eagle had anything to do with what happened.''

''No one but us.'' Orion pointed at Joseph, then at his own chest. ''I knew George Washington's track the instant I saw it, so I knew he'd been there. I figured he'd taken you.''

Horrified, Diana stared at him. ''You didn't tell the colonel that. Please tell me you didn't. Tell me that you didn't back up that lying private's story.''

''I told no one anything, except Joseph,'' Orion said soothingly. ''We came here without making any kind of report. I didn't want to say anything until I had all the facts.''

Diana's shoulders slumped in relief. Now she understood why Grey Eagle had viewed the arrival of his brothers with such trepidation. She'd never considered that he might be blamed for the deaths of the soldiers; evidently, he had considered it very seriously.

''Diana, there's something I have to ask you,'' Joseph said gently.

She raised her gaze to him, suddenly wary. ''Ask.''

''Did Grey Eagle force you to come here?''

Her heart started pounding. ''No. I came freely.''

''We need to know the entire truth,'' Orion put in, his tone as low and kind as Joseph's was. ''For all our sakes, but especially for Grey Eagle's.''

''He didn't force me,'' Diana said firmly.

''So, after a terrible, exhausting ordeal, you didn't want to return to the fort,'' said Joseph. ''Instead, you embarked upon a dangerous three-day journey with a man you didn't know, to come to a large Cheyenne village.''

Diana stared down at her hands. ''He didn't force me.''

''Did he threaten you?''

''No!'' She looked up at Joseph then, saw the concern in

his eyes, and she could not withhold the truth from him. "Grey Eagle wasn't threatening as much as he was, well, *determined*. He had given his word, and nothing would steer him from his path. He didn't force me. He merely pointed out that he *could* force me if need be. I came with him willingly."

"He gave you no choice," Joseph said harshly.

"I came willingly," Diana repeated, more forceful herself. "Your brother saved me from brutal rape and certain death, Joseph, and I will always be grateful to him for that. He treated me with kindness and concern during the journey here, and continues to do so. I have no complaint against him, nor will I tolerate any being made from other quarters."

Joseph's stern expression relaxed. "Very well. I'll ask you no more about it."

Throughout the entire discussion, Jubal had calmly puffed on his pipe. Now he pulled the stem from his mouth and spoke. "The little one's been safely born, Diana. Will you be goin' back to the fort with Joe and the Hunter?"

Diana swallowed a groan. Why did Jubal have to bring that up now? She turned to him. "I don't know."

Her answer seemed to surprise both Beaudines. "We assumed you would be," Orion put in.

"You're welcome to stay with us as long as you like, girl," said Jubal. "I told you that when I asked you to come with me and Sparrow after your pa died."

"Thank you," Diana whispered. She faced Joseph. "When are you leaving?"

"Tomorrow morning, early."

So little time to decide! Diana twisted her hands together. "Can I let you know then?"

"Of course." Joseph looked at her strangely. "Do you like it here among the Cheyenne?"

"So far, I do." She did not add that life in the encampment—even the little she'd experienced—was far better than life with her uncle and aunt had been.

Joseph nodded. "I've always liked it, too."

"And I," Orion added. "Sarah and I spent our first married winter with the Cheyenne."

"She told me," Diana said with a smile. She glanced away, wondering where Grey Eagle was, wanting to go after him, not daring to roam about the encampment by herself. "I'll leave you men to your pipes and tobacco." She scrambled to her feet.

"Sleep well, Diana," Joseph called after her. "We'll talk more in the morning."

"Good night, gentlemen." Diana ducked into the lodge, and heaved a sigh of relief when the hide that covered the entry fell into place and hid her from Joseph Beaudine's probing and too-perceptive eyes.

Chapter Twenty-Three

Grey Eagle came up from under the surface of the waters of the bathing pool to find a tall man standing on the bank. The light of the nearly full moon allowed him to see that it was Orion.

"Howdy, little brother," Orion said quietly, as if he did not want to disturb the peace of the night. "Mind if I join you?"

"Come on in."

Orion stripped and waded into the water. "I love these heated pools. I wish there was one at the fort." The waters closed over his shoulders and he sighed with contentment.

Grey Eagle did not respond. The silence between them grew lengthy, and finally Orion said, "What's going on between you and Joe?"

After a long pause, Grey Eagle said, "Nothing was until today. Today, Joseph seems to have forgotten that he is no longer in the Army." He did not add that the aggressive attitude earlier displayed by Joseph had angered him—that and the accusatory questions.

"He's not being real tactful about it, Eagle, I'll admit, but he's trying to keep you out of trouble with the Army."

"I am not in trouble with the Army."

"We didn't know that for sure until we found out what really happened at the cabin." Orion hesitated. "You still might have some problems, if the colonel finds out you forced Diana Murdoch to come here with you."

Strangely hurt, Grey Eagle stared at him. Had he misjudged Diana so badly? "She told you that?" he asked, careful to keep his tone neutral.

"No."

That one word eased Grey Eagle's bewildering hurt.

Orion continued. "She didn't have to. In fact, she wouldn't. She defends you, little brother, yet she can't lie. Joe and I could read enough between the lines to figure out that you didn't give her a choice about coming."

"I gave my word to Sweet Water and Sparrow."

"And a Beaudine always keeps his word."

"That's right," Grey Eagle snapped, not liking the edge of sarcasm in Orion's voice. "I would not allow Diana to cause me to break my word." He glared at his brother. "What do you want, Orion?"

"I want to understand why you virtually abducted Diana Murdoch, a woman you didn't know before that day at the cabin. It was dangerous, Eagle, and foolish. You're lucky that, for some crazy reason, she likes you enough to protect you." Orion shifted his position in the water so that the moonlight fell more fully on his face. His long black hair swirled in the water around his shoulders. "There were other women here to help with the birthing, so that reason won't justify abduction, even if Sweet Water especially wanted Diana with her. Why did Sparrow want you to bring her?"

Grey Eagle feared the true reason would sound foolish, but he decided to give it anyway. "You know that Diana and her father saved Sparrow from Painted Davy Sikes and Con Horton."

Orion nodded. "Bless them for that. I wish we'd been there when it was discovered who she was. Those two bastards would not have felt too good by the time we finished with them."

"I agree. Anyway, Sparrow stayed with the Murdochs for a couple of months while her broken leg healed. Even after

Gideon's death, Diana took care of her. They became close friends—sisters, almost. When the time came for Sparrow to go home, both she and Jubal begged Diana to go with them. Diana refused, and stayed with her uncle and aunt.''

"She couldn't have been happy there.''

"I'm certain that she was not. Sparrow knew it, too. She told me that if Diana stayed with the MacDonalds, or returned to her mother's home in St. Louis, her spirit would die. Sparrow begged me to bring her back.'' Grey Eagle shrugged. "So I gave my word that I would.''

Orion's eyes narrowed in thought as he studied Grey Eagle. "That's still not enough reason to justify the terrible risk of kidnapping a white woman and bringing her to a Cheyenne encampment. I know you too well, Grey Eagle. So does Joseph. You're holding something back.''

Now was one of the rare times in his life when Grey Eagle silently cursed the close, uncanny connection shared by all of the Beaudine siblings. The dream of Diana as his woman, as his wife, was so precious to him that he did not want to share it with anyone—not even his brothers, who he could trust not only with his life, but with his deepest secrets; his brothers, who were understandably concerned about him.

"Talk to me, little brother,'' Orion softly invited. "Let us help you.''

Grey Eagle scrubbed his hands over his face and gave in. He met Orion's gaze. "Diana is the Woman in the Clouds.''

Orion gaped at him. "The one you've seen in visions since your first vision quest? The one with the Eagle?''

"Yes. She wears the mark of the Eagle on her shoulder, here.'' Grey Eagle touched the place on his own shoulder. "She knows the Spirit of the Eagle. She can call him to her side— I saw her do it. So did the five Ute warriors who attacked us. Diana and the Eagle saved my life that day.'' His words reminded him of his wounded leg, and he bent the knee, pleased that he felt only a twinge of pain from both wounds.

"You couldn't know that when you took her.''

"Sparrow told me of the mark, so I suspected it from the beginning. Then I saw the mark myself. I saw *her,* and I knew.

From that moment on, she was destined to come with me. I would not let her go." He paused, staring at Orion. "I will not let her go now, not with you and Joseph, not even if she wants to go." He expected Orion to protest, but his brother did not. Instead, Orion spoke calmly.

"Well, you're in luck there, because I don't think Diana wants to go back to the fort, at least not right now, and Joseph has no reason to force her." He ducked his head under the water and came back up.

Hope flared in Grey Eagle's heart. As nonchalantly as he could, he asked, "What makes you think she doesn't want to leave yet?"

"Because she didn't jump at the chance. She seemed almost dismayed that Jubal brought it up, and she told Joe she'd give him her answer in the morning." Orion raised a brow, humor twinkling in his eyes. "Forget all that mystical Eagle stuff; I think the simple truth is that you and Diana like each other." He broke into a grin, his even white teeth gleaming in the moonlight. "Wait 'til I tell Jubal and Joe, and Mama and the girls, and Sarah . . . hey!" His final word ended on a sputter as Grey Eagle pushed his head under the water.

"Brothers," Grey Eagle muttered. He released Orion's head and waded out of the water. The night air felt cold against his wet body, but he felt better inside. He donned and adjusted his breechclout, then looked to Orion, who floated lazily in the pool. "Thank you," he called quietly.

"You're welcome, little brother."

"Where will you and Joseph sleep tonight?"

"In the lodge of Raven's Heart—they have more room than Jubal does right now."

"Then I'll see you in the morning. Good night, Orion." Grey Eagle gathered up his leggings and moccasins and headed back toward Jubal's lodge.

Black Moon clutched her deerskin dress to her naked breasts and, hidden within the protective shadows of a stand of fir trees, watched Grey Eagle leave. Disappointment pounded on her, as did resentful anger at the Hunter for coming when he did.

Everything had been going so perfectly! She'd stripped off her dress, left her moccasins and leggings by the tree, had taken the first cautious, eager steps to join Grey Eagle in the warm, sensual depths of the pool, certain that he would not turn her away this time. Under such erotic conditions, what man would? Or could? Once in the inviting waters with him, she would be able to freely caress and explore his irresistible body, she would have his hard, throbbing maleness inside her at last—then she heard someone's approach. Not daring to move for fear of being discovered naked, she'd been forced to hide in the shadows while Grey Eagle and the Hunter talked.

How she wished they'd spoken in Cheyenne rather than English!

The white woman's name—Diana—had been said several times, and Black Moon drew blood from biting her lip in frustration at not understanding their conversation. But she hoped they discussed the woman's leaving. Then she prayed that the Hunter would leave Grey Eagle alone again. Now, she watched the handsome object of her desire disappear in the trees.

Black Moon ground her teeth in fury as she pulled her dress back over her head, not caring if the Hunter heard her or not. She snatched up her moccasins and leggings and trudged back in the direction of her brother's lodge, thinking of one plan to ensnare Grey Eagle, then discarding it as another came to her frantic, frustrated mind.

So intent was Black Moon upon her scheming that she did not see the man standing in front of her until she was almost upon him. She stopped and stared, the wild hope flaring in her breast that Grey Eagle had waited for her, followed by a dizzying plummet of disappointment when she realized it was not him.

Why did Calls the Wind stand in her path?

Impatiently, Black Moon brushed past the stocky, silent warrior. To her astonishment, he caught her sleeve and tugged lightly, then released her. Among the Cheyenne, that simple action constituted a flirtation.

Surely Calls the Wind was not interested in her. Even if he was—as most of the men in the village were, she knew—how dare he presume to flirt with her? Black Moon stopped and looked back at him, a withering remark on the tip of her tongue. But there, with the moonlight on the warrior's face, she saw something in his expression, a heated knowing in his eyes, that gave her pause.

Had he followed her earlier? Had he spied on her in the shadows, watched her wantonly strip off her dress for Grey Eagle? Had he been a witness to her humiliation in having to leave the pool area without accomplishing her goal?

Black Moon flushed with mortification and fear, desperate to remember if there had been enough moonlight under the trees for him to have seen anything. It had seemed so dark!

But if Calls the Wind had seen her, if he told others, she would be ruined. If her aggressive and immodest pursuit of Grey Eagle became known, no man in the tribe would marry her, no woman would befriend her. Her own brother would most likely put her out of his lodge.

She swallowed the nasty remark she'd been about to make and struggled to keep her expression impassive. For a moment longer, she stared at Calls the Wind, searching his equally expressionless face for some sign of what he knew, of what he had seen. He gave her no hint, but merely returned her stare.

Unnerved, Black Moon whirled about and hastened toward the safety of her brother's lodge.

The time had been right to make his first move, just as the Old Ones told him. Calls the Wind watched Black Moon hurry away, distressed that the woman took no care of her bare feet. He longed to run after her, to sweep her up in his arms so that her pretty little feet would not be assaulted by a rock or a burr.

How beautiful she had been! Enough moonlight had filtered through the trees to show him that Black Moon had removed her dress, that she modestly hid herself in the shadows as she prepared to bathe. His impatient loins had urged him to join her in the waters, but he was determined to merely watch tonight. Then the Hunter arrived, spoiling his plans—the Hunter and Grey Eagle.

He'd seen only the Hunter come down the path, but Grey Eagle was there, too—he knew Grey Eagle's voice, heard the brothers speak their strange-sounding white man's language. How could he have missed seeing Grey Eagle on the path?

Suddenly, the suspicion poked at him—that Grey Eagle had been in the pool first. Had Black Moon followed Grey Eagle here?

Could it be? After Grey Eagle told Two Bears that he was not interested in Black Moon as a wife, could she still be hoping?

Calls the Wind frowned. He'd assumed that Grey Eagle was out of the way. If that was not the case, measures would have to be taken.

Then Calls the Wind smiled. Black Moon had stopped, had looked at him when he tugged on her sleeve. She did not scold him for his boldness, or order him to leave her alone. She didn't smile, either, he admitted, but she had not discouraged him. That was very encouraging.

The Old Ones were right, as he had known they would be. He had taken the first important step. Now he just had to be certain that he took no wrong steps in his courtship of the lovely Black Moon.

Thankfully, the Old Ones would guide him, just as they always had.

Calls the Wind took a deep breath, empowered with the heady feeling of love. Nothing could stop him now. And if it turned out that Grey Eagle might try, then Grey Eagle would die.

When Grey Eagle arrived at Jubal's lodge, no one remained at the outside fire, which had burned down to coals, so he ducked inside. There he found Sweet Water leaning against a backrest, nursing her daughter, while Jubal sat at her side, watching with love and pride. The mountain man nodded a greeting, which Grey Eagle returned.

Diana he found in her bed, her back to the fire, snuggled so far under her new buffalo robe that only the top of her head peeked out. From its position near her feet, the puppy raised its head, opened one sleepy eye, and nestled back down. A fierce disappointment flashed through Grey Eagle; he wanted to see Diana's face, perhaps even talk to her, apologize for his earlier taciturn mood. Now he would have to wait until morning.

He laid aside his leggings and moccasins, pulled his breechclout off, and crawled into his lonely bed, wishing with all his heart that it was *their* bed.

Jubal's quiet voice reached his ears. "Do you think she'll leave with your brothers in the mornin'?"

With a quick glance at Diana's motionless form, Grey Eagle rolled over onto his stomach, raised himself up on his elbows, and faced his friend. Under no circumstances would Diana leave in the morning, but, since he did not know if she truly slept, he refrained from saying so. He could well imagine her reaction to such a statement from him. All he said was, "I hope not."

"Di-an-ah not leave," Sweet Water announced in a loud whisper, then a doubtful, distressed look came over her round face, and she looked at Jubal. "She want to see baby. She not leave."

"I don't think so, neither, wife," Jubal reassured her with a smile. "If she tries, we'll ask her to stay for a while."

Vastly relieved, Grey Eagle collapsed his arms so that his chin rested on his joined hands. If Diana chose to leave in the morning, he would not have to make a scene, because Jubal and Sweet Water would do it for him. For just a moment, he allowed his lips to curve in a small, triumphant smile—but when he looked up, he knew Jubal had seen it. The mountain man's sharp eyes bored into him, then one eyelid closed in a slow wink.

Grey Eagle flashed him a full grin before he buried his face in the soft fur of his buffalo robe.

He had allies.
Diana didn't stand a chance.

Frozen in her fetal position under a robe that had suddenly become much too warm, Diana pressed a fist to her smiling mouth, as if the others in the lodge could hear a smile.

He hoped she would stay.

Jubal and Sweet Water wanted her to stay.

She was welcome here.

Grey Eagle wanted her to stay.

For a while, she would stay.

Chapter Twenty-Four

"You're certain?" Joseph asked Diana the next morning. They stood with Orion on the riverbank. Joseph held her hands in his and searched her eyes with his warm brown ones.

Deeply touched by his obvious concern, Diana squeezed his fingers. "I'm certain, Joseph. I want to watch the baby for a while, make certain no complications arise . . . no." She stopped herself and smiled. "I'm making excuses to stay when the simple truth is I *want* to stay, to spend some time with the baby, with Sweet Water and Jubal and Sparrow, and . . ." She hesitated, and could not say Grey Eagle's name, not even to his brother. "And with the Cheyenne." Her grasp on Joseph's fingers tightened even more and her voice dropped to a whisper. "I *need* to stay. Since my father's death, life at the fort has been . . . difficult. Here, I am welcome."

"Oh, Diana." Joseph drew her into a brotherly hug. "I wish we—my family—had been there in your hour of need. If Knute had known how unhappy you were with your aunt and uncle, how you and Sparrow were treated, he and Thomas would have taken you to our home, would have watched out for you and cared for you until our return, and you would be there still. They had no idea."

Diana blinked away the sudden tears that filled her eyes and returned Joseph's hug. "Thank you, dear friend. In future times of trouble, I will know to turn to your family."

"It is good that you know that."

Did Diana imagine it, or was there a definite note of satisfaction in Joseph's voice?

He set her back. "We must go. The sooner we get to the fort and make our report, the better."

"Fare you well, Joseph Beaudine." Diana smiled up at him. "Please give my love to everyone, and my congratulations to Annie Rose."

"I will." Joseph smiled with the unique and endearing pride of an expectant father.

Orion gave her a quick hug, then stepped back and looked at her so intensely that Diana wondered what could be wrong. "Orion?"

"You look so different in deerskin, with your hair down in a braid and ornamented with feathers, and wearing shells in your ears."

With an uncertain laugh Diana asked, "Is that good or bad?"

"It's definitely good. You are beautiful, of face and of heart. I can perfectly understand why my brother is so taken with you." He grabbed both of her hands in his.

Diana blushed, bright red, she was certain, if the heat in her face was any indication. Embarrassed as she was, a gladness touched her heart at Orion's words. *Grey Eagle was taken with her.* She managed a shy smile.

Orion leaned forward and kissed her cheek. "Fare you well, little sister, until we see each other again." He gave her hands a final squeeze, then walked away to join Joseph.

Diana put her hands to her hot cheeks. *Orion called her 'little sister.'* The gladness in her heart was joined by a growing hope.

Grey Eagle approached his brothers, leading their two saddled horses. The tension between him and Joseph had eased at breakfast, when Joseph apologized for being so military-like, and Grey Eagle had granted that he himself had not been easy to talk to, either. Now, he handed the reins to Orion, then turned to Joseph.

"Safe journey to both of you," he said.

Joseph settled his hat on his head. "You know Mama Florrie is going to skin us alive for not bringing you back, at least for a visit."

"And our sisters are going to help her," Orion added mournfully. "And probably our wives."

"You two can handle a pack of women," Grey Eagle assured them.

Orion and Joseph shared a telling look.

"Not a pack of Beaudine women, Eagle," Orion protested. "They're mighty fearsome."

"That is true," Grey Eagle admitted, fighting a smile.

"When will you bring Diana back to the fort?" Joseph asked, all traces of humor gone now.

"That will be up to her. I will tell you one thing, though." Very soberly, he looked first at Joseph, then at Orion. "By summer's end, she will be my wife."

Neither brother showed any surprise.

Joseph calmly asked, "Does Diana know this?"

"Not yet, but she will."

"Well, I'd ask her before I started making any plans for a wedding celebration and a new lodge. Women like to be included in such things as their own marriage."

"I'll ask her," Grey Eagle snapped, his annoyance toward Joseph growing again. He didn't add that Diana's answer would be 'yes,' no matter what.

"Touchy, isn't he?" Joseph directed his question to Orion as if Grey Eagle weren't standing right there.

"Sure is," Orion answered cheerfully. "A might arrogant, too. Do you suppose that comes from the Cheyenne half of him?"

"It comes from the Beaudine half," Grey Eagle growled. "Neither of you has any business talking to me about arrogance. Just ask your wives." He pointed to their impatient horses. "Now get going. Daylight's wasting."

"Yes, sir." Orion snapped a salute at him and vaulted into the saddle. Thunder, his great stallion, danced about, clearly ready for a run, while Joseph's sweet mare, Grace, champed at the bit as he climbed into the saddle. The group of people who had stood back to give the brothers some privacy now closed in around them, calling out good-byes and good wishes in both Cheyenne and English.

The two men splashed across the river. Most of the crowd broke up, but Jubal, Sparrow, Diana, and Grey Eagle watched until Joseph and Orion paused at the top of the rise. Both brothers raised an arm in final farewell, a gesture that Grey Eagle and Jubal returned. The two men disappeared, leaving a strange loneliness in their place. At least it felt strange to Grey Eagle.

He turned to Diana, and it struck him anew that she had chosen to stay for a while. It took all the self-restraint he possessed to keep from reaching out to pull her into his arms, to hold her close and stroke her hair, to tell her how glad he was that she stayed. He would not do that, for fear that if he did, she would take her new mare and race after Joseph and Orion. So, instead, Grey Eagle asked Jubal to accompany him on a hunting expedition, and the two men walked off to make their plans, leaving Diana and Sparrow alone.

Grey Eagle glanced back just once, then wished he hadn't. He saw Sparrow pull on Diana's hand, chattering excitedly about a visit to the new baby. He also saw a hurt look in Diana's large, beautiful eyes as she stared after him. That look troubled him greatly, because it gave him the uncomfortable feeling that he'd just done something very wrong. For the life of him, he had no idea what it could be.

Not a word, not even a warm look—Grey Eagle had given her no sign at all that he was glad she stayed. Diana had come away from the river terribly upset, and fought to hide her feelings from her friends. She'd begged Sparrow and Little Leaf to allow her to help with some of their numerous chores, and now she pulled viciously on a tanned buffalo hide that had been draped around an upright pole. She clutched the two edges of the hide in her hands and alternated pulls between her right arm and left, drawing the hide back and forth around the pole with the hoped-for result of a softened hide. It was hard work, for the hide was heavy, but she was grateful for the labor. Otherwise, she might break something out of pure frustration.

She'd told Joseph the truth that morning. She did want to stay in the encampment for a while, to visit with Jubal and Sweet Water and Sparrow and Little Leaf, to help with the care of the new baby, to learn some of the ways of the Cheyenne. But she also stayed because of Grey Eagle.

Her feelings for him were wonderful and confusing—and so very fragile, like a tiny wildflower seeking purchase for its delicate roots in a patch of rocky soil. At first, when she'd realized that Grey Eagle was becoming special to her, she had determined to tear that flower of sentiment out of her heart and throw it away. And she had tried, to no avail.

She'd thought at first that she was drawn to him for the oldest reason in the world—that of Man and Woman. His beautiful male body called to her, and her traitorous female body desperately wanted to answer.

But it was so much more than that now. His kindness, his integrity, his courage—were not such things far more important in one's mate than physical beauty? Such things made up a person's character, and it was on the cornerstone of character that lifelong relationships were built.

Lifelong.

Diana realized that her arms ached ferociously, and she allowed the heavy hide to fall. As she rubbed her upper arms, she looked about the peaceful, bustling village.

If her wildest, most secret imaginings came true, and she learned that Grey Eagle had some special feelings for her, would he offer marriage? Would he want her to live with the Cheyenne for the rest of her life? Could she do that—give up her family, her culture, her language?

Of course, he had one foot in the white world, too. From what she had seen this morning, Grey Eagle was devoted to his brothers, and no doubt to the rest of his family. Perhaps he would agree to do as Sarah and Orion had done the first year of their marriage—winter with the Cheyenne, then move back to Fort Laramie for the emigration and trading season, maybe even travel to St. Louis every few years so she could visit her sister.

That she could do.

Diana squeezed her arms in a final burst of irritation, then bent to retrieve the hide. She was a fool, spinning daydreams in her head, asking silent questions for which there were no answers. Until she knew exactly how Grey Eagle felt about her, there was no point in dreaming. She had hope for a future with him, but she also knew that she was risking the kind of broken heart from which she might never recover—just as her father had never recovered from her mother's cruel indifference.

A distance away, another woman labored over another buffalo hide, using her scraper with the same angry energy Diana used with her hide and pole. Black Moon knelt beside a hide staked to the ground, and with her scraper attacked the particles of flesh and fat that clung to the hide, causing them to fly about. She was famous in the tribe for the speed with which she could clean a green hide and prepare it for tanning, and never did her hands move so fast as when she was angry.

Why did the white woman not leave with Grey Eagle's white brothers?

The previous day, Black Moon had been overjoyed at the arrival of Joseph Beaudine and the Hunter, certain as she was that they had come to take the white woman away. All afternoon she'd made her plans, in the evening had put them into motion, and then everything had gone wrong.

Now, to make matters worse, the woman called Diana chose to stay, and the foolish Beaudine brothers—including Grey Eagle—did not force her to leave.

Black Moon sat back on her heels and wiped her hand across her forehead. Under the cover of her arm, she glanced about the village, searching, relieved when she did not see Calls the Wind. The thought of what the man could do to her exalted position in the village terrified her—she who was afraid of nothing. If only she knew for certain what he had seen!

But there was no way to know, not until Calls the Wind made some kind of move. And until—unless—he did, she would act as if nothing unusual had happened, and proceed with her plans. That decided, Black Moon attacked the buffalo hide with renewed vigor, determined that, before the end of the summer, it would be used in the construction of her new marital lodge—the one she would share with Grey Eagle.

Over the next several days, Diana settled into her life in the Cheyenne village. She learned many of the rules of Cheyenne society, such as the fact that the position at the back of the lodge was the warmest, and therefore was the place of honor and given to guests. Every person who came to one's lodge was offered food, no matter the reason for or length of their visit. When entering a lodge, women moved to the left, men to the right. It was considered the height of rudeness to pass between another person and the fire; one did so only when absolutely necessary, and with profuse apologies.

She learned that each day started with the men and boys waking the camp with their boisterous, noisy dash to the creek for their 'strengthening' bath, and that shortly after breakfast, most of the older boys and the men—including Grey Eagle— left the encampment for most of the day in order to hunt, while the women were kept busy with the never-ending and cheerfully shared chores of child care, meal preparation, and maintaining the home.

Because it was important to her that Sweet Water rest and see to the baby, who Jubal had finally named Mary Sweet Rose—Mary after his sainted mother, Sweet to honor his wife, and Rose because he'd always liked the name—Diana insisted upon taking over as many of the household chores as she could. Those chores kept her so busy during the course of a day that she had little time to miss Grey Eagle, although she was always aware of his absence.

The evenings and nights were a different story—when he was absent in a different way.

Her heart leapt with joy to hear the yips and shouts of the men returning from their hunt; her eager eyes searched for him in the milling, excited crowd. Although it was usually with no more than a glance or a nod, she felt that he acknowledged her presence before he led George Washington off to be cared for, and she would sigh with happiness.

He would join her and Jubal and Sweet Water at the lodge, always polite, and never warm. Still, she waited for any look, any smile from him. Sometimes she was rewarded; other times, she was not. Always, she was grateful for any notice he gave her. The evening would pass in relative peace, then all would retire, and the pattern would repeat itself the next day.

In times of introspection, though, while scraping a buffalo hide, or slicing an elk haunch into thin slices to be dried in the sun, or, late at night, staring at the patterns of the dying fire that danced on the hide walls of Jubal's lodge, Diana became angry with herself for accepting Grey Eagle's meager attentions as eagerly as a cur would accept a scrap of meat. And she would swear to herself that, starting with the very next day, she would not wait for his return throughout the day, she would not search for him in the crowd, she would not hope that her fingers touched his as she handed him a bowl filled with the supper she had made for him, she would not watch his face as he slept.

Each day, she betrayed herself.

Each day, she became more bewildered, and more withdrawn.

He'd admitted that he hoped she would stay; she'd heard it from his own mouth. So why would Grey Eagle show her no friendship, no warmth, now that she had? He'd been kinder to her when they hardly knew each other. Diana longed to return to those few short days, as tense and uncertain as they had been.

She named her puppy Rosie, after Jubal's daughter, and Rosie became her constant companion. Even more than Sparrow or Sweet Water, Rosie knew of her heartache and confusion, for

Diana poured out everything to the growing dog. Rosie was an attentive and sympathetic listener, but she was remiss in offering advice, a shortcoming for which Diana readily forgave her.

In those first two weeks with the Cheyenne, Diana missed her father more than ever, missed his unconditional love and sage advice, and there was no cure for that. She began to think seriously of asking Jubal to take her back to the fort—maybe in another week, or maybe in two, when Sweet Water was fully recovered from the rigors of childbirth, when the baby was a little bigger. The thought gave her no joy, but returning to the fort was probably the best thing to do, given Grey Eagle's obvious and complete lack of interest in her.

Holding himself back from Diana Murdoch those first two weeks was the most difficult task Grey Eagle had ever set for himself—even more difficult than keeping himself from seducing her when she'd been his captive, and he'd been certain at the time that nothing could be more difficult. But he wanted her to experience life in the encampment without influence or interference from him.

The Cheyenne way gave its people a good life, but one that was by no means easy. It was important to him that Diana understood that, that she had some idea of what she was getting into when she became his wife.

She'd wanted to stay for the sake of her friends—Sweet Water, Sparrow, Jubal, and the baby. Despite what Orion confided about her liking him, Diana had given no indication that he had played a role in her decision to stay. Grey Eagle did not see that as a deterrent, at least not in the beginning, for she treated him in a very Cheyenne-like manner—reserved, modest, and polite. Her attempts to learn the ways of the Cheyenne touched him, and made him proud.

He suspected that someone had explained to her the intricate, indirect method of Cheyenne courtship, because she also gave him many subtle reasons to take heart.

He knew she looked for him when the men returned from

the day's hunt, and that she was glad to see him; she never said so, but her beautiful, honest eyes could not lie. He knew that it was she who kept the lodge in such neat order, that it was she who cooked foods the way he liked them. He knew that, late at night, she watched him when she thought he was asleep, because he watched her, and often found her eyes shining in the faint light of the fire coals.

By the end of the first week, Grey Eagle was very pleased with how things were progressing. Diana had taken to the Cheyenne way of life with an ease that had astonished him; she conducted herself as the ideal picture of a Cheyenne woman. If at times he missed her flares of temper and her feisty, fascinating spirit, he consoled himself with assurances that she would allow more of her true self to emerge when she felt more comfortable in her new environment.

By the end of the second week, Grey Eagle knew that he was losing her, and he didn't know why.

Perhaps Diana had decided that the Cheyenne way of life was not for her, although that was not evident in her behavior or manner as she tidied up after the evening meal.

Perhaps she truly had no special feelings for him, had stayed only for the sake of her friends, and the time of her visit was drawing to a close.

Whatever the reason, there was no doubt that Diana had withdrawn from him, emotionally and spiritually. She had gone back to the Clouds. To make matters worse, there had been no sign of the Eagle since that day Diana called him to her side.

Was she as lost as he? Did her heart ache as his did?

Grey Eagle knew that he was in grave danger of losing the most important thing in his life. He knew, as certainly as he breathed, that if he lost Diana, the Woman in the Clouds would never come to him again. Perhaps the Eagle would never come again, either.

He was a warrior. All of his life, he'd fought for what he believed in, for what he wanted.

Grey Eagle wanted to fight now, for Diana. But who was he to fight? Diana herself? The Eagle? Her spirit? His spirit? And with what weapons?

He watched her across the fire as she took up her sewing—women always had something to sew, it seemed—and the sadness in her eyes broke his heart.

For the first time in his life, Grey Eagle had no idea what to do.

Black Moon helped her sister-in-law clear away the evening meal, and wondered why she had ever been worried. It was obvious that Grey Eagle and the white woman were at odds.

Grey Eagle did not wait for the white woman along the path to the creek, or to the bathing pool. He did not tug on her dress, indicating his interest.

The white woman joined the others when they welcomed the men back from the hunt each night, but she did not offer Grey Eagle a cup of fresh water like Sparrow did, nor did she wait to walk with him.

There was no closeness between them, nothing special in their manner toward one another, not even in the most subtle of ways. They rarely spoke to each other. In fact, Grey Eagle and the white woman seemed uncomfortable in one another's presence.

As for the other worry, in two weeks there had been no word or message from Calls the Wind. He had not gone to the tribal elders with stories of what she had done, nor had he attempted to flirt with her again. Black Moon sometimes caught him watching her, but he always stood at a distance, his face expressionless.

A triumphant smile curved Black Moon's lips, which she hastily covered with one hand. She did not want to invite questions from her prying and jealous sister-in-law, nor did she want her brother's attention drawn to her.

Just the same, she was very pleased. Everything was going according to plan. Now, all she had to do was find a way to get Grey Eagle to accept the love amulet Buffalo Woman had made for her. Then he would be hers.

Chapter Twenty-Five

Later that same evening, Grey Eagle sat on his bed, wearing only his breechclout.

"This shouldn't hurt at all." Diana spoke quietly, as if she did not want to awaken the baby, although little Mary Sweet Rose was wide awake and gurgling happily at Sweet Water's breast. She knelt between his legs, with the surgical scissors poised over the nearly healed wound on the inside of his thigh. The cool fingers of one small hand seared his skin when she touched him, while her other hand manipulated the scissors to snip the stitches that had helped his torn flesh to heal. Then she shifted her position and removed the stitches from the other wound.

She'd lied.

The removal of the stitches hurt a great deal, but not because of Diana's gentle medical ministrations. It was her closeness that pained Grey Eagle, the scent of her clean, shining hair that lashed him, the beauty of her healed face appearing golden in the firelight that tormented him.

How long ago that day seemed, when they had worked together to remove the arrow, when she sat between his legs and kissed him for the first time. His soul cried out to her, begged her to kiss him again.

Instead, she moved away, gracefully, as she always moved, which not everyone did within the confines of a tipi. She stored her medical instruments in their case, then took her puppy— Rosie, she'd named it—outside for a few minutes. Woman and pup returned, and Diana crawled beneath her buffalo robe, while Rosie took up her usual position at Diana's feet. The familiar wiggling of Diana's hidden body told Grey Eagle that she had removed her deerskin dress, but he knew she still wore her chemise and drawers, because, much to his amusement, she did at all times, unless the garments were drying after being washed, which she did every other day.

He pulled his breechclout off and lay on his back under his own robe, staring at the few tiny stars that peeked through the open smoke flap of the tipi. The sadness he'd seen in Diana's eyes washed over him.

"I've had just about all of this I can stand," Jubal muttered.

Grey Eagle looked at his friend without raising his head. What was the man talking about?

Jubal sat on the edge of his bed, wearing only his breechclout, his elbows resting on his knobby knees, his lips clamped around his pipe. His long grey hair was tangled, and his eyes fairly sparked with annoyance. "Grey Eagle, let me ask you somethin'."

The man sounded serious. Grey Eagle sat up, allowing his robe to fall to his waist, and swivelled about to face his friend. "Ask me whatever you wish, Jubal."

"Are you gonna wed up with that woman or not?"

Grey Eagle's breath caught in his throat, forcing him to cough. "Excuse me?" he croaked.

"Are you gonna wed Diana or not?"

At that, Diana sat up as if she'd just discovered that the lodge was on fire, and she, too, faced Jubal, clutching her robe to her breasts. Sure enough, Grey Eagle saw the straps of her chemise, appearing to be very white against her shoulders.

"Jubal, what did you say?" Diana's voice sounded hoarse and angry.

"I've asked twice already, but I'll ask again, just in case one of you two lovesick fools is hard of hearin'." Jubal spoke with the exaggerated patience of a teacher explaining a lesson to a slow child. He used his pipe stem to emphasize his words. "I said, are you two intendin' to wed or not?"

Grey Eagle said, "Why do you ask?" at the same time Diana said, "That is none of your business." Their eyes met over the fire. Diana blushed and looked away, and Grey Eagle dropped his gaze to the flames, feeling as uncomfortable as hell.

"I'ma askin' 'cause I care about the both of you, and it *is* my business, 'cause you're in my lodge, and you're drivin' me to drink. The only trouble is, there ain't nothin' stronger'n tea around here. Now, listen up, the both of you." Jubal again stabbed the air with his pipe stem. "For near two weeks now, you been circlin' each other like two cats with their tails tied together, neither one sure what the other's gonna do. You're both ready to claw, and you're both ready to snuggle up and purr, only you don't know what the other wants, so you don't do nothin'." He crossed his arms over his chest. "And I'ma gettin' tired of it."

Grey Eagle glanced at Diana; she gaped at Jubal, seemingly unable to speak. He was in no better condition, for he had no idea how to respond to Jubal's colorful—and he had to admit, justified—tirade.

Jubal pierced him with his sharp gaze. "What are you gonna do, Eagle?" He spoke quietly, presumably out of respect for his still wide-awake infant daughter, but Jubal's voice thundered inside the lodge as surely as the Christian God's must have when He handed down the stone tablets to Moses.

Grey Eagle stared at the man he loved as a second father, and everything suddenly fell into place. The answer was so obvious. An incredible peace came over him. "I'm going to wed her," he said firmly.

"Well, I'm glad to hear it!" There was a sarcastic note to Jubal's tone, but Grey Eagle did not miss the flash of joy in the mountain man's eyes.

"Excuse me," Diana snapped. "Do I have any say in this?"

"You just settle down, girl. You'll have plenty to say, if I know you at all. But not right now."

"Jubal—"

"He'kotoo'estse!"

Grey Eagle put a hand over his mouth to hide a smile. Evidently, Diana remembered the Cheyenne words for 'be quiet,' which he'd told her one night on their journey here, because she lapsed into silence at Jubal's similar command. Rosie snuggled up to Diana and licked her chin in a show of support. Diana released her hold on the robe to grab the pup, and the robe fell to her lap, making the mounds of her breasts visible beneath the thin cotton of her chemise.

"Listen up, son," Jubal commanded, drawing Grey Eagle's attention away from Diana. He pointed his pipe stem at Grey Eagle. "You're movin' in with Raven's Heart tomorrow, and there you'll stay 'til Diana decides whether she'll have you or not."

Grey Eagle stiffened. "I'll ask her now."

"No, you won't. You ain't gonna put her on the spot like that. You made your intention clear, Grey Eagle. Now you're gonna court Diana proper-like, and give her time to make up her own mind." He looked at Diana, who stared back at him, her eyes wide, as if she were in shock. "That's when you'll speak your mind, girl—when he's courtin' you. You say whatever you want to him then. If you like him special-like, tell him so. If'n you don't, have the kindness to tell him straight up, so he don't go gettin' false hopes." Jubal stretched and yawned. "All this yakkin' done wore me out. Now, you two lay down and hush up, and let me'n my wife'n my sweet little baby get some sleep. Eagle, bank them coals, will you?"

As if he didn't have a care in the world, as if he hadn't just turned Grey Eagle's—and Diana's, no doubt—world upside down, Jubal crawled under the buffalo robes he shared with Sweet Water and Mary Sweet Rose. Murmurs were heard, and little snuffling baby sounds, then the Sage family settled into silence.

For a long time, Grey Eagle did not move. Neither did Diana. Rosie fell asleep in Diana's lap, and still she did not move.

Finally, just when Grey Eagle was about to obey Jubal's order to bank the the coals, Diana spoke in a small voice.

"Well, I guess he told us, didn't he?"

"I guess he did."

Diana said nothing in response; she merely shifted her position and lay down again. Rosie moved to Diana's feet, where she turned in a circle a few times and curled up in contentment.

Grey Eagle banked the coals, then lay back himself, his hands resting on his chest. For several long minutes, the lodge was silent except for the final shifting and popping of the coals. A question came to Grey Eagle's mind, and he could not keep it inside.

"Diana." He whispered her name.

She answered in a whisper. "Yes?"

"Remember when you told Joseph that you had problems with that lieutenant because you did not welcome his suit?"

A pause. "Yes."

Grey Eagle's heart started pounding. "Will you welcome my suit?"

There was a longer pause. Then the beautiful word he needed to hear came from the dark mound of Diana's buffalo robe, in both of his languages.

"*Heehe'e.* Yes."

True to his word, the next morning Jubal helped Grey Eagle carry his belongings to the lodge of Raven's Heart and Little Leaf. Diana hated to see Grey Eagle go. Perhaps things had been awkward between them, but at least she'd had the comfort of knowing she would see him each day. Now she had no idea what to expect. In morose silence, she built up the fire in front of Jubal's lodge, and was delighted to see that the mountain man carried Sparrow's bedding when he returned.

"Are you certain you want to share your lodge with four females, Jubal?" she teased. "Five, if you count Rosie. You are terribly outnumbered."

"I'll be terribly pampered, is what I'm thinkin'," he

announced. "I might get to likin' all you womenfolk fussin' over me."

Sweet Water, who sat nearby on a buffalo robe with the baby, merely snorted.

Jubal tossed Sparrow's bedding into the tipi, then bent down to plant a noisy kiss on his wife's cheek. "Don't you like to fuss over me, honey?" he wheedled.

"I fuss, all right," Sweet Water assured him. Then she flashed him a cheeky grin. "Jubal-honey."

Diana joined Jubal in his laughter while Mary Sweet Rose cooed and kicked her plump little legs.

Sparrow ran up, clutching some of her things to her chest, her pretty face lit with a smile. "I stay here while Grey Eagle courts you!" she announced happily.

"I know, Sparrow. I'm so glad." Diana drew the girl into a warm embrace, then released her. "Do you need help setting up your bed?"

"No." Practically bubbling with excitement, Sparrow disappeared into the lodge.

Diana joined Sweet Water on the robe, unable to resist picking up the naked infant. She cuddled Mary Sweet Rose in her arms and looked at Jubal. "What happens now? What will Grey Eagle do?"

Jubal lowered himself to the robe as well, and reached out to offer his daughter a finger to grab on to, which Mary Sweet Rose immediately did. "He'll court you, the Cheyenne way. And you let him, Diana. Don't give in too soon, or else he might get more cocky than he already is—you know, too big for his britches."

"Grey Eagle don't wear britches," Sweet Water reminded him.

"That don't matter," he said, waving her words away. "You know what I mean. Every woman deserves to be courted. Don't you make it too easy for him, you hear me, girl? Make that man work for what he wants."

"I won't play the games of a coquette," Diana warned.

"No, no, I don't mean you should lie to him. Just let him court you according to Cheyenne tradition. You'll like it. Am

I right, Sweet Water?'' He winked at his wife, who smiled broadly in return.

"You right, Jubal-honey.''

Diana laughed. "Very well. Just what is the Cheyenne tradition of courting?''

Jubal stroked his beard thoughtfully. "When you go get water, he might be waitin' for you near the creek. When you go to fetch wood, he might be waitin' along your path. He won't say nothin', but he might tug on your sleeve. That's how a Cheyenne man lets a woman know he's interested. If she don't like him, or ain't interested in him special-like, she'll ignore him or tell him to leave her alone, and that pretty much ends it right there. But if she wants to encourage him, she'll stop and talk, or invite him to walk with her.''

"It would be nice to walk with Grey Eagle,'' Diana said wistfully.

"Then ask him.'' Jubal paused. "Now, don't expect him to offer to carry your water, or your wood, like a white man would, 'cause that ain't the Cheyenne way. Menfolk have their duties, and womenfolk have theirs, and each is proud to do their part. A man's duty includes protecting his woman, and he can't do that too well if he's caught with his arms full of wood. A Cheyenne woman would lose respect for a man who offered to take on her chores.''

That seemed odd to Diana, but she did not argue. "I don't mind carrying the wood.'' She bent down to give the baby a quick kiss, and wondered if the day would come when she would sit in the sun with her own child—hers and Grey Eagle's. The thought sent a familiar rush of heat to her belly, so strong that she closed her eyes against it for a moment, then she looked up at Jubal. "Thank you for bringing everything out into the open, Jubal. My heart was breaking.''

"I know, girl.'' Jubal patted her shoulder. "If it makes you feel any better, so was Grey Eagle's. He thought you was deliberately tryin' to behave as a virtuous, unwed Cheyenne woman would, which pleased him, and so he responded like a Cheyenne man, while you was thinkin' he ignored you because he had no interest in you at all. You was lookin' for him to act like a white man, 'cause that's what you're used to.''

Diana frowned, and it wasn't because Mary Sweet Rose found her braid and gave it a vigorous tug. "He and I are so different, Jubal. Look how deeply we misunderstood each other, simply because we've been raised differently. Is there hope for us to be happy together?''

"Oh, I think so, just like me'n Sweet Water get along all right.'' He smiled at his wife. "If you have a basic respect for each other in addition to lovin' each other, and you talk things out when there's trouble—and there's gonna be trouble, I promise you—then the two of you'll do fine.''

Diana took a deep breath, and felt full of love and hope. "Do you think he'll start the courting right away?'' she asked shyly.

"He will if he's got any brains in that thick skull of his. Grey Eagle wants you powerful bad, Diana, just like you want him. Ain't no sense in waitin' to get things started.''

Another hated blush heated Diana's cheeks, and she lowered her head to nuzzle the baby's soft hair.

" 'Sides,'' Jubal continued, "the whole village knows somethin's up. Ever'one'll be watchin' to see when he makes his move. Yes, sir, this should be a very interestin' courtship.'' He leaned back on his elbows, clearly pleased with himself.

Diana realized that Mary Sweet Rose was rooting at her breast. Somewhat embarrassed by the baby's innocent and intimate actions, yet thrilled with the hope of motherhood at the same time, she handed the infant to Sweet Water. "I think she's hungry.''

Sweet Water gathered her daughter close and opened the top of her dress.

Suddenly impatient for the courting to begin, Diana scrambled to her feet.

"Where you off to, girl?'' Jubal asked.

"To get some firewood,'' came the quick reply.

Jubal leaned back again, his mouth curved in a wide, satisfied smile.

* * *

With a hide water bag swinging from her fingers, Black Moon sauntered along the shady path to the section of the river she liked to use. What a lovely day it was, she thought. A perfect day to approach Grey Eagle when the men returned from the hunt later that afternoon, to offer him—in front of everyone, including that stupid white woman—a cup of fresh water. It was a bold and risky plan, but she was confident that he would not humiliate her by refusing her cup. For him to do so in front of the village would be unpardonably rude, and Grey Eagle was far too noble to be rude. Black Moon took delicious pleasure in so cleverly using one of his most admirable traits against him.

A shadow fell across her path, and she looked up. Her throat tightened and her heart started pounding.

Calls the Wind stood only a short distance from her, his dark eyes upon her as if he wanted to devour her. He wore the beaded leggings and elaborate headdress that one usually saved for special occasions, his chest was painted to highlight the scars he had earned in the Sun Dance, and he carried a long coup stick with many marks. Black Moon knew at once that he had dressed to show her that he was a respected warrior. A worthy mate.

He wanted to court her.

Infuriated that the man would choose today, of all days, to finally make his interest known to her—today, when she needed to concentrate all of her energy and power on Grey Eagle— Black Moon stomped by without so much as a glance at him. Only the memory of what Calls the Wind might have seen that night at the pool kept the angry words she wanted to shout at him in her thoughts rather than on her tongue.

"Have you not even one kind word for me?" he asked quietly.

Stunned, Black Moon stopped in her tracks. He had dared to speak to her when she had not given him permission to do so? She whirled to look at him. "You are too bold," she said haughtily. "I will tell my brother. He will see that you do not speak to me again."

Calls the Wind gave a slight shake of his head. "Two Bears encouraged me to be bold. He said you would not otherwise turn your thoughts from one who does not want you."

A flood of fury roared through Black Moon, causing her teeth to clench and her hands to close into fists. Her brother had discussed such private matters with another man? With Calls the Wind, of all men? Calls the Wind, who all of his life had been quiet and reserved, even as a boy; who had earned honors for his bravery but never boasted; who had brought the broken body of her husband to her after his fatal confrontation with an enraged bull buffalo. Like a sturdy, thick-trunked tree, Calls the Wind was always there, in the background, and she gave him no more thought or notice than she would such a tree.

Now he wanted to court her? And her brother encouraged him? Black Moon swallowed, hard, before she dared to speak, afraid that in her outrage she would sputter or shriek.

"Two Bears had no right to discuss such matters with you," she coldly informed Calls the Wind. "I did not give him permission to do so."

"He is your brother, and responsible for you. Two Bears is free to discuss your matters with any he chooses."

He dared to argue with her! No man had ever done that, with the exception of her dead husband and her deceitful brother. Black Moon bit down on her lip, not knowing what to say, because Calls the Wind spoke the truth. How did one argue with the truth?

After a moment's hesitation, Calls the Wind continued. "Allow me to court you, Black Moon. I am a worthy husband for you. I will spend the rest of my days making you happy and proud."

"No." Black Moon turned toward the river.

"If you wait for Grey Eagle, you will wait forever."

Black Moon froze. How did he know of her feelings for Grey Eagle?

Calls the Wind went on. "Even now, he waits for the white woman on her path. He will tug on her dress, like this."

Black Moon felt the slight tug at her shoulder. "You lie," she snapped. "He cares not for her."

"He cares." Calls the Wind moved around Black Moon until he stood in front of her. His expression was one of sympathy, and that infuriated her. His next words infuriated her even further. "Just this morning, he moved into the lodge of Raven's Heart, on the grey-haired one's instructions, so that he may court properly. All of the village knows. Grey Eagle will ask for the woman called Diana, and she will have him."

It could not be true! Black Moon pressed a shaking hand to her forehead. She needed to think!

"I will court you." Calls the Wind spoke firmly.

"No! " she spat.

"I will. I will have you as wife, lovely Black Moon. One day you will take off your dress for me, as you did that night at the pool." He reached out and lightly touched her cheek, then pulled his hand away.

Black Moon stepped back, terrified. "What night?" she gasped.

"The night the Hunter was here. I saw you near the pool. I shamed myself by wondering if you had gone there to meet Grey Eagle, even when I knew you would not lower yourself in such a way. You had merely come to bathe, but the Hunter came, and his brother, and you left."

A sense of relief so strong that her knees almost buckled shook Black Moon. *He had not seen everything! He had no hold over her!* She was free of Calls the Wind, or would be when she made it clear to her brother that she would not have him.

"I must go." Again, she brushed past him, determined to get to the river and back to her lodge as quickly as possible. She needed to discover the truth about Grey Eagle and the white woman.

"I will court you." Calls the Wind's stern voice followed her.

"No!" she shouted over her shoulder.

"You will be my wife, Black Moon. The Old Ones told me." His voice had taken on an eerie note of conviction.

"They lied!" Black Moon pushed through a thicket of willows, relieved when the supple branches closed behind her, knowing they blocked Calls the Wind's view of her. Her eyes narrowed in furious determination. Two Bears would not enjoy the coming discussion they would have.

Calls the Wind stared after Black Moon in horror. *She accused the Old Ones of lying.* Steps had to be taken immediately to counteract the damage Black Moon's insult would surely cause.

Frantic now, Calls the Wind raced along the path and back to the lodge he shared with his aged mother. First, he would go to the sweat lodge, to purify himself and his thoughts. Then he would go on a vision quest and fast, for several days, if need be. He would plead with the Old Ones to tell him what they wanted in atonement, and he would do it.

Black Moon did not know what she had done. For her sake, he would make amends with the Old Ones, no matter the cost.

The Old Ones did not lie.

They *could* not lie.

Chapter Twenty-Six

As Jubal predicted, as Diana hoped, Grey Eagle waited for her in the shadows of the newly leafed cottonwood trees at a far bend in the river. Following Jubal's instructions, Diana tried to ignore him as she closed the distance between them, determined that she would march right by—and would keep on going—if he did not tug on her dress or do *something* to get her attention.

But the closer she got, the more difficult it became to take her eyes from him, to keep her lips from curving in a smile. He looked so good, standing there in the dappled sunlight, wearing unadorned leggings, his blue breechclout, and his hair-pipe breastplate. His glorious hair was clean and shining, and hung free to his waist, and Diana was thankful that he did not adhere to the Cheyenne custom of dressing his hair with bear grease.

Then her hungry gaze fell upon his face, his so handsome face, and she saw the warmth and longing in his green eyes, which he made no effort to hide; those—combined with the immeasurable relief she felt because so many of the troubles between them had been explained away last night and this morning—made it impossible for her to remain unresponsive.

A smile spread across her face, and Diana had the strange sense that if she would just raise her arms and try, she could fly as Franklin did.

She walked up to Grey Eagle and stopped, and simply stared at him.

He struggled with a smile—she knew he did—and he reached out to lightly tug her sleeve.

Diana could not keep the impulsive and honest words inside. "It is so good to see you."

Grey Eagle blinked, and his hand moved from her sleeve to brush an errant strand of hair behind her ear. His fingers toyed with her shell earring for just a moment, then his hand fell away. "You saw me last night. And this morning."

"Not like this. Not with the confusion and hurt of days of misunderstanding gone. Now it is you I see. And you look good." A husky note came into her voice.

His eyes searched hers. "I understand what you mean, Diana. You look good, too. You look beautiful."

She smiled, shyly this time, and said, "Thank you." After a surprisingly awkward moment between them, not unlike two young sweethearts suffering through their first dance lesson, Diana remembered more of Jubal's instructions. "I guess you're interested—in me, I mean—because you pulled on my dress."

Grey Eagle raised a quizzical eyebrow, and Diana felt foolish for stating the obvious. "Would you like to walk with me?" she finished hurriedly.

"I would, very much so."

They fell into step together, and Diana felt that the world fell into step, also. She breathed deeply, in happiness and in gratitude, and vowed to kiss Jubal when she returned to the lodge.

"I must ask you about something," Grey Eagle said. His voice rolled over her, warm and intoxicating.

"Please ask."

He hesitated for a moment, then said, "The morning Joseph and Orion left, from the look on your face, I think I hurt you, and I'm not certain how."

Diana blinked, surprised that he even remembered how her face looked that morning, which now seemed so long ago.

"I'd like to know what I did," he continued, "in the hope that I will never do it again."

Diana glanced up at him, and was touched by the sincerity she saw in his expression. She spoke gently. "It was what you did not do that hurt, Grey Eagle."

He frowned. "What did I not do?"

"You gave no sign that you were glad I decided to stay." She paused, then, when he said nothing, went on. "I know I used Sparrow, and Sweet Water, and Jubal, and the baby, as reasons to stay, but your presence here played a large role in my decision." Diana was struck by a niggling doubt, and she looked up at him again. "Surely you knew that."

"I did, even though you never said so. On some arrogant level, I knew."

Diana smiled at that. They walked on for a time, then Grey Eagle broke the companionable silence.

"I wish now that I had done that morning what I wanted to do, but I was afraid it would send you racing after Joseph and Orion, begging them to take you to the fort."

"What was that?" Diana came to a halt and watched him closely, feeling that his answer was terribly important.

He stopped also, then faced her, one hand running lightly down her arm. "I was so happy that you stayed, Diana. I wanted to take you in my arms, right there, in front of any who watched, and tell you so."

Her heart started thudding, a slow, happy thudding. Diana ran her tongue over her suddenly dry lower lip and did not ponder the wisdom of her next words. "Do it now."

The fingers that caressed her arm gripped her, and he brought his other hand up to her other arm. He stepped closer, so that their bodies almost touched, but just caressed her arms as he studied her face. Then his powerful arms closed around her and he pulled her close.

Diana rested her cheek against the cool corduroy of his bone breastplate and put her arms around him. His hair tickled her hands and forearms, and she gave herself the freedom to play with those appealing locks just a little, then she tightened her hold on him. He felt so good!

Grey Eagle held her close with one arm tight around her, and with the other hand he caressed the back of her head. "I am so glad you stayed," he whispered, his breath warm on her ear, and tears pricked Diana's eyes.

"Oh, so am I," she breathed. She raised her face to his, and their mouths met, tenderly at first, then with increasing urgency and passion.

When at last Grey Eagle freed her, Diana felt dazed. His hands cradled her cheeks, her hands clutched his forearms, and they looked into each other's eyes, both of them panting.

"I must go join the hunt," he said, resting his forehead against hers.

"I know."

"May I call upon you tonight?"

Diana leaned away from him. "That doesn't sound very Cheyenne," she teased.

"No, it doesn't."

His hand ran lightly up and down her arm, under the wide sleeve of her deerskin dress, driving her mad. "You may call upon me," Diana told him breathlessly. "Would you like to join us for supper?" she added, then stopped herself. "Is that Cheyenne-like?" she asked doubtfully.

"Yes," Grey Eagle answered with a laugh. "It is always Cheyenne-like to offer food."

"That's right. I remember now." Diana sighed. "I'm doing this courtship thing all wrong. Jubal is going to scold me; I just know it."

"What could you be doing wrong?"

"I'm certain that I'm too forward. I lack the modesty of a virtuous, unwed Cheyenne woman."

Grey Eagle stepped back, his hands still holding her upper arms. "Jubal told you that?" he demanded.

"No, no. He told me that was how I acted earlier, that you thought I was doing so deliberately, when in truth I was wounded and didn't know what to do."

His fierce expression relaxed. "Don't worry about doing

anything 'right,' Diana. That led us both into trouble. Be your-self—Cheyenne or white doesn't matter. Just be Diana.'' He surprised her with a quick kiss. ''I'd rather argue outright with you, like in those first few days, than have both of us hurt in silence.''

''So would I. Any time you want to argue, just tell me. I'm certain we can find something to bicker over.'' Diana lost the battle with the smile she was fighting.

''Vixen!'' he growled, and pulled her close for another quick kiss, then set her back. ''Be off with you. You keep me from my duties.''

''And you keep me from mine,'' she retorted happily. ''Go now. Good luck with your hunt.'' Suddenly, the stories Sparrow told her of how Black Moon's husband was killed while on a buffalo hunt flashed in Diana's mind, and her voice took on a serious tone. ''Come back safely to me tonight, Grey Eagle. I shall wait for you.''

He touched a forefinger to his lips, pointed that same finger at her, and was gone.

Diana looked about the quiet glen. The cottonwoods rustled in the slight breeze, and the river gurgled contentedly nearby. The sun seemed to kiss everything in sight, including Diana's heart. With a sigh of genuine happiness, she turned and headed back to the encampment, the fringe of her skirt swishing against her leggings as she walked.

Sparrow had been right—she now loved the freedom of movement made possible by her deerskin dress. Still, she always wore her chemise, and, most of the time, her drawers. Perhaps the day would come when she would not feel the need to do so—when she shared a lodge with no one but Grey Eagle.

Grey Eagle took his time as he made his way to the small meadow where he had earlier turned George Washington and his other horses loose to graze. The sky seemed impossibly blue this morning, the sunlight was warm on his back, and his prospects for a successful courtship looked very promising. He made a mental note to thank Jubal for the role the mountain man had played in easing the tension between Diana and him. It was possible that he owed his future happiness to Jubal's blunt, caring interference.

In the distance, Grey Eagle heard George Washington whinny a welcome. That sound was quickly followed by another, more curious call from the stallion, and Grey Eagle instantly knew that someone else was in the vicinity. His hand dropped to the hilt of his knife and he moved into the shadows.

A moment later, he saw Black Moon emerge from a thicket and look about, as if she searched for something—or someone. She looked upset, and Grey Eagle was surprised that his immediate reaction was irritation. The manipulative woman may have caused him trouble in the past, but she was still a Cheyenne, a dutiful and loyal member of a close-knit tribe. Perhaps something was truly amiss.

He stepped back out into the sunlight and waited.

Her frantic gaze fell on him and she broke into a run, slowing only when she reached his side.

"Tell me it isn't true," she breathlessly begged, grabbing his forearm in a fierce grip. "You are not courting the white woman. You cannot be."

Grey Eagle's jaw tightened as he pried her bruising fingers from his arm. "It is true," he said harshly.

Black Moon stood back, staring at him with haunted, hopeless eyes. Her shoulders slumped, as if she had caved in on herself.

Against his will, Grey Eagle felt a stab of sympathy. "Many weeks ago I told your brother that I am not the man for you. Did he not relay my words to you?"

"I could not believe those words." Her voice was wooden, her eyes dull.

Grey Eagle had never seen Black Moon in such a state. Angry, yes; fighting mad, proud, arrogant, even cruel. But not . . . broken. The sight was disturbing. "Collect yourself, woman." His tone was firm, but not unkind.

"I cannot, not without you." An ember of life animated her, brought a flush to her pale cheeks, caused her hands to close into fists, and she cried, "Why do you—the only man I choose—not want me when every other man does? What is wrong with me?''

"Nothing is wrong with you!" Helplessly, Grey Eagle spread his hands. "It was not meant to be. There is no more to it than that.''

"Did the Old Ones tell you that?" she sneered.

The subtle shift in her tact induced Grey Eagle to answer cautiously. "They did not need to. I know it here." He laid his fist over his heart. He did not add that it was the Spirit of the Eagle who spoke to him more often and more clearly than the Old Ones did. Mentally, he shrugged. Perhaps they were all the same.

Something he said must have sparked something in Black Moon, for she straightened her shoulders and a familiar flare of arrogance lit her eyes. "I will not give up."

"You must. There is no hope."

"If you will not court me, I will court you!"

Grey Eagle stared at her. Surely she was not serious. "You must not. You will ruin yourself in the eyes of the entire tribe, Black Moon.''

"I don't care!" She took a step toward him, her eyes wild.

"You must care," Grey Eagle ordered. "There are many fine, worthy warriors in the village who would be proud to call you 'wife.' Do not destroy yourself over me. I am not worth it.''

"You are!" she cried, taking another step toward him.

Grey Eagle grabbed her upper arms to prevent her from coming closer. He stared into her tear-filled eyes, willing her heart to hear him. "I am not worth destroying yourself over. No man is. No woman is. *No one is!*" He gave her a firm shake. "You are Cheyenne. Act like it.''

Black Moon stiffened. She stared at him. The wildness faded from her eyes, and she pulled away from his grasp. Without another word, she brushed past him and regally walked away, her head held high.

Her leaving should have brought him relief, but Grey Eagle only felt more troubled. Her swift mood changes and abrupt departure made him suspect that Black Moon was unbalanced in some way. Even if she was not unbalanced, she was unpredictable, and that, combined with the rage he knew she was capable of, made him wary. Because her efforts with him had been unsuccessful, it was not unreasonable to suspect that Black Moon might turn her anger on those he cared about—such as Diana.

Grey Eagle whistled for George Washington. Before he left to join the hunt, he had to warn Diana.

She looked up from the pot she stirred over the outside fire and was surprised and delighted to see Grey Eagle standing before her with George Washington's reins in one hand. Diana held a hand up to shield her eyes from the sun. "Well, hello," she said. Her welcoming smile faded at the somber expression on his face. "What is it?"

"We must talk."

Diana's stomach knotted. What could be wrong so soon after their wonderful courting session just a short half hour ago? It was something serious. She knew enough about the Cheyenne to know that strict rules were followed by courting couples— in public, anyway—and that no man would so boldly approach his unchaperoned intended outside her lodge without very good reason. "Of course."

"Is Jubal here?"

Before Diana could answer, Jubal stepped out of the lodge. "What's goin' on?" There was no bantering or censure in his tone—only sober concern, as if he'd known at once that something was wrong.

Grey Eagle answered with a question of his own. "Is Raven's Heart here?"

Jubal shook his shaggy grey head. "He's out with the huntin' party."

"Sit with us," Grey Eagle said to Jubal, grabbing Diana's hand. He guided her to the robe spread on the ground near the fire, where Sweet Water and the baby had earlier rested. The three sat down, the men cross-legged, Diana with her legs curled to one side. Rosie trotted up, her tail wagging, and settled next to Diana's hip.

Grey Eagle looked at Diana, his green eyes intense and piercing. "Perhaps I should have spoken to you sooner about Black Moon, but there seemed to be no urgency." He paused.

"Until now," she softly observed.

"Until now."

"Then speak to me now, Grey Eagle." Diana calmly waited.

He told her everything, including all that had happened before he met her. When he finished, Grey Eagle looked at Jubal. "She was crazy today, Jubal. I fear she might try to harm someone close to me."

Jubal tugged thoughtfully on his beard. "Like Diana."

"She would be the most likely target, but Black Moon knows of the love I feel for Sparrow, for Sweet Water, for Mary Sweet Rose, for Little Leaf." He slapped one knee in frustration. "And chances are she will do nothing at all."

The thought of anyone harming Grey Eagle's loved ones— who were also her loved ones—made Diana's blood run cold. "Can we take the chance?" she cautiously asked.

"It ain't that much of a chance, Diana. A Cheyenne liftin' his—or her—hand against another Cheyenne is just about unheard of." Jubal waved *his* hand, encompassing the village with the gesture. "You've seen the brotherhood here, the labor cheerfully shared, the generosity of one toward the other. That ain't no show. The censure, the humiliation, the risk of exile that a Cheyenne would face for harmin' his tribesman is more than most folks could bear. The chances are real good that Black Moon won't harm a fellow Cheyenne." He pointed at her. "You ain't Cheyenne."

As relieved as she was that she might be the only potential target, Diana could not stop herself from adding, "Neither are you, Jubal. And if we want to get picky, Grey Eagle and Mary Sweet Rose are only half Cheyenne."

"At this point, the only thing I want to do is be watchful," Grey Eagle said. "Black Moon is the most admired woman in the village. I cannot believe that she would throw away the years it took her to reach that position because of me. The price is simply too great, and there is no motivation that I can discover to justify her doing so.''

"I agree," said Jubal.

Grey Eagle stood up and gave Diana a hand. When he pulled her to her feet, he did not release her hand. "Let us all be on our guard.''

She nodded.

"I'll warn the others," Jubal announced. "You tell Raven's Heart when you catch up to the hunt.''

"Agreed." Grey Eagle brought Diana's hand to his mouth and kissed it.

"Not very Cheyenne-like," she murmured.

"Must be the Beaudine in me," Grey Eagle said with a grin. He let her go and reached for George Washington's reins.

"I like all of you," Diana innocently assured him, then, at Jubal's knowing grin, realized how easily her words could be misinterpreted. *Oh, Lord.* She knew it would be futile to stop the coming blush.

Grey Eagle swung up into the saddle. "I like all of you, too, Diana Murdoch." There was a decidedly lascivious gleam in his eyes, which caused Diana's blush to deepen.

When Jubal laughed out loud, Diana shot a glare at him over her shoulder, then looked back up at Grey Eagle. "I'll see you tonight," she said. Shyly, she kissed the tip of her finger and pointed at him.

The flare of heat in Grey Eagle's eyes warmed her to her toes. "Yes, you will," he said, his voice deep and rich. He touched his mocassinned heels to George Washington's sides and urged the stallion to a trot.

Diana watched him until he was out of sight, surprised that Jubal watched with her. "Do you really think the risk is minimal, Jubal?" she asked quietly.

"Yep, I do, girl. But we won't take no chances." He paused. "Did I hear you two say you'd be seein' each other tonight?"

"I invited him to supper. I hope that's all right."

"You know it is." With a pleased smile, Jubal disappeared back inside the lodge.

The sounds of a murmured conversation drifted out, and

Diana knew he was filling Sweet Water in on what had happened. Even though the sun still shone brightly, a chill raced down her body, and Diana wrapped her arms around herself.

She remembered the vicious hatred in Black Moon's eyes that day at the pool.

She knew very well that Grey Eagle was a man worth risking one's reputation for, worth fighting for.

She would be on her guard, as he urged, but that was all.

As she did for the fierce winter storms that had lashed the hills and prairies around Fort Laramie months earlier, Diana had a healthy respect for Black Moon. To take the storms—or Black Moon—lightly was to court disaster. But neither was worthy of fear. To be on one's guard against a potential enemy was not the same thing as fearing that enemy.

Diana was not afraid of Black Moon.

If necessary, she would fight for Grey Eagle. And she would win, for she had the Power of the Eagle on her side.

And the power of love.

Chapter Twenty-Seven

Grey Eagle came for supper as the last of the sunlight faded from the western skies. He was accompanied by Raven's Heart, and Little Leaf soon followed with a cast-iron stew pot filled with delicious-smelling soup. As the group gathered around the fire in Jubal's lodge, Diana was struck by the infectious spirit of friendship and goodwill that prevailed.

She sat nearest the entryway on the women's side of the lodge, her bed serving as a seat for Little Leaf and Sparrow in addition to herself, and Rosie, of course. Sweet Water and Jubal shared their bed with Mary Sweet Rose, while Raven's Heart and Grey Eagle sat across the fire from the women. A month ago, Diana could not have imagined such a scene, especially with her in it. But there she was, in a Cheyenne lodge, wearing a deerskin dress and shell earrings, sharing a delicious supper of roasted rabbit, elk and wild turnip stew, and tea made from wild mint, with a group of people she had come to love. That such a scene could be a part of her life from then on—which it would be if she married Grey Eagle—was amazing to her.

When the meal was finished, the men left to check on the horses while the women tidied up. Diana hoped that joining her for supper did not constitute 'calling on her' in Grey Eagle's mind. Surely he would come back for at least a little while before the evening's end.

The women shared a quiet half hour, playing with the baby and chattering about the coming summer hunt, when the tribe would break into smaller groups. Diana enjoyed the time with her friends, but grew impatient to see Grey Eagle.

"Diana." Jubal's voice called from outside the lodge.

The hide covering the entry was tied back, and she peered out the opening. Jubal crouched near the fire circle, adding lengths of wood to the coals. "Yes?" she asked.

"Someone wants to see you."

Diana stuck her head farther outside and looked in the direction Jubal pointed. Grey Eagle stood near the lodge, wrapped in a red wool trader's blanket, watching her impassively. Her heart started pounding with anticipation.

"Well, are you gonna come out or not?" Jubal demanded.

"I'll be right there." Diana ducked back inside and pulled the tie from the end of her braid. He had come calling! Excitement and happiness bubbled up in her as she searched for the brush Grey Eagle had left with her.

Sparrow giggled and held up the brush. "I will see to your hair."

The fact that both Sweet Water and Little Leaf wore broad smiles was not lost on Diana. It was good to know that her friends approved of her relationship with Grey Eagle. She forced herself to sit still while Sparrow brushed out her hair.

"Leave hair down," Sweet Water commanded.

"I intended to," Diana told her. She gave Sparrow a quick hug, then eased through the opening. Rosie followed right at her heels and trotted over to Grey Eagle. He bent to scratch the puppy's ears, then straightened again and looked at her.

"Good evening, Diana." His voice caressed her with its warmth, and she decided that she loved the sound of her name coming from him.

"Good evening," she answered shyly.

Grey Eagle held one of his arms out to the side, a clear invitation to step closer. Diana glanced back uncertainly at Jubal.

He nodded. "Go on, girl, if you want to. I always liked this part of courtin', when a couple gets to stand real close together and share a blanket."

She stared at him. "I'm not supposed to seek him out or start a conversation, but I can get under the blanket with him?"

"Yep, but only right here, just outside the lodge, and only when there's a chaperone, and you have to stay standin'."

Diana could not believe it. She would be able to touch him, to hold him, right there. Jubal had warned her that she would like courting, and he was right—she did. She stepped nearer. Grey Eagle put his arm around her shoulders and drew her close. Her arms encircled his waist, and she realized that he still wore the buckskin shirt he'd worn at supper. They were both covered from shoulder to foot with the blanket, bound in an intimate cocoon.

"I like this," she whispered.

"So do I." Grey Eagle's arms tightened around her.

After a few minutes of holding each other and stroking each other's back, Diana asked, "What do we do now?"

"We talk. For hours, if we want to."

She was silent for a moment, then asked, "Can we kiss, too?"

What sounded to Diana like a chuckle rumbled in Grey Eagle's throat. "That is not the Cheyenne way, but I think we will kiss." As if to prove his point, he lowered his mouth to hers for a quick, warm kiss.

"I definitely like this." Diana snuggled against him.

"What shall we talk about?" Grey Eagle asked.

She thought for a moment. "Tell me about your childhood."

"All right. Then you can tell me about yours."

"Mine wasn't very happy," she warned.

"Life is made of good times and bad, Diana. I want to share all of life with you." He kissed the top of her head.

"And I with you." She rested her head against his chest, and he began his story in a low voice.

The hours flew by. Finally, Jubal called out that it was time to say good night, and Diana realized that her legs ached from standing still in one position for so long. She glanced around and saw that the village was quiet. When she turned back to him, Grey Eagle's warm mouth waited for her, and he captured her lips with his. Now her knees felt like they would buckle, and Diana clung to him. He kissed her gently, and with such tenderness that tears formed in her eyes.

"Always leave your hair down for me in the evening," he whispered.

As simple as his request was, there was also something erotic about it, and Diana shivered with pleasure. "I will."

"Good night, Diana." He kissed her again, softly, and was gone, taking his blanket with him.

Diana pushed her hair back from the side of her face and watched until he disappeared between two tipis, then she looked about for Rosie. The pup slept near the fire. At her whispered command, Rosie followed her into Jubal's lodge. Once inside, Diana crawled to her bed and lay curled on her buffalo robe, her hands clasped tightly at her breast.

She was in love.

Earlier, when she'd made the silent vow to fight for Grey Eagle if necessary, she realized that she had the power of love on her side. She knew then that she loved him. Now she also knew she was *in love* with him, which was subtly different.

The feeling of being in love was so special, so precious, that she did not want to move for fear of it fading away.

"Are you all right, girl?" Jubal's voice came from the direction of his bed.

"I'm fine," Diana whispered, hoping he would not talk more. She did not want to share the moment with anyone.

"I told you that blanket part was fun." There was a definite teasing quality to Jubal's voice, and Sweet Water made a noise that sounded suspiciously like a giggle.

Even in the dark, Diana blushed. "Good night to the both of you," she said firmly.

Since it was Sparrow rather than Grey Eagle who now slept across the coals from her, she pulled her dress off and neatly folded it before she scrambled under the robe. The intimate moment of discovery had ended with Jubal's teasing, but some of the magic still remained. She would hold on to that magic throughout the night, until she saw Grey Eagle again the next day, when the magic would be renewed and strengthened.

For two weeks, Grey Eagle courted Diana, slowly and patiently, when what he wanted to do was carry her off to a secluded glen, lay out his finest robes for her, remove all of her clothes, and his, and make her his wife. However, under Jubal's watchful and occasionally annoying eye, that was not possible. The mountain man had taken to heart his role as Diana's guardian, just as Sweet Water had taken on the role that would have been filled by Diana's mother.

Grey Eagle knew that Sweet Water had enlisted a group of her friends to work on the buffalo hides that would become Diana's lodge when they married. An urgency motivated the women, because the tribal elders would announce any day now that the time had come to begin the summer migration, and the women wanted to finish the assembly of the lodgeskin before the camp broke. Normally, the tribe would have started the migration several weeks earlier, but a large herd of buffalo had moved into the area, and the decision had been made to stay longer than usual at the comfortable winter campsite.

Sparrow's grandmother, an undisputed expert in lodge construction, had taken Diana on a pole excursion, and even now, the logs which would become the lodgepoles lay stripped of their bark and drying in the sun not far from Jubal's lodge. Grey Eagle also knew that Sparrow worked long and lovingly on Diana's doeskin wedding dress. The girl possessed a genuine talent with beading and was earning a reputation as an artisan among the Cheyenne. Diana herself was occupied with some project, but she would not tell him what it was, and if he happened to come near when she worked on it, she immediately put it away.

Grey Eagle grew impatient.

That night, when he called upon Diana and held her close under the cover of the blanket, he found it difficult to keep his mind on any topic of discussion. Finally, he gave up trying.

He lifted her chin, cutting her off in midsentence, and kissed her.

Diana could not breathe. Grey Eagle had never kissed her like this—hungrily, without mercy, in a way she had not known it was possible to be kissed. His mouth moved over hers, then to her cheeks, chin, forehead, and eyelids, then to her ear, and to her neck, and back to her mouth, leaving a trail of fire in its wake, leaving her quivering with desire.

"Thank you for letting your hair down for me," he whispered hoarsely. His fingers plowed through her long locks, massaged her scalp and neck, caressed her shoulders and back, moved lower to touch her hips and bottom. He pulled her against his hips, and she felt his male hardness press against her stomach. A longing flashed through her, almost unbearable in its intensity, and left Diana limp in his arms.

"You torture me," she scolded in a weak whisper. The blanket had fallen to the ground, and the night air seemed cold in contrast to the heat she felt inside.

"And you, me, sweet Diana." He kissed her mouth again. "Such torment is a taste of the pleasure we will share when we are wed."

And when will that be? The words begged to be let out, but Diana choked them back. After the hours and nights of talking together in the safe little world created by the security of the wool blanket, she had grown so comfortable with Grey Eagle, so close to him—emotionally and spiritually as well as physically—that she could speak freely to him about almost anything. But that one question she did not dare voice. In both the Cheyenne and the white cultures, it was up to the man to propose marriage.

He bent and retrieved the blanket, then moved away from her. "I must go."

She understood why—perfectly—and so took no offense at his suddenly abrupt manner. The love and the passion between them had reached such a height that it was almost painful for them to be together when they could not express that love and passion with the joining of their bodies. "Grey Eagle."

He hesitated, then turned back to her.

Diana took a step closer to him and dropped her voice to a sultry whisper. "The next time you come calling with that blanket, leave this in the lodge of Raven's Heart." She tugged meaningfully on the fringed hem of his shirt.

Grey Eagle stared down at her, and when he responded, his voice sounded rough and strained. "Yes, ma'am." One hand shot out to grab the back of her neck, and he kissed her hungrily, then he turned away and was soon gone from sight.

Shaken to her soul, Diana turned and blindly stumbled into Jubal's lodge, desperate for the sanctuary offered by her bed and the heavy buffalo robes against the onslaught of emotion and desire that overwhelmed her. As she lay there, wishing for sleep, she kept remembering the four long days—and four long nights—she'd had with him, alone in the wilderness, and she moaned to think how she had squandered them.

He came to her later than usual the next night, after darkness had fallen. At first, Diana feared that Grey Eagle's tardiness was the expression of some kind of reluctance to see her. When she gladly went to the shelter of his inviting embrace, though, she realized that he had obeyed her command to leave his shirt with Raven's Heart, and it dawned on her that perhaps his tardiness was an attempt to allow them to take immediate advantage of the darkness.

She did not hesitate to do so.

When his arms—and the blanket—closed around her, and she embraced him in return, Diana found her nose against his naked chest. She could not stop herself from pressing her lips to his warm skin, as she had wanted to do from the first moment she saw him without a shirt.

Grey Eagle gasped, as if in pain, and he grabbed a handful of her hair.

By now, Diana knew enough about his body to know that she had caused him no hurt. A surge of feminine power engulfed her, and she allowed her hands and lips to roam the enticing expanse of his chest. When she encountered one of his small, masculine nipples, she curiously touched its hardness with the tip of her tongue. Grey Eagle moaned, and tugged on her hair hard enough to force her face away from his chest.

His mouth bore down on hers, nipping and licking. He plunged his tongue into her mouth, bruising her in his passion. When he raised his head, neither of them could breathe. The blanket lay rumpled at their feet.

Diana stared into his eyes, and felt his soul touch hers.

Grey Eagle bent and dragged the blanket up around them again, holding her close. She felt his chest heave under her cheek. His lips moved against her hair as he spoke. "The Cheyenne can take months, even years, to court. I can't, Diana. I've known from the first day I met you that you would be my wife. I hope that now you know it, too." He looked down at her then, used a gentle finger to raise her chin. In the dark of the night, his eyes looked black. "Marry me." His voice was a whisper, filled with the promise of all her tomorrows.

Diana's heart lurched. "I will marry you."

He kissed her again, reverently this time.

"When?" she asked.

"As soon as the women are prepared to help you raise our lodge. According to Cheyenne custom, now that we have agreed to marry, we can do so at any time—tomorrow, even. Tomorrow night we could once again share my buffalo robes, but we'd have to stay with Jubal and Sweet Water until our own lodge is finished. Since I wish to be alone with you on our wedding night, we will wait."

"I'll speak to Sweet Water, first thing in the morning. The women have been working so hard; it can't be much longer."

"It better not be," Grey Eagle growled in her ear, sending shivers of delight down her body. "I must go, now, before I carry you and this blanket off to the cottonwood grove and be done with it."

His words painted an enticing picture in her mind. "I've always thought the heated pool would be a nice place to be with you," she casually suggested, and was rewarded by Grey Eagle tightening his hold on her. His obvious desire for her made Diana want him even more.

Again, he was the strong one. "I will see you tomorrow,"

he said firmly. He kissed her one last time, hard, then pulled
the blanket from her shoulders and walked away.

Trembling, Diana made her way to her bed. She fought to
calm her breathing, which proved to be a real battle, because
she could not get Grey Eagle out of her mind, nor could she
free her body of the warmth of his body. She slipped off her
dress and pulled the robe over her, grateful that Jubal did not
tease her tonight.

She was to be married.

The wonder of it stole over her, and Diana wished with all
her heart that her father was there to share in the moment.
"You'd like him, Papa," she whispered, tears pricking her
eyes. She blinked them away. This was not a time for sadness,
but for joy. Wherever he was, Gideon was happy for her—
Diana knew it in her heart.

She was to be married to a good man whose love for her
was honest and deep and holy. She was to be married to a
beautiful man who made her breathless with wanting him.

As she shifted her position to accommodate Rosie, her chemise rode up around her hips in a most annoying fashion, and
Diana remembered the afternoon when Grey Eagle forced her
to rest in the nude while her soaked garments dried. The feel
of the soft buffalo robes against her naked body had been
intriguing and uncomfortable at the same time, perhaps because
at the time she was innocent to simple sensuality. Now, Grey
Eagle had awakened her not only to sensuality, but also to
sexuality, and to a deep, abiding love. Diana had never felt so
alive.

With a sigh, she wiggled about and adjusted the chemise,
certain that it would take her a long time to fall asleep. The
fire Grey Eagle had started in her with his love, and fed with
his desire, gave no sign of going out any time soon.

Diana learned that it was surprisingly simple to marry when
following Cheyenne tradition. Jubal explained that, because
neither she nor Grey Eagle had parents or close relatives present—who would have exchanged gifts had they been there—

the ceremony would consist of Grey Eagle coming to get her and taking her to the new lodge.

"That's it?" she had asked disbelievingly.

"Yep, that's about it."

Now, three days later, she rested in Jubal's lodge, freshly bathed, wearing only her chemise, while Sweet Water brushed her drying hair. Diana felt surprisingly calm, considering.

This was her wedding day.

Earlier, immediately after the morning meal was finished, Sweet Water, Little Leaf, Sparrow, and a few other women, including Grandmother, had helped her set up her new lodge on the outskirts of the encampment. An honored warrior who was also a medicine man blessed the empty lodge before any set foot in it, then the women furnished Diana with gift after gift of necessary household items, until their generosity brought her to tears. Sparrow helped her move her belongings from Jubal's lodge to hers—her lodge!—and now all that remained to do was get dressed.

Because her bedding had been taken to the new lodge, Diana sat on Jubal's bed, where Mary Sweet Rose slept at her side. She touched the baby's soft, soft hair and marvelled at the perfect beauty of her little face. Perhaps she would have a baby of her own some day, a beautiful little girl or boy, a baby that she and Grey Eagle would make together. The thought heated her face and caused her belly to tighten with pleasurable anticipation.

As if she'd read Diana's mind, Sweet Water said, "You have baby next summer, too."

"Maybe I will," Diana murmured. She looked up from the sleeping infant and the dreams for the future the little girl inspired when Sparrow hurried through the entryway.

"Grey Eagle comes soon! Grandmother and I come to help!"

Diana knew that Sparrow had been making her wedding dress, but she was not prepared for the creation of white doeskin decorated with ermine tails and intricate blue beadwork that the girl laid out on her bed. For the second time that day, Diana was moved to the point of tears by the love and kindness shown her.

She insisted upon wearing her chemise under the dress, but agreed to forego her drawers. Sparrow presented her with soft moccasins and beaded leggings to match her dress, and, in her Cheyenne finery, Diana felt as lovely as any bride, in any culture.

There was a bit of a flap when Grandmother wanted to anoint her clean hair with bear grease. Diana's gentle explanation that she wanted to go to her husband's bed without beauty aids, so that he would know her as she truly was, helped soothe the old woman's ruffled feelings. Grandmother smiled again when Diana asked for her assistance in securing the shell earrings— earrings Grandmother herself had made as a gift for Diana when Sparrow was returned to her people. Sweet Water brushed out Diana's hair one last time, Sparrow attached a white feather ornament just behind her right ear, and the women announced Diana ready for her wedding. To her amusement, Sparrow also tied a rawhide strap decorated with white feathers around Rosie's neck. The puppy wagged her tail and yapped with excitement.

Diana stood in the warmth of a wide ray of sunshine that came through the smoke opening at the peak of the lodge, and waited for Grey Eagle to come for her. Intense feelings washed over her, some expected, some surprising. On this day, of all days, now, just before her marriage ceremony, when her father should have been there to give her away, she missed Gideon with a paralyzing grief. She also missed her sister, which was to be expected. What surprised Diana were the feelings that surfaced regarding her mother. While she didn't actually miss Felicia, she felt a deep sorrow that her relationship with her mother had never been a good one.

Even if it had been, she doubted that her mother would have approved of Diana's choice of a husband. Her mother's parents certainly would not have. Diana bit her lip against an irreverent smile. How she would love to take Grey Eagle to St. Louis, to introduce him to her mother and grandparents, and their so-important circle of friends.

Jubal ducked through the entryway, speaking as he did. "Your man has come for you, girl—" He stopped, and stared.

"Lord almighty, girl, you are just plain ... beautiful. There ain't no other word for it."

"Thank you." Diana clasped her hands together, suddenly nervous and shy.

"Your pa'd be so proud." Jubal blinked rapidly, as if something was caught in his eye. "Ah, hell, Diana. He *is* proud. I can feel Gideon's spirit here. I just wish it was him standin' before you now rather'n me. It was his place to take you out to your man."

"I wish he could be here, too, Jubal." Diana held out her hand. "But I know my father is glad that you're here to act for him, and so am I."

Jubal grabbed Diana's hand in both of his. "Well, I'm just as proud as a cock rooster to march you on out there, girl. You weddin' up with Grey Eagle has made me very happy. Let's get you married now."

Diana could not help but smile. Leave it to Jubal to comfort her in the face of sorrow, ease her nervousness, touch her heart, and make her smile, all within the span of a minute or two. She tucked her arm in Jubal's.

He looked at her, his wise old eyes probing. "You got a good head on your shoulders, Diana Murdoch," he said soberly. "You got some idea of what you're gettin' into, weddin' up with this man who's torn between two worlds."

She nodded.

"No doubts? No second thoughts? Like the white man says, 'Speak now, or forever hold your peace.' "

A deep and calming peace filled Diana at his words. "I have no doubts, Jubal; no second thoughts."

He gave a satisfied nod. "Then let's do it."

The women in attendance to Diana left the lodge first— Sparrow, Grandmother, and Sweet Water, who carried Mary Sweet Rose. Then Jubal stepped outside. He called Rosie out before he thrust his hand back in to Diana. She held on to him as he guided her through the entryway, then she straightened. The entire population of the encampment surrounded the lodge, with Grey Eagle in the forefront. He stood before her, resplendent in his Cheyenne finery, and the sight of him took her breath away.

Evidently, Sparrow had been more busy than Diana knew, because Grey Eagle wore a wedding shirt that bore some resemblance to her dress. The buckskin that made up the body of his shirt was not bleached as white as her dress was, and the pattern of the multicolored beads was different—bolder, more masculine—but there was no question that the work was Sparrow's. With the shirt, his dress leggings and moccasins, and his glorious hair ornamented with a lone eagle feather and falling free except for the two narrow braids behind his ears, Grey Eagle was magnificent.

Diana could not take her eyes off him. Like a statue he stood, tall and proud, and very Cheyenne. Love swelled in her heart, until she felt that she could fly, and the call of the Eagle echoed in the clear air.

She raised her eyes to the heavens then, searching, and there, above the rise, she saw him, lazily riding the circular currents.

Jubal was right, she realized. Gideon *was* there, as surely as Franklin was. The deep, nagging sense of grief left her, and Diana faced her husband with a free heart.

Grey Eagle heard the Eagle, too, and had seen him.

Instantly, Diana knew it, just by the look in Grey Eagle's green eyes. She felt it again, as she had that day on their long-ago journey. The pulsing connection—between him and her, between them and the Eagle; between them, and the Eagle, and the earth and the sky.

From far away, she heard Jubal's words.

"Diana Murdoch, do you wish a marriage between you and this man?" Jubal held her hand in a tight grip, calling her back from the Clouds.

"I do," she said fervently. "I do."

With his free hand, Jubal took one of Grey Eagle's. "Grey Eagle Beaudine, do you wish a marriage between you and this woman?"

"Yes, I do." Grey Eagle's voice was clear and proud.

Jubal drew their hands together and stepped back, releasing

them to each other. ''Then go to the lodge that has been blessed for you, and may your days together be long upon the earth, and always happy.'' He repeated his words in Cheyenne, and the gathering erupted in a loud cheer.

Grey Eagle pulled Diana into his arms and, in a very un-Cheyenne-like manner, swung her around until her feet left the ground. She clung to him, laughing, and he set her back on her feet, suddenly sober, and took her face between his hands and kissed her.

The crowd descended upon them, offering congratulations and best wishes, and later, massive amounts of food were served. Grey Eagle and Diana sat together on a robe in front of Jubal's lodge, each picking at the food piled before them. Rosie ate far more than either of them did.

After a while, the aching need grew in Diana until she wondered how much longer she could stand it.

At that moment, Grey Eagle looked at her, as if he sensed her discomfort. ''You don't seem to be very hungry,'' he commented.

With no hesitation, Diana responded truthfully. ''Not for food.''

Grey Eagle's eyes widened slightly, then, without a word, he gathered her up in his arms and stood. Her arms went around his neck. Purposefully, he strode across the encampment, past family and friends, past tipis and cook fires and robes spread in the sun.

Behind them, Diana heard Jubal comment, ''It's about damn time. I wondered how long they'd wait.'' Then his voice rose. ''Sparrow, catch that puppy. Those two lovebirds need some time alone.''

Diana buried her face against Grey Eagle's neck and smiled.

A moment later, he stopped and set her down. Standing behind her with his hands on her shoulders, he leaned forward so that his cheek touched hers, and together they looked at the lodge before them.

The new lodgeskin appeared pristine in the afternoon sun, perhaps because it lacked the smoke stains that darkened the tops of all the other lodges. From the west, a low rumble of thunder rolled toward them, bringing with it a cool breeze and the promise of rain. George Washington was staked nearby, as was Diana's mare, who she called *Nokeeho*—the Cheyenne word for 'squirrel'—a name she had chosen because of the young mare's chestnut coloring and playful disposition.

Looking upon the tranquil scene, Diana did not think she had ever seen any place so welcoming.

"Let's go home, wife," Grey Eagle said against her ear.

A thrill went through her. *Home.* Such a beautiful word, Diana thought, as she took her husband's hand and followed him through the hide-covered entryway that led to a new life.

Chapter Twenty-Eight

Grey Eagle stepped through the entryway and moved to the right, releasing Diana's hand as he did. It was evident that someone had recently been there. A low fire burned in the rectangular fire pit, and a smoldering sinew-bound stick of sage and sweet grass lay on the flat stone that served as an altar of sorts and sent its aromatic, curling tendrils of smoke toward the open smoke vent. A covered cast-iron pot sat near the fire, and a water bag so recently filled that it still dripped hung from one of the lodgepoles. Someone had thoughtfully ensured that he and Diana would not have to leave the lodge until the following morning unless they chose to.

Diana moved to the left and looked about anxiously. She leaned forward to smooth a corner of the robe covering their bed, and Grey Eagle realized that she was trying to make certain that everything was perfect. No doubt she wondered if he was pleased with the home she—with the help of her friends—had made for him.

He examined the interior more closely. The bed he would soon share with Diana lay at the back of the lodge, waiting for them. Covered with buffalo robes, with the red wool 'courting' blanket folded neatly at the foot, the bed looked large and comfortable. One backrest stood at the head of the bed, another at the foot. Hides of varying kinds hid most of the grass-covered ground, his belongings and Diana's lay neatly arranged along the lined walls, and a stack of wood was piled just to the left of the entryway. His gaze fell on Diana. She stood near the bed, watching him.

"I am fortunate to have such a lodge," he said. "Especially one made with so much love."

Diana visibly relaxed. "I think it is very cozy. I like it." She clasped her hands together, nervous now, he could tell. "Either Sweet Water or Sparrow brought us some food." She nodded in the direction of the covered pot. "Do you want something to eat?"

Grey Eagle allowed his gaze to roam over his wife. How beautiful she was, in that incredible dress, with her hair down for him. Her cheeks were kissed with pink, her lips moist and inviting, and her eyes—her arresting hazel eyes—studied him in return. He saw the love and the passion in their depths, and finally answered her question. "I want you, Diana Beaudine."

Her eyes widened slightly, then she sat down at the foot of the bed and removed one of her moccasins. When she pulled her skirt up over her knee and freed the garter that held up her legging, Grey Eagle's breath caught. Hurriedly yet with care, he pulled his wedding shirt off over his head and laid it aside. Now she had the other moccasin off, and worked with the other legging. Grey Eagle untied his own leggings, and in an instant, his leggings and moccasins rested with his shirt. Wearing only his breechclout, he moved to the head of the bed and sank to his knees.

Diana glanced back over her shoulder at him, and bit her bottom lip. Shyness and desire warred within her, he could tell. She grabbed the hem of her dress and pulled it up her thighs, leaving her white, lace-edged chemise in place. With subtle shifting, she worked the dress from under her bottom and paused. The skirt of the dress lay in folds at her waist. She looked back at him again. "Will you help me, please?"

He moved behind her, still on his knees. When she raised her arms, he eased the lovely dress over her head and off. Her hair fell down around her, covering her shoulders and breasts. Grey Eagle carefully draped the dress over a backrest, then turned back to Diana. Her hands reached for the hem of her chemise, and he stopped her.

"No. Leave that. I will take it off you."

Her hands stilled, and she waited. Grey Eagle removed the white feathered ornament from her hair and set it aside, then helped with her earrings. Again, she stilled, waiting for his direction, her back straight, her gaze downcast. Kneeling behind her, he pulled her hair to the back of her neck and placed a kiss on her exposed birthmark—the Mark of the Eagle. His mark. Diana shuddered, and her breathing became shallow and fast.

Grey Eagle caressed the slender lengths of her arms, and noticed that her hands and forearms were lightly tanned. He brought his hands back up to set them on her shoulders and looked down at her, saw the hardened tips of her breasts pressing against the thin chemise. Slowly, his hands slid down from her shoulders, pressing against her, down, down, until his fingers touched those teasing peaks, and she gasped. He went further and took the delightful weight of her firm, rounded breasts in his hands. Diana placed her hands over his, as if to keep them in place, and leaned back against him. Grey Eagle wondered if she could feel his hardened length pressing against her back. When she sensuously moved her upper body back and forth against him, he wondered no longer. Now his breathing speeded up.

Diana moaned. That small sound, combined with the feeling of her tightened nipples pushing against his palms, made him suddenly impatient to taste those hard buds. His hands dropped to the hem of her chemise, and he pulled the garment up and off her, flinging it aside. He sat back on his heels and looked at her. Diana remained still, her back to him, her dark hair reaching to her hips. Grey Eagle extended his arm past her left side, offering her his hand. She placed her hand in his, and swivelled around to face him, her bare legs curled to one side. Thick strands of her hair hung over her breasts, concealing them from his gaze. He pushed those strands back behind her shoulders, then rested his hands flat on his thighs.

His gaze roamed over her, bringing a blush to her cheeks, but she did not lower her eyes or attempt to cover herself. Grey Eagle delighted in everything he saw. Her long dark hair contrasted with her pale skin, as did her taut, rosy nipples and the small, teasing patch of dark hair just visible at the juncture of her thighs. Her breasts were not large, but were pleasingly full, her waist very narrow, her stomach flat, her hips femininely flared. Diana's body was as beautiful as he had known it would be—as beautiful as her face, as beautiful as her spirit. He sighed in contentment, and waited for her to make the next move.

At first, she just watched him. Then she inched closer, moved so that she was also on her knees, sitting back on her heels, facing him. She leaned forward to lay her hand over his heart, and Grey Eagle knew his heart lurched, as if it leapt toward her. He closed his hands into fists, to keep them from reaching for her tantalizing, so-close breasts, because it was her turn to touch.

She touched.

Her hands moved to his shoulders, then down to his elbows and back up, and she rose to a kneeling position. Grey Eagle's eyes closed as Diana explored his upper body, her small hands heating him with a fire like he had never known. She stroked his hair, running her fingers through the strands, then put it back over his shoulders and moved her hands to his chest. They played over him, first firmly caressing, then stroking with feather-light touches—his chest, his ribs, his stomach, his hips. His breathing became ragged when she worked the knot loose on the rawhide cord from which his breechclout hung. His eyes flew open and his stomach grabbed when she tugged at the piece of cloth. He raised up to a kneeling position so that she could pull the breechclout and cord away, which she did, and he kept his eyes on her face.

Diana met his gaze, then she looked down, slowly, lower and lower. Her eyes widened and her cheeks pinkened. Then she looked up to his face again. She leaned forward and placed her lips on his, and Grey Eagle's restraint broke. He pulled her to him and crushed her in his arms, at last feeling her bare breasts against his chest, her stomach against his, their thighs touching.

Diana had never known such feelings. Her hands moved through Grey Eagle's hair as her mouth moved with his, slanting, her lips parting, her tongue teasing his. His hands cupped her buttocks and pulled her tight against him, so that his eager manhood was caught between them. She rotated her hips in the instinctive, ancient dance of love, and together they fell sideways onto the waiting robes.

His hands were everywhere. He pushed her onto her back, pushed her hair away from her neck and shoulder, caressed those places with lips and tongue until she whimpered. Then, his mouth—his wonderful, maddening mouth—moved from her shoulder to her collarbone, then down farther, across her chest. He kissed the first swelling of her breast, then downward his tongue trailed, and stopped. He held there, his mouth poised over her straining nipple, his warm breath tormenting her, and when Diana felt that she could take no more, when she was ready to beg him to touch her there, his warm wet mouth closed over her, and she cried out at the shock of pleasure that rocketed through her.

She could do no more than lie there helplessly as Grey Eagle lovingly assaulted her with his hands and his mouth. His long hair trailed over her body, its softness teasing her in its own way. One of his hands worked lower, over her stomach, down her hip, down her thigh and calf. Her hands grabbed his head, her fingers moved through his hair. He bent her knee on the way back up, his fingers working along the inside of her thigh. Her eyes closed. His mouth worked on her breast, and his long fingers inched ever closer to her most secret place, teasing her, tormenting her. An exquisite tension built in Diana, and she whimpered again, begging him for something, not knowing what it was that she needed. When his fingers touched her at last, gently parted, gently stroked, gently probed, she cried out again and bucked against him as a gentle explosion pulsed through her, leaving her stunned and gasping.

She opened her eyes to find him watching her, an expression of love and satisfaction on his handsome face.

"I knew you would be passionate," he whispered.

"What did you do to me?"

"I loved you."

"I want to love you," she said breathlessly. "I want to give you the same pleasure."

"You will, sweetheart. Right now." He spread her legs farther apart and moved between them. For a moment, he sat back and stared down at her sprawled body.

Diana felt the heat in his eyes move over her, and she fought the urge to cover herself. If it gave him pleasure to look at her body, then she would allow him that, even if she felt little pokes of embarrassment.

"You are so beautiful," he said softly as he lowered himself over her, and his words and manner made her feel beautiful.

He rested his weight on her, his elbows propped, his hair falling around her face in a dark, sage-scented curtain. She felt his pulsing length against her abdomen and shifted her hips in invitation. She wanted him inside her.

Grey Eagle moaned at her movements. He pulled back, and she spread her thighs wider. His hand went lower, to offer guidance, and she felt the soft tip of him rub up and down. Diana concentrated all of her attention on the joined parts of their bodies as he pushed into her, just a little.

"I might hurt you," he said, hoarsely. "God knows I don't want to, but I might."

Diana's arms tightened around him. "It's all right."

He pushed a little deeper. "You are so warm and wet," he breathed. "You feel so good." He pulled back, then entered her completely with one swift thrust.

Again, she cried out, and bucked against him, against the sharp pain. Grey Eagle lay over her, in her, without moving, and whispered words of comfort in Cheyenne.

He was huge. Diana felt her body shifting, her muscles stretching to accommodate him. The pain receded, and was replaced with heat, and she knew a fierce gladness that she had given the gift of her virginity to this man, now, at this time, in this place. It was all so *right.*

She moved her hands lower, to his taut buttocks, and pressed against him. "You feel so good," she whispered, deliberately repeating the words he had just said to her, wanting to assure him that she was fine, that he could proceed.

Grey Eagle moved slowly at first, carefully, building the tension in Diana anew, until she began to move her hips in time with his. She rocked with him, her inside muscles tightening around him, and he moved faster. His breathing became ragged and audible, and Diana knew the same exquisite tension was building in him. Higher and higher he took her, and she took him, until she cried out again, in ecstasy, and his low shout of triumph echoed at the same time. He collapsed on top of her, and Diana clung to him. Her heart pounded against his, his rapid breathing matched hers, and she felt him spasm deep inside her, and knew his seed had filled her. She kissed his shoulder as a great tide of joy washed over her.

"Welcome, *na-ehame,*" she whispered. *My husband.*

Once more, Grey Eagle raised up on his elbows and looked into her eyes. "Thank you, *na-htes'eme.*" *My wife.* He kissed her, then relaxed upon her again.

They were wed.

They spent the rest of the afternoon in each other's arms, talking and dozing. The storm that had threatened from the west came with blustery thunder and a light rain. Diana loved that storm, loved the feeling of being safe inside her own snug house, safe in her husband's arms, no matter the weather outside. At sunset, they dressed again in their wedding clothes—Diana did not wear her chemise—and took a walk along a secluded section of the river, hand in hand. The air was cool and fresh following the storm, and the dying sun painted incredible colors on the remaining clouds.

Diana took a deep, happy breath. "You saw Franklin, didn't you?" she asked, although she already knew the answer.

"Yes. It was kind of him to give us his blessing on our wedding day."

She smiled. "I hadn't thought of it like that. I may have married a poet, Mr. Beaudine."

His fingers tightened on hers. "I don't think so," he said with an answering smile.

She felt so incredibly close to him, in a way she had never felt with anyone else. Of course, no one else had been her lover—that alone could explain her feelings. But Diana suspected it went deeper than that, and she was glad that she had a lifetime to explore the feelings Grey Eagle brought out in her. "I think my father was here today, too," she said softly, thankful that she had no hesitation about saying such a thing to her husband.

"I'm certain that he was, Diana."

She looked at him, surprised and moved. "You're certain?"

Grey Eagle nodded. "I'd be there with my daughter, no matter where I had to journey from. I'm sure Gideon feels the same way. Love does not die."

To Diana, his words were very profound, and comforting. "No, it doesn't."

After a pause, Grey Eagle asked, "Do you think your father would approve?"

"Of you? Oh, yes. He would have liked you very much. I think you two would have been great friends." She smiled at the mental picture of Grey Eagle and Gideon together.

"What of your mother?"

Diana sighed. "I don't think she would be pleased."

"Because I am half Cheyenne?"

"Because she is a snob."

Her answer seemed to catch him by surprise, because all he said in response was, "Oh."

She swung his hand up and kissed it. "Now, Nora would like you, once she got over the shock."

"Your sister?"

Diana nodded. "She would think you very handsome."

"And that carries weight with her?"

"Yes. She is young—only sixteen—and very spoiled, I

fear.'' Diana slanted a teasing glance at him. ''But I have outgrown such foolishness. I do not think you handsome at all.''

''You don't?'' Grey Eagle seemed genuinely perplexed. ''All the other women do.''

''You arrogant oaf.'' Diana lightly punched his arm. ''Well, all right, I think you pleasant-looking.''

Grey Eagle dropped her hand and put his arm around her waist, drawing her close. ''Only pleasant-looking?''

She nodded, fighting a smile.

His fingers moved against her ribs. ''You're sure?''

''Yes.'' She tried to squirm away from him. ''Don't you tickle me.''

Grey Eagle brought his other hand into play, and she was helpless against his strength and his fingers. His tickling brought shouts of laughter from her. ''Admit it,'' he growled. ''You think me exceedingly handsome.''

''Oh, I do!''

''That's better.'' Grey Eagle backed her up to a tree, suddenly very serious. ''It is good for a man to laugh with his wife.'' He took her face in his hands and searched her eyes. ''I love you, Diana.''

Her arms went around him, and she held him, tightly. ''And I love you, Grey Eagle, more than I thought it possible to love.'' For several minutes, they embraced each other as the day darkened around them. ''And I actually think you are beautiful,'' she finally whispered against his chest.

''I knew that.''

She swatted his backside. ''Arrogant oaf.''

''Yes, dear.'' He stroked her hair. ''Are you hungry? For food, I mean.''

Diana smiled. ''Yes.''

''Then let's go eat.'' He draped his arm over her shoulders. ''You need to keep up your strength.''

''Why?''

''Because I intend to love you all night long, wife.'' He planted a wet, smacking kiss on her cheek, and led his happy, willing wife in the direction of their lodge.

*   *   *

From the other side of the river, Black Moon watched them go. Hatred and jealousy boiled inside her, making her feel physically ill.

He went through with it. Grey Eagle married the white bitch.

"Your marriage will be short-lived," she snarled in a whisper, even though the couple had disappeared from view. "You both will pay for this day, and you will pay dearly." Quietly, she backed away and headed in the direction of her brother's lodge.

A few minutes later, Calls the Wind looked up from the knife he was sharpening. He sat outside his mother's lodge, keeping her company while she labored over their supper. Calls the Wind had a genuine affection for his aging mother and did not mind sitting with her, especially when doing so afforded him the opportunity to keep a surreptitious eye on the lodge of Two Bears, which was only a short distance away. Even now, as he watched, Black Moon stormed toward her brother's lodge.

His beloved was clearly upset, as was evident in her stance, and in the sharp words she said to her sister-in-law before she ducked through the opening and disappeared. When Black Moon did not reappear after several minutes, Calls the Wind calmly returned his attention to his knife.

He would allow her to be upset today.

Grey Eagle had married only hours ago, and even though Black Moon's feelings for the man were unrequited, Calls the Wind could understand that she would be distressed, because now, all hope was gone. Even Black Moon could not deny the truth any longer.

In a day, maybe two, he would join the line of hopefuls who waited outside her lodge every evening. Each man hoped to ensnare Black Moon in the folds of his blanket, and every evening, each man failed.

Calls the Wind would not fail.

He had fasted for days, had scarified his calves with the point of his knife until the blood ran. He had earned the forgiveness of the Old Ones for Black Moon's indiscretion with the pain of hunger, and with the blood of his body.

Now that the last obstacle had been removed, she would have no reason to put him off.

What if she found a new reason?

The words taunted him, even though they came from his own mind. Calls the Wind's jaw tightened, as did his grip on the knife in his hand.

Black Moon would not find a new reason, for her own sake.

He had been patient for years.

He would be patient no longer.

Later that evening, after another bout of lovemaking, Grey Eagle lay on his back under the soft buffalo robe and held his wife close. Her head rested on his shoulder, and her fingers made light, caressing circles on his chest.

He felt blessed.

There was no other word for it. He was blessed with the presence of Diana in his life at all, and was even more blessed because, for some unfathomable reason, she evidently loved him as he loved her.

"I have a gift for you," he whispered against her hair.

"You gave it to me already," she drowsily responded. Her hand wandered lower, to touch him most intimately. "I loved it. Thank you, husband." Her lips touched his chest in a kiss.

Blessed.

"Diana."

Something in his voice must have told her he was serious, for her hand returned to his chest and she looked up at him, all signs of playfulness and fatigue gone. "I'm listening, Grey Eagle."

He sat up, carrying her with him. "Wait here." With no self-consciousness, he rose naked from their bed and crossed the interior of the lodge to where some of his belongings rested against the hide wall. He crouched down and searched through a pack until he found a small velvet bag. With the bag in hand, he returned to his marital bed. Diana sat up, waiting for him, clutching the top robe to her breasts.

He knelt beside her and gently pulled the robe from her grasp. "Do not hide yourself from me, wife. I take great pleasure in gazing upon your beauty."

An endearing blush reddened Diana's cheeks. "I also take pleasure from looking at you," she admitted softly. "Be patient with me, Grey Eagle. Nudity is not a common practice among the whites, even when they are married and alone in the privacy of their bedrooms."

"That is their loss." He shifted to a sitting position, with the bag in one hand.

"I agree." Diana smiled at him. "I have a gift for you also, husband." She darted out from under the cover of the robe, retrieved something from a bundle, and returned to his side, hiding the item behind her as she sat down. Her eyes were bright with the excitement of a child on Christmas morn, and Grey Eagle fell even more in love. "You first," she urged.

He gave her the bag, which she clutched in her hands. "My father gave this to my mother on their wedding day," he explained. "When she died, he put it away, until my twenty-first birthday. That day he gave it to me in the hope that one day I would love a woman as much as he loved my mother." His hands closed over Diana's. "I do now. This is my wedding gift to you, dear wife. I hope it brings you pleasure."

"Thank you." She stared into his eyes, blinking away tears, then looked down at the bag. With great care, she pulled open the satin drawstring cord, and turned the bag upside down. A mass of pearls tumbled into her waiting hand, eliciting a cry of surprise and wonder from her. "Grey Eagle! What is this?" She held up a three-strand choker made from creamy white pearls, and two dangling earrings. Even in the flickering fire-light, the quality and value of the jewels was evident.

Grey Eagle shrugged. "I've told you that my father came from a wealthy family; he had the means to purchase such a gift. Because he wanted to honor her as his wife in the white man's tradition, yet give her a gift that would have some significance in her Cheyenne world, he chose his marriage gift to my mother with great care.'' He reached out and touched the pearls that glowed in Diana's hand. ''You've surely seen the hair-pipe chokers that many of the Cheyenne wear.''

Diana nodded. She moved her fingers, causing the pearls to shift and sparkle in the firelight.

''My father commissioned this choker—and the earrings— to be made in the Cheyenne style, but with the jewels of the white man. Only my mother wore them before you. Now they are yours.'' He hesitated. ''I hope you like them.''

''They are beautiful.'' Her voice sounded curiously hoarse. ''Thank you, Grey Eagle. I shall treasure them all the days of my life. Help me put them on.'' She held the pearls out to him with one hand and gathered her hair away from her neck with the other.

Grey Eagle fastened the choker in place, and was unable to resist the impulse to plant a kiss on her inviting flesh, then hooked the long earrings in her ears.

She released her hair. ''How do they look?''

Diana's question was innocent, he knew. But as he watched her in the golden glow of the firelight, saw that light caught and reflected by his mother's pearls, the beauty of the jewels paled in comparison to the beauty of Diana's naked body. ''Beautiful,'' he managed to croak.

With one hand touching the choker as if she could not quite believe that it was indeed hers, she smiled somewhat sadly. ''I should have given you my gift first.''

''Why?''

''My gift comes from my heart, Grey Eagle, but it cannot compare to yours.''

Stricken by the thought that he may have unintentionally hurt her, he said, ''Let me be the judge of that.'' He held out one hand in demand.

Diana reached behind her and pulled out something furry. Hesitantly, she put the item in his hand. ''I made them myself,'' she said in a small voice.

Grey Eagle held up to the firelight that which she had given him. There were two items, it turned out, both identical, both very soft, both with strips of beading down the sides.

"Jubal told me a story of how you once bet him a knife you really liked against a pair of gaiters Sweet Water made for him," Diana said. "He said you lost that bet. I couldn't get you a knife to replace the one you lost, so I made you a pair of gaiters. Sweet Water showed me how to fashion them, and Sparrow coached me on the beading, but I made them myself." She finished on an almost defensive note.

The gaiters were made of soft, plush beaver pelts, and the beadwork on the sidebands, while not executed with Sparrow's skill, was still admirable. That Diana would make him such a thoughtful gift in the short time she had been among the Cheyenne touched him deeply. Grey Eagle stared down at them, his throat constricted with a suspicious lump. "These are the most precious gift I have ever received," he said, and meant it. He raised his eyes to her. "Thank you, Diana." He pulled them on over his bare feet and adjusted them around his calves. With the leather binders she had provided, the gaiters fit perfectly, and he knew they would keep him very warm when winter again came howling down upon them in a few short months.

"You really like them?"

"I really do. Do not compare them to my mother's pearls, sweetheart. Anyone can pay someone to make something. These I shall always treasure, because you made them yourself, just for me." He drew her into his arms and kissed her tenderly.

Diana threw her arms around him. "I do love the pearls, Grey Eagle. They are special because they belonged to your mother, and were from your father."

"Then we both chose good gifts."

"Yes."

Diana pressed her breasts against him, and Grey Eagle willingly fell back on the buffalo robes. He looked up to find his wife straddling his hips in a most bold and intriguing manner. Her long, love-tangled hair framed her face and upper body, her shapely breasts jutted out proudly, their darker tips pebbled and hard, and his mother's pearls glowed against her skin. To his astonishment, he felt himself stirring against her again.

Diana, with her innocent love and honest passion, had inspired him to levels of performance he would not have believed possible.

He wore nothing but beaded beaver pelt gaiters, and she wore nothing but pearls, as they loved each other once more.

Chapter Twenty-Nine

The next morning, there was great excitement in the village. The tribal elders announced that the time had come to begin the summer hunting season. In four days, the tribe would split up for its annual migration.

Hectic days of preparation followed. The women worked together to finish the numerous hides that were in various stages of the tanning process, while the men worked with the horses and ensured that all weapons were in good order. Scouts rode out in several different directions and would return in a day or two with information on which would be the best way for the groups to go. Because Diana and Grey Eagle did not have many possessions, they offered their services to the families of Raven's Heart and Jubal. The days passed quickly, and, to Diana, the nights passed even more quickly—too quickly, in her opinion.

She loved knowing that she and Grey Eagle would be alone in their own lodge when darkness fell, free to explore each other in any way they chose. They passed hours in conversation, learning more about each other's past experiences and present philosophies, and they spent hours making love, which taught them more about each other in a different way.

Grey Eagle learned that if he lightly nibbled on Diana's collarbone, his touch would sent shivers of delight down her body, bringing her nipples to tight, enticing buds and raising goose flesh on her legs. He loved the sensitivity of her body, loved how enthusiastically she responded to him.

Diana learned that the back of Grey Eagle's neck was very sensitive, perhaps because it was always covered and protected by his hair, and that if she kissed him there, he would become very still. If she teased his ear with her tongue and warm breath, he would shiver. If she kissed her way down his chest and stomach, he would moan. And one night, when she felt adventurous and took her mouth even lower, he writhed in surprised pleasure.

The love between them grew.

The night that was to be the last spent in the winter encampment arrived. After sharing supper with Jubal and Sweet Water, Grey Eagle escorted Diana back to their lodge, where George Washington and Nokeeho were picketed, then he went to check on his other four horses, who were with the tribal herd. Diana packed a few more household items in hides and secured the bundles with thin strips of rawhide, until all that remained unpacked was their bed and the articles they would need in the morning.

She looked around the interior of the lodge and felt a sense of sadness. Only four days had she and Grey Eagle lived there, but she felt that those four days had been a honeymoon of sorts, a magical time of discovery and love, and she was loath to leave the place. The knowledge that the interior of their lodge would look exactly the same when they settled in their next camp gave her comfort.

Grey Eagle still had not returned. As Diana sat on the bed waiting for him, an idea that had been niggling her mind all day blossomed. A slow smile spread across her face, and she reached for the red wool blanket. Now hoping that he gave her a few more minutes, she went to work.

After a discussion with Jubal about how they thought the camp might break up—which families would travel together, how many small groups would be formed—Grey Eagle started back in the direction of his lodge, anxious to be alone with Diana. He'd covered about half the distance there when a figure wrapped in a red blanket materialized out of the dark shadow of a cottonwood.

"Grey Eagle."

He recognized the honeyed voice of his wife, and his heart leapt in joy. "Diana." He reached for her, but she stepped back, holding the blanket tight around her body.

"Come with me."

He obeyed, staying close by her side. Her manner puzzled him, but did not cause alarm—yet—because she did not seem to be upset or distressed. Skirting the outside edge of the village, she led him down a path that he realized would take them to the heated pool. A bolt of excitement shot though him, tightening his stomach and stirring his manhood.

When they came into the clearing where the pool was, Grey Eagle was glad to see that no one else was there. A few feet from the water, Diana said, "Please wait here." Again, he obeyed.

She walked the short distance to the edge of the pool. There, she stood and stared down at the steaming waters for a moment, then turned to him. The pale light of the waxing moon kissed her indistinct features, and Grey Eagle was reminded of how she had looked when she'd come to him in the clouds. He knew Diana was the Woman, had known since the first day he'd met her, but still, the wonder that he had found her in the flesh struck him anew.

She looked at him, the force of her love touching him across the distance that separated them. He wanted to close that distance, but made himself wait for what she had planned. Diana dropped the blanket, and Grey Eagle's eyes widened, for she wore nothing but her long, glorious hair. Her pale body seemed to glow in the moonlight, and she looked to him to be a goddess—of the night, of the water, of love. He instantly became hard, and when she held out her hand to him, he moaned.

Slowly, he approached her, his hungry eyes drinking their fill of her beauty. He took her hand with one of his, and laid his other hand over her heart. Her hardened nipple pressed against his palm, and he heard her sharp intake of breath. Under his hand, her heart thudded, and filled him with the joy of her life. How glad he was that she was alive, that she was his. He drew her into his arms and kissed her, relishing the feel of her naked body under his hands. There was something very erotic about him being fully dressed when she was nude.

She pulled away from him and took a few backward steps into the water. "Join me," she invited, her voice a sultry whisper.

Grey Eagle was reminded of another time he had been tempted to join the Woman in the water. Then she had been an apparition, and the water had been freezing. Not so now. He wasted no time in stripping off all he wore.

Diana backed farther into the water, until it came up to her waist. Grey Eagle watched her gaze travel down his fully aroused body, saw her sensual smile of satisfaction, saw her hand raise in invitation again. Into the warm, welcoming waters he went, fighting the urge to throw himself at her. Instead, he circled her, drawing ever nearer. He reached out to stroke her hair, wrapping the rose-scented lengths around his hand. He bent and kissed the Mark of the Eagle, and she shuddered.

That little movement broke his restraint. Grey Eagle moved to face her, and took her head in his hands. He kissed her, tenderly at first, then more and more hungrily, suddenly ravenous for all of her. His mouth moved down her neck, then to her shoulder. He grabbed her waist and lifted her higher, helped by the buoyancy of the warm water, and trailed his mouth down her chest. She gripped his shoulders, braced her weight, and made it easy for him to reach her nipples. He latched on to one, and she moaned, soft and low, arching her back. The wet ends of her hair teased his hands.

He could stand it no longer. Holding her close with one arm, guiding her hips with his other, Grey Eagle lowered her down the length of his body. Her eyes widened as he lowered her farther still, right onto his waiting shaft. Slowly, he filled her. His eyes drifted closed as he felt her slick, snug warmth tighten around him. They clung to each other—her arms around his neck, her legs encircling his hips, his arms holding her upper body, his legs slightly spread for balance.

With a gentle rhythm, they rocked together, and the slow leisure of their movements combined with the sensuous, liquid warmth surrounding them took them to incredible heights of pleasure. Diana cried out. Her body grabbed him in tiny, involuntary spasms, as if it wanted to pump the seed from him, and it succeeded. His release came and Grey Eagle let out a long, low cry, feeling as if he poured his soul into Diana along with his seed.

Both breathless, they clung together as the waves of pleasure receded and left a deep sense of loving peace in their place.

"The pool was a good idea," Grey Eagle whispered hoarsely, amazed that he could speak at all. He loved the feel of her breasts pressed to his chest, of her legs embracing his hips and holding him inside her.

"Yes." Diana sighed the word more than spoke it. She loved the feel of his chest against her breasts, the strength of his arms around her, of his legs as he supported her weight, the pulsing power of his manhood deep inside her. "Thank you for indulging me, husband. I did not want to leave this place without experiencing this with you."

He nibbled her neck. "You are most welcome, wife. It would have been a terrible loss to have missed this." He began to move her through the water. Eventually, he pulled himself from her, and, like two children, they explored the expanse of the pool, sometimes floating, sometimes splashing, sometimes holding each other again.

Much later, when the constellations had moved a great distance across the night sky, Grey Eagle helped Diana out of the water. The cool air was refreshing, but chilling, and after gathering Grey Eagle's clothes, they shared the warmth of the red blanket as they made their quiet, careful, barefoot way back to their lodge.

The encampment was broken the next morning. In what to Diana was a surprisingly short period of time for such a tremendous undertaking, the tipis were emptied and the lodgeskins removed, leaving forlorn conical skeletons of lodgepoles piercing the morning sky. The poles came down next, and Diana learned that there was a direct correlation between the number of horses a man owned and the size of his lodge.

No matter how many buffalo hides a family had—or children, for that matter—if they did not have a sufficient number of horses to pull the travoises that were made of the lodgepoles and carried the family's belongings, their lodge was small. The wealth of a Cheyenne family was determined by the number of their horses.

The tribal horse herd was now gone, having been split up among its individual owners. Many of the horses pulled a travois behind them, as did some of the larger dogs, and other horses carried men, women, and older children. Small children were secured in the safety and comfort of a travois, as were several old people. In a little less than an hour, an encampment of approximately two hundred people was ready to move. Diana was amazed.

She waited on Nokeeho's back, sitting in her Cheyenne saddle. The high pommel and equally high cantle would take some getting used to, but the saddle was reasonably comfortable. She wore one of her doeskin dresses, and the fringed hem rode above her knees. It seemed strange to think that not so long ago, the idea of her stockings and drawers being displayed while she very unladylike rode astride had troubled her. Now she freely rode astride, with her bare knees exposed, and thought nothing of it.

The gathering broke into four groups. Dogs—including Rosie—barked excitedly, children laughed and shouted, farewells were called to friends and family. Then the groups moved out, each in a different direction. Diana was grateful to see that the sullen and beautiful Black Moon, along with her brother and his family, went with a band that headed south, as did an odd young warrior named Calls the Wind and his sweet old mother. She and Grey Eagle stayed with a group that included Jubal and Sweet Water, and Raven's Heart and his family.

They headed in an easterly direction, and soon the other bands were gone from sight. A strange silence settled over everyone, or perhaps it just seemed that way to Diana after spending weeks in a lively, sometimes boisterous village. And so began her first summer with the Cheyenne.

One morning a week later, Diana left her lodge with two empty water bags. She had not gone far when she heard what sounded to her like a baby crying. What troubled her was that the crying seemed to come from the middle of a thicket of willows and young cottonwoods, some distance from the small encampment of fourteen tipis. No one else was in sight.

She set down the bags and cautiously entered the thicket. To her astonishment, she found a cradleboard hanging from a tree branch, and securely strapped to the board was a very unhappy Mary Sweet Rose.

"Oh, sweetheart," Diana crooned as she pulled the cradleboard from the branch and into her arms. She rocked the board and searched the area for Sweet Water, unable to believe that the devoted Cheyenne mother had purposely left her infant daughter so isolated and unattended. Finding no sign of her friend, Diana left the thicket with the baby, whose howls had subsided to indignant whimpers.

Diana spotted Sweet Water in front of her lodge, tending a cook fire, while Jubal leaned against a nearby backrest and contentedly puffed on his pipe. With comforting murmurs to Mary Sweet Rose, Diana crossed the small encampment, aware that some of the women paused in their work and watched her pass. Sweet Water looked up as Diana approached, and the smile of welcome faded from her round brown face.

Suddenly aware that something was wrong, Diana came to a halt. "I found Mary Sweet Rose hanging from a tree, all alone," she announced.

"She still cry?" Sweet Water demanded.

"Yes, she was crying. That's how I discovered her."

Mary Sweet Rose continued to fuss, her sounds of discontent growing louder. Diana rocked the cradleboard again. "I thought you'd want to see to her," she said pointedly.

Sweet Water stood up, her face set in the closed Cheyenne expression Diana knew so well, and was coming to dread.

"Baby need learn to not cry," Sweet Water snapped, and took the cradleboard from Diana's grasp. "You leave her be." She marched off, back in the direction of the willow grove.

Stunned and hurt, Diana watched her friend go, unable to believe what she'd just heard. She turned to Jubal, who watched her impassively. "What did I do wrong?" she asked. "And what did she mean, the baby can't cry? All babies cry."

"Cheyenne babies don't," Jubal said around his pipe stem. "They're taught from the day they're born that cryin' ain't gonna get 'em what they want. All it'll get 'em is bein' left alone for a while."

"But that's so cruel!" Diana blurted out.

Jubal took the pipe from his mouth. "Don't be makin' judgments on things you don't understand, girl," he warned. "Have you seen any abused Cheyenne children?"

"No." Diana crossed her arms over her chest and looked down at her mocassinned feet, feeling very much like a naughty schoolgirl being called to task, still not understanding what she had done wrong.

"Cheyenne children are the happiest, best-behaved, most loved children I've ever seen," said Jubal. "About the only thing they ain't allowed to do is cry. And that's because one cryin' baby can endanger the whole camp."

Diana frowned in disbelief. "How?" she demanded.

Jubal took another puff on his pipe, his stern gaze unrelenting. "That cryin' could be heard by the wrong people, Diana, like a passin' party of enemy raiders. And surely you've noticed in your time among the Cheyenne how polite they are to each other."

Reluctantly, Diana nodded.

"It'd be mighty rude for me'n Sweet Water to allow our daughter to raise a ruckus and disturb our neighbors, now wouldn't it?"

"She's only a baby," Diana protested.

"So? That don't mean she can be a bother to the rest of the band, and maybe a danger, too." Jubal sighed. "I know this is difficult for you to understand, but it ain't as cruel as it seems. Babies learn real fast that cryin' ain't gonna work.'' He raised a bushy eyebrow at her. "You got a fence to mend with Sweet Water. She's in a huff 'cause she feels that you interfered with her motherly duties.''

"I suppose I did," Diana admitted, guilt and self-doubt washing over her. "I'll go find her right now.''

Jubal nodded in satisfaction, and Diana went in search of Sweet Water. She could not condone leaving a baby alone in the bush to cry itself out, and yet she could understand the reason behind the Cheyenne doing so. The thought that her dear friend was upset with her made Diana feel terrible, and she wondered if she would ever truly belong with the Cheyenne.

The rift with the kind-hearted Sweet Water was mended, and later that night Diana confessed her folly to Grey Eagle as they prepared for bed. By the time she finished with the story, they lay together, her head resting on his shoulder as he stroked her hair. In conclusion, she said, "I couldn't believe that Sweet Water would deliberately leave her baby there alone, and yet I guess that's what I thought she'd done, and I was filled with indignation. Then it turned out that she had a good reason for doing what she did, and I interfered where I had no right to.''

Grey Eagle's arm around her tightened in a hug. "All is well now, Diana. Don't trouble yourself any longer over it.''

"But I hurt my friend." She raised up on one elbow to look at his face. "And because I'm your wife, I made you look bad in front of the tribe.''

"No, you didn't. Your friend has forgiven you, and all is well.''

Diana lay back down again. "Not really.''

"What else is wrong?''

With a sigh, Diana wondered if she should share with him something that had been bothering her for days.

"Talk to me, sweetheart," he coaxed.

She gave in. "With the exception of Jubal and Sweet Water and Sparrow's family, no one will accept my help with sickness and injuries. They treat me with respect, yet all turn to the aging Buffalo Woman for medical assistance.''

"They have turned to her for years, Diana. You cannot begrudge her that.''

"I don't begrudge her at all. I'm certain she has earned the high regard with which the others hold her." She did not mention that Buffalo Woman herself was cool in her manner toward Diana, and that no matter how hard Diana tried, she could not get the woman to warm up to her. "Although she and I have learned through different schools, we both have knowledge of value, and I wish she would allow us to work together. When that boy fell from his horse and broke his leg yesterday, Buffalo Woman would not accept my offer of the laudanum to help with his pain. He suffered needlessly, Grey Eagle, and that troubles me deeply.''

"I know. Your concern for others is one of the things I love about you, wife. But no one accepts change easily, Diana, and your methods of medical treatment are different from those of the Cheyenne in many respects. Your surgical instruments may be admired, but they are also feared." Grey Eagle kissed her forehead. "Give them time, and the Cheyenne will come to accept and love you as Sparrow and Sweet Water do.''

"Do you really think so?" she asked doubtfully.

"I know so." He shifted his position so that he lay on top of her, braced on his elbows. His long hair fell over her breasts and arms, soothing her with its sage-scented touch. "Now let me love you," he whispered, nuzzling her neck, "so that you can smile again.''

Diana sighed and wrapped her arms around him. In no time at all, she was smiling again.

Chapter Thirty

Over the next two months, life settled into a comfortable routine for the band of nomads. Following a day or two, or perhaps even several days, of travel, a good campsite was found or chosen, tipis were set up, and the constant procurement of food continued. Sometimes the band stayed at one campsite for a day or two, other times for a week, once at a particularly lovely place for two weeks.

Diana became proficient in the setting up and taking down of her tipi, to the point that she was amazed at herself. She also did not mind the work of cleaning, cooking, and preserving the bounty of game Grey Eagle brought home to her, nor did she mind the gathering of roots, bulbs, fruits, and herbs that was part of life for a Cheyenne woman. Her command of the Cheyenne language slowly improved, and she worked with Sparrow and Sweet Water on their English. They traded days of language—one day they spoke only Cheyenne together, the next, only English, and so on. She needed much more help with her Cheyenne than her two friends needed with their English.

In time, Diana came to understand how the Cheyenne believed they were closely connected to the spirits of the earth and to nature, how grateful they were for the bounty of their world, and how successfully they lived within the boundaries of that world. She also realized how much the Cheyenne were at the mercy of nature, how completely dependent they were on the availability of game—especially the buffalo—not only for their food, but for their clothing, shelter, utensils, and tools. There was no nearby mercantile or butcher shop they could visit in times of drought or flood or storm, and she vowed she would never again take for granted the luxury of being able to purchase one's supplies and foodstuffs so easily, as most white men could.

Now that she had lived among them, the respect for the Plains Indians that had been planted in her by her father grew to new heights.

In early August, Diana's band of Cheyenne were joined at a particularly fertile and lovely campsite by another band. She recognized many of the people by sight if not by name, and was dismayed to discover that Two Bears and his family were part of the band. For a few weeks at least, Black Moon had come back into her life.

Sweet Water confided to Diana the gossip she'd heard on that subject. With the blessings of both his mother and Two Bears, the young warrior named Calls the Wind had courted Black Moon vigorously throughout the summer. The beautiful widow steadfastly refused the man, much to the anger of her brother and the humiliation of Calls the Wind. Still, the silent, stocky warrior would not give up. All in the tribe admired him for his patience and persistence with Black Moon, who was beginning to lose some of her elevated social standing for her unkind treatment of a courageous and worthy man, especially since she accepted no other suitor.

Diana heard the news with disappointment. Although she avoided Black Moon, and Black Moon also stayed out of her way, Diana was not convinced that there would be no trouble. The look she caught on Black Moon's face one morning as that woman stared after Grey Eagle only reinforced her concern. Black Moon never spoke of Grey Eagle, nor to him, nor approached him, but from that one fleeting look of unbearable longing, Diana knew that Black Moon still carried very strong feelings for her husband. She warned Grey Eagle and the others to be on their guard, and looked forward to the day when Black Moon's band went its own way again.

A week later, Diana and Sparrow labored in a lush meadow with several other women and girls, digging bulbs and roots. Rosie rested nearby, the growing dog's tongue hanging as she recovered from her valiant and vain effort to run down a rabbit. The chore of digging was tedious, but it struck Diana that even the most mundane, sometimes exhausting chores—such as tanning buffalo hides—were almost if not actually fun when the duties were cheerfully shared, as Cheyenne women did.

She spotted a nearby dogbane plant. "We should collect some of that," she said to Sparrow. "I've heard that the roots of the dogbane can be boiled into tea and used as a purgative. It would be a good thing for me to have on hand." Not that any of the tribe would come to her for aid, she thought sadly.

Sparrow shook her head. "I cannot touch it, Diana. It makes redness on my skin."

"You're allergic to it?"

"What is al-ler-gic?"

How to explain that? Diana wondered. "If a person is allergic to something, it makes them sick each time they touch it, or eat it. The skin itches, and a rash forms, and sometimes hives—large welts like bee stings."

"Then I am al-ler-gic to dogbane. That is how I kept my skin red last winter."

Diana stared at her. "You deliberately caused the rash my father treated you for?"

Sparrow nodded. "The two smelly white men did not know I speak English. I hear them talk, know they want to use me, but not if I have red skin. So I kept my skin red. When I came to you and your father, there no longer was the need."

"Sparrow, you are a very clever girl." The admiration in Diana's voice was genuine. By a simple if uncomfortable means, Sparrow had saved herself from months of rape.

Sparrow smiled, shyly, but Diana could tell that her words of praise delighted her young friend.

The morning was lovely and warm, and time seemed to pass quickly. Diana was surprised to see how full her bag of roots and bulbs was already. She was pleased with her morning's work, and knew that Grey Eagle would be pleased with the meal she set before him tonight.

Then, very faintly, she heard it.

The call of an eagle.

She sat back on her heels, listening.

"What is it?" Sparrow asked.

"An eagle. Maybe it's Franklin." She had not seen Franklin since the day of her wedding. Diana eagerly searched the skies.

Sparrow frowned. "I hope it is not Franklin."

Diana looked at her in surprise. "Why not?"

"Because Calls the Wind dug an eagle trap over there, by the buffalo wallow." Sparrow pointed with one hand and shaded her eyes with the other as she looked upward. The girl was clearly worried.

A sharp stab of fear bolted through Diana's stomach. "What is an eagle trap?"

"Brother Eagle is holy to the Cheyenne," Sparrow explained. "That is why his feathers are so valuable. It would be disrespectful to use a weapon to kill a holy Brother, so instead, a man digs a pit and hides there, with a baited grate covering it. Brother Eagle is hungry, so he comes to eat the bait, and the man reaches through the grate and captures Eagle's foot."

Diana dreaded the answer to her next question. "Then what?"

Sparrow's young face took on a sorrowful expression. "Then he twists Brother Eagle's neck. I am sorry, Diana, my sister."

The eagle called again, much closer this time. Diana scrambled to her feet. It was Franklin. She could feel him. *Oh, God.*

Terror wrapped itself around her heart. "Please get Grey Eagle," she begged Sparrow.

"Where is he?"

"At our lodge, working on his rifle. Hurry, *na-semahe.*" *Little sister.* The term of endearment came easily to Diana's lips. Sparrow raced away. The other women and girls took notice, and called quiet questions to one another.

Ignoring them, Diana desperately searched the skies as she ran toward the buffalo wallow. She spotted an eagle, watched as it circled ever closer in the hot morning air. Whether the magnificent bird was headed toward the trap or toward her, Diana could not tell. She cried out to Calls the Wind in Cheyenne, shouted his name, but did not know the words to ask him to dismantle his trap.

She came to a stop a short distance from the buffalo wallow. Just ahead, Diana saw the bloody carcass of a young deer tied to a grate made of thick branches. She pressed a hand to her suddenly roiling stomach, as if that could ease the sick feeling there.

''Franklin!'' she called, watching the eagle circle above her. Without taking her eyes from Franklin, Diana bent down and released the garter that held up her right legging, then tore the legging off, loosening her moccasin in the process. She kicked the moccasin away as she thrust her right arm into the tube of soft deerskin. The legging made a poor arm guard but was better than nothing at all.

Diana held her arm out to her side at shoulder height, praying that Franklin was more drawn to her than he was to the carcass. ''Come to me, Franklin,'' she called. Her eyes closed, and she reached for him with her heart. ''Come to me.''

A series of surprised shouts and cries sounded behind her at the same time a rush of air blew tendrils of hair around her face. Diana opened her eyes and watched Franklin come in for his landing. She braced herself and her arm, determined that she would hold him up, and leaned her head away from his nearest flapping wing. His talons clutched her arm painfully, but she did not move. For all his size, Franklin was amazingly light. He neatly folded his wings and shuffled his feet on the shifting legging, then calmly looked at her.

Almost faint with relief, Diana reached up with her left hand to touch his feathered chest. ''Hello, sweetheart.'' From the corner of her eye, she saw the grate holding the deer carcass move, and, a moment later, Calls the Wind pulled himself out of the pit. He stared at her in awe.

"Diana."

Grey Eagle's voice touched her, drew her to carefully turn around. He stood not far from her. Behind him, the entire population of the encampment—including Buffalo Woman and Black Moon—had gathered, and all stared at her with the same fearful wonder that Calls the Wind did. Only Grey Eagle and Jubal did not appear to be in shock.

Suddenly afraid that she was guilty of some terrible transgression in the eyes of the Cheyenne, Diana said to Grey Eagle, "I didn't want him killed." Her tone was quietly defensive.

"I know, *na-vekee-hesta.*" *My sweetheart.* "You've done nothing wrong." He took a few steps, then stopped when Franklin flapped his wings once, as if in warning. "Will he let me approach?"

Deep in her heart, Diana was suddenly certain that Franklin would allow Grey Eagle near. She felt the magical current flowing around her, the Spirit of the Eagle binding her and Franklin together, and she knew the Spirit would welcome Grey Eagle to their circle. "Yes," she answered.

Grey Eagle came forward slowly. He wore only his breechclout and moccasins in the heat of the day. His hair moved on the warm wind, as did the eagle feather tied to the end of one braid. His eyes, so green in the sunlight, found and locked on hers.

Diana held out her free hand to him. He took it in a tight grasp, and touched the place between Franklin's eyes with his other hand.

The powerful circle of love was complete.

For several minutes they stood there, until Diana's arm began to tremble from the effort of keeping it outstretched and level. As if he knew of her discomfort, Franklin shuffled his feet and moved his wings. Grey Eagle stepped back, and Franklin lifted off of Diana's arm.

"Fly away, Franklin," Diana whispered as the eagle rose higher. "Fly far away from eagle traps. Stay safe, so that you may visit us again."

Grey Eagle held tight to her hand, and together they watched until Franklin was a dark speck in the cloudless sky. His call echoed back to them one last time, and the eagle was gone.

Diana blinked, then looked down at her aching arm. The now torn legging had slid off over her hand, and she saw that her arm bled from a few deep talon scratches. Then she looked to the ground, and found a perfect, lone eagle feather.

She picked it up and turned to face Calls the Wind. Grey Eagle released her hand. Slowly, taking care with her one bare foot, Diana walked to Calls the Wind and held out the feather. "Thank you for not killing my friend," she said quietly.

Grey Eagle translated her words to Cheyenne.

Calls the Wind stared at her, then accepted the feather. *"Ne-a'eshe,"* he said solemnly, thanking her.

Diana nodded in response before she retraced her steps to Grey Eagle's side. His arms closed around her, and she clung to him, suddenly exhausted. "Please take me home," she whispered.

Without hesitation, he swung her up into his arms and carried her across the meadow. Her arms closed around his neck and she revelled in the security and safety he offered her. The members of the tribe stepped back and created a path for them, and Diana heard Grey Eagle ask Sparrow to retrieve her legging and moccasin.

Then they were in their lodge, and he laid her on their bed. He removed her other moccasin and legging, brought her cool water, made certain that the sides of the lodge were rolled up high enough to allow a cooling breeze to blow through. Sweet Water came and helped Grey Eagle cleanse and bind the bleeding gouges in her forearm. Then he sat at her side and held her hand until she fell asleep.

After that memorable incident, Diana's acceptance by the Cheyenne was ensured. Even Buffalo Woman was won over at last, and called on her with a gift of some medicinal herbs. Women and girls stopped by for cups of mint tea and friendly chats, sought her out for small medical treatments, and included her in their midday meal gatherings. Calls the Wind wore his new eagle feather with pride, and treated Diana with the greatest respect.

All accepted her wholeheartedly now, with the exception of Black Moon. Diana did not mind, for she would not have trusted an overture of friendship from that woman. She was grateful that Black Moon kept her distance.

Life was good, Diana thought drowsily a few nights later as she lay at Grey Eagle's side. Life was very good.

Calls the Wind waited for Black Moon along the path that led to the area where the women gathered wood. A week had passed since the incident with the eagle, and it was the first time since then that he approached her. He did not wait for an invitation to walk with her, for he knew it would not come. Boldly, he fell into step with her. Her mouth tightened into an irritated line, but other than that, she did not respond to his presence.

He fought a surge of anger, and forced his voice to remain calm. "There can be no question now that the white woman knows the Spirit of the Eagle. There can be no question that she is meant to be Grey Eagle's woman."

Black Moon favored him with a withering glare.

Calls the Wind tried again. "They are bound together, Black Moon, by the Eagle, and here." He laid his fist over his heart.

She looked away from him.

He was beginning to lose patience. "Your desire for another woman's man shames you, and is wrong in the eyes of the Cheyenne. I know what it is to love one who does not love you. I know how that hurts. I will help you forget about Grey Eagle, if you will only let me."

Now Black Moon stopped, so suddenly that the long fringe down the side of her dress swung madly. She faced Calls the Wind, and he was shocked by the hatred he saw in her beautiful eyes.

"You know nothing," she ground out, her voice low and deadly. With that, she spun away from him and marched on.

Deeply troubled, Calls the Wind let her go. It was clearly time for another fast.

Two days later, Diana was awakened very early by the sounds of shouts and screams and barking dogs. The interior of the lodge was lit only by the glow of the fire coals. Rosie growled, and at first, Diana assumed it was the start of the men's daily rush to the river. Then she realized that there was a different edge to the sounds, that horses screamed, too. Grey Eagle was up in an instant, securing his breechclout. He snatched up his knife and his rifle and cautiously peered past the edge of the hide door. Gunshots sounded. Rosie scrambled past him, barking.

"Protect yourself," he ordered tersely, and was gone.

Her heart in her throat, Diana hurried into her deerskin dress and bound her hair at the base of her neck with a piece of rawhide. She took up the pistol and, as Grey Eagle had done, looked out the entryway.

There was so little light in the eastern sky that it was difficult to tell what was happening. The shouting and shooting had moved away, toward the river, and she slipped outside. A riderless, fear-stricken horse with wild eyes raced by, and Diana saw that the lodge farthest from the river—one that belonged to a member of Black Moon's band—was on fire. There was no sign of Grey Eagle.

The encampment had been attacked, but by who?

What of Sweet Water and the baby? What of Sparrow and Little Leaf?

Diana hurried to the closest tipi. There was no sound from within. "Sweet Water," she whispered loudly.

"Diana!"

Diana sighed with relief. She entered the lodge and found Sweet Water sitting on her bed at the back, a knife brandished in one hand. Mary Sweet Rose lay wide-eyed beside her, but did not cry. The value of the Cheyenne training their babies to silence struck Diana then like nothing else could. "Jubal has gone with the men?"

Sweet Water nodded.

"We've been attacked, but by who, I don't know."

"Pawnee." Sweet Water spat the word, her voice heavy with disgust.

That single word caused Diana to shudder. She knew that the Pawnee were longtime enemies of the Cheyenne, and notorious for the brutality of their attacks. With pistol in hand, she joined Sweet Water on the bed, keeping the baby between them. The sounds of battle faded, then died away. Now came the cries of distress and mourning.

Jubal stuck his head through the opening. Relief flared in his eyes, but his voice was brisk. "The bastards are gone, along with a bunch of our horses. Come on out, women. Diana, get your bag. Folks have been hurt. And killed." Then he added, almost as an afterthought, "Grey Eagle's fine." He backed his head out and was gone.

Diana and Sweet Water hugged each other in relief, then set about following Jubal's orders.

For the first time, Diana saw Grey Eagle and George Washington in war paint. The sight was fearsome.

Across her husband's face, a black line of paint ran from earlobe to earlobe, over the bridge of his nose. Above that line, his skin was painted red up to his hairline. Below the line ran black vertical stripes spaced an inch apart. Alternate black and red circles ringed his arms, just as black and red stripes ran down his naked thighs. George Washington's eyes were encircled with black, while his nose and legs sported black and red stripes. Red handprints had been placed on his hindquarters.

Grey Eagle rode bareback, and wore only his breechclout and his moccasins in addition to his war paint. He carried nothing but his weapons, while a single buffalo robe, rolled and tied over George Washington's rump, held the bag of food he had accepted from her. A water bag hung from the rope. With those meager provisions, he was going to war.

Diana stared up at him, and knew a fear like none she had ever known, not even when her own life had been threatened by Lieutenant Thatcher. "Come back to me," she said quietly.

"You know I will, *na-hteseme.*" He leaned down and caressed her cheek, then straightened and looked at Jubal, who stood next to Diana. "We'll get the horses back and avenge the deaths of our people. You and Sweet Water get to Fort Laramie as fast as you can and warn my brothers and Colonel MacKay that the Pawnee are raiding."

Jubal soberly nodded. "Will do, Grey Eagle. Watch your back, now. Your woman expects you home, and in one piece." He put a comforting arm around Diana's shoulders. "And alive," he added.

Grey Eagle nodded and took up the reins. His intense gaze seared Diana to her soul. *"Ne-mehotase,"* he said. *I love you.* He touched his forefinger to his lips and pointed it at her, then turned George Washington's head and rode after the other painted warriors, taking her heart with him.

"Ne-mehotase," Diana whispered as her eyes filled with tears. "Please come back."

Chapter Thirty-One

Two members of the tribe had been killed. The old mother of Calls the Wind was struck down by a blow to the head with a war club as she tried to run from the attackers, and a young warrior died fighting for his horse. The wails of grief that reverberated through the village haunted Diana and brought back sad memories of her father's funeral.

Calls the Wind spent time alone with his mother's body, then turned her over to Little Leaf to be prepared for her final journey. When he again came out of his lodge, he was painted for war, and the rage in his dark eyes was a terrible thing to see. He gave all of his mother's possessions, including her lodge, to the family whose tipi had burned, threw himself on the back of his painted war-horse, and, with a blood-curdling war cry, raced after the rest of the revenge party.

Jubal and Sweet Water took only minutes, it seemed, to prepare for their journey to Fort Laramie and were soon on their way, with Mary Sweet Rose strapped in her cradleboard and tied to her mother's back. Diana hated to see them go, but she had little time for sadness.

The rest of Diana's day was taken up with the care of the wounded. With Sparrow on hand to act as translator when needed, Diana and Buffalo Woman sponged bumps and bruises with a soothing tea made from lavender hyssop leaves, cleaned and bandaged cuts and gashes, and removed two arrows and three bullets from injured men, one of whom was Black Moon's brother, Two Bears, who had been shot in the thigh. All of their patients were ordered to drink cups of willow bark tea.

After a quiet supper shared with Sparrow and Little Leaf, Diana retreated to the loneliness of her own lodge. She lay under the buffalo robes that carried faint traces of Grey Eagle's sage scent and was very grateful for Rosie's warm and affectionate presence.

She watched the dying fire and was tormented with worry about her husband. Was he safe? Was he warm? Was he comfortable? If he wasn't, there was nothing she could do for him. Diana had never known such fear and worry, such a complete sense of helplessness. Finally, she could stay awake no longer. Just as she started to fall into sleep, she felt a strange and universal kinship with all women throughout the ages who had watched their men go off to war. Her last thoughts were a prayer for the safe return of the entire Cheyenne war party, and especially that of Grey Eagle and Raven's Heart.

The second day following the attack passed much as the first had, filled with the care of the wounded. Diana felt confident that all of her patients would live, barring the development of any complications. As she prepared to spend another lonely, restless night in her lodge with Rosie, she began to seriously consider Little Leaf's invitation to stay with Sparrow and her until Grey Eagle and Raven's Heart returned.

Sometime in the night, Diana was awakened by a scratching on the hide covering of her lodge. Rosie lifted her head and growled low in her throat.

"Di-an-ah." Her name was called in a voice she did not recognize.

Diana slipped into her chemise and crawled to the entryway. To her astonishment, it was Black Moon who crouched outside. Black Moon motioned that she should come, and held up a stout stick that Diana recognized as the one Two Bears used as a crutch.

"Has Two Bears taken a turn for the worse?" Diana asked, then realized the futility of her question. Black Moon spoke no English. She tried to find the words in Cheyenne, and was finally able to understand that Two Bears' wound had opened and was bleeding heavily. Diana was puzzled, because when she had checked on Two Bears earlier in the evening, he seemed to be healing well. But there was no telling what could happen with a deep wound, as his was.

Diana pulled her deerskin dress on over her chemise, slipped into her moccasins and leggings, and grabbed her medical satchel. With a firm command to Rosie that the dog stay in the lodge, she slipped outside.

Black Moon waited for her a short distance away. Diana followed her around the outskirts of the camp as quietly as she could. Then she realized that Black Moon had veered from the path that led to Two Bears' lodge. She looked back over her shoulder, trying to get her bearings in the darkness, and when she faced forward again, she could see the white gleam of Black Moon's somehow wicked smile. A second too late, Diana saw the crutch as it swung toward her. Pain exploded along the side of her head, and she crumpled to the ground.

Diana had never known such pain as that which danced with vicious delight in her head. She moaned, then realized she was gagged, and that her hands were tied in front of her. In an instinctive attempt to ease the sick feeling in her stomach—and to protect the baby she hoped had taken root there, for her monthly flow was a week late—she curled into a fetal position. In addition to Black Moon's voice, Diana heard two other familiar voices, all speaking Cheyenne. What were Painted Davy Sikes and Conway Horton doing at the encampment? Didn't they know that Sparrow was here? Didn't they know what the Cheyenne would do to them if it was learned who they were?

She struggled to a sitting position and with her bound hands pushed her hair back off her forehead. The tangled mass was sticky with a congealing wetness that Diana knew was blood. Black Moon had done some damage with that crutch. Diana managed to loosen the knot on the gag enough to pull the filthy piece of cloth down over her chin. With aching eyes, she surveyed the area.

A low fire burned nearby, shedding light on a small and unfamiliar clearing as well as on four horses and the two men with whom Black Moon spoke. Diana wondered how long she had been unconscious and how far she had been taken from the encampment. Would it do any good to scream? The fire gave her reason to doubt it. Sikes and Horton had not managed to stay alive on the frontier as long as they had by being so stupid as to build a fire where it could be seen by their enemies.

Black Moon looked up. Her expression changed to one of triumphant gloating. She spoke rapidly in Cheyenne. Sikes and Horton both turned, and Sikes sauntered over to her side.

"Well, how do, Miss Murdoch." A look of mock concern came over his tattooed face. "You ain't lookin' so good."

"Miss High-and-Mighty looks like a gawddamned Injun, that's what she looks like," Horton taunted as he approached. He pushed his ugly whiskered face close, and Diana fought to keep from gagging when the man's body stench and foul breath reached her nose. "You're gonna be sold as a slave, missy, just like that little girl you wouldn't let me have." Horton reached out with his meaty hand and cruelly squeezed her breast. "But I'll have you first."

"Not here, you won't," Painted Davy growled as he kicked Horton's hand away from Diana. "There ain't no time now."

Horton glowered at him, but moved back. "When we do have time, I get her first, Painted Davy." His hand fell to the handle of his knife. "That's the way it'll be."

"Fine." Painted Davy waved him off, then bent down to take Diana's arm in a firm grip. He jerked her to her feet.

"Is this her idea?" Diana asked, gesturing with her bound hands toward Black Moon.

"Yep," Painted Davy answered. "She sure hates you. Says you stole her man. She's gonna tell him you got sick of life with the Cheyenne and wanted to go back to your friends at Fort Laramie, just in case he wants to try to find you. But we're taking you north instead, to the Crow. We'll winter there, and when we tire of you, we'll sell you, just like she wants.'' He dragged her toward one of the horses. ''And in case you're wonderin', we're too far from the camp for anyone to hear you scream.''

Black Moon approached with several folded items and the medical bag. Diana recognized the black skirt and bodice she'd worn that long-ago day when she left Fort Laramie, as well as her cloak and the battered wide-brimmed hat. Black Moon had evidently returned to the lodge before joining her cohorts. She threw the items at Diana.

''He will be mine,'' she taunted in Cheyenne.

Diana understood that. ''Never,'' she said, also in Cheyenne.

Her calm reply seemed to enrage Black Moon. With a snarl, she grabbed Diana's wide sleeve and shoved it up over her shoulder, exposing the birthmark. Before anyone knew what she intended, Black Moon pulled her small eating knife from her belt and buried the blade in Diana's shoulder. Diana cried out in agony.

''I will cut the eagle from you!'' Black Moon screamed in Cheyenne. She jerked the knife free and took aim again.

''Christ almighty!'' Painted Davy grabbed Black Moon's hand and forced her back. ''Are you loco?''

Diana sagged against the side of the horse. She was able to twist her arms in such a way that her bound hands reached her shoulder, but she could not stem the flow of blood from the wound.

''Con, pick up the stuff this crazy woman threw. We ain't leavin' any sign of Miss Diana.'' Painted Davy roughly guided Black Moon across the clearing. ''Go on, now,'' he said in Cheyenne. ''Get out of here.''

Black Moon angrily pulled her arm from his grasp, threw Diana one last triumphant look, and walked off.

Diana pushed away from the horse. ''Please translate for me, Mr. Sikes, exactly what I say, so there is no danger of her misunderstanding me.''

Painted Davy nodded.

"The Eagle knows what you have done," Diana called out. "He will find you."

Painted Davy spoke in Cheyenne.

Black Moon halted just as she reached the edge of the circle of firelight. She glanced back over her shoulder, her eyes wide with fear. Without a word, she hurried into the darkness.

Con Horton crammed Diana's things into a pack on one of the horses, then heaved his bulk into his saddle. Painted Davy came to Diana's side and looked at her closely, with no compassion.

"If you can't ride, I'll tie you to the horse, stomach down."

Diana swayed, feeling ill and faint, to say nothing of the terrible pain that pounded in her head and throbbed down her arm. "I can ride," she insisted, terrified that if she was tied to the horse in the manner Painted Davy threatened, she would lose her baby, if she was indeed pregnant. She would ride, or die trying.

"Then get on up there." Painted Davy ended up practically throwing her onto the bare back of her horse. He tied her feet with a length of rope that passed under the horse's belly, then climbed into his own saddle, the reins to Diana's horse in hand. "Let's get the hell outta here." He kicked his horse and started off. Con followed Diana, leading the packhorse.

Desperately, Diana gripped her horse's mane as best she could with her hands tied. If she lost consciousness, if she slipped or fell off, she could be seriously hurt or killed, with her feet tied as they were. She had to stay on that horse's back, for the sake of her baby. Grey Eagle's baby. Their baby.

She *had* to survive this.

She *would* survive this.

They rode the rest of the night and through the morning. Diana slumped over her hands, lost in a fog of pain and delirium. At some time during the night, Rosie caught up to them, and now followed Diana's horse, her tongue hanging and her sides heaving. For some reason, the men didn't shoot at the dog or chase it away, for which Diana was most grateful. She would have been no help to Rosie if the dog had needed it.

When Painted Davy finally called a halt, the sun was high overhead and the day hot. Diana hardly noticed that she was pulled from the horse's back and dumped on the ground under a cottonwood. Immediately, she curled up on her side, and Rosie lay down beside her. Diana could manage no more than a whispered greeting. The breeze rustled the leaves of the tree that towered over her, and she dozed off.

She awakened to Rosie's low growls and found Con Horton leaning over her, an evil leer on his face.

"It's time to pay up, Miss High-and-Mighty. You'll be glad to have me 'tween your legs after you been screwing some gawddamned Injun buck." He fumbled with his trousers with one hand and pushed her dress up her thigh with the other.

Rosie bit his hand. Horton howled in rage. Wide awake now, Diana rolled away from him and sat up, galvanized by fear and desperation. Wildly, she looked about for any kind of help. Painted Davy sat nearby, casually nursing a cup of coffee, a grin on his face.

"Don't look at me," he drawled. "Con'll kill me if I try to cut in line."

"That's right," Con growled. He lunged for Diana's leg. She kicked him in the head and scrambled farther away, then somehow got to her feet. Rosie stood guard in front of her, growling, teeth bared, head lowered.

Horton cursed and fumbled for his pistol. "I'm gonna kill that damned dog."

Painted Davy laughed at Diana. "I just can't get used to the proper and snooty Miss Murdoch as a squaw. Captured by the Cheyenne, then takes one as her lover. Who'da thought it?"

Diana took an unsteady step backward, her eyes not leaving Horton's face, her heart pounding with fear even as a righteous anger grew in her. The big man lurched to his feet, holding his trousers up with one hand, and finally freed his pistol.

She stepped back again, wishing Rosie would get behind her, knowing the protective dog never would. "If you touch me, Grey Eagle will kill you."

At the same instant, both men froze, Horton with his pistol waving slightly, Painted Davy with the cup halfway to his mouth.

"What'd you say?" Horton croaked.

"I said my husband will kill you if you hurt me. Or my dog," she hastily added.

"That ain't what you said. You said a name. Gawddammit, who's your man?"

"Grey Eagle Beaudine."

Diana's quiet, proud words had the effect of a bolt of lightning on her two captors. Painted Davy stared at her in horror, and Con Horton's face drained of color, even as the hand that held his weapon fell to his side.

In the silence, from far away, Diana heard the call of an eagle, and was infused with hope and a strange sense of power.

"Damn." Painted Davy flung down his coffee cup. "That Cheyenne bitch lied to us. She said it was a lowly warrior, no one important, but she'd been promised to him from childhood and still wanted him."

"We took a Beaudine woman." Horton returned his pistol to its holster and secured his trousers. "Painted Davy, we took a Beaudine woman. We're dead men."

"Shut up, Con. Just shut the hell up and let me think."

Diana was astonished at the change that had come over the two men just at the mention of Grey Eagle's name.

"Where is Grey Eagle now?" Painted Davy demanded.

She could think of no reason to lie. "With a war party going after Pawnee raiders who attacked our village."

"So he's not at the encampment."

"No." Diana paused, and when Painted Davy said nothing more, she continued. "You can't take me north to the Crow, not if you want to live past next week. Grey Eagle will come after you, and so will his brothers. They will find you."

"She's right, Painted Davy."

"Shut up, Con."

Diana tried to think of some way to press her advantage, but her head hurt so badly that it was difficult to follow a cohesive train of thought. She sank wearily to a sitting position on the ground. Rosie nestled at her side, still on full alert.

Where could she go? Back to the village? Black Moon had attacked her once already; there was no guarantee she wouldn't do so again. Grey Eagle could be gone for several more days, and with Jubal and Raven's Heart also gone, she had no man to speak up for her against the lies Black Moon would surely tell.

For the sake of the baby, if there was one, Diana dared not go back to the village until she knew Grey Eagle was there to defend her. Where to go? Then the answer came to her: Fort Laramie. Black Moon was going to tell Grey Eagle that Diana had left him and gone to the fort. He would come looking for her. Joseph and Orion were already there, and Jubal and Sweet Water soon would be. "Take me to Fort Laramie."

Both men looked at her.

"That ain't a bad idea, Painted Davy," Con said. "Remember what old Will Mayhew told us last week when we ran into him on Beaver Creek? He said her family put up a reward to get her back from the Injuns. We can take her in and collect that money. That'll make up for not bein' able to sell her to the Crow."

"And we'll run right into Captain Joe and the Hunter," Painted Davy snapped.

"Do they know she wedded up with their brother?"

"No, they don't," Diana put in. *Not for certain, anyway,* she silently added.

Horton was beginning to get excited. "Let's take her in, Painted Davy. We'll dump her off, get the money, and hightail it outta there before the Beaudines know we was there."

And you'd better head for Australia, Diana thought wearily.

"It might work," Painted Davy admitted. "All right. Let's do it."

"Will you please untie my hands?" Diana asked.

Again, both men looked at her warily.

"It was my idea to go to the fort," she pointed out with exaggerated patience. "Why would I try to escape now?"

Con Horton pulled out his huge knife and used it to saw the

rawhide that bound her hands. Diana rubbed her raw wrists, surprised that the relief of being freed brought threatening tears. She could not cry in front of those two brutes. She would not cry until she was safe again.

The eagle called again, farther away now.

"Do you want something to eat?" Painted Davy asked grudgingly.

The last thing Diana wanted was food, but she needed to keep her strength up. "Thank you, yes. And something for my dog. I'd also like to wash the blood from my head and my arm and do what I can for my wounds."

"All right, all right. Just make it fast. Con, get some water."

Horton glowered at him. "She ain't the gawddamned queen of England."

"She's in bad shape," Painted Davy argued. "We'd best get her fixed up some, or the Beaudines'll kill us anyways."

"I suppose you're right." Horton stomped off with a canteen, swearing under his breath.

As Diana waited for her captors-turned-escorts to bring food and water, she gathered Rosie into her arms and rested her cheek against the dog's sun-warmed head. Grey Eagle had given her the puppy months ago with the explanation that Rosie would watch over her. She'd had no idea then how true his words would prove to be.

Two days later, after darkness had fallen, the lights of Fort Laramie came into view, flickering in the distance. Never before had Diana seen such a welcome sight. Painted Davy and Con Horton had not treated her kindly, but neither did they inflict any additional damage. Painted Davy had even gone so far as to rig up a harness of sorts, fashioned from an old blanket and strips of rawhide, to hold Rosie on the horse in front of Diana when the dog tired. Diana patted Rosie's back and assured her that she would soon be let down.

They entered the compound and rode straight to Colonel MacKay's headquarters.

"Wait here," Painted Davy ordered. He stepped down from

the saddle and pounded on the door, then spoke rudely to the private who answered his knock and pushed his way inside. The door closed again.

Diana swayed on the horse's back, not certain how much longer she could last. All of a sudden, the door burst open, and the private rushed outside.

"Miss Murdoch? Is it really you? It's me, Private Ross, miss. Here. Let me get your dog first."

Rosie was pulled from the harness. Diana looked down at the kind face of the young man who held up his arms to her. If he was shocked or appalled by her appearance and her clothes, he didn't show it. "It is so good to see you again, Private Ross. How is Private Dawson's leg?"

"He's just fine, miss. You're the one who needs help now. Please let me help you."

"Very well." Diana slid off the horse into Ross's steadying arms. Her knees buckled when he set her down, and Ross swept her up and carried her inside the headquarters office where she and her father had come so long ago to resolve the problem with Thatcher. She expected to find the colonel there, but, with the exception of the angry-looking Painted Davy, the office was empty. Ross carried her through a side door and into the colonel's private parlor. "I can walk," she insisted.

Ross carefully set her on her feet. Rosie impudently marched in and sat at Diana's feet.

"Miss Murdoch!" Colonel MacKay hurried to her side and took her right hand. Diana winced when he jarred her arm. "Oh, my dear, what has happened to you?"

"It's a long story," Diana murmured as she looked about the room. A beautifully dressed young woman sat on a sofa, sobbing into a handkerchief. An older, equally well-dressed woman wearing large hoops stood next to the young one, patting her shoulder in an absentminded manner. She stared at Diana, clearly horrified.

With her free hand, Diana brushed her matted hair off her bruised forehead and smoothed the skirt of her blood- and travel-stained deerskin dress. The older woman's rude perusal irritated her. She straightened her spine and met the somehow familiar woman's shocked gaze. "Do I know you, madam?"

The younger woman wailed again. The sound was getting on Diana's dangerously stretched nerves, and she thought of the courtesy exhibited by the Cheyenne in teaching their children from infancy not to cry loudly.

"Diana, of course you know me." The older woman hesitantly reached out, then let her hand fall to her side.

The room started spinning, and Diana suddenly felt very hot. The woman repeated her name, and it seemed that the sound came from a very long way.

"Mother?" she whispered, and collapsed into Private Ross's sturdy arms, claimed at last by the blessed peace of unconsciousness.

Chapter Thirty-Two

Diana awakened slowly, taking stock of her aching body bit by bit. Her feet were bare against each other, her legs curled together, her hands clasped at her breast. A solid warmth against the back of her legs told her that Rosie was there. She lay covered with robes on a comfortable bed. Her head pounded without mercy, and her right shoulder felt on fire. With a moan, she shifted, and felt a tugging at her neck. Where was she? What had happened? Cautiously, she opened her eyes.

Sweet Water's beloved face smiled down at her. "Diana."

"Hello, my friend." Diana swallowed, wondering why her voice sounded so rough. "I've had the most terrible dreams." She pulled her left hand from under the covers and was surprised to see her arm encased in a long white sleeve that ended in a ruffle at her bruised wrist. Something tugged again at her neck, and Diana irritably grabbed it, then realized that she wore a high-necked nightdress and was covered with blankets rather than buffalo robes. She turned dismayed eyes on her friend. "They weren't nightmares, were they?"

"Nope." Jubal stood at the head of the bed and now leaned down into Diana's line of sight. "It sure is good to see your pretty eyes opened, Diana. We've been sick with worry over you."

Everything gelled in Diana's confused mind. "I'm at the fort."

"Yep. One of the officers gave up his room to you. Your mama's here from St. Louis, and so's your little sister."

Diana frowned. The sobbing young woman on the sofa must have been Nora. What were they doing at Fort Laramie? "Where is Grey Eagle?"

"We don't know for sure, but there ain't no doubt he'll be here before long. And he'll be madder'n hell—ah, a wet hen when he gets here. It ain't gonna be pretty."

"Did the war party return safely from the Pawnee?"

"Sure did. Old Will Mayhew just got back from the wilderness. Said he spent a night with our band of the Cheyenne. They recovered the horses, took a few more, and killed three Pawnee. In answer to your next question, Grey Eagle is fine." Jubal paused, then added, "Except he's awful riled."

Sweet Water laid a cool cloth on Diana's aching head. "Not talk so much," she scolded. "Diana tired."

"You're right, wife. I'll go check on our daughter." Jubal bent down and placed a kiss on Diana's cheek, then left the room.

Sweet Water gently washed Diana's face with the cool cloth. "What happen to your arm?" she asked.

"Black Moon stabbed me. She said she was going to cut the eagle from me."

Sweet Water's mouth tightened. "Bad white men tell colonel the Cheyenne hurt you. I didn't believe. Now I do."

"Of the Cheyenne, it was Black Moon alone. Where are Sikes and Horton?"

"They leave fort yesterday morning, early, before we know you here. Your mama give them money."

Yesterday morning? "Sweet Water, how long have I been asleep?"

"Long time. Over one day. That why we worry."

She'd lost a whole day. Overcome with exhaustion, Diana

closed her eyes. That meant she was one day closer to seeing Grey Eagle again.

"Who are you?"

Diana awakened to the sound of an imperious, demanding voice.

"I am Sweet Water."

"Well, you may leave at once."

She'd know that voice anywhere. "My friend will stay, Mother," Diana said tiredly. She opened her eyes and saw her mother standing tight-lipped at the foot of the bed with her arms folded across her chest. Felicia wore a lovely, wide-hooped gown and was, as always, impeccably groomed.

" 'Thou shalt honor thy mother and thy father,' Diana Murdoch. Obey your sweet mother and send this ... person ... and that dog away at once."

Rosie growled. *Oh, Lord*. Diana turned her head and, just beyond Sweet Water's expressionless Cheyenne face, could make out the fashionable form of Belinda Mullen. The woman flashed a disgusted look at Rosie, then in Sweet Water's direction.

"My name is now Beaudine, Belinda. Mrs. Beaudine. And it is you I will send away." Diana weakly waved her arm. "I insist that you leave at once."

"Diana!" her mother snapped.

"Well, I never!" Belinda huffed.

Diana struggled to a sitting position, while Sweet Water moved to arrange the pillows at her back.

Belinda looked at Diana's face, and her own pretty face paled. "You look dreadful, Diana."

"I also feel dreadful, and I'm certain my mother will think my behavior dreadful." Diana stared at Belinda. "I have no patience for your pretended concern. Leave my room at once, and do not return."

"Diana!"

"Stay out of this, Mother. This is one battle you won't win." Just repeating the words Grey Eagle had said to her so often gave Diana strength. She was filled with an intense longing to see her husband.

Felicia guided Belinda to the door. "Perhaps it is best that you leave for now, my dear. Diana is not herself."

"I am quite myself, Mother, more than you know," Diana said firmly. "I will not change my mind."

Felicia closed the door behind Belinda's retreating form and turned to face Diana. Sparks of fury seemed to fly from her brown eyes. "How dare you speak to that nice lady in such a way?"

Diana rolled her eyes. "I'm not surprised that you and Belinda have become close friends. You have so much in common." She could not keep the sarcasm out of her voice.

"I find your manners and your mood sadly wanting, Diana." Felicia's hands found her hips. "Clearly, you have been on the frontier much too long. It is good that your sister and I undertook the horrors of the journey here in order to bring you home. And what is this nonsense about your name being Beaudine now?"

"Why did you offer a reward for my return?"

Diana's complete change of subject caught Felicia off guard. "Well, of course, we had to, your grandparents and I. Why wouldn't we? You are my daughter, and their granddaughter. You belong at home with us."

"Have you met Joseph and Orion Beaudine?"

"Yes. What does that have to do with anything?"

"Did they not tell you that I was safe and happy at the Cheyenne encampment? That I chose to stay there?"

"Yes, they did, and I knew at once that you had been coerced or forced. You would never *choose* to live with savages."

How ironic, Diana thought wearily, resting her head against the pillows. When she—and Gideon—wanted Felicia to come, the woman refused. Then she came when Gideon was dead, when Diana had nothing left to say to her.

"I am married to one of those 'savages,' Mother. He is the third of the Beaudine brothers, his name is Grey Eagle, and his mother was a Cheyenne woman. We were wed over two months ago."

Felicia's face blanched. "This cannot be."

"Oh, it is, I assure you. I would be with him still had I not been beaten, stabbed, and kidnapped, taken by force from my home and my husband. But don't worry. You'll get to meet your new son-in-law soon, because he will come for me."

Felicia reached for a ladder-back chair and sank down on its edge. "I will have the marriage annulled," she said, almost to herself. Then her eyes narrowed. "You were not wed. There was no priest or preacher to perform the ceremony."

"I was wed before the Cheyenne, and before the eyes of God."

"That is not legal." Felicia jumped up from the chair. "I'll have this farce of a marriage annulled."

Diana almost felt pity for her frantic, furious mother. "It is legal, Mother. And I am of age." She hesitated. "And the marriage has been consummated, joyously and many times over. There is nothing you can do."

Felicia flushed bright red and clamped her mouth shut, then whirled about and rushed from the room.

"You tell her good," Sweet Water said proudly.

"Yes." But Diana felt no triumph. How sad that her mother could not congratulate her on her marriage. She closed her eyes in an attempt to close out a world that had become painful on many levels, for it was only in sleep that she found any relief.

The next afternoon, a conference was held in Diana's sick-room. She sat up in bed with a thick shawl around her shoulders and held a sleeping Mary Sweet Rose. Rosie curled up at the foot of the bed, as usual, her head resting on her paws as she kept an interested eye on things. Diana's hair had been washed and now lay in clean scented waves over the shawl. Although her head still ached, as did her healing arm, she felt better than she had in days.

Colonel MacKay was there, as was Captain Rutledge, Joseph and Orion Beaudine, Jubal Sage, Sweet Water, Felicia, and Nora. The three women sat on chairs, with Sweet Water's placed next to the bed. Felicia held her head high and her lips pressed together, while Nora stared down at her hands, which were clasped in her lap, and mercilessly wrung a handkerchief.

Nora had been to visit Diana but twice. Both visits had been of short duration and very uncomfortable. Diana hated to see how shy her sister was with her. Perhaps it was too late to counterbalance Felicia's damage. She drew her attention back to the ongoing discussion.

"You're certain he's coming?" the colonel demanded of Joseph.

"Oh, yes. And he won't be alone, Colonel. Grey Eagle's bride was taken from him. There will be repercussions."

"But that Cheyenne woman who arranged all this was going to tell him that Diana left him," Felicia protested.

Joseph turned cold eyes on her. "Grey Eagle won't believe that for one second, Mrs. Murdoch. Beside the fact that Black Moon is a liar, your daughter and my brother are deeply in love and completely devoted to each other. He knows she would never leave him. I repeat, his wife has been taken from him. The Cheyenne believe that revenge must be exacted for such a transgression."

Diana found it almost comical how the discussion—which had everything to do with her—went on around her as if she wasn't there.

"Will the Cheyenne attack the fort?" the colonel asked.

Felicia gasped at the question, no doubt thinking of the fort's lack of protective outer walls.

Joseph looked askance at Jubal, who shrugged and stroked his long beard as he answered.

"I don't think they'll attack outright, but they'll be ready to. Grey Eagle will want to hear from Diana exactly what happened, and he'll decide what to do then."

Colonel MacKay sighed. "As you know, gentlemen, the federal government is working tirelessly to make a treaty meeting with the Plains tribes a reality, hopefully within the next month. The last thing we need right now is trouble with the Cheyenne." He looked at Joseph, then at Orion. "Are you two willing to go talk to your brother? Explain what happened and see if you can help smooth things over?"

Joseph and Orion shared a look, then Orion nodded. "Jubal, we'd ask that you stay here and watch over Diana. That way, if by some chance we miss Grey Eagle and he gets here before we find him, you can talk to him."

Jubal snorted. "Yeah. As if there's a chance the Hunter can't find his own brother, especially with Joe along to help."

Diana smiled at that.

"Well, let's get to it then." Colonel MacKay awkwardly patted Diana's shoulder. "I'm glad to see you looking better, Mrs. Beaudine. We'll get this all straightened out." He smiled at her, but the worried look did not leave his eyes. "Captain Rutledge, if you would accompany me to headquarters, please. We have plans to make. Good day, Mrs. Sage. Mrs. Murdoch. Miss Murdoch."

"Yes, sir." Captain Rutledge sent Diana an encouraging smile, then followed the colonel from the room.

Joseph accepted the hand Diana held up to him and sandwiched it between his own. "We'll find him and bring him to you, little sister." He bent and kissed her cheek, then bent lower to kiss Mary Sweet Rose's forehead.

Orion stepped up next and also kissed Diana. "All will be well. You just get better, Diana."

Diana smiled up at them. "I will. Godspeed, brothers." A comforting warmth encircled her heart at the word that came to her so easily. Joseph and Orion *were* her brothers now.

The Beaudines left. Felicia stood up, and Nora followed her mother's lead.

"I guess nothing more remains to be said," Felicia said sharply.

"I guess not," Diana answered. She watched as her mother spun around and marched from the room without another word. Nora paused at the door and looked back at Diana, her large eyes filled with tears, then followed Felicia. A moment later, the outside door slammed.

Jubal broke the silence that settled over the room. "No offense, Diana, but I just can't see that woman with your sainted pa."

His comment was a sad truth, and Diana only shook her head. "I can't, either, Jubal. I can't, either."

Private Dawson rubbed his tired eyes and glanced hopefully at the eastern horizon. He was rewarded with the sight of the first faint glow of light. The last hour of night guard duty was always the worst. It was as if he could hear his pillow calling out to him. He stifled a yawn and again shouldered his rifle, which seemed to have grown heavier, then continued with his rounds.

It had been five days now since Miss Murdoch—Mrs. Beaudine—had been brought in by Sikes and Horton, the bastards, and the colonel claimed her half-Cheyenne husband was coming for her and bringing a war party with him. Watches had been doubled, and tensions in the fort ran high. So far, there'd been no sign of any of the Beaudine brothers, not even Joseph and Orion. Dawson would be glad when the situation was resolved, once and for all. There was enough to worry about with the big treaty meeting coming. He wished that gathering was being held at Fort Kearney instead of Laramie. There was no telling what might happen with a large group of Indians from various tribes all in the same place, at the same time.

A little later, he met up with Ross, who shared night guard duty with him. Together they watched the eastern sky. Once the light got started, Dawson thought, it moved rapidly. "Well, one more time around the perimeter should about do it, Ross."

"That's what I figured. See you soon."

Dawson nodded and moved on. People were beginning to stir in some of the buildings. He saw lights in a few windows, smelled the smoke of cook fires, heard muffled voices and clanking dishes, and from somewhere a woman shouted in a shrill voice to hurry with the firewood.

The sun was ready to break over the horizon, and the bugler stumbled sleepily to the flagpole, hoisting up his suspenders as he went. The crisp notes of reveille sounded in the still air and set dogs to howling.

Ross approached him again. "Well, we made it through another night." He yawned. "I hate night guard duty."

"Me, too." Dawson rubbed his eyes again and squinted at the rising sun. Then he stiffened.

"What is it?" Ross asked.

"I don't know." Dawson shaded his eyes with one hand and looked into the sun. "Someone on horseback. Looks like a lone warrior. I can see feathers on his lance."

"Damn," Ross muttered. "He's centered in the sun. I can't tell if he's wearing war paint or not."

To Dawson, there was something eerie about that still figure. "You think Mrs. Beaudine's husband has come for her?"

"Alone? Maybe. Whoever it is, there's something on his mind, 'cause he's makin' an entrance. I'd better go get Captain Rutledge."

"Good idea. I'll stay here."

Ross ran off, and returned a few minutes later with Captain Rutledge.

"Any change, Private?" Rutledge asked as he approached, still buttoning his blue coat.

"No, sir. He's just been sitting there, as still as a stat— Wait. Now he's moving."

As the three men watched, the warrior slowly raised his lance in an arc.

"What was that?" Ross wondered.

"A signal," Rutledge answered.

Dawson swallowed hard. "I got a bad feeling about this."

"So do I, Private Dawson. Private Ross, get the colonel."

"Yes, sir." Ross turned to go, then halted. "Jesus God."

The three soldiers watched in horrified silence as the hilltop on either side of the lone man filled with a line of evenly spaced warriors on horseback.

Dawson followed the line to the left to see how far it extended and was speechless as he turned a complete circle.

"My God, sir, we're surrounded," Ross breathed.

Questions and cries of fear rang out across the compound. People came from buildings and stared at the hills.

"We must take immediate steps to avoid panic among the

civilian population,'' Captain Rutledge snapped. ''Private Ross, get the colonel. Ask him to meet me in front of the barracks. Run, man!''

''Yes, sir!'' Ross took off.

Captain Rutledge cupped his hands around his mouth. ''Bugler! Sound the alarm!''

The startled man stared at him for a moment, then put the bugle to his lips and blew.

''Dawson, stay here and keep an eye on that man in the center. He's the one running the show. I want to know where he is at all times.''

''Yes, sir.''

Captain Rutledge ran for the barracks, where soldiers in various stages of undress poured out of the door, all with rifles in hand.

Dawson returned his gaze to the dramatic sunrise and knew he would never forget that sight as long as he lived—assuming, of course, he lived beyond today.

There was no question in his mind now.

Grey Eagle had come for his bride.

Chapter Thirty-Three

Diana stood next to her bed and absentmindedly patted Rosie. Sweet Water sat on a chair, nursing Mary Sweet Rose, and together they waited for Captain Rutledge or Jubal to bring word that it was time.

Grey Eagle had come for her.

She wished she had the lovely wedding dress Sparrow had made for her. But she did not. Felicia had destroyed—burned, she'd announced with glee—the deerskin dress Diana had worn here, and even though she didn't know for certain that the dress could have been cleaned of its bloodstains, Diana had wanted to try. She wanted to go to her husband dressed as a Cheyenne.

Instead, she wore her best 'white man's' dress, made of lavender silk. There had been another argument with her mother over Diana's refusal to wear a corset and hoops, and another when she refused to try to cover up the ugly bruise that discolored her forehead, and yet another when she insisted upon wearing her hair down. Diana asked Sweet Water to pull the hair back from her face in two narrow braids behind her ears, as Grey Eagle wore his hair, because it made her feel close to him. Felicia had left in a snit, and now, at last, Diana and Sweet Water waited in relative peace.

As she stared out the window with unseeing eyes, Diana acknowledged a tiny fear. What if Grey Eagle believed she had run away? Was that why he brought with him a war party large enough to surround the fort? Would there be bloodshed and death on both sides because of Black Moon's selfish, cruel scheming?

Diana rested her hand on her flat belly. Her tardy monthly flow had not yet started, and with each passing day, she became more certain that she did indeed carry Grey Eagle's child. Would he be pleased?

It had been little more than a week since she'd last seen him, and it felt like a lifetime had passed instead. Diana missed him terribly—missed the loving looks in his green eyes, his loving touch, his sense of humor, the long discussions they'd shared, the bed they'd shared. She missed just watching him, for the sheer pleasure of enjoying his beauty.

A knock came on the door.

"Come in," Diana called.

Jubal stuck his head in. "Time to go, Diana. Your man's waitin'. With any luck, we'll be able to avoid a war today."

Diana's heart started pounding. She gave Jubal her hand, and, without further word, they left the room, followed by Sweet Water.

The sunlight seemed very bright when Jubal led her through the door outside. Most of the inhabitants of Fort Laramie were gathered on the parade ground and Diana felt their eyes on her as she passed. She spotted Angus MacDonald in the crowd and was surprised to see that the man's face was even more bruised than hers was.

"What happened to him?" she asked Jubal in a whisper.

"He ran into my fist." Jubal held up his right hand, displaying skinned knuckles.

Diana stared up at him in amazement. "You hit him?"

Jubal shrugged. "If anybody ever needed a kick in the chops, it's that bastard, for what he done to you, 'scuse my language. I figured you to be too much of a lady to hit him, and I figured Grey Eagle would probably kill him, so I decided it was my responsibility to see that he was showed the errors of his ways."

"Did he learn his lesson?" Diana asked, trying to suppress a smile.

"I don't know. Angus strikes me as a mighty slow learner."

They came around the corner of the officer's quarters and Diana paused at the sight before her.

The Cheyenne had refused to enter the actual compound, so they waited a distance from the headquarters building. As all the Cheyenne did, Grey Eagle wore his war paint. So did George Washington. Grey Eagle and his stallion were positioned front and center. Joseph and Two Bears—whose presence surprised Diana—flanked his right, while Orion and Raven's Heart flanked his left. No man smiled a greeting.

Between the line of warriors and the buildings of the fort was a line of mounted cavalrymen, all with their swords drawn and held at attention. Behind the cavalrymen stood a line of infantrymen, all with rifles and standing at attention. Front and center on the side of the Army waited Colonel MacKay and Captain Rutledge, both mounted.

A warm summer breeze fluttered flags and feathers alike, and an eerie silence hung over the entire scene. Diana was certain that everyone could hear the nervous beating of her heart.

Jubal again started walking. He led Diana to the colonel's horse, then released her and stepped back. She shaded her eyes and looked up at the officer.

"May I go to him?"

Colonel MacKay frowned and leaned down from his saddle. "You're certain he won't hurt you? There's no chance that he would believe that other woman?"

"None. I know my husband, Colonel. And he knows me. I am anxious to see this resolved."

"As am I," the colonel agreed, and straightened. "Go with God."

Diana turned and faced the formidable row of Cheyenne, surprised that she felt no fear of them, but only respect. Then she looked at Grey Eagle, and her breath caught.

He was magnificent and fearsome at the same time, and Diana felt a fierce surge of pride that he was her man. Tall and proud he sat on George Washington's bare back, his hair moving in the breeze. He stared at her with the intensity she so well remembered, and Diana longed to run to him, to pull him off his stallion and into her arms. But she did not. She, too, carried herself tall and proud, and waited.

With his lance, he motioned her closer. Diana advanced, then stopped near George Washington's head. The stallion nickered in welcome and pushed at her shoulder with his nose. Diana longed to respond to the horse's caress, but felt it best not to. She was aware that Rosie stood at her side, and did not take her eyes off her husband.

Grey Eagle addressed her in Cheyenne, loudly, so that his fellows could also hear. "Did you leave our lodge by choice, as Black Moon has said?"

Diana answered as clearly. *"Hova-ahane."* No.

"Were you taken by force?"

"Heehe'e." The rest of her statement was long, and she looked to Jubal for help. He stepped closer and loudly translated as she spoke. "I left our lodge believing that Two Bears needed my assistance, and was taken before I reached him."

"How were you taken?"

"Black Moon struck me with the crutch Two Bears used." Diana pointed to the bruised side of her head. A low murmur ran through the line of Cheyenne. "Then two white men took me from her and brought me here, even though she instructed them to take me north and sell me to the Crow."

The murmurings grew louder.

"I have been told that Black Moon stabbed you. Is this true?" Grey Eagle asked.

"Heehe'e. She said she would cut the Mark of the Eagle from my shoulder."

Many of the Cheyenne now broke into louder discussions.

"Before my sister is condemned for such an act, I would see this wound," Two Bears shouted in Cheyenne.

Diana understood him and turned her back to Jubal, pulling her hair forward over her left shoulder. He unhooked the top of her bodice far enough so that she could drop the material off of her right shoulder. She showed the scabbed wound first to Grey Eagle, whose mouth tightened into an angry line, then she turned her shoulder to Two Bears. Whether it was the unharmed Mark of the Eagle or the wound next to it that caused his face to pale, she did not know.

"My apologies for my sister's treachery and cruelty," Two Bears said stiffly, "to both Grey Eagle and his Eagle Woman." He pulled his horse's head around and rode away, followed by several of his friends.

With a sigh of relief, Diana leaned her head against George Washington's shoulder. Suddenly, her legs felt weak.

Grey Eagle leaned down and touched her cheek. "Greetings, *na-htes'eme.*" Wife.

No word had ever sounded more beautiful to Diana. "Greetings, *na-ehame.* I have missed you."

"And I, you." He held down a hand to her. Diana gladly took it, and he swung her up behind him. She wrapped her arms around her husband's waist and leaned her cheek against the long strands of sun-warmed hair that covered his naked back. "I would ask one question of you, Colonel," Grey Eagle said more loudly. "Do you know in which direction Painted Davy Sikes and Conway Horton headed?"

"They said nothing to anyone here."

"They mentioned spending the winter with the Crow," Diana said quietly.

Grey Eagle turned and spoke to the remaining Cheyenne. When he finished, five raised their rifles and whooped, then set off to the north. Diana wondered how much time Sikes and Horton had left.

"I am satisfied with the return of my wife," Grey Eagle announced.

"Then I am satisfied also," Colonel MacKay answered. "Troop, dismissed!" He nudged his horse forward and held out his hand, which Grey Eagle took. "Good to see you again, Grey Eagle. I'm sorry it's been under such trying circumstances."

"Thank you for your help, Colonel."

"Are the two of you willing to stay here at the fort long enough to make official statements on all that has happened, both with this incident and the one at Bridger's cabin that started it all?''

Diana and Grey Eagle answered him at the same time. ''Yes, sir.''

''Good. We'll talk later then.'' He saluted and rode away.

Grey Eagle turned George Washington around and faced his brothers and the remaining Cheyenne. ''Thank you for your help,'' he called out in Cheyenne. ''My wife and I will return to the encampment in a few days.''

With a great deal of whooping and shouting, the remaining warriors rode off, led by Raven's Heart. Joseph and Orion guided their horses into place beside George Washington, and the group entered the compound.

''I hope you don't mind, Diana,'' Grey Eagle said over his shoulder. ''I promised my brothers we'd stay for a visit, so that Mama Florrie doesn't kill them.''

She could not keep from smiling at the contrast between Grey Eagle's fierce appearance and his words that spoke of love and respect for his stepmother. ''I'd like that,'' she said.

''We'll like it, too,'' Orion put in. ''Mama was awful upset when we came back without you two last time.''

Diana smiled at him, then asked her husband, ''Do you know that my mother is also here? And my sister?''

''Yes,'' Grey Eagle answered. ''I look forward to meeting them, even if your mother won't like me.''

They now rode past the covered porch of the headquarters building, and Diana's gaze fell on the women there. Felicia stared at her, an expression of both anger and astonishment on her red face. Nora stood at her side, gaping, and Belinda Mullen was being helped to her feet, apparently after fainting. ''Don't worry about it,'' Diana said quietly. ''She doesn't like me, either.''

''Well, I like you,'' Grey Eagle assured her. ''And as soon as we get to a private room—one with a door that can be bolted—I intend to show you how much.''

Some of the ache faded from Diana's heart, and she tightened her arms around her husband. ''I would like that,'' she whispered, and pressed a kiss to his back.

Rosie gave a happy bark as she trotted next to George Washington, and Diana heard the faraway call of an eagle. She turned and looked toward the sound, and saw the distant outline of her father's headstone. The eagle called again, and she smiled. Franklin had told her that long-ago day that all would be well.

She knew now that he was right.

Epilogue

St. Louis, October 1851

Diana Beaudine followed her husband as he expertly led her in the graceful steps of the waltz. She knew that everyone present that night at her grandfather's elegant mansion gawked at and whispered about her and Grey Eagle, and, naughtily, she enjoyed it. She couldn't help but gawk at her husband herself.

He wore formal white man's dress tonight, complete with trousers, silk shirt, grey cravat, and a black frock coat. His hair, ornamented with his two narrow braids and his lone eagle feather, fell down his back to his waist, and Diana noticed several ladies casting longing glances at those shining locks. She could sympathize, for she never grew tired of playing with Grey Eagle's hair.

She presented a picture herself, she knew. Tonight Diana wore a deep forest-green ball gown, with hoops but still no corset, in deference to the coming baby. Her waist had thickened but she was only in her third month, and Grey Eagle alone knew her secret. The bodice of the gown was cut daringly low, exposing the swell of her breasts as well as the dark Mark of the Eagle and its accompanying badge of glory, the scar left by Black Moon's knife. Her hair was done up in an elaborate arrangement at the back of her head, her neck encircled by the exquisite pearl choker that had belonged to Morning Sky. The matching pearl earrings dangled from her ears, and she wore her beaded wedding moccasins and leggings. Sparrow was right—white man's shoes were uncomfortable.

"What are you thinking?" Grey Eagle asked her with a smile.

"Actually, I was thinking of what a handsome couple we make. We are quite the hit of the ball."

"I agree. And, believe it or not, I think even your mother is pleased."

Diana searched for and found her mother on the opposite side of the room. Felicia looked radiant, as always, and she seemed genuinely happy. "I think she's enjoying the notoriety of having, shall we say, such an unusual son-in-law?"

Grey Eagle shrugged. "I'm just glad the two of you have come to some kind of truce." The dance ended, and he kept Diana's gloved hand in his as he made for the side doors that led to the garden. "I need some air."

"So do I." Diana smiled at those they passed on their way outside, and could not help but think of all that had happened since that day in August when Grey Eagle came to Fort Laramie for her.

Two Bears had returned to the encampment and publicly censured Black Moon. He stopped short of evicting her from his lodge, but her standing in the village—and perhaps even her life—was ruined. In the end, it didn't matter, because two days later, Black Moon was discovered lying on a nearby hillside. She had been strangled with her own braids, her body lovingly laid out. Calls the Wind lay next to her, a peaceful look on his face, the knife he had plunged into his heart still gripped in his hand. Perhaps it was not the way Calls the Wind had imagined his time with Black Moon would be, but he was with her now, bound together forever in death.

The great meeting of the Plains tribes and the Army had finally happened. Called the Council of 1851 in the St. Louis newspapers, over ten thousand Indians from several different tribes had gathered on September first for the treaty meeting with high-ranking Army officers and government officials. All three Beaudine brothers as well as Jubal Sage had served as interpreters. In the end, the Indians conceded far more than the whites did, and, on September seventeenth, the Treaty of Fort Laramie was signed. The fact that no bloodshed took place among some of the tribes who were hated enemies was remarkable in and of itself.

Grey Eagle led Diana to a bench in Felicia's elaborate garden, and they sat down. He draped his arm around her shoulders. For a moment, they were quiet, then Diana brought up the treaty, something that had been on her mind since she'd read the papers this morning announcing its ratification. "Do you think the Fort Laramie Treaty will stand?" she asked.

"For a while, like most treaties," her husband answered. "In the end, it will be broken, as they all are."

"By the whites?"

Grey Eagle shrugged. "Perhaps. It is usually the whites who break the treaties, but not always." He took up her hand with his free one. "Joseph believes that trouble is coming."

"Do you agree?"

"Yes. It cannot be avoided. There are simply too many whites, and the Indians cannot pull themselves together to present a united front."

"They need a man like George Washington to lead them."

Grey Eagle smiled at that. "They do, but even if a man such as George were to come forth, I doubt the different tribes can overcome their differences, jealousies, and grudges, even in order to survive."

Diana remembered the life she had shared with the Cheyenne and felt a deep sadness that her adopted people faced such a serious threat in the future. "If it comes to it, husband, will you choose the side of the white man, or the side of the Cheyenne?" Her fingers tightened on his as she waited for his answer.

"I will not deny either of my parents, Diana. I don't quite fit in either world. I am accepted by the Cheyenne, and tolerated by the whites, but I belong to neither. The only thing I belong to is my family. I will choose my family's side.'' He brought her hand to his mouth for a kiss. ''By marrying me, you no longer belong in the white world, either, nor will you ever completely belong in the Cheyenne world. Which side will you choose?''

She did not hesitate. ''I choose you, Grey Eagle, and your family. Where you live, I will live. Where you fight, I will fight. Where you die, I will die.''

''And our children?''

''They will be raised as you were.''

Grey Eagle pulled her more securely into his arms. ''I am blessed in you, *na-htes'eme.*'' He placed his hand over the mound of her left breast, over her heart, and tenderly kissed first the mark and scar on her shoulder, then her mouth.

''*Ne-mehotatse, na-ehame,*'' Diana answered. *I love you, my husband.* In her husband's loving embrace, she at last understood what home really meant.

No matter where they went, as long as she was with Grey Eagle, Diana was home.

From far away, she heard the call of an eagle, and was certain she imagined it, for she and Grey Eagle were in the middle of a large city. But then a picture of Gideon smiling at her flashed in her mind, and the call echoed once more.

Gideon and the Spirit of the Eagle had come again to touch them with the power of love.

Dear Reader,

Like most authors, some of my stories are a little more special to me than others. Grey Eagle's story is one of the special ones. The Spirit of this story (for lack of a better term) came to me over twenty years ago, and some of the scenes you read in this book were written then and are printed now with few changes. That demonstrates how powerful the "birth" of this story was.

My subsequent study of the history and society of the Cheyenne Indians only reinforced that Spirit, and left me with a profound respect and affection for a truly remarkable people. If you share some of my fascination for the Cheyenne, I can recommend a few books for further study.

The Cheyenne Indians, Volumes One and Two, by George Bird Grinnell, is widely held as the definitive resource on the Cheyenne tribe. Mr. Grinnell (1849–1938) lived during the time of the vanquishing of the Plains tribes and even accompanied George Armstrong Custer's Black Hills expedition as a naturalist in 1874. The sources for his books were the aged Cheyenne who could remember the old days and the old ways. Originally published in 1923, his two volumes make for fascinating reading.

Equally intriguing is the book entitled *The Mystic Warriors of the Plains,* by Thomas E. Mails. This thick, lush, beautiful book filled with engrossing narrative and wonderful illustrations was invaluable to me in my research, and I was impressed with and touched by Mr. Mails' obvious respect, admiration, and affection for the Plains tribes. I highly recommend it. Even the casual student will find it to be an entertaining read.

For those of you who are curious about my use of Cheyenne words and terms, I found, much to my delight, a Cheyenne-English dictionary at a nationally famous bookstore in Denver called The Tattered Cover (1-800-833-9327). They stock translation dictionaries for most if not all of the Native American tribes.

My research on eagles proved equally interesting. Eagles can grow to a height of three feet, with a wing span of six to seven feet, and yet they only weigh between eight and ten pounds because they are mostly, well, feathers. It is difficult for them to carry more than two pounds of prey, so they are restricted to a diet of fish, small game such as prairie dogs, rabbits, and mice, and carrion, like that used by Calls the Wind in his eagle trap.

During the course of my research, I found myself wishing that time travel was truly possible. Knowing what I know now, I would have cherished the opportunity to live among the Cheyenne in the old days, as Diana did, before their culture was nearly destroyed by contact with and subjugation by the white man. It is my sincere wish that I conveyed in this book the respect and admiration I feel for the Cheyenne people. I also hope that the story of Grey Eagle and Diana—and Franklin— touched your heart in some small way and reminded you of the healing, strengthening, and glorious power of love.

All the best,

Jessica Wulf
P.O. Box 461212
Aurora, CO 80046
(if you write, an SASE
would be appreciated.)

ABOUT THE AUTHOR

Jessica Wulf is a native of North Dakota and has spent most of her life in Colorado, where she now lives with her husband and two dogs. She has a B.A. in History, as well as a passion and fascination for it, and often feels that she was born in the wrong century. *Grey Eagle's Bride* is her sixth novel.